I would like to dedicate [illegible]

LISA – for being the b[illegible] world, for all her support and, mostly, for her love.

AISLING – for being the best friend I have always needed, for all the positive encouragement and for her dreams.

Karen Campbell

THE KNOWING

AUSTIN MACAULEY
PUBLISHERS LTD.

A CIP catalogue record for this title is available from the British Library.

ISBN 978 184963469 4

www.austinmacauley.com

First Published (2014)
Austin Macauley Publishers Ltd.
25 Canada Square
Canary Wharf
London
E14 5LB

Printed and Bound in Great Britain

Chapter One

I awoke from the same nightmare I had been having for weeks, reached over to turn on the lamp and lit a cigarette. Sighing, I lifted my pen and notepad and began to write. I had seen it all tonight, from the meeting to the murder, which meant that the girl was now dead. I had seen the killer place the single red rose on the girl's body and knew, whoever he was, that he had just killed again.

I sighed again. I would have to go to the police in the morning.

****

The next morning, I sat cold and alone in the waiting area of Strathclyde Police Headquarters in Pitt Street, Glasgow. The news lately had been full of little else but the man behind the murder of three young women in the Glasgow area. The pressure was really on the police to find him, and I was sure my assistance would be gratefully met, as it had been in the past. What they did not know, however, was that he had actually killed five. There was a girl listed as 'Missing', but I knew she was dead. By his hands. And then, there was the poor girl I saw being strangled in my dream last night. Five, all gone.

A sour-faced woman in a grey suit, nice legs, approached me and scowled. "You're here about Charlton Heston?"

"Yes."

"Come this way, please," she said, gruffly and I followed her.

We went into a small interview room with a table and four chairs, and I sat down across from her. Early thirties, I guessed, good skin, clear blue eyes, tidy brown bob. Attractive, but still scowling.

"What can I do for you, then, Mrs…?" she trailed off.

"Miss Keith. Jen. Where's DI McLean? I normally speak to him," I told her.

"Do this a lot then, do you? Help the police with their enquiries?"

I started to redden, feeling like a fool, and the dislike set in. Good legs or not. "Look, Sergeant…"

"It's DI, if you don't mind. DI Coutts. McLean's been transferred. So, now you have me. Well… What can I do for you?" She began to drum her fingers on the desk, impatient.

I counted to ten in my head. I had a job to do here. Stay patient, I told myself. "DI Coutts, I'm a psychologist but…" I struggled for the proper words, "I also 'see' things."

"You 'see' things?" she repeated, her scowl turning to derision.

"Yes, I'm psychic," I blurted out.

I could see her eyes roll, 'oh no another nutter'.

"Look, Miss Keith, thank you for wanting to help, but I think we will manage."

"But that's just it – you're not managing. You haven't even found the fourth body, and he did it again last night." I could be patient no longer.

I had her attention now. "What fourth body?"

"Amanda Cairns. She's been missing for a month."

"And how do you know she's dead and not just run off somewhere?" she asked, calm and precise.

"Because I've seen it! If you can let me hold something of hers, I might be able to tell you where to find her," I pleaded.

"Hold on, you can't expect me to believe this."

"Look, I've helped McLean before. Check your files. Remember Kylie Wright? Two year old, went missing in Govan? How do you think you lot found her? Because I told McLean where to look. I'll be on record as an assisting psychologist."

"Wait here."

She got up and left. I was getting mad now. I knew how stupid I looked, walking into a police station, declaring I had visions. I probably would not have believed myself either, but

McLean had, eventually, and I was pissed that he wasn't here, that I had to go through all this convincing once more.

He had taken me for a drink once, and we had got on well. He called me a 'waste of a good woman' because I 'kicked with the other foot', as he had put it, in his kind, machismo way. I had noticed it had not stopped him checking out my cleavage.

My thoughts were interrupted by the reappearance of DI Coutts. I noticed the lightest of blusher, emphasising her cheekbones. And as much I disliked her, I could not stop my eyes moving to her lips, just for a second, and thinking how soft they looked.

"Okay, I've checked what you said, Miss Keith," she said, sitting back down.

"Call me Jen," I offered.

"Jen. Seems you did help with the Wright murder, profile gathering."

"Well, we wouldn't want the press to hear about psychic input, would we?" I joked, still nervous and on edge.

She laughed. I found her beautiful then, and that disturbed me.

"So, what is it you want to tell me?" she asked, in a friendlier voice.

"The man you are looking for is late forties to early fifties. He's going bald, slightly overweight, lives with an elderly parent – probably his mother – and he holds down a job," I told her.

"I can get that from any criminal profiler." The derision had returned.

"He's a gardener."

She became serious, and watched me intently. "What makes you say that?"

"That's where he gets the roses."

"Roses."

"You know, the ones he places on his victim's breasts. With the signed card," I added.

"How do you know that? That information has not been released."

I sighed. "I've seen it!"

"So, tell me, why does he use the name Charlton Heston?" Was she testing me?

"He sees himself as a real man, macho, powerful, like 'Ben Hur'. You can't get DNA because he wears a rubber suit, with a hole cut for his penis. And he wears a condom, of course." I closed my eyes. "He looks ordinary. He walks with baggy trousers and a long raincoat. He has a hammer in the pocket. He's lurking in the woods. I see a cemetery close, and the girl appears. She is about twenty, a big girl, fat. I think she is walking home, drunk from a night out. He comes from behind and hits her on the head with the hammer, she falls and he pulls her into the woods, deep out of sight. Oh yes, he has the gloves to match. I can see them as he is dragging her. He takes a carrier bag from his pocket and removes his coat and trousers, neatly folding them into the bag. The girl groans and he hits her again on the side of her head. I think I can hear her skull crack. He rapes her and sodomises her, and then puts his clothes back on. He takes his rose and card, pulling up her top. She's not wearing a bra, and he slaps her face. He checks the rose, like he is proud of it, before he places it on her." My eyes snap open.

"Then I wake up," I add, in apology.

She is staring at me. "That's it," I say.

She springs to life, pulling a small notepad from her pocket. I catch the curve of her breast in her well-cut suit.

"Can I have your details, please?" she asks.

I give her them, realising I have been wasting my time. She still thinks I am a crackpot and, as she ushers me out, assuring me she will be in touch, I feel the urge to cry.

****

Later that evening, I opened a bottle of wine and the sadness crept in. I can never save them. I always see it too late. I sip my wine and turn on the television. The news. Strathclyde Police today found the body of a nineteen year old… I switch it off. I can't bear to listen. I have seen it all and done the best I can do. My heart goes out to the parents of that dead girl.

My door knocks and I jump. I don't get visitors. Not now, not since Julie left. I plod to the door, and open in. With surprise evident in my voice, I say "DI Coutts! Ah, come in." I am embarrassed to be caught wearing my old blue pyjamas.

She steps in and I smell her perfume. It is New West for Women, and I know it has been applied recently.

"What can I do for you?" I ask, the tables turned. For what reason has she come to me?

"Call me Kate," she smiles and I feel nervous. Or is it excited?

"Kate, would you like a drink?" I offer.

"Yes, thanks. I'll have a coffee."

I flee to the relative comfort of my kitchen and switch the kettle on. I don't drink coffee, but I keep a jar for visitors. And, as I rarely get visitors, I hope it has not congealed. Returning with her cup, I find her looking at the photographs I had out in frames. Me with Julie. Me with my degree. Me with Julie. I wish I had got around to moving them away from prying eyes.

I hand her the cup and tell her to please sit down.

"Have you seen the news?" she asks.

"I couldn't watch it," I say, curling back into my seat.

"We found her."

"I know," I say, sadly.

"She's still alive, I wanted to let you know."

Still alive? But I had been so sure she was dead. And so had Charlton Heston! That's why he had left her. "Alive?"

"She was still in surgery the last I heard, but we found her, thanks to you. If she had lay there much longer, I don't think she would still be with us."

I start to cry. She wasn't dead. I cover my face with my hands and sob. The poor girl.

Kate comes to me, and holds me and says, "There, there." I cry into her good grey suit, making a wet patch, and I think about how good she smells, wearing the same perfume that my Julie had worn, and I cry a bit harder.

Two years since I had been held by a woman, two long, hard years of heartbreak and loneliness. Now I could feel the stirrings again, of my want, of my need, to be held.

"Feel better now?" she asks, softly.

I try to laugh. "Yes, I suppose," wiping my sleeve across my nose.

"How long have you 'seen' things?" she asks.

I sniff. "As long as I can remember, really. I cried for a week when I was five because I knew our dog was going to get run over."

"I didn't believe you, you know, when you first came in this morning," she says, like I had not already guessed that.

"I know you didn't. What changed your mind?" I ask, looking straight into those clear blue eyes.

"The red rose. And I saw the torture on your face when you were telling me. Call it a hunch," she smiles.

I laugh. "Hunches separate the good cops from the bad."

She laughs with me again, and I am struck by her beauty. Maybe I could start to like her a little.

"Who's that in all the photos with you?" She nods at them.

"Oh," I say, feeling the old sadness when I think of Julie. "That's my ex."

"Girlfriend?"

"Yes." Now she would panic and make an excuse to leave.

"How long were you together?" she asks, not panicking and not leaving.

"Eight years."

"Why did you split up?"

"She was having an affair," I say, flatly.

"Couldn't you see it?"

I cannot decide if she was mocking me, or was just plain nosy. "Actually, I couldn't. I never saw the year of lies, and I couldn't smell another woman's perfume in my bed. Perfect, eh? I can see strangers getting raped and murdered, but not the fact that the woman I loved was deceitful right under my nose."

"How did you meet her?"

"Here's the thing," I explain. "I was twenty, still a student, and I saw her about to get in a black taxi at Queen Street station. I ran over, screaming at her 'Wait, wait! Don't get in! Get out!' She got out and some fat bloke in a suit got in, instead. 'Explain' she said, not exactly happy. 'Just watch', I told her. So we did and off the taxi trundled, straight into a smash from some car jumping a red light. The car smacked the taxi about where she had been sitting, and the fat man got out, a bit wobbly, but okay. It was her that I had seen, though, and she would not have been okay. I knew those few seconds had made all the difference."

"It must be hard for you to live with this not knowing," she remarks.

"I've got used to it. Do you want another coffee?"

"Yes, please."

I go back to my kitchen and told myself to quit it. Was I so hard up that I had to flirt with the first attractive woman I saw? But she *was* the first woman I had been attracted to in two years. When I had thrown Julie out, I had been broken-hearted and vowed never to get involved again. That level of hurt I could do without. I had opened to her, told her about my gift, and she had believed me because she had seen it. She had never laughed at me, she had loved me; but then, in the end, my gift had torn us apart.

For months, I had seen that toddler get abducted and abused. A tragic waste of an innocent, young life. It had upset me so much and I had thrown myself into my work to forget. I had neglected Julie and she had sought her needs elsewhere, until I had finally cottoned on. What had she said, so full of hate? "I thought you would have seen the signs before now."

No, I told myself, DI Coutts was wrong for me. She was a policewoman, a sceptical one at that, and she was only here to do her job. But, I asked myself, did that job entail holding me when I cried and asking me about my personal life?

I breathe in deeply. Whatever reason she was really here for didn't matter. I was *not* going to fall for her. I walk back into my living room and she is sitting back on the couch, as though she had sat there for years. She runs her hands through her hair, a small unreadable smile on her lips, and I shiver.

It is the most erotic thing I had seen in years.

I sit at the opposite end of my couch from her, and take a sip of my wine. I do not know what to say. I have butterflies in my stomach, something I have not experienced since my youth, and it makes me ache.

"How did you find her then?" I ask, trying to fill a quiet space to relieve my tension.

She winks at me. "Got a map. Checked out woods next to cemeteries. A reported missing this morning. Didn't take too long. But it would have, if you had not come forward, so thank you." I can see she meant that.

"Welcome. I just wish I could have prevented it; prevented them all."

"Who's to say you haven't prevented more? When he finds out this girl is still alive, maybe he will panic, make a mistake."

"Don't you understand?" I shout, standing up. "He's laughing at you, laughing at us all. He thinks he is cleverer than the police, that he will never be caught." I stop suddenly. "What's in your bag?"

She lifts her bag and begins to open it. "It's a picture of Amanda Cairns, the girl who's been missing a month."

I feel the surge. "Give me it, give me it!"

I hold the picture and, as the vision comes to me, I speak. "Amanda Cairns. She knocks a door and he answers. I can see him. Glasses, pencil thin moustache. She's trying to sell something, and he lets her in. A voice shouts from a room away, 'Who is it?', and he says pleasantly, 'A salesman, mother, don't worry, dear.' He takes Amanda into his front room. His window… She begins to talk to him, and he's smiling. I don't want to look, I don't want to see!"

"Tell me," I hear Kate whisper.

I know tears have sprung into my eyes. "He leaves the room to get something, I don't know what and she walks to the window. She's looking out at… Then the hammer hits her, many, many times. She never had a chance to scream. She goes down and he hits her until she is dead.

"Then he has her.

"He still has her, that's why she's not been found. He's kept her! He has her in an eight by eight box in his other front room. She is under dirt or compost – oh god, he waters her!"

"What did she see from the window, Jen?" Kate is gently coaxing.

I think hard. What did she see? "She saw a sign. Underground."

"Which one, Jen?"

"Cessnock."

"I've got to go." I am awake. "Thank you," she says, and grabs my face, kissing me on the cheek. She takes the photograph. She runs out, and this time it is me watching from a window as she jumps into her car and pulls away, wheels skidding.

This night, for the first time in weeks, I go to sleep with a face in the forefront of my mind that did not belong to a murderer. It belonged to Detective Inspector Kate Coutts.

****

Not the next day, but the next, I bought the paper on my way to work.

'Charlton Heston caught!'

'Cessnock rapist snared!'

So she had done it. She had believed me and they had got him. Now Glasgow and Amanda Cairns could sleep easily once again. I knew he had kept Amanda because she had turned up unexpectedly on his doorstep, delighted with the opportunity. A quiet loner that would not hurt a fly, his neighbours said. I threw the paper in the nearest bin and went to my car. I was pretty sure I would see it all again one day, and I should be happy that I would get some peaceful sleep for the time being.

Then why was my mind full of Kate Coutts?

****

It was perhaps a month or six weeks later, and I was again sitting in my old blue pyjamas, sipping wine and watching 'It's a Wonderful Life' when the door knocked. I briefly toyed with the idea of ignoring it, but I finally heaved myself off the couch to answer.

DI Coutts.

"Hello, you," I said, because I did not know what else to say. "Come on in."

"I brought you something," she smiled, her perfume intoxicating me.

"Not a red rose?" I grimaced.

"No," she replied, leaning in for a kiss. "Me."

Chapter Two

I was walking down Sauchiehall Street in the chucking rain, trying to remember what Kate had told me to buy in for her weekend party. She had some friends coming round to the flat I lived in, that *we* lived in now, and I was desperate to impress. But for the life of me, I could not remember.

I still had tomorrow. I'd wrap my arms around her later, when she finally dragged herself in from her job, and I would soothe her and then I would confess like the criminals she interviewed every day, and she would laugh.

I was lost in dreams of Detective Inspector Kate Coutts, as I had been since the day I met her. I had helped her solve a murder case and find a missing girl, and now we were lovers, living together in my little flat. I still had my old blue pyjamas and I still drank more wine than I should have, but I was happy now. The photos of me and my ex, Julie, had been replaced by pictures of me and Kate, and some of our kitten, Jonah, that she had got me for my birthday.

I loved having something to love. I loved having someone to love. And they loved me back. Life could not get any better.

So, it was with a smile on my face that I walked down a drizzly Glasgow street and bumped into a woman who would change my life.

Our shoulders smacked off each other and I dropped my bag of shopping. I mumbled "Sorry" as I stooped to pick it up, and automatically turned my eyes to see who I had hit. The girl – she was around her mid-twenties – smiled at me and said "I'm really sorry", but my eyes had already gone past her to the young boy that stood next to her.

I put him about five, and I knew he was a spirit. He laughed at me. He knew I could see him and he mocked me. By now, the woman/girl had walked on, and he mouthed "Can't catch me", and then ran along to catch up with her. I stood up and followed them down the road with my eyes.

She, walking oblivious; him, following her every move.

I went home with a headache.

****

Kate came home at six, early for her. I had already opened a bottle of wine and I saw her frown a bit. I wanted to scream at her, at anyone, "It's alright for you, you don't have to see what I have to see", but I didn't.

"Kate. Something's going on. I saw something today and I don't see things for no reason."

"I thought you hadn't had anything since we met?" she questioned, ever the copper.

"I haven't, until today. I bumped into a woman – well, a girl, really – and she had a spirit following her."

I looked at Kate and I knew how hard this was for her to understand. Although I had helped her, there was always that element of scepticism, and I resented it. Why could she not trust me?

"Did it say anything?"

"Aye. He said 'Can't catch me'. I know what it means."

"What, babe?" she sounded distracted as she reached into the oven for the meal she knew I would have cooked for her.

"It means someone is going to die."

She took a bite into the curry I had made and answered, "Why do you think that?"

"Because he has been gaining strength. He is taking strength off that woman, and he is nearly ready."

She continued to spoon curry into her mouth. "So, are you telling me that because you bumped into somebody today, you now think there is going to be a murder?"

"I don't *think,* I *know*!"

Since we had got together, nothing had happened to me. No more Amanda Cairns. We did not talk about it. But now it was back I knew the nightmares would start, and I started to panic Kate would go the same way as Julie did, and I did not want to lose her. I loved her, but I could not ignore the messages I was given.

"How much have you drunk?"

"Oh, for God's sake, Kate, I am not saying this because I am drunk. I am drunk *because* of this!"

She sniggered then and said "So, what's your excuse for the last six months?"

That incensed me and I grabbed her wrist. I let myself feel her blood pumping until it was pumping with mine, shut my eyes and let the work begin.

"I'm in my bed, hiding under the covers. *No, Daddy!* I am so scared. I know he is going to hurt me. Like he hurts me every Saturday night when he has been out with the boys. The door creaks, and daddy comes in, with his trail of beer permeating the room. I pull the quilt right over my head, as if it will protect me. He pulls it down and breathes his beer fumes. 'Hi honey'."

I recoil, because Kate has slapped me in the face and I see her crying…

"That's enough!"

She left then, and when she came back later that night, I was already sleeping, locked into a nightmare, recurring, recurring, of bumping into a girl in Sauchiehall Street, and the boy becoming a monster; but when I woke I was alone, always alone.

****

I got up the next morning to go to Glasgow University for my Psychology lecture, and I saw Kate sleeping on the couch. I stood for a moment, watching her lovely face with her eyes closed and mouth slightly open, and I regretted how I had hurt her the night before. But I had had to, to make her see, to make her believe once again that I was not a crank.

I got dressed and left her a note, asking to leave me the list for her party that night. I could not bring myself to wake her, as it was early and I liked to go on the tube to Hillhead and get a cup of tea before I faced the hordes of inquisitive students.

She had never told me her father abused her.

****

I had a busy day, and when I got home at three, I found Kate's reply to my note, and swiftly took off to the local supermarket to get what she wanted. Then I came home and began to prepare for the party, cleaned and cooked, and then I went for a shower.

The curtain opened and I saw her standing, grinning. "Well, aren't you a sight to behold?"

She stripped and joined me and, as her hands wandered over my naked, wet body, I knew the night before had been forgiven. For the moment.

After, she helped me in the kitchen and we laughed and hugged, and no one could have known that the night before I had discovered her father fucked her.

As the guests arrived, we welcomed them, introductions were made and I noticed Kate said I was a psychology lecturer and not a psychic, or medium. Not even I would have known what term described me.

As it turned out, it would not matter, because after the meal, I was taking the plates back into my kitchen, and when I went in with the last lot, the little boy was standing in my kitchen.

I dropped the plates.

"Hey, lady," he said. And time stopped for me.

"What are you doing here?" I stood frozen.

"I've come to give you a clue, 'cause you'll never catch me."

"Why would I want to catch you?'

"Oh, you know you do; it is written all over your face."

"You have to go. I can help you find peace."

"I don't want peace. I want revenge."

"No," I murmured. "You need peace, and I can help you find it."

"Oh," he sneered. "You can tell me why she aborted me and kept that brat?"

"Yes."

"You are full of shit. I am going to get your Kate."

"No! You don't touch my Kate!"

He laughed and walked away, through my kitchen door and out through the hall, and then he was gone.

"Jenny?"

I heard the voice calling my name, so distant. "Jenny!"

I focused and saw Kate, her face disapproving, her friends crowded round the kitchen door. They had heard me talking to myself.

"Kate, the boy was here."

"Oh Jenny, for God's sake. Why now?"

It was a long night. Her friends left quickly and I felt awkward. Her friends thought I was mad, talking to myself in the kitchen, and she was embarrassed and did not know how to act. I felt like I was mad, and not for the first time.

"Kate, you have to believe me – something is going to happen. You are a policewoman, you can stop it."

"Stop what? Some imaginary crime in your head? I have no proof of anything, so how can you expect me to believe you?"

That cut like a knife through my heart. "Do you want me to hold your wrist again?"

I saw her flinch and wished I had not said that, but it was the only way to make her see that I would hurt her if it would stop someone dying.

"Stop this, Jenny. It's over now. I don't know what happened when you helped me find that girl, and to be honest, I don't want to know. It just is. You cannot go on pretending you can… Well… See dead things… It's like a fucking movie."

And all at once, I knew she was scared and that saved me. From hurting her more, because I would never hurt her unless I had to.

"You're in danger, Kate."

"Oh fuck you, Jenny. I am a policewoman. I am in danger every day of my life. Don't think you can excuse your behaviour tonight by some feeble excuse. My friends think I am with a nutter who has conversations with herself."

"And what do you think?"

"I don't know what I think."

She left and I went to bed, to be welcomed in sleep by my recurring nightmares. There are always some things that you can count on.

****

I fed Jonah, and the days went past and I did not see Kate. I worried about her, but I could not sense his power had grown and I did not try to phone her because I knew, wherever she was, that she was safe.

Three weeks later, when she still had not been in touch, I realised the extent of my love for her. Not that I did not know it before, but when you wake up day after day, and the person you love is not there, and they should be there, it begins to hit home. I loved Kate. I loved her with a sense of me that had never been able to truly love someone before. I was scared that I would see the end, and I had never been able to see it with Kate.

I had never even been able to see it with Julie either, but Kate was much more real to me.

But she was safe, and if she was not with me that was safer for her, so I could suffer the solitude in my bed if it meant she was alive.

Of course, in my line of work, things are never as simple as that, and it came to a conclusion.

I awoke in the morning and the thud in my head hit me. It was like a hangover, only I had not been drinking. I had not drank since she left me.

My head pounded and I tried to get something from what I was feeling, but it was like the messages were too heavy and my brain could not cope, and so it pounded and pounded. I had a glass of water from the sink and ran my fingers through my hair.

'You have to get to Kate,' a voice inside said to me. I do not ignore voices inside me anymore. People tend to die if I do.

I phoned her office, calmly, and they told me she was already out on calls. The panic started to rise. They would not tell me where she had gone.

I dressed quickly and got a taxi to the police station in Kelvinbridge that she now worked at. I found a name in my head, another woman who had heard me talk to myself in the kitchen, and asked for her. I was clutching at straws. But she remembered me, and she came out to talk to me. She took one look at my face and ushered me into a private room.

"I need to find Kate," I said.

"She doesn't want to talk to you," she answered. Coldly, I thought.

"Look, it doesn't matter if she wants to talk to me or not, I *need* to talk to her. This is life or death."

She openly laughed in my face, the guffaw of an entire unbeliever.

I grabbed her wrist. "Just get the coke to the flat at 109 St. George's Cross for ten o'clock. I'll make sure the pigs are not around. If not, then you are going to have to pay a wee visit to the Godfather, and he won't take kindly to his supplies being messed up. Do you get me, Benny?"

I looked into her eyes and saw her face had gone white. "Now, you tell me where Kate has gone."

"How the fuck…?"

I had no time to dally. "Just find where she has gone!" I screamed at her, and she quickly went to find out.

She came back even whiter. "She's not answering her mobile phone… But we think she has gone to a flat in…"

I closed my eyes and felt the utter panic rise up in me like a tidal wave. My Kate. Where was she?

"Ibrox…"

A flat in Ibrox? I ran and I ran and I ran, until a taxi took me there.

I stood at the great stadium that was Ibrox and breathed in for her smell, for her perfume, for a scent of her trail. His power had grown. I felt it and he was drawing me in. It wasn't Kate he wanted – it was me!

A mist had begun to settle around the flats, confronting me and I walked in a haze. I was drowning in a darkness, and every street seemed the same, walking round in circles, crying in my head for my Kate.

Until I stopped in front of a flat that seemed vaguely familiar.

'I am looking out the window, looking at an underground station. I don't know which one… It's dark and…'

****

I awoke later in a darkened room and again, the panic overtook me. Where was my Kate? Had I managed to save her? Then the panic for myself hit and I tried to get my eyes accustomed to the dark around me. Where was I? I felt a lump on my head and assumed I had been hit, perhaps passed out and been taken to some closed room.

I got to my feet and began to move, with my hands on the walls feeling for a door, or a light switch or a human body. Nothing. I was alone in a fortress.

Or at least that's how it seemed, until I came to the lump on the floor. My Kate. My Kate, alive.

Breathe Kate, breathe Kate! She coughed some phlegm into my face and I smiled. A face full of snot was better than a room full of death.

"My love!"

"Jen?" she coughed.

"Listen to me," I said. "We are in a room. Can you move? Is anything broken?"

"No."

"We have to find a way out. Are you with me?"

"Yes. How did we get here?"

"I don't know. Have you got a phone or anything?"

"No, she took it off me."

"She?" I thought it was a boy I was looking for.

"Yes. She was going to tell me about…"

"About what?"

“Oh, it doesn’t matter now,” and she laughed and laughed. A bit too long.

“For fuck’s sake, Kate! C’mon, we have to get out of here!”

I think I scared her then, because she got to her feet and we began to feel for doors, and then, of course we found one. Because to be able to get in, you have to be able to get out.

And I think a part of me knew what was coming.

Kate was a trained policewoman, so when she said she could kick a door in, I stood back and let her. True to her word, she booted it down. And there we were, her arm around me, protecting me.

She had never protected me before.

I saw a woman with a boy behind her. Kate saw a woman.

And this is where she will think I am mad because I didn’t want to talk to the woman. I needed to talk to the boy.

“Jonah, it’s okay now.”

Kate looked at me. “Jen… The kitten’s not here.”

I felt her grip on me lessen slightly.

I had to ignore her, or he might have killed her, and I knew he was capable of killing her. He had grown and he could come into a human and I would be unable to stop that.

“Jonah, she loves you”

“She doesn’t!” he spat.

“She does, I’ll show you!” And at that, before I knew what I was doing, I was inside the head of the girl and I was showing him her putting flowers on the makeshift grave she had made for her aborted child. I showed him her tears of regret and the anguish her future life has entailed, and he watched me and started to degenerate. His tears were washing him out. Her arms were coming around him and he was letting her cuddle him, and just for a second – just for a second – they were solid, and they embraced.

It was only then that I saw the knife pressed against Kate’s throat fall down and a loud roar of “Put your hands in the air!” resonate.

****

DI McLean sits in my living room and we recount the events of the week before. I don't know how he got there. So, he tells me.

"I come in, right." The machismo bull is on overdrive. "And Kate is there with a knife held to her throat, and medium here," – he points to me, and laughs – "is having a conversation with herself."

"Yeah," Kate says, because she is brave now the threat has been removed. "What was that all about?"

I smile because it is all I can do.

"So, I shout 'Put your hands up!' and the bitch dropped the knife and started to cry, and then it was all over."

It was all over.

Kate came over to me, and smiled, put her arm around me – to protect me – and I let her and I smiled back.

But I saved her, and DI McLean saved me.

A man saved me.

But it's not the end. It is never the end.

Today DI McLean came to my flat and insisted that we go shopping, so we did as I am easily led.

I had bought the new Killers CD, and then I saw a familiar figure.

It said, "You can't catch me."

Chapter Three

The woman had the knife at Kate's throat and was pressing harder and harder. I could see the line of blood grow clearer and clearer and hear Kate's moans grow louder and louder.

"You can't catch me!" he laughed.

The moans grew into screams until I realised it was me screaming myself awake, and Kate saying, "Shush, it's okay. I'm here, nothing will hurt you."

****

About six months ago, I had been out shopping and I had seen a spirit that would haunt me. It had ended up in Kate being kidnapped by a young woman, who was in the power of a child she had aborted many years before. This child had caused her not only to take Kate hostage but to take me, and when we had been able to confront her, she had taken a knife to Kate's throat whilst I had reasoned with the spirit.

And somehow, my saviour had appeared in the form of DI McLean. And he *had* saved us. It had taken me a few weeks to get it out of him that he had managed to be there out of pure luck, as he had overheard me in a police station demanding to see Kate and had followed me.

He liked being thought of as the one that saved me.

How could I correct him?

****

Things seemed to happen in cycles with me and I began to have nightmares, even though I had seen nothing. Kate was as sympathetic as you can be when you get woken every night and have to get up for work the next day. Part of me knew that she still thought I put it on, even after I had showed her what I had seen about her life. She blocked out what she could not handle, and she blocked out her childhood. It was easier that way for her.

It was not easier for me, though. But, it did make me love her more.

There were things in my head that would not go away, and I could not block them out like Kate could. I had seen a spirit and it had said it would get Kate. It had not got Kate, but I knew it had also not gone.

When I see a spirit, it normally means someone is going to die. No one had died.

Kate said that the girl – the one who had the abortion, whose name was Lorraine – had been going to tell her something but had stopped. And then Kate had laughed.

And I remember that I had not liked that laugh.

He – Jonah – the same name as our cat – had wanted to know why she had aborted him and kept "the brat".

I supposed I would have to try and find out.

****

With an attempt at subtlety, I asked Kate if she had managed to find out anything about Lorraine since she had been sent to Carstairs, the nice mental hospital we have in Lanarkshire for our friendly goons.

No. She had not wanted to know any more.

A corridor closed.

When I reach a corridor closed I ask myself, what can I do to find another way down? And so, after asking Kate, I did the next best thing and I asked DI McLean.

He of course had a much healthier appetite and had made some enquiries.

They were about to release Lorraine because she had not shown any signs of mental illness and therefore was better. I said fuck a lot when I heard that. Rob, DI McLean, had shrugged and said that's how the justice system worked and I should get used to it as he had. He offered to take me out for a drink and I thought 'Why not?' and went.

After several glasses of wine, my tongue ran away with me. "Kate doesn't believe me, you know. She thinks I'm mental. Even though I have told her the truth, she still thinks I make things up."

He smiled into my eyes, "I believed you."

I laughed "Aye, after I gave you every detail you needed. You didn't at first."

"I believe you now and I always will. You don't lie."

"No, I don't."

He leaned over then and kissed me on the lips.

****

Several nights later, Kate and I were curled into each other on the couch. She was making me watch a horror called 'The Dead Zone' and as I watched it, I thought, 'I'm him, I am Johnny'. I think she did it on purpose to torture me.

The phone rang and she answered because no one phoned me. It was Rob and she handed the phone to me with her eyebrows perched up.

"Hello?"

"I need your help," he said. "Can I come over?"

"Of course." How could I refuse?

Kate glared at me when I told her, and there were things I had not told her, but we all have a bit of the psychic in us and she had a bit of a hissy fit.

"Why did you say he could come? We were having a nice night, and we never get any time together."

"Well, I couldn't say no, could I?"

****

Rob's hand snaked round my neck and I could not help myself but respond. I felt my fingertips grip his waist and then I saw it.

He was sitting there, looking at his table. Pictures of me. Everywhere. He just kept looking.

He just kept looking…

****

He came over and got right to the point. "There's a man been reported missing. I know, I know – don't look at me like that, Kate, we get lots of reported missings and they all turn up, blah blah. I just think this one is different, and I wanted Jen to touch his picture." He looked at me with pleading eyes. Pleading eyes that I now knew were full of his love.

Kate guffawed and I felt my temperature rise. Oh, it wasn't that when you came to me with a picture. I suppose that was different.

"Let me see, Rob." She had never heard me call him Rob before, and I caught her sharp glance from the corner of my eye. Maybe it would make her believe me, and maybe it would make her love me more.

He handed me the photo. I took it and turned my back on Kate and I faced him, and then my eyes closed and the visions came. "Samuel MacGuire… He is dead… He went out, he drank a lot and had a good time and he sang and laughed and he walked home by the water and he started to sing some more and he raised his arms and he faced the waves and… He fell in and then he stopped singing and… I can't breathe… I can't get up… Mammy." My face stung from a smart slap.

"Leave her alone, Rob! It's not fair, you keep doing this to her!" Kate shouted.

"You did it too!"

"Just get out! This is my home now." And Rob left.

I slumped onto the couch and Kate came over and she took me in her arms and cuddled me tight, so tight it almost hurt, but I still let her.

****

The next morning I got a text from Rob. It said, 'Hi, I hope ur ok. We had a sighting in the Clyde, looks like we found the body. Sorry to have to do that 2 u last night. Kate doesn't like me. Fancy a pint some time?', and I replied, 'I am glad he has been found. Sure, pint sounds good.'

And then, I thought, why am I hiding him? I have done nothing to be ashamed of. My conscience said 'You kissed him back', and I knew this was true. Even though I loved Kate and I had never loved a man, I liked him and he cared – I could see that. And, most importantly, he believed me.

And so it went that I hid him. Kate worked nights and sometimes I met him for a drink, or he would drop in to the flat to see me, and even though I like lazing about in my old pyjamas, I did not feel intruded upon when he came. It was comfortable. That alone should have made me feel uncomfortable.

****

Rob and I were drunk in some pub in Byres Road. We were laughing and falling onto each other's knees over something stupid, and I thought then, for one fleeting moment, how easy it would be to love him: he believed me and I did not need to convince him. I gulped and looked into his handsome blue eyes, and he must have recognised some need in me because he stopped laughing and he looked straight back into my eyes.

And I knew then that I could love him, but I did not want to. I wanted my Kate. But it was too late, and he was kissing me and I was kissing him.

And I did not think, and I let his kisses and his love wash over me and I let him take me back to his flat and I let him… I let him.

I got a taxi home at 6am and Kate was asleep in our bed with Jonah curled into her hair. I felt the pangs of guilt hit me, as the alcohol wore off. Oh Lord, what had I done?

I went to the toilet and threw some water on my face, and glared at myself in the mirror, full of self-hatred.

And then I saw him.

Laughing at me. He said "Ha ha ha, can't catch me. You betrayed your lover. Ha ha ha."

I turned to shout but he was gone. I shivered.

I knew things were going to get bad now. And I could feel the distant thumping of a headache.

****

That morning, a few hours later, with a shit of a hangover, I stumbled out of bed. Kate was at the breakfast table, eating some toast and drinking coffee. I hate coffee, it makes me feel sick, and I took a deep breath to relieve the pangs of nausea.

She smiled at me, and I felt even more shit. "Jen, I didn't think you would manage to get up today, the state you rolled in."

I smiled back. I could not speak. I could not open my mouth for fear of blurting out what had happened the night before. But, if I told her, she would leave me and I did not want her to leave me and so I could not tell her, and I made the decision to lie to her. How much more could I hate myself?

"I'm sorry. I had a few too many and ended up in a taxi back to Becki's and…" I shrugged. "I woke up and came home. I'm sorry."

She finished her coffee, and stood up, smoothing down her skirt. I looked at her legs and thought how much I loved them wrapped around me and how dirty I felt for shitting on her. I had never done that in my life before, and I saw the guilt written all over my face. I went to her and I held her tight in my arms.

"Jen, you reek of drink. Go back to bed and sleep it off."

I thought, 'Yes, I will, I don't need to work today', and smiled a smile of utter shame and went back to bed. As I heard the door shut behind her, and Jonah crept into bed with me, I began to cry and fell asleep.

****

"You lied to me."

"What?" I was barely awake. Moments were coming back to me… A man between my legs, his pleasure, my disgust… Oh God, I *had* lied to her.

"Kate..."

"Fuck off!"

I heard her sob start before the phone went dead. And then I saw it all.

Jonah was laughing at me... Oh God, he had chosen Lorraine because she had aborted a child and he took over that child because he knew I would meet Lorraine and he had to reel me in to get me. What a fool I had been, as it became clearer and clearer, but hazier and hazier. He did not think he was Lorraine's child, he thought he was MINE!

But I had never had a child, or been pregnant... This made me fuzzy in my head.

But it did not matter what I thought; it was what Jonah thought that counted and he wanted to get back at me, I saw that now. He wanted to rip my heart from my chest and make me bleed.

My Kate... He would go for my Kate. I knew this and he had told me this. The woman I loved, the woman I would put before anything, the woman whose side I would rush to. He knew this and I knew he had her.

I had to find her. Again.

****

I rang the man I had betrayed her with, because, after all, he was a policeman, and I said, "Rob, help me find Kate."

He said "Tell me where you are" without hesitation, and I thought, 'Where am I? Where is she? Where should I be?' I closed my eyes and I tried to feel Jonah.

Nothing.

Fuck.

I took a deep breath and I tried to feel Kate.

Nothing.

I hyperventilated and tried to feel Rob.

Bingo.

"Kelvinbridge Park. Look for her."

And then the helpless fog descended and I was running, in a taxi, and running some more. And all the time, my heart was beating for my love, my love, my love, she whispers…

****

Who do you choose?
All or nothing?
Who do you choose?

****

I am there. I see Kate, and I see Rob and I see Lorraine, and I see Jonah.

Jonah is in Lorraine and she speaks and says, "Do you remember Kate when I told you she would love a man and you laughed?"

Oh God.

Rob looks at me.

"Ask her," Lorraine says. "You thought it funny at the time."

We are in a shed that the maintenance man drinks tea in. No one can see us. I see that Kate and Rob are tied up and I do not know how they got there. I cannot see everything!

Kate looks at me, with tears streaming down her eyes. "Jen, she is lying…"

I find that there is a weight on my heart and I cannot lie. "I love you, Kate."

Jonah/Lorraine gets angry "No, Jennifer, tell her you fucked him."

Kate looks at me, her tears are still rolling, "You did, you fucked him last night and you came home to me and…" She breaks into fresh tears.

I close my eyes and hate myself. I love this woman and I want to save her life because Lorraine does not have a knife this time, she has a gun.

Lorraine laughs and laughs and laughs, but it is Jonah laughing really. "You betrayed your lover. That's what you get for getting rid of me."

He still thinks he is my child, a child I have never had, and I realise I have to humour him. "I am sorry, Jonah. I am so sorry. Please forgive me. I will do anything to make this better."

Kate continues to cry and Rob is taking it all in, looking for a way out I hope.

"Anything?"

"Yes," and I am fearful as I say this.

Jonah struts and pushes his chest out. "Pick," he orders.

"Pick what?" I answer, helplessly.

"Pick one of these two to live," he says and absently points the gun.

It is Sophie's Choice, and I am Sophie, and how do I pick? How do I pick? My lovely Kate, who did nothing wrong but get involved with me. Rob, who loves me with all his heart and would do nothing but try and make me happy.

"I can't pick!" I scream.

"Pick," he says. "Or they will both die."

I have no reason to doubt him. "Oh God," I break down, "Why are you doing this to me?"

He threw his head back and laughed. "Because I can, because *you* did. You chose. Now choose again. You have 'til ten." And then he began to count.

Kate? Oh God, if I said Kate, he would kill Rob. Rob? If I said Rob, he would kill Kate. He is bluffing, if I say Kate because I love her most he will kill her.

"8… 9…"

"Rob!" I scream. "I pick Rob!"

Kate screamed in anguish and I shouted, "I'm sorry, I'm sorry, I'm sorry."

And then Jonah laughed and shot Rob three times in the skull, and shot Lorraine and it was over.

****

Except nothing is never over.

And my period is now five weeks late.

Chapter Four

For the third time that morning, I ran to my toilet and retched. I was meeting Kate for the first time since the inquiry following Rob's death at the hands of Lorraine, the suicidal maniac. Or helplessly possessed human as I saw her. I was a bag of nerves.

Of course there had been an inquiry. A policeman had been murdered. I had given evidence about this. How had I managed to "just be passing a hut in the middle of Kelvinbridge Park"? I was looking for my partner, DI Coutts, and had had an iPhone tracker which led me to that area. I had heard muffled noises, which had led me to investigate. At my point of entry, Lorraine had gone mad and shot DI McLean and herself.

I had not seen Kate since then, despite leaving messages for her to contact me. I knew she felt betrayed. I had admitted sleeping with him, I had chosen him over her. But could she not see I had picked him to save her? I knew Jonah would kill whoever I had wanted to save, so I had shouted "Rob!" to save my darling Kate. I would have to make her see.

I ran to the toilet and threw up again. As I left my flat to meet her, I counted nine weeks late and sighed.

****

My heart leapt as I saw her approach. Her strong calves pounded the pavement and I felt longing inside me. I fought back the urge to cry as my eyes feasted on the love of my life, a woman I would do anything for.

We sat across from each other, drinking tea (me) and coffee (her). I tried not to feel sick. She looked at me like she hated me. I died inside. The shame. I loved a woman and slept with a man – could I go any lower?

"I trusted you, Jen. Can you imagine what it felt like to have some nutter kidnap me and tell me, for the second time, that you had betrayed me.

"You know, I didn't believe her that time when you came and found me. She told me then you would betray me with a man, and I had laughed because I knew you. I knew you loved me and would never be unfaithful, never mind be unfaithful with a man. It just wasn't you.

"And then it was all true and you admitted to sleeping with… Rob… And then you picked him, you picked him."

I interrupted. "It wasn't like that, Kate. I knew if I picked you, Jonah would have killed you. I had to say Rob."

She leant in close and whispered, "Who the fuck is this Jonah, because I know it's not the fucking cat."

I hated her using bad language.

"Jonah. The spirit I told you of months ago. When Lorraine first had you by the throat, I was talking to Jonah then, to convince him not to kill us.

"Don't you remember? And then Rob came in, but by then I had shown Jonah that his mum loved him and hadn't wanted to abort him, and he melted into her. See, you don't see any of that. You never believe me, even when I have said stuff about you. I'm not making this up. I wish I was."

I sat back, exhausted at my outburst.

"I believed you when you said you loved me. I never thought you would sleep with a man. I *trusted* you."

I felt a prick of tears in my eyes. "I'm sorry. I don't know how to say how sorry I am. I touched him and I knew he loved me and you were being distant." I sounded like my ex, Julie, and I felt even more disgusted at myself.

"So that excuses it?" she shouted, and I noticed heads had turned to look in the small coffee bar.

"No," I hung my head in shame. "It doesn't, but I love you. I will do anything for you to come back. Please. I am begging."

She shook her head. And I thought I saw tears in her eyes too. "I don't know, Jen. It's all too sore."

****

I stood in the shower, rubbing my tummy. Inside there something was growing, and I panicked because I knew what it was. It was the seed of Rob's love. His child. A child which, if I had it, would mean I would never have Kate again. I began to cry and retch at the same time. I loved Kate and I did not want to be without her, but I did not believe in abortion. And yes, dammit, I had loved Rob – not in the same way, but he was my friend and he was dead, and this was a way of keeping him alive.

I lay in the bottom of the shower for a long time and sobbed. And I held my hands on my stomach whispering, "My baby, my baby", and I cried even more.

****

I had made up my mind even before my GP confirmed I was pregnant. I had always known, I suppose. And instead of crying, I began to smile because inside me was a life growing. A life that was half of me. A life that I would love forever. I would have this baby on my own, even if it meant never seeing Kate again, and I grew used to this being okay because I had my child inside me. My little eleven-week-old lump of nothing that meant everything to me.

I think I sort of became happy.

****

I got a call from a woman called Nina Grainger. She had been a friend of Kate's, who had heard me talking to "myself" in our kitchen and thought I was mad. She was the one whose arm I had held and knew she was not a truthful person. She told me she was calling on official police business about a suspected murder in Aberdeen and asked if I was willing to help.

It's not in my nature to say no, so I agreed. I have a gift that can help. And sometimes it cannot, but I have to do what I can and I will never say no.

Nina told me to get to Aberdeen – my expenses would be met – and she would come get me if I texted her my arrival time. I had nothing to go on, but I had been faced with worse scenarios and did not sense anything wrong.

The next day I listened to my iPod on the scenic journey to Aberdeen, which I found quite relaxing. I had already texted Nina when my train was arriving, and she had confirmed she would meet me and see me into a hotel. As was my habit, even though she never replied, I had texted Kate to tell her that I was en route to Aberdeen to help her friend Nina, and that I hoped she was okay. No response.

All went according to plan, and when I was safely ensconced in my room, Nina explained that the wife of a Glasgow drugs baron had gone missing and he suspected a local rival. Why were we in Aberdeen then, I asked. He lived there but had his underlings deal with his criminal empire in various parts of the country and so the nearer we were to him, perhaps the better the "signal" I could get. I nodded in agreement.

"Here is a picture of her," she offered, and I took it. "Her name is Benita and she is forty seven. Was forty seven."

I held the picture in my hand and studied the hard, blue eyes of the woman smiling back at me. I felt nothing.

"I'm sorry," I said. "I'm not getting anything."

"It's okay," she smiled. "Tomorrow, I will pick you up and take you to his house."

"Does he know about me?"

"Yes, but it's been explained it may not work."

"Oh, okay," I said relieved. There was nothing worse than a grieving relative begging for information on their departed loved ones, and I tried to avoid that if I could.

Nina left and I settled into my room, got a bottle of wine from room service, and watched some rubbish on telly.

I woke up, and Rob was sitting at the end of my bed. "Hey, Toots."

It was an old joke. "Don't you call me Toots! It's Jenny. J-E-N-N-Y. Jenny."

"You have to leave here and go home," he said.

"Why?" I asked, understandably curious.

"Because my baby is at risk."

I flushed. "I'm only helping out on a murder. I'm not doing much." I don't know why I was making excuses rather than wondering why he was in a hotel room in the middle of Aberdeen. When he was dead.

"I love you, Jenny. I know it means nothing now because I'm dead, but I do, and I am not going to let any harm come to you. Or my child."

I took a deep breath. "I'm not going to let anything happen to our child."

He smiled sadly. "You have walked into a trap, my love."

I was getting narked. "Don't call me your love. I am not your love."

"Oh, you are my love and there is nothing you can do about it. But this isn't really about you. It's about Kate, so listen to me. Closely…"

****

I had my bags packed, ready to do a runner after what Rob had told me. Nina Grainger was on the payroll of James McManaman, known as "Big Jimmy". Known as the Godfather. When I had gone into Kelvinbridge Station looking for Kate and had held Nina and detailed one of her drug drops, she had shat her pants and wanted me out the picture before I dropped her in it. So she had lured me to Aberdeen, far enough away from Glasgow for her to be implicated, and now I was going to be taken to Big Jimmy's, where I would likely never see the light of day again.

What I didn't know at that point was that she had assumed I had told Kate about this, and so she also wanted Kate out of the picture. Or Big Jimmy did; it was all the same.

I opened the hotel room door and Nina was standing there, about to knock. "Going somewhere?" she said, eyeing up my bag.

I have learned how to play cool and replied, "I assumed after I had solved the mystery of the missing wife, I would be free to go home."

She smiled. "Yes. Come on, my car's outside."

Rob had told me to get out of Aberdeen, and tell Kate exactly what Nina was all about. He knew Kate was an honest copper and would do the rest.

"And under strange skies… we cling… on lost trails…"

I was driven to Big Jimmy's house. Mansion, in fact. I sat, looking cool as a cucumber, panicking to high heaven inside about how I was going to get out of this one. Nina introduced us to the bodyguards at the gates and they let us in. It was a fortress! My hand instinctively went to my tummy and began to rub.

Nina picked up on this and asked, "You okay?", nodding at my stomach.

"Yes. I think I must've eaten something dodgy at the hotel."

She laughed. "That's the sheep-shagging cooks up here for you."

I forced a smile. They are not going to hurt my baby. They are not going to hurt my baby.

I will do whatever it takes. They are not going to hurt my baby.

We arrived at the front of the house and were ushered into a huge living room. I did not need to fake how impressed I was. Drug dealing obviously paid well. Before long, Big Jimmy joined us.

He was, indeed, big. About 6'4" tall and just as wide, he was an imposing figure. "You must be Miss Keith, our psychic. Come here and shake my hand, lass." I did as I was told. "Has Nina told you about my wife?"

"Just that she is missing. It's best I don't know more, really. Don't want my judgement impaired,"

I tried to smile but think I grimaced. Great, good going, Jen, keep it up. Don't want to get shot here and have your brains splattered all over this nice expensive Persian rug, as that will just be a total bitch to clean.

"She *is* missing. She went shopping down in Glasgow and the fucking weegies have got her, I know it, the small-balled cunts."

I tried not to blush at his language and nodded.

"What do you need?" he asked, and at that, I realised his wife really was missing and, as much as he maybe wanted me out of the picture, he wanted his wife back.

"If you have a photo, and maybe something of hers that she has worn recently, that would be a start," I offered.

He flicked his head at Nina and off she trotted, obviously familiar and comfortable with his large house. We were alone.

"Most people are scared of me, you know," he said. "Why aren't you, lass?"

"Should I be?"

He laughed. "How do I know you're real? You could be a fake. Can you tell the winning lottery numbers?"

Now I laughed. "If I knew them, do you think I would be living in a wee two-bed flat?"

He smiled, then quickly it faded. His eyes turned to slits as he considered me. "Tell me something then. Convince me."

Convince me or I'll kill you, I thought.

I walked over to him, my heart hammering behind my ribs and I grabbed his wrist. I closed my eyes, took some deep breaths and off we went.

"Hard man? I'll show YOU a fucking hard man! Your father battered you with a walking stick. The police brought you home, you were only young, maybe fourteen or fifteen. You hated it there with your parents – your dad with his walking stick and bottle of whisky, your mother, eyes blacked, shaking from head to toe. Your sister. Maddie? Hunched over the sink, hands red raw. Jimmy will get out of this. Jimmy will be rich. Killed your first man at eighteen, strangled with your own hands. Oh God, your own father."

I felt myself fall over as Big Jimmy pulled himself away. He was ashen, the effect the truth has on disbelievers. He was about to speak when Nina walked in with a photo of the wife and a scarf. Jimmy had gotten himself a drink and was glaring at me. I rubbed my stomach. My baby.

"Give her them," he grunted at Nina and she came and handed me the photo and scarf.

I had a feeling I was in deep shit. Pardon my language. I took the photo and scarf and turned my back on them. I tried to feel something, but nothing came. I jammed my eyes shut hard. Not a dot.

When I opened them, Rob was standing in front of me. "Make something up."

"What?"

I heard Nina say "Who she talking to?"

Rob said, "Stop speaking out loud, they can hear you. His wife isn't dead. Make something up. You need to get out of here."

Jimmy said "How the fuck should I know? She's your medium."

"What?" I repeated, shaking my head a bit.

"Jesus, Jen, shut up! You have to say something so that they think they still need you. You need to get out of here alive. If you don't, they will kill you."

I took another deep breath, for all it was worth. "Your wife, oh shops. Diamonds and gold. She's happy. Then something… I can't see… Someone… She's in a car… She's being driven, it's dark and I think she… She's okay, she's alive."

Big Jimmy had gotten up and was coming at me. "She's alive?"

Oh for fuck's sake. Why was Jonah now here?

I had turned, hearing Jimmy's footsteps and saw Jonah laughing beside him.

"Worked it out yet, medium?" he asked.

"Worked what out?" I asked.

Jimmy looked puzzled. "Who the fuck are you talking to now?"

"A spirit," I answered tersely, my fear having gone.

I could see Jimmy turn around and look at the nothing he saw.

"Where's my fucking wife?" Jimmy roared.

"I don't know."

Jonah giggled "Work it out, medium."

"I don't know what I'm supposed to be working out!"

"You're supposed to be working out where the fuck my wife is!"

It was like trying to listen to the telly and radio at the same time.

I pointed at Jimmy. "Your wife is somewhere in Glasgow." I pointed at Jonah. "I don't know what I am meant to work out."

Nina spoke then. "Jimmy, if your wife is in Glasgow, I'll find her. We should get Jen home."

"The deal is off," he said. "I need her. She can help me find Benita."

****

I sat on the train home from Aberdeen with more questions than answers. A drug dealer would "be in touch" about his missing wife, and Jonah, the spirit of an aborted child, my aborted child, asked me if I had "worked it out yet". I did not know what I was supposed to work out. I had my child in my belly and I was not going to get rid of it. I had been lured into some sort of trap and Rob, my saviour of before, had talked me through it, to save his unborn child.

Where was Kate? Why had Rob said it was all about her?

I sat on the train and Rob appeared.

He said, "Have you worked it out yet, medium?"

Chapter Five

It's always the same. I awake from the dream, screaming something. And this time I am screaming the name of a woman who used to be my lover.

"Julie!"

And my lover now, Kate, wakes me and says "Shush, it's alright", but she is not amused. I would not be amused either if she had woken me shouting her ex's name.

But, it was not her, it was me. As usual, so I was finding, I was becoming the sinner in a sinner/saint relationship. And that annoyed me a little, too.

"Jen, you okay?" she whispered.

"Mmm," I mumbled.

We both fell back asleep and did not mention it. Until the next night. "Julie!"

I sat bolt upright, annoyed now at being awake. Some sort of foggy memory was skirting around my recognition.

Kate sighed. "Julie again?"

"Mmm," I mumbled and tried to go back to sleep. I slipped my arm around Kate, but something had begun to nag me. So I lay awake a wee while…

I remembered a time of being with Julie. I remember dancing up close to her, grinding our hips together. I remember sitting in my flat, drinking wine and laughing. I remember lying on top of her and a shiver running through my whole body as I kissed her neck. I remember not knowing she was fucking someone else, someone else in my bed, and I know how much that hurt me. I would never forget that.

"Jen?"

"Yes, my love?" I replied, as I toasted some bread.

"Why are you dreaming of your ex?"

"I don't know. I haven't worked it out yet," I answered, in all honesty.

"Do you think that's fair on me?"

Before I answered, I had to think. Did she think I could control my dreams? Had the experiences we had shared not taught her anything about me?

"What do you mean, babe?" and as I said it, I moved in for a cuddle.

She moved quickly, so as not to avoid me obviously, but to avoid me.

"Well, how would you feel if I started shouting my ex's name?"

"I'd think you had my psychic gene," I joked. Her silence shut me up.

Until the third night in a row, when I again woke shouting "Julie!"

"We have to find her, Kate. There's a reason I'm shouting her name. I just can't quite grasp it yet. You know, like you are walking in fog and you know the road is just around the corner but you can't see it…" I was babbling.

"You want me to find your ex-girlfriend?" she asked, at 3 o'clock in the morning, through a thin veil of patience.

"Yes," I said, feebly.

"Okay," she sighed and went back to sleep.

****

I got off the train at Queen Street station in Glasgow with a thousand questions battering around my small brain. I bought a Subway and went looking for a taxi. As it drove away, I wiped some mayo from my chin and fleetingly remembered that I had met Julie at this taxi rank. I got home, unpacked my case, threw some clothes in the washing basket and opened the fridge. A bottle of white wine was chilling. I would leave it for later.

After pottering around for a bit and checking my answering machine (nothing), I decided to clean the bath, and then later I could relax with some candles, a good book and that cold glass of wine.

I was on my hands and knees scrubbing with the ever-reliable 'multi-purpose cleaner' when I had a shooting pain in my left hand and dropped my cloth. The pain slowly subsided and began anew in my head. It went the way it always does and the pain became a vision.

I saw my Julie standing in a long line on a hot summer's day, laughing and joking with a woman beside her. They go through entrance gates and wander on. I watch them meandering, get a pint in a plastic beaker and walk on.

My concentration is broken by a banging at my door. I open the door to Kate, who barges in past me, leaving a scent of her perfume, New West for Women. The perfume my Julie wore…

"Where have you been?" she demands. "I've been worried sick."

"I sent you a text. I told you I was in Aberdeen with Nina. I'm just back."

"Nina!" she spat.

"I know. I have to talk to you about her. Do you want to sit down or stand shouting at me in the hall?"

She stormed through to the living room and sat where she had always sat. I yearned for her to sit there forever.

"And what do you mean, you were worried sick? You haven't been in touch since I last saw you. You can't be that worried."

"I've been watching from afar."

"Spying on me? Making sure I don't go off with anyone else?"

"No. I just like to know you're okay."

"Why?"

"Because I love you, that's why! Look, never mind that. What were you doing in Aberdeen?"

I sat down next to her and let my story unravel. I would leave out the bit about Rob. "Nina Grainger rang me and asked if I would help her on a missing person's case. You know me, I said yes and she asked me to go to Aberdeen, she would book me a hotel, etc. Anyway, that time when I was looking for you, when Lorraine got us, I had gone into your station and I spoke to Nina. I'd touched her and felt she wasn't an honest person.

"That was confirmed in Aberdeen. She is in cahoots with some crime lord called Jimmy McManaman, whose wife is apparently missing. I'm not sure how – drugs at the least."

"I know," she said, softly. "I've been investigating her for months." She put her head in her hands. "Jesus, Jen, you cannot keep running around putting yourself in danger. Leave it to people who are trained. You could have been killed."

"Look, she knows I know. And she thought I had already told you. It's you they want out of the picture, not me, I'm just a crank. Who would believe me?" I put my hand on her thigh, gingerly. "You need to have her arrested. I'm worried for you."

She looked up, and a tear slid down her cheek. "You're so good."

She broke my heart. "I'm not good. I just love you and I don't want anything to happen to you. I want…" I choked. "I just want you back."

She kissed me. "I'll come back."

****

We lay naked in bed, smiling into each other's eyes. I was so happy I could burst. I leaned over and kissed Kate's forehead and she smiled, and I felt the nest of butterflies flutter in my stomach. She was beautiful.

"What are you going to do about Nina and Jimmy?" I asked. I had a feeling I would somehow end up involved in all that was to come.

"I'll have to speak to my boss. You know I can't really tell you anything, but I want you to move into my flat, just for the time being, to be safe."

"I thought you had rented it out?"

"I had but the tenants left and I needed somewhere to stay, so I moved back in when we… split up."

I hated those words. I had seen my life without Kate and I did not want to imagine it again, not now that I had her back in my arms.

"What do you know about Jimmy's wife?"

"I don't know anything about her, except from a photo. I know she's alive – that's all."

"We think she has been kidnapped by a rival gang, possibly to kill, possibly to extort cash."

"Can't I help?"

"I don't want you involved, Jen. That's my final word." Sealed with a kiss so that I could not argue. Why would I want to argue and spoil that kiss?

****

The next day I had promised I would throw some stuff together and take it to Kate's flat, and get some food in after my afternoon lectures. I was true to my word and found myself happily humming in Kate's kitchen. Jonah sniffed about, unhappy at being transported in his box and had a poo in his litter tray to exact his revenge. I was happily ensconced in cleaning Kate's fridge, when I was hit with the pain in my head again. I put my hand up to my head, and when I drew my palm away, my sight blurred into a vision.

Julie. Leaning into a fridge.

This fridge.

Kate never told me if she had managed to find her.

****

I had forgotten about that. I had stopped screaming Julie's name in my dreams, and I had forgotten. Kate had never mentioned it and it slipped my mind. How could I be so careless? What were these visions trying to tell me? And I still hadn't told Kate I was pregnant. I didn't know if she would stay with me knowing that, and I could not bear to lose her again when I had only just got her back. If I loved her hard enough, she would stand by me. And we could be a family. Maybe I delude myself a bit. It was just such a beautiful picture in my mind that I would not have it ripped away. Not yet.

I rang Julie's parents and got a number for her. They had always been fond of me and had briefly stayed in touch after we parted, until it just became awkward. I rang Julie. She was surprised to hear from me, but agreed to meet me the following week. I didn't know what I was going to say to her, but I figured something would slip into place. Things always came to a head. Things always resolved. Usually.

Kate came in from work and threw her arms around me. "All well, my gorgeous woman?"

"All's well," I replied.

As I put out some dinner for her, I told her I had rung Julie and was meeting her next week. I would never lie to her again.

"You can't," she said, flatly. "You can't meet her."

"Why not?" I asked, puzzled. "Oh God, baby," I realised, putting my arms around her from behind, as she sat in front of her plate. "I'm not going to go off with her, or suddenly think I love her again. It's you I love. It's just, well... Do you remember ages ago when I used to wake up shouting her name? I never got to the bottom of that and I've had a few more odd things happen. I'm just hoping if I see her I'll get the answers as to why."

"No. I don't want you to."

I stood back. "Kate, what's going on? This isn't you."

She took a deep breath. "There's something I haven't told you about Julie. Fuck!" Her mobile started ringing. "Yeah... Where?... On my way. I have to go. The investigation with Nina has taken a turn. She's been found holed up with Jimmy's wife. We're going in. I'll be back as soon as I can, don't wait up."

She ran out the door. What the...? I grabbed my coat and ran after her. What hadn't she told me? I jumped in my car and sped off after hers, my mind racing.

Then Rob was in the passenger seat and he said, "Have you worked it out yet?"

"No. Leave me alone. Go away."

"I'm so sorry," he said and disappeared. Just what I needed. A miserable ghost.

I saw Kate run into what looked to me like an empty warehouse. There were other cars, and I assumed other officers, but I couldn't see anyone. I ran as hard as I could, and I caught Kate running up some stairs.

"Kate!" I shouted.

She stopped at the top and turned, her face aghast with horror seeing me. "What are you doing here? Get out!"

And then I was back into my old dream. I saw Julie walking with another woman. They stood at entrance gates, and paid their way in. They meandered and bought a pint and walk on. The woman looked back over her shoulder. It was my Kate.

I open my eyes, reeling. "You *know* her?"

I stagger back and my foot loses its placing. I fall backwards down the stairs. That is the last thing I remember.

****

I wake up in a hospital bed.

Oh God. My baby.

Chapter Six

I am having a dream. I know it is a dream, so I am not panicking. Yet. I cannot see myself, but I am driving in a car, not my car, and I am going someplace that has lots of green around it. It's not a bad dream and, because I know it's a dream, I try to make things happen the way you can in a dream that you own. I try to imagine slowing down, but the car speeds up and a small knot of anxiety begins to build. I put my foot on the brake pedal but nothing happens, and the car is speeding faster and faster. I am beginning to flail at the steering wheel and, out of nowhere, from mist that has just appeared, I see a stag with huge antlers staring right into the windscreen, and before I know it, I am swerving the car and I am veering off the road.

And then it goes dark again, and there is a pain in my head. I am groggy and trying to rouse myself. I do not like this dream anymore. I feel cold and the coldness is working its way up from my feet, washing over my legs, I feel my hips and stomach pinch from a frost all around my skin, like a million small darts stabbing me. I cannot move my head. And the cold and wetness is continuing to move up my body. The wetness. And now the anxiety is not a knot, but a paralysing fear, as I realise I am in water and I cannot move, and the water is filling me. I try to open my eyes and search the darkness. I cannot make a thought in my mind. I am overtaken by the freezing cold that is all around me. I open my eyes. The last thing I see before I close my eyes is the girl coming towards me....

I awoke in a cold sweat. Why?

That was not my dream.

****

Oh God. My baby.

I awoke in a cold sweat and saw Kate sitting in a chair, beside a bed that I was in. Of course, I was in hospital. I had fallen down some stairs.

"Kate, my…"

"Your baby is fine," she finished for me. I closed my eyes with relief. My little peanut was still there, growing away inside me. And then I remembered seeing my Kate with my Julie.

"What happened?" I asked.

"You took a step backwards and lost your footing, by all accounts. I ran to help you and called an ambulance, you were out cold. But you're fine, don't worry, and you can go home any time you like."

"Nina?" I managed.

"Nina got away," she sighed.

****

That day, she took me home and she put me to bed and brought me in a cup of tea.

"You want to know, don't you, Jenny?"

"Yes."

"I thought you might have seen some signs."

I remembered my Julie, full of bitterness, saying the very same thing.

"I'm just a person, Kate. I don't know everything. So, come on, when did you start sleeping with my ex?" I saw her wince but didn't care.

"Shouldn't I be asking you when you were going to tell me you were fucking pregnant?" she spat back. Let battle commence.

"I was going to tell you but I was scared. Can't you understand that? I had only just got you back, and to turn around and say, 'Oh, by the way, I'm having Rob's kid' wasn't an easy thing to find the right time for."

"So it's his?"

"Oh my God, who did you think was the father?"

"How should I know? You went behind my back once. That I know of."

"That's not fair, Kate."

"Yes, it *is* fair. You lied about sleeping with him. I had to find out from a nutter. A nutter! Who then shot herself!" She laughed with bitterness.

"How do I know what else you lied about?"

"I've never lied to you! *You* lied to me!"

"Oh? What did I lie about?"

"You lied about being with Julie."

"Think very carefully, Jenny. When did I ever say anything about Julie?"

I thought carefully and she was right. She never told me about her past relationships, just a word here and there.

"You could have still said."

"Said what, Jenny? 'Oh, your ex? Yes, she's my ex too'. Would that have made you feel better? It's the past, and that's where it belongs."

I know Kate and I know she does not like to relive the past.

"Tell me now then. I need to know."

She sighed. "We were together for a couple of years, okay? It was no big deal and very casual for a long time."

"How did you meet her?"

"I saw her profile on 'Gaydar Girls'. We messaged a few times, and went for a drink. She was honest, told me she was with you but it wasn't working."

Wasn't working? That would be the first I knew.

"*When* did you meet her?"

I could see her rummaging about in her brain. "A couple of years before I met you."

And that is why I could not smell another woman's perfume in my bed. They wore the same one.

"Why did you split up?" I asked.

"We wanted different things. It was never going to work."

I really did believe her but there was only one way to be sure… I grabbed her wrist and saw my Julie, crumpled in tears, sobbing hysterically and screaming “I can’t do it!” and my Kate, shaking her head sadly, and walking away.

“Stop doing that!” she pulled herself back violently.

I knew a girl once called Violet, who liked to say her name had a silent ‘n’ but that’s a different story…

“Are you going to stay with me?” I asked, because I had to know. I loved her and I had to know.

A song came on the radio. She sang. It was ‘The Chain’ by Fleetwood Mac. I love Stevie Nicks. And I love Kate, and I have to know.

“That depends.”

“On what, Kate?”

“On whether or not you keep the baby.”

“I’m keeping the baby.”

“Then you can’t keep me.”

****

I think I cried myself to sleep that night and the next night and the next. Kate left to go to her work, but she always came back again and she looked after me; she cooked for me and she brought me cups of tea and she run me baths. But she never touched me. The days were ticking by, and she was waiting for me to say I would have an abortion.

It was a choice. All or nothing.

What do you chose? All? Or nothing?

Every day when she came back to me in her flat, the relief washed over me. I felt sore when she left me, a pain that started in my heart and did not know where it wanted to end. How could I live a life without her? Who can turn their back on love? I knew I would never love again in the way that I loved her, that I would never find the one to die by the sea with. There would be no one else to grow old with, my heart so full of love for her.

How could I ever love someone else when I would always ache for her underneath?

All or nothing.

****

I recognised Julie straight away when she came walking over to greet me in the way she always had. She kissed me on the left cheek. And the butterfly explosion that used to be in my stomach was no longer there. She was wearing a hat that I bought her, because it was February and February in Glasgow is not warm. We were in the Polo Lounge, and ordered a pot of tea for two.

"So, how have you been, Jen? I didn't expect to hear from you."

She took her hat off. Her hair was stuck down at the front and I fought the urge to move it. That is what I would have done before, but not now.

"I'm fine. Look, I didn't ask you to meet me for old time's sake. I need answers."

I could see the look of uncomfortableness stretch across her face and tried to reassure her.

"No, Julie, not about us. Well, not really. About you and Kate. The one you left me for."

"How did you find out about her?" she asked, looking genuinely puzzled. Then a look of realisation hit her and she said, "Ah, you saw it?"

"No. I'm with her."

"What?"

"Kate is my partner."

"Well, knock me down with a feather and bugger me backwards. I knew she would get you in the end."

Now it was I who was puzzled. "What are you talking about?"

"Jenny, she was practically obsessed with you."

"Wait, wait. Start at the beginning. Don't leave anything out to spare my feelings, please."

She sipped some tea. "I met her through 'Gaydar'. You were never about. You spent all your time with that copper, McLean, on that kid's murder. It wasn't that I didn't love you, Jenny. I guess I'm just shallow and wanted attention."

"It's okay," I soothed, taking her hand across the table. I could do this because I did not love her any more. If I had loved her, I would have felt unfaithful, but she was more like an old friend that I had known since childhood, safe.

"Och, you know how it goes." No. I didn't. "We met a few times, I thought she was pretty. Things progressed…"

I interrupted. "You told her about me?"

"Not exactly. Not in the beginning. After we had… slept together… I told her I lived with a woman. She wasn't concerned, it was very casual. For a long time we just met for sex because I still loved you." Her face pained. "And then I sort of, you know, started to love her and wanted more." She paused.

"Right? And then what?"

"Has she not told you any of this?"

I pursed my lips. "No."

"Well, then I brought her to the flat when you were out and she saw your photos and she asked about you. Who were you? How had we met? What did you do? Where were you? Everything and anything."

"You told her about my gift, didn't you?"

"Yes. I had to. It was how we met, after all. Taxi. Don't get it." She smiled. "It's funny how you can remember the beginning but never the end."

"The perfume."

"What about it?" she said.

"Who wore it first?"

"Me," she laughed. "You bought it for me."

Yes. Yes, I *had* bought it for Julie. I had forgotten that. So Kate had smelled it on my Julie and taken it as her own.

"What happened then?"

She took a large intake of breath. "After I left you, I moved into her flat and, for a year, things were great. But I wanted a child."

Uh oh.

"We talked about it and she wasn't keen, but I took matters into my own hands and used a gay friend – do you remember Geoff? I used him and a turkey baster. I thought she would be okay. But she wasn't." Her eyes mist over and I knew she still loved my Kate. Like I loved her. "When I told her I was pregnant, she hit the roof. And I mean went fucking scripto! She wanted me to get rid of him and I refused, and there was a kind of stalemate and then she left me."

"When was this?"

She crumpled her eyebrows, in exactly the way I used to love when she was thinking, and said, "Around the time of that Charlton Heston killer."

I feel like I had been punched in the stomach. Around the time I walked into Pitt Street station and met Kate in the flesh for the first time.

"Don't you want to ask me about the baby, Jenny?"

****

I know it is Kate's day off because she did not want me to go out today. She did not know I was meeting Julie. I did not lie. I just omitted a detail.

Two can play that game, I thought. There is so much I want to say to the woman I love who, in some ways, I simultaneously hate.

And it is as I am walking that I realise I am being followed. I should feel scared but all I can feel is anger. Kate with Julie. Julie pregnant. Kate saying no. Kate with me. Me pregnant. Kate saying no. I hear my name being called and I am exasperated.

"What?"

"Do ya remember me, lass?"

Holy shit. It was big Jimmy McManaman, and he was crying. "Ah canny live withoot ma Benita. Ye need ta tell me where she is, hen."

Feck. Where was my miserable ghost Rob now, when I needed him?

I had no choice but to take Jimmy up to Kate's flat. He was inconsolable. It was quickly established that Jimmy did not care about police involvement, but that he just wanted his wife safely returned. He did not know that Nina had his wife;

he trusted her. Kate set him straight. He punched a hole in her kitchen door and then quickly apologised and took a fifty pound note from a wad in his pocket and laid it on the table, for 'her trouble'.

"Ring her, Jimmy, and set up a meet. I'll come with you. She won't know. We can get Benita back."

That was all the convincing Jimmy took, and he rang Nina. Act normal, we had emphasised. I casually strolled behind Jimmy and rubbed his shoulder, hoping to get a view of what might happen. I didn't.

"Nina, what the fuck is going on, hen? Where urr ye…? Am in fucking Glesga… Weegie bastards… Where urr ye? Right. Am coming. Don't fucking move!"

"She's…"

… at a flat in Ibrox. Oh for fuck's sake, how many times?

****

Middleton Street. I have been here before in the fog. It smells of marijuana and chicken pakora. Not entirely unpleasant.

I am with Jimmy. The plan is that he and I shall go in and confront Nina. Between the two of us, and Kate pulling up the rear, we can take her. Kate is calling for back up when we know for sure she is there.

And, of course, she is there. She opens the door to a flat and we troop in.

"Why's she here?" she asks, pointing at me.

Jimmy roars impressively. "Because I fucking want her here!"

I am clumsy and lose my footing often. I trip over a loose floorboard and fall into Nina. And then I get a pain in my head and my mouth is running away with me before my brain can shut it up. "Where is my Jimmy? Tell me, you fucking pig! He will kill you for this, kill you – do you get that? Fucking skin you alive. Get that away from me, you pig bitch!"

"Jimmy, she's killed her!" I scream.

And then all hell breaks loose. Jimmy lunges for Nina. Kate throws herself in the door. Jimmy has Nina on the floor with his hands on her neck and Kate says, “Jimmy, off her, leave it to us. OFF!”

Strangely, he gets off her and stands up. Nina remains on the floor. Kate walks over to check Jimmy is okay, and I see Jonah.

“Mummy, she wants you to kill me,” he says.

“No!” I scream, as Nina reaches for the gun in her jacket. “No, I chose *you*, Jonah!” and Nina shoots me in the stomach.

****

I worked it out.

****

I am in a dark room and I cannot move my limbs. There is rope around my ankles and wrists, tying me to a chair. A naked man walks into the room, licking his lips and says, “Well, what do we have here?”

****

I awake from the nightmare and my hand goes to my empty stomach.

Chapter Seven

I know I am in my bed but I am a dead weight on the mattress. I cannot move. Except my head. I can turn from side to side, and as I turn from side to side, I see a video camera set up in the corner of the small, dark room next to a single bed. I can see the red light flashing. A bed-sheet has been nailed over the window. I can smell damp. I realise I am naked and tied, sitting on a chair. My feet are tied to a leg of the chair and my arms behind my back, wrapped too tightly in a rope that is chafing my wrists. There is a rag in my mouth, stuck with tape, so my cries are muffled. I am petrified.

The door opens and in walks the man, naked. “Well,” he says “And what do we have here?”

I lower my head in the shame of my nakedness, and see my body.

But it is not my body. The legs are too skinny and the knees too bony. My toenails are dirty and I only have four toes on my right foot, as there is no little toe. I bring my eyes up from my knees to my skinny thighs and I see I am a boy. A young boy. I have no pubic hair. I am barely developed.

I begin to struggle as the smiling man takes a step closer. The chair begins to tip and I try to scream, but it is noiseless, and as I am falling, he is getting closer with that smile.

The chair falls back and we topple. I am helpless. I smell him before I see his face lean over. “Action!”

****

I wake in my bed. Cold and alone. I know I have tried to scream, the way you try to scream in dreams and nothing happens. And when the reality of being awake hits me, I open my mouth and let the scream emerge.

“Shush,” she says, because she is never far away. She barely leaves my side. “I’m here, you’re safe.”

But she had been there before, and I had not been safe, and I had lost my baby.

****

I think it was three months ago that Nina Grainger shot me in the stomach and caused me to lose my baby. It might have been four months ago. I am so burdened by grief that I cannot tell day from night. These things happen in split seconds and when Kate had turned and saw Nina drawing a gun, she had drawn hers – I did not know she even carried a gun – but Nina had got her shot off first before Kate's hit her. Kate had not shot to kill, she had shot to disarm, and now Nina was locked up, awaiting trial for kidnap and murder amongst other things.

It did not make me feel any better because Jonah had been there and he had said, "Mummy, she wants you to kill me." Not "Mummy, she is going to kill me". A small but crucial difference.

She.

Kate.

My Kate. That I loved with all my heart.

That I *had* loved with all my heart.

I do not know if I even have a heart any longer.

****

She came every day and she washed me and she fed me and she talked to me. I let her. Nothing could rouse me from the depression of losing my baby. I never even asked her why she came. And some days I think I would not have noticed if she had not.

Time has no meaning when you are in the throes of grief. Every minute, every second, is just an ache inside. A heaviness that won't shift. A bunch of questions that all start with 'If'. If I had done this, or if I had done that differently, I might have a big fat belly right now and feel some small persons feet pushing into my bladder, making me want to pee.

I had nothing. All or nothing. I had chosen all, and I had got nothing.

I did not care if I never saw Kate again. I looked at her when she would dress me with my dead eyes, and wondered why she was here. What brought her back? Guilt? I never spoke to her. But she still came. I noticed her eyes were dead eyes too now.

****

I was alone. The TV was on, but I was not watching it. It was just a noise in the background to give the impression of normality. From the corner of my eye, I saw a familiar shape and turned my head to Rob.

For the first time in as many months, I felt the first thing akin to an emotion. I choked with the feeling inside of me. I could feel the tears sting me and blinked to prevent them. This was the daddy I had let down. After he had warned me, too.

"I'm sorry, I'm sorry," I began to cry.

"No," he smiled and a light grew all around him. I felt my mouth open in awe, and he reached his hand towards mine and a string of light hit me. A warm feeling, of deep happiness and love washed over me. "It's okay, Toots. I've got Jonah, he is with his daddy now."

"But… but…" I stammered.

"You chose him, he saw that. It's fine."

"I don't understand, Rob. Of course, I chose him. He was my baby. How could I not?"

He smiled "Jonah is only young, and he got confused. I wasn't there to show him, but I am now."

"Show him what?"

"Time isn't the same here, Jenny. It's hard to explain. There is no future and no past, just one big now. Jonah was here before me, but he wasn't really. You lost him and he lost his way a bit. All he could focus on was the love he felt off you, and that love was for Kate. Before that, he had got mixed up with Lorraine. He just got muddled up.

"He did not have your love to focus on until he met you, and that's when he felt a force drawing him to you. You have to understand he is only a baby and doesn't know. He saw Lorraine, and her life and he thought he was hers, but it was only to draw you in, he didn't get it. Then Lorraine passed and he knew that wasn't right. So, he focused on Kate, the strongest emotion that he could get, and he saw her asking someone else to choose, and she chose the life. He saw Kate asking you to choose, and he knew he was not the life and he got it wrong. He thought you had chosen her and not him, and he hurt.

"It was his hurt that his mother didn't want him."

The tears flowed freely down my face. "But I *did* want him!" I sobbed.

"He knows that now. Don't you, Jonah?" and Rob turned and looked into the light. I saw my baby, my Jonah, come walking to me, with the biggest, happiest smile I have ever seen on a child's face.

"Hi, Mummy," he simply said.

I broke into fresh sobs. "Hi, baby," I managed.

"I'm okay now, Mummy, I've got my Daddy," and he turned his radiant smile to Rob. The look of love passed between them and I cried some more.

"Mummy, you can't be sad now. I'll see you again one day, and we can smile together."

My heart broke down the middle. I couldn't speak.

"Jen, you really can't be sad now. You have work to do."

I could not remove the lump from my throat. Just let me hold him one time! My little boy. Blond hair, blue eyes, a dimple in his chin. I want to feel my arms around him and breathe in the scent of him. I don't want to feel empty inside.

Rob turned again to me and let the light wash over me. I could live in that light.

"Jenny, it is not your time to be with us, but one day it will be. You have to start living again. You have a link between our world and yours, and you need to use it. You have it for a reason."

I began to breathe in deeply. Everything was okay. In a way. It was certainly better than it was yesterday.

"I will. I'll live," I said.

****

Seeing my slow return to trying to live a life, Kate decided to take me away for the weekend. We would go to Ayr for a couple of days and walk along the beach. She had grown up in Ayr, and loved the beach. She was excited to show me the places that she loved, and I could see she hoped her excitement would jolt some feeling in me. We had never spoken about what would happen with us, I just accepted that she came to my flat every night and slept on the sofa and then left for her work. I never asked myself why because I had been so absorbed in my own misery and, when it finally occurred to me, I felt bad because I knew she was a good person and whatever made her think the way she thought, was because of what had happened to her to make her the person she was.

That was not my fault, or her fault.

I began to look at her again, with a small glow in my heart. I watched the way she squeezed the teabag to make the cup of tea exactly the way I liked it, and then added the milk. I watched the way she handed me the cup at the kitchen table and then ran the spoon under the sink to prevent the staining, because she knew stained spoons annoyed me. I had told her that once. I had only needed to tell her once. Because she listened to me and she thought of me, in the smallest of ways.

She put the washing up liquid upside down in the cupboard so I did not have to squeeze. She put the lid back on the toothpaste. She changed the loo roll when it was almost done. She emptied the hoover. I had forgotten all those nice things about her…

We strolled along Ayr beach and there was a bit of a breeze, so she put her arm in mine and we shared some body heat.

I smiled at her and said, "I love you."

Her reaction surprised me, because she burst into tears and threw her arms around me.

"Oh Jen, I never thought I would ever hear you say that again!"

I held her back. She was, after all, the woman that I loved.

And I did love her. Yes. I loved.

It all came flooding back. My love.

I tightened my grip on her. "Thank you, Kate. Thank you for not abandoning me."

She cried and cried into me. Almost like the first time she had come to my flat. When I had cried into her.

"I will never abandon you – don't you see that?"

Yes. I saw it. I saw it all. She would never abandon me. And the answer why was a simple one word answer.

Love.

We walked along the beach and we kissed and we did not care who saw, and we smiled and I felt life breathe itself back into me. The shows were on on the Low Green and we decided to take a whirl or two. I had some candyfloss and she licked the sticky bits off my chin and I laughed some more. I felt completely alive and happy. I could not remember when I had last felt like that.

As we walked around the rides, Kate saw a booth and dragged me in that direction. "Come on, look, it's a fortune teller. You can probably tell *her* fortune," she laughed.

The warmth of happiness that had enveloped me, fled, and I was enveloped in a feeling of dread. "No."

"Come on," she pulled, not seeing it.

And then it was too late, and the woman appeared from behind the curtain of her booth that served as a door. She looked me straight in the eye and said, "I've been waiting for you."

I walked forward, in that dreamlike way that I should be used to but am not, and she pointed at Kate. "Not you. Just her."

Kate shrugged and removed her arm from mine, and I found myself walking in behind the curtain and sitting down.

She sat across me, a table with a crystal ball in the middle. How much more clichéd could this get?

"My name is Damian." She looked around her. "Forget all this shit. This is just for tourists. It's the ones like you that matter."

I said nothing.

"Gimme your hand," she demanded. I edged my hand across the table, a purple velvet cloth let it slide easily over and I found myself thinking, almost ironically, 'Is this not what I do?' I looked into her grey eyes, and saw the smile at the edge of them. She saw me looking and smiled back, disturbing the nest of butterflies that had been sleeping.

She was very attractive. And I could not look away from her.

"You have had a loss," she said.

"Yes," I agreed, for as much as I know things, I hate charlatans.

"It's not a true loss. The happiness is on the other side."

"Mmm," I muttered.

She laughed. "You don't believe me! How can *you* not believe me? All that you have seen?"

I shifted uncomfortably in my chair. "It's not easy."

"I know you love her. And I know she loves you."

Anyone could have said that, seeing us. A fortune teller that did not make. "Okay."

She looked me in the eyes and said "Jonah", and then that got my attention.

"You don't need to worry, he's happy with his dad. Do you believe me yet?"

"Yes."

She tilted her head. "Hmm, Kate. She has known you a long time, longer than you have known her."

I said nothing.

"Julie has the answer. You need to speak to her."

"What? Why?"

Her grip on me tightened. "There's not a lot more I can see," she peered into me. "It's very black… I'm not sure… Can you swim?"

Chapter Eight

Sometimes I can go for months and never have any dreams. Well, not ones that I can remember. This was not one of those times. The black bags under my eyes were getting bigger and I was beginning to wish for a dream like the movie 'Inception'; at least I would have an excuse for not being able to understand the rubbish I was getting. I would pad to the kitchen in my bare feet, trying not to trip over Jonah, who would inevitably be weaving in and out of my legs, miaowing for food. I would stick the kettle on, light up a cigarette and leaf through whatever magazine was lying on the table. Some nights I would have a cup of tea and read for an hour, and then go back to bed, trying not to disturb Kate.

I was trying to rebuild my life after losing my baby, Jonah. It wasn't easy, but I knew he was with his dad, Rob, and that they had each other. I could feel the love between them just by thinking about it and remembering the string of lights surrounding us. It was my summer holidays, as the University I lectured at was closed, so my days were my own – or nights, depending on Kate's shift. We had grown close again after our weekend away in Ayr, and every single time she kissed me, I felt that butterfly explosion inside.

That's why it surprised me when Julie rang me and asked if I fancied a cup of tea – she knew better than to suggest a coffee – and I agreed. Julie once said to me that people can grow to love each other over a pot of tea. Damian, the fortune teller I had met on the shore front at Ayr, had told me Julie had the answer. The answer to what I did not know, but I am forgetful and it had left my mind. I was more concerned with being in love all over again with my delicious Kate.

Then the dreams began.

****

I am in the room but I am not in the room. I am watching the smiling man lean over a computer and point to the screen, with his companion nodding. They shake hands. It is a bond sealed in Hell. I zoom in on the computer screen and I see the scene being unplayed. The boy is tied to a chair, with a bed in the corner of the room and a bed-sheet is nailed over the window. He only has four toes on one foot. The smiling man comes into the room and I smell the fear from the boy. I notice the red marks all over his body and the dried blood on the inside of his thighs. The boy kicks back and the chair topples over, and he falls backward.

This does not stop the man smiling. He flicks his head and checks the red light of the video camera is on.

He unties the boy and throws him on the bed. The boy is lying on his stomach and the man climbs atop… And the boy would be screaming if not for the gag in his mouth, but the veins in his neck are popping and I know he is suffering. When the man is almost finished, he shifts his position until he is able to get his hands around the boy's neck, and he begins to squeeze. He is throttling the boy and moving his little neck back and forth, and the boy's face is red and his eyes are bulging. Finally, the man finishes and the boy is purple and still.

I awake with a start. I grab my notepad from the side of the bed and begin the trudge to the kitchen. I think I have just seen a snuff movie being made.

****

And the next night I have the one where I am so cold. I know it is not my dream, but I am there anyway and the coldness surrounds me all the same. I want to scream but I am unable to, and when I finally open my eyes and sit bolt upright, I open my mouth and let the scream out.

And there are two screams, because Kate is also sat bolt upright, screaming.

We stare at each other.

"Did I just have your dream?" I ask.

"Yes," she answers, quietly, and I trudge to the kitchen and make a tea for me and a coffee for her.

"What do you think it means?" I ask.

"I don't know. I've sort of had it before."

"You've had it before? When?" I am naturally curious.

"I've had it on and off all my life. A recurring nightmare, if you like. I dunno what it means, babe." She tried a lopsided smile. "I was hoping maybe you would know."

I shrugged my shoulders. "Beats me."

"Thanks for the coffee. I need some shut eye. I'm in Liverpool tomorrow."

"Oh yes," I leaned over and kissed her and suppressed my irk at the taste of coffee.

****

Kate left for Liverpool early the next morning. She was staying overnight. It was a work thing and I wasn't allowed to know anything, as usual. I think she feared I would make a better detective than her, but in truth, that was rubbish. I jumped at the cat's shadow, but Kate was fearless – one of the many things that I loved about her.

I met Julie that day for another cup of tea.

We caught up on old times and laughed a lot. It was easy. We were comfortable. We had known each other a long time. But I had to know.

"Julie, did Kate ever have a recurring nightmare when she was with you?"

Her face changed almost instantly. "Yes."

"Well?" Jesus, talk about trying to get blood from a stone.

"Well what, Jenny?"

"What did she tell you about it?"

"Shouldn't you be asking her this?"

"I only found out last night that the dream was hers."

"What do you mean?"

"I mean, I have had the dream before but I knew it wasn't my dream, and then last night, I had it and I woke up screaming, and she was doing exactly the same. It was really spooky, actually."

"Are you not used to being spooked yet?" she laughed.

"No, I hate it. I wish this would go away."

"Then you would never have met me. Do you regret meeting me?"

"Of course not," I blushed. "So, what do you know about this dream?"

She shifted slightly in her seat. "Jenny, I don't think it is my place to tell you."

"You have to!"

"Okay, but don't let her know that I told you. In fact, don't let her know that you know. She hates weakness." She sighed. "Kate has had this dream throughout her life. I don't know how often, but I know it terrified her. She only ever had it with me twice, and the first time she had it was the first time in years she said and she blabbed that night. I'm sure it was just her fear that made her lose control and tell me. She's trapped in a car underwater and she is drowning, but she sees a woman swimming towards her. Then she wakes up. She thinks that woman saves her, and she thinks that woman is you."

"Me?"

"Yes, you. The very first time I brought her to our flat – your flat, sorry – she saw your pictures and her face just went white. I never saw that look on her face ever again. She became obsessed, I'm telling you. Asked everything about you. Pissed me off a bit to be honest. I suppose it was inevitable she would end up with you."

"Was it?"

"Of course," she answered. "She thinks one day you are going to save her."

****

Later that night, when I was curled on the sofa watching 'Eastenders' in my old blue pyjamas and having a sneaky bottle of wine, my Kate rang me.

"Hi lover," she said. "Is my woman well?"

I smiled. "I'm well. How's Liverpool? You okay?" God, I missed her.

"It's not as nice as our Glasgow bedroom, let's put it that way." I could hear the smirk in her voice. "Jen, darling, can you do me a favour?"

"Sure."

"An old friend of mine needs somewhere to stay for a bit. Can you meet him in town and take him to my flat? He's gonna live there for a bit."

"Course I can, babe. Is everything okay?"

"Yes, yes," she reassured. "He's just had some changes to his life… It will be fine. He's lovely, you don't need to be worried."

We signed off and I grudgingly got off the sofa to go put some clothes on and meet her friend. His name was Logan and he would be waiting outside Queen Street Station for me, knowing my car that Kate had told him the details of. I threw on some old jeans and a jumper, gargled some mouthwash to get rid of the smell of wine, and set off to meet him.

I pulled up to Queen Street Station a wee while later and saw a skinny man with a mop of brown curly hair and a large holdall scanning the streets. He broke into a smile seeing my car and loped over, throwing himself in the passenger seat, after depositing his bag in the back.

My jaw dropped. "Lisa?"

"It's Logan now, honey. Give us a cuddle, Jen!"

****

When I was eighteen, I left home and went to live in student digs in Glasgow for my University course. Although I have always been comfortable with my own company, I was eighteen and crying out for some loving, so I took myself along to the student gay and lesbian group and met Lisa, my first girlfriend. Lisa had deep brown eyes, long curly brown hair and was completely wicked. I loved her instantly and we quickly became inseparable.

She taught me many things, and one was to never be ashamed of who I was. Lisa had a big mouth and never let anyone get the better of her.

After a few drinks – and she drank a lot – she got a bit feisty and several times, we had legged it away from a potential beating. After a few months, it became obvious that Lisa was not the happy-go-lucky chick that I had initially thought she was. There was trouble in her mind, trouble too deep for her to deal with. I took her to the doctor once about her drinking, and they gave her some pills, but no one probed. Including me, I suppose.

Lisa went her way, dancing and drinking, but I had exams to study for and we drifted apart. Just before the end of my first year, she came to see me and told me she was going away 'to get her head together'. That was the last time I ever saw her. Until tonight.

****

I brought Logan back to my flat. I wasn't going to let her stay on her own at Kate's. I mean him. Wasn't going to let him.

I got us some wine and settled down on the sofa to find out what had been happening.

He fluttered his eyelashes. He was totally camp. "I know you're *dying* to find out what's been going on, so I'm not going to disappoint you, darling."

I shook my head, laughing. Still as mad as a pound of mince. "Spill the beans, then – don't tease the lesbian."

"Well, I was *such* a mess back in the day. You know what I was like, pissed out of my face, taking God knows what drugs. I had to get away, chick. Glasgow was bringing me down. I went down to London for a bit. but that was worse and then I came home to my mummy and daddy and they sent me to a shrink, and gender reassignment it was!" He gulped down his glass. "Any more?"

I brought the bottle through from the kitchen. "But you never wanted to be a man, did you?"

"Course I did. Why do you think I was such a bad lesbian?" he laughed.

"Have you… you know… Got bits?"

"Why do people always think it's fine to ask me about my genitalia? I don't ask you about yours."

I was about to apologise, when he added, "It's fine, because I love you. I don't mind. I had to live as a man for a couple of years, then there were the hormones. Then I got my tits off – what a fucking relief that was. I could legitimately say I'm off my tits!"

"Did it hurt?"

"Course it hurt, honey – you don't get two lumps removed without some pain – but that's nothing, let me tell you, when they demolish your twat and give you a knob."

My ribs began to hurt from laughing. We spent the rest of the night laughing and catching up. Lisa – Logan – had not had an easy time of it, trying to be accepted as transgender in the small northern Scottish town of Lossiemouth, full of RAF men. But she – no, he – was a man now and had come to Glasgow to start fresh, to find love, a job. To be normal.

"How do you know Kate?" I asked, because I had to.

"I shared a flat with her for a while, after I stopped seeing you. She was the first person to really listen to me, and she was the first to say, 'I think you are a man in the wrong body'. I never forgot that, so I always stayed in touch, dropped her a letter here and there, then an email. She's a good egg."

"I know," I smiled. "*My* good egg. Now, bed!"

****

I am dreaming. Again.

It's the same room, with the bed-sheet over the curtain. I am an imaginary pair of eyes looking in. I cannot see anything on the bed and the camera is switched off. I can hear a muffled sort of crying and sniffing. I try to make my view of the room larger, but the dream is not obeying at the moment. I can hear arguing outside the door, loud voices raised in anger, but I cannot distinguish the words.

And then I see him in the corner, almost melting in with the dark of the walls. Knees pulled into his body, ankles tethered together, gag in his mouth, hands bound. Shivering and whining, I would recognise that hair anywhere.

It is Logan.

****

Kate came back the next day and swiftly moved Logan into her flat, with some ground rules. She knew him well too, it seemed. When she got in from her landlord duties, she said we were going to the fair on the Green and who am I to say no when my woman is happy? So off we trotted, and went on some rides and laughed into our candyfloss. Nothing out of the ordinary.

I was watching Kate's back as she lifted a pretend rifle and tried to hit some shapes that were moving. I turned my head and saw a familiar pair of smiling eyes, beckoning me over. Damian, the fortune teller.

"I wondered how long it would be until I saw you again. Step in. This is no chat for frivolous ears."

I felt a gnawing inside me but had no power to resist, as my legs had turned to jelly but were taking me into her booth nevertheless. I sat myself at the seat I had taken that windy day in Ayr and saw the same smooth velvet cloth across the table.

Damian sat down. "You dream about me, don't you?"

I shook my head. "No."

"You will eventually. Did you get your answers from Julie?"

"Yes."

"I knew you would," she smiled. "Have you started your advanced swimming yet?"

I knew she meant the dream of Kate's. That had slipped my mind. "No… I forgot you asked me that."

"You need to start, hen. You can't forget again, got it?"

"Yes. Look, I'll put it in my phone," which I duly did. I am not blonde, but I think I should be. I was not sure this woman had a gift like mine, but after the cold dream, learning some life-saving skills could not hurt.

She leant across and took my hand. “Are you expecting a ring on this hand?” It was my left she was holding.

“I don’t know… I’ve never really thought about it.”

“You won’t get it. And if she asks you, say no. Remember, no.”

I nodded. Even with the things that have happened in my life, I find it hard to believe others.

She had been smiling and then her smile froze and she said, “Who is Lisa? No. Logan?”

“A friend.”

She let go of my hand and leant back in her seat. “Him. You need to help him.”

****

There is a song by The Butterfly Explosion, an Irish band I found on Myspace, and in their song ‘Crash’, they sing:

“I can’t let go
I can’t let go
I can’t let go
I can’t let go”.

It is a beautiful song that touches the inside of my soul and makes me melt with love.

****

And I am back in the dream, and my body is filled with a million darts of ice-cold stings. I cannot move my body and the water is surrounding me, and I see the girl coming towards me but I cannot stay awake. The cold is claiming me. The girl, coming closer, not just any girl… Closer… I am fighting to stay awake. She is grabbing my hand.

I can’t let go.

****

I awake from the dream and I am quietly crying. I go through to the kitchen, leaving my Kate asleep with her mouth slightly open, notepad in hand, and boil the kettle while I jot down what I can recall. I must remember to get a new notepad.

I make myself a cup of tea and sip, letting the tears fall slowly down my cheeks. My heart aches. I see the tenderness in my woman when others see the hardness. I see the way she throws her arm possessively over me in her sleep, not knowing she is doing it, making a little content noise when she gets me close to her. The way she always cuddles into my back and kisses it goodnight before we drift off. I see my vulnerable woman and her walls of pretence. Somehow, I got beyond those walls and I know the beautiful heart that she has. But I don't think I have got beyond every wall.

And this dream worries me. I cannot help be overtaken by sadness when I have it. And that is why I am crying. It is better that I get it out now, when Kate is asleep than in front of her, when she will question me and I will not be able to withstand her questioning. I cannot lie to her. I can omit but not lie.

A song begins to play in my head, as I cry for my darling.

"I don't need to know now
I don't need to know 'cause you're never far
Because you're never far.
So, eyes that told me so much
Lies
As words are woven
You'll ever stop.
Darling, we'll never start."

I went back to bed and laid my head on her chest and wet her T-shirt with my tears, but she did not wake up, and for that I was glad. I liked seeing her untainted and happy in sleep.

I would not let go.

****

"Just one drink, okay?" she urged me.

Kate insisted we go out and meet Logan for a quick drink. She never asked much and I felt obliged to go. But I was scared.

I had a level of happiness and I did not want anything to spoil that. After losing my Jonah, I did not think I could withstand another loss. My Kate was everything to me and I had been having so many strange and unusual dreams of late, nothing good could be coming. Was it wrong to want to stay in my bubble for a little while longer? Do I wear rose coloured glasses?

We got a drink at the bar, and as I turned to say something to Kate, Logan walked in.

With the smiling man, the video camera man.

That is when I fainted.

'Nothingness is all.'

Chapter Nine

I came to with Kate leaning over me, asking if I was okay. I quickly died of embarrassment as I realised that I had fainted on seeing the smiling man walk in with Logan. She helped me to my feet as I insisted that I was fine, and a glass of wine would help me recover.

We got a table, and Logan said he would sort out the drinks while Kate fussed over me. I did not want her to worry over something I had dreamt about. We still never talked about my gift and I knew it made her uncomfortable, despite what had happened in our past. Despite me knowing that she had a recurring dream in which she thinks I save her life. Julie had told me that after prompting, but I had never brought it up with Kate. I knew she loved me – I could see it in the way she looked at me and the way she held my gaze at intimate moments. I hated to think of my Kate suffering, and I knew her childhood had not been a bed of roses, after I had held her arm and saw her dad abusing her. She never spoke about it, and I never asked. Her imperfections made her perfect.

I was trying my best to pretend that everything was normal. I had learned, after Jonah visited me in my kitchen what seemed a lifetime ago, and I had spoken to him in front of Kate's guests, that people did not always appreciate my gift and tended to think I had mental health issues. Which was fair enough. I would probably think the same if I saw someone talking to thin air. Kate and I had a difficult time then, and I was not going to do anything to jeopardise our relationship. Like entangling her in my weird dreams.

The smiling man and Logan came over, and Logan introduced him as he passed our drinks as Simon Dunstable. I must remember that name, I thought, trying to make a mental note.

You are a paedophilic murderer, I also thought.

Logan had not taken long to reacquaint himself with Glasgow's nightlife and had met Simon at Bennett's.

The night passed in one of those blurs where I tried to remember things, but the more wine I had, the harder that became.

I remembered these things:

Simon Dunstable said he was a national businessman, but not in what business.

He was charming, mannerly, polite, and almost quite funny.

I got very drunk and Kate practically carried me up the stairs to our flat.

I began to sing a Fleetwood Mac song, over and over again until I shouted at the top of my lungs.

Kate undressed me and put me into bed, and I heard her in the kitchen as I sang to myself and then I muttered under my breath when she came to bed smelling of coffee, before passing out.

****

When I was a young girl, I used to have dreams about songs. They were nice dreams because they were harmless. Just songs I liked. Or songs I had never heard of, but once I found them when I woke up, I loved them. My gift was giving me the gift of music. My first cat was called Severina after the song by The Mission, that I heard in my dreams for a week.

That was the first night of the dreams of music and it began with a line, a single line. It was not a band or a song I knew. And it ended with the same single line.

'Release.'

****

I got up the next day, and Kate had already left for work – she had taken the car the night before so did not have my problem of a hangover – and I began to sing to myself as I fed the cat and boiled the kettle for a cuppa.

I got my cup of tea, switched on the PC and went onto iTunes. I downloaded The Editors.

And all day I sang "Release, find your peace, my love."

I thought it was just a great song.

****

When you are happy, you do not notice the passage of time. You reflect one day and think, oops, a year has gone past, where did it go? You never think of the small things that happen, you never think this is the last day that I will spend with someone. But, one day, that will be true. For everyone there is a last day. Nothing ever lasts forever. I get up every day and I tell Kate I love her before she goes to work, because it might be the last day I see her.

I worry because she is a policewoman. Not because I have a gift.

I cannot see the end for everyone.

Just a few murdered souls.

****

We were at the breakfast table. Kate said, "I hope you weren't singing to me last night."

I blushed because I cannot sing. "What was I singing?"

She mimicked me "Pale shelter."

Eek. Tears for Fears. Another favourite track of mine. I half-laughed, sipping my tea.

"I hope I wasn't singing to you, either."

****

I had a week before Uni started up again, and for once, I remembered something, but only because I had put it on my phone. I went to the baths and stripped into a bathing costume for my first life saving swimming lesson. As I walked shyly from the changing rooms to the pool, I wished I had shaved my legs.

I was the only one in the class.

And my instructor was Damian.

She stood, svelte, in a red bikini, and laughed.

"You finally remembered, then?"

I did not find that funny.

I had my lesson, but I could not concentrate for the smile at the end of her eyes. She held her hand on my stomach for just a second too long. And it felt good.

I muttered to myself, as I got changed, stinking of chlorine, and left the changing rooms to head for the exit. I should have known better, because Damian was waiting for me, with that twinkle in her eye.

"Come on, we are going for a cup of tea."

"Why?" I asked, genuinely puzzled.

"Because," she said, smiling into my eyes, "People can grow to love each other over a pot of tea."

And I would have choked, but my mind was overloaded with the words of that song 'Pale Shelter.'

We went for a cup of tea all the same, and I asked her because I had to. That is the way I am. I am jittery and nervous and say the wrong things at the right time. But, I am honest.

She looked me in the eyes, and I swear she could see into my soul. "It's funny. I do the stalls at the fairs as Crystal Chris, but I make it all up – it's easy when you know how." She looked down into her cup, almost apologetically. "I know you're different. You don't make it up."

I shook my head, to clear some cobwebs. "But I don't understand, Damian. You said things to me that you couldn't possibly know."

"I know. I don't know how I knew them. Maybe I do have a wee gift after all. Scone?"

I shook my head no, and she put some strawberry jam on hers. Quite a bit of strawberry jam, actually. I watched her take a bite and said awkwardly, "You have a bit of, er, jam on your…" pointing my finger. She began to move her tongue around her mouth.

"Got it?"

"No, it's…" I moved my finger to her chin and wiped the jam. "… There."

She looked into my eyes and held my gaze, until finally I looked down into my tea, embarrassed again.

"Tell me about your girlfriend," she said.

A good change of subject. I happily rambled about Kate, and she refilled my cup while I yapped on.

"Do you think she is the one for you?" she asked.

"Do you?" I asked, half-joking.

"No," she smiled, reaching across the table and taking my hand in hers. "I am."

****

That night, Kate came in from work, bringing a bottle of wine home with her. That worried me, as she hardly ever drank.

"You okay, babe?"

"Yes, my love," she answered, pouring out two glasses. "Just a shit time at work. No, not that. It's not work, work's fine. It's just what I have to see sometimes gets you right in the stomach."

I could imagine. I saw vile things in my dreams, but my Kate saw them in real life.

She threw herself down on the sofa and I came behind her and rubbed her shoulders. "Want to talk about it?"

"No, it's fine. You don't need to hear it. Tell me about your day."

I had that little argument in my head when you say, do I tell her the whole truth, half the truth or a teeny bit of the truth? Will she believe me if I tell her the whole truth? Will she find out if I tell her a half-truth and then think I was hiding something?

I am ridiculously bad at decision making. I therefore opted for the truth, knowing she probably would not like it, but at least I would know that I had been honest. I never wanted to lie to her ever again, and it was not as if I had actually done anything.

"I started my advanced swimming lessons today and you will never guess who my instructor was. Do you remember the fortune teller at Ayr and the Green? It was her. Apparently, she only does the stalls for the extra money in the summer months, and she's a swimming teacher really."

Kate threw a sideways glance over her shoulder at me. "The pretty one? That will explain the broad shoulders then, if she swims."

"Yes, well," I went on nervously. "She was waiting for me when I came out the changing room afterwards, and we went for a cup of tea."

She laughed. "God, you and your cups of tea."

"That's it really. She's nice and funny and I think we will probably end up friends."

"And what is it you are nervous about, Jen?"

"Nervous? What do you mean?"

She laughed again. "You forget I *know* you. What are you nervous about? Do you like her, is that it? Do I need to worry?"

She did know me. But she didn't know all of me. It's impossible to know another person completely. They will always surprise you.

"No, I don't like her – not like that. I love you. She just said something funny, that's all. She thinks she is the one for me."

She turned right round then. "Do you?"

"I cannot imagine another woman in my heart except you." I walked round the couch and sat down beside her. I took her hands. "I know I did that one thing behind your back but I promise you, I will *never* do anything like that again. I need you to believe me. I am telling you because I don't want secrets and lies between us. Please, trust me."

"I do trust you," she said, softly, and I saw how soft and vulnerable she was, and my heart ached. That's when I leaned in to kiss her soft lips, and that's when I got the shooting pain in my head, bringing the vision.

****

The little girl in the black jacket is standing holding the lady's hand – her mother's, I think. Everyone is dressed in black and the blonde peroxide on her mother's head stands out. They are standing at the side of a grave and the mother is weeping silently. The Minister is reading from his Bible, and there are a lot of faces being wiped by hankies. The rain pours down, and runs down the cheeks of the bereaved with their tears.

The coffin is lowered into the grave. A small coffin. A baby's coffin. The little girl stares as the coffin disappears. She is not crying. She is tugged round as her mother turns to walk away, retreating from the elements and her grief.

The little girl is my Kate.

****

A couple of weeks later, I wake up to hear Kate shouting, "Where's my phone?"

I sit up and scratch my head. I have the creases of the bed sheets still ironed into my face.

"In the kitchen? Next to the kettle?"

"Got it!"

"What time is it? Where are you going?"

She came running into the room. "I'm doing an overnighter in Birmingham. I told you last week."

Did she? I really need to start writing things down. Which reminded me I needed a new notepad.

"Oh, okay. Well, I'll miss you. Phone me later, yeah?"

She smacked a kiss on my forehead. "Always. Be good." And off she went.

****

I had lectures that day and dragged myself onto the tube for a quick sandwich and tea in Hillhead before the walk up to my classroom. I was wondering what I would do with my night, thinking I would catch up on the soaps and have a sneaky wee bottle of wine.

My last class of the day had about twenty students, and they were generally very good. Quite a chatty bunch. At the end, one girl stayed behind for a quiet word. She wanted an extension on her essay due in at the end of the week. I am not normally one for granting extensions and told her so.

"I know, but my wee brother had an accident, Jenny, and he had to get rushed into hospital."

"Oh, what happened?"

"We don't really know, but he had to have his little toe amputated. He won't talk."

Somewhere, something deep inside of me began to buzz.

"Fine. You can have over the weekend. Monday morning okay?"

"Thanks, Jenny." She smiled and left.

I gathered my things and knew I was forgetting something. I actually *knew* it.

A notepad. I needed a new notepad!

I made a mental note to get one on the way home.

****

I went to bed that night, a little bit squiffy having finished my bottle of wine, after Kate had phoned to check in. I fell asleep quickly, with Jonah at my feet.

And I dreamt of the little boy tied to the chair, with the smiling man walking into the room. And I was the eyes of that little boy as he hung his head in shame, following them down his dirty legs to his feet. And to that one foot with only four toes.

I woke up with a start and reached for my notepad, which I didn't have as I had forgotten to buy one. I went back to sleep.

****

When I awoke the next morning, I did not remember that I had dreamt.

Chapter Ten

"Yea, though I walk through the valley of the shadow of death,
I will fear no evil: For thou art with me;
Thy rod and thy staff, they comfort me."

"Jen!"

"What?" I mumbled, coming to from a sleep.

"You're quoting the Bible again."

"Oh sorry," I managed, as Kate turned back over to try to sleep. I had been waking her up reciting the Bible. "Will you do me a favour, Kate?"

"What?"

"Will you buy me a notepad? I keep forgetting."

"Yes," she sighed. "Now, go back to sleep."

I cuddled into her and felt the heat from her back and I felt happy.

I am not religious in the slightest, and had never read the Bible.

****

It was my last class of the day and I noticed I had a student missing. Gail Dunstable.

"Where's Gail?" I asked the class. I thought she was avoiding handing in her next assignment, having been late with the previous two, despite me granting extensions. I think of a drop out as a failure.

There were some shifty looks among my students until one piped up.

"There's something up with her brother, Jen."

Alarm bells slowly started to ring in my head.

"What's wrong with her brother?" I asked, with a kind of trepidation.

"He's disappeared."

I fell down into my chair and put my head in my hands. There was something I was missing here.

****

When Kate came home that night, I was sitting in the kitchen at our table, drinking a cup of tea, chain-smoking and flicking through the pages of *Take A Break*. Normally, I like to do the crosswords, but I could not concentrate. That little alarm bell in my head was beginning to ring louder and louder.

"Have you had any kids reported missing?" I asked, before she could even take her coat off coming in the door.

"Don't I get a kiss?"

I gave her a half-hearted kiss. "Well? Have you?"

"No, I haven't. What you going on about, darling?"

I followed her into the kitchen. "I don't know. Your dinner is in the microwave. Just a weird feeling I have."

She looked at me quizzically and I knew she hated this part of me that saw things. "What is it?"

"I dunno – just a weird feeling that I have missed something."

"I meant what's my dinner?"

She had remembered to buy me a notepad.

****

"Love each other as I have loved you. Greater love has no one than this, that he lay down his life for his friends."

I woke up with my usual start, and Kate was not there. She had not come home. But my notepad was there, and I wrote this down.

****

Then I woke up again and Rob was sitting at the end of my bed.

"Hey, Toots."

What now?, I thought. Do I not have enough problems in my life without the man I betrayed my girlfriend with appearing on the end of my bed? The man who is the father of my dead baby. The man who loved me, that I did not love enough back.

I groaned. "Rob, no – go away."

"You need a jolt. I can't believe you are so ditsy."

"I'm not ditsy, I'm half awake." And where was Kate anyway?

"You have missed things," he said, and his sad eyes bored into me.

That woke me up. "Missed what?"

"I can't. Don't you understand it yet?"

"No. Quite frankly, I don't. Its…" I looked at the clock, "… 4.22 am and you are sitting on the end of my bed. What am I missing?"

I think if he could have reached out and touched me, he would have. Instead, he said, "I'm not permitted to tell you. You are given the messages. *You* need to work them out, but you have been missing them."

"Great. Big help. Cheers," I answered, moodily. That's it, get me up in the middle of the night and expect me to decipher cryptic messages.

"Jenny, I can't, but it's all there. You can stop it going further."

"Stop what?" I am generally a patient person but enigmatic ghosts push my limits.

"Read your dreams," he said and vanished.

I got up to make a cup of tea, tripping over the cat and banging my head. I took my cuppa back into bed and lit a fag, muttering what I would not do for a quiet life.

****

That morning I woke up to a song in my head called 'The Summoning Of The Muse' by a band called Dead Can Dance. It was the type of song I would expect to hear in a church.

I do not know if I should believe in coincidence.

What is coincidence if it is not a message from the dead?

****

Kate was sleeping on the couch, still in the clothes that she had left in the day before and I boiled the kettle and made her a coffee. I knew she would be starting work again soon. I put her coffee on the table in front of her and sat down to look at her. Her mouth was open slightly, her beautiful eyes were closed and flickering slightly. Her hand curled under her chin. My love.

The smell of the coffee must have got to her, as her eyes flickered and a small smile creased the ends of her lips.

"How long have you been sitting there?"

"Just a minute. I like to take in your beauty."

She leant over for her coffee, and sipped. "We had a kid reported missing last night."

Alarm bells.

"Is that why you didn't get in until late?"

She sipped again. "No. There was a murder as well. Crazy night."

Bang. Bang. Bang.

"What can you tell me about the murder?"

She did not notice my distress, and I am glad, because I was trying to hide it.

She puffed and I noticed, for the first time ever, the bags under her eyes.

"It was a woman called Jean McPherson. She was just coming home after a night out. Jesus! It's so sad. How can people do this to each other?"

I was about to answer when I saw Rob, in the corner of the room pointing furiously at his watch.

It was not a message – it was a warning.

****

After my swimming lesson the next day, I had lunch with Damian and invited her for dinner with Kate and I. She had a right good laugh at that, and told me there was no way she was coming over to mine to watch me play wifey with my girlfriend – she would wait.

She said, "I can wait. Because one day you are going to need me and I will be there. Like a fly on shit." She had laughed some more.

****

The day went into the next day, and my life continued as normal. I awoke my from my dreams, and I wrote down what I remembered at the time, and I went back to sleep. I cooked Kate's dinner, and when she wasn't there I put it in the microwave for her. It was a simple and easy life. It was what you did. You got up, you fed the cat and cleaned its litter tray and took the bin out, and you went to work and you came home and you made dinner. If I was lucky, I got an hour or so with Kate before her lids became heavy.

If I was really lucky, I had the insistence of her fingers.

****

I was applying the finishing touches to my make-up in a bathroom mirror. I put my lipstick on and puckered my lips into a tissue, dabbing off the excess. I grabbed the hairspray and shut my eyes as I sprayed a frantic amount around my head. I checked myself again. Looking good.

I heard someone calling me and I shouted, "I'm coming. Two minutes."

I opened the bathroom cabinet and took out a sanitary towel, and quickly pulled down my pants and stuck it on. I pulled them back up and lifted my tights that had been draped over the edge of the bath. I thought, please don't let me get a ladder now.

I caught my reflection one last time in the mirror and rushed out the bathroom door. A woman was standing saying, "Come on, we will miss the bus."

I nodded and went into a bedroom. There were bunk beds and a kid asleep in each one. I leant over and kissed them both softly, not wanting to wake them. I crept out the room, leaving the door ajar.

I walked with the woman to a bus stop and we giggled and took a sneaky nip from a bottle of vodka she had hidden in her bag. The bus took us from Scotstoun into the city centre, and we went into a bar and had a drink. We walked to another bar and had another drink and another drink.

And then we went dancing.

In reality, I am tossing and turning and murmuring in my sleep.

But I did not wake up.

And I am the woman again, and we are getting into a taxi. Me, the woman I am with, and the well-dressed man. The woman gets out and staggers a bit as she is quite drunk, and we drive away. I feel no fear.

The man and I leave the taxi and he pays. We begin the walk to my tenement, and he knows a shortcut and I follow blindly, trusting implicitly.

We are hidden by some garages and he tries to kiss me. I kiss him back. But I have a husband, and I know I should not be doing this. The alcohol is impairing me, and when I try to protest, he struggles with me. And I am on the ground and he is ripping my clothes, and I am trying to scream but no one can hear me and he is pushing his hand over my mouth. He has his hands around my neck and he is squeezing.

In my head, I do a flip and I see through the man's eyes.

He has just finished raping her and he takes off her tights and ties them around her neck and squeezes some more, just for good measure.

He leaves her towel visible to show her shame, and walks away.

"Yea, though I walk through the valley of the shadow of death,

I will fear no evil: For thou art with me;

Thy rod and thy staff, they comfort me."

I wake up and grab my notepad and rush to the kitchen, where I see the light is on and Kate's face is on the table. She is fast asleep. I flick the switch on the kettle and begin to scribble furiously.

I saw his face.

****

The next morning, I was waiting for Kate to get up. It was her day off, and I needed to talk to her about my dream. The door knocked and I went to answer it.

A woman in her fifties, with peroxide blonde hair stood there. "Hello, I'm Sheena."

I don't know any Sheenas. "I'm sorry, I don't think I know…"

She butted in. "Kate's mother. You must be Jennifer."

"Jen. Um, do you want to come in? Kate's still in bed but I can get her up."

"Thanks, I will so come in," and in she came.

I led her into the kitchen and told her to make herself a cup of tea and I would get Kate.

I went to wake her, which I hated doing as she worked so hard and never got a chance to rest properly.

"Babe, wake up – your mother is here."

I have never seen anyone go from fast asleep to wide awake in so short an instant. "What? My mother? Are you shitting me?"

"No, she's in the kitchen."

"Fuck. Go keep her busy."

I duly went to the kitchen and saw Sheena waiting for the kettle to boil. "Oh you found it, great. So… How are you?"

"I'm good thanks, Jennifer."

"Jen."

"Just thought I would drop in and see how my eldest was," she boomed. She had a very powerful voice, and an imposing character.

I smiled helplessly, waiting for Kate to come in. Eldest?

"Mum, what you doing here? I told you never to come to Jenny's."

I began to watch the verbal game of tennis.

"Can't a mother come and see her daughter?" Sheena asked, pouring the hot water into her cup.

"I know you better."

"Och Kate, you still have a stick up your arse, I see. Doesn't she, hen?" She turned to me for affirmation. I tried to suppress a giggle. "I just want to stay for a wee while, a wee holiday."

"No chance."

"Kate! Of course your mother can stay!" I put in.

Kate glared at me. "One night. That's it."

Sheena broke into a big smile. "That's ma girl. Give your old ma a cuddle" and she went to Kate and bear-hugged her. Kate was as stiff as a board. Then Sheena turned to me and hugged me.

"Marriage must be respected by all and husband and wife faithful to each other. God will punish the immoral and the adulterous."

Sheena let go of me and I felt the red flush work its way up my face. I had not known I was speaking.

"Oh, for crying out loud!" That was Kate.

"Do you mind explaining that one to me, hen?" She looked at Kate. "Is your girlfriend some kind of religious freak?"

I was dying of embarrassment and afraid to open my mouth. Kate sighed. "No, she's a medium."

I was secretly proud beneath my shame at spouting biblical quotes to a stranger, that Kate had revealed what I was.

"Are you really, now?" Her mother looked at me with interest. "Talk to the dead then?"

"Not exactly. They talk to me."

Her mother laughed uproariously. "Oh my! I like you, hen. This one is a keeper, hen, not like that…"

"Enough, mother!" Kate butted in.

Not like who?, I wondered.

****

Her mother fell asleep that night on the sofa, and Kate stormed to bed in a foul mood. Her mother's presence had not been looked on favourably, and she had scowled all day. I thought her mother was quite funny actually, and we had a bit of a joke at Kate's expense. Which probably, looking back, had not helped her black mood.

As I laid a blanket on her mum, my hand brushed her shoulder and I got the faintest of electric shocks.

"Go to your room," she slurred and the young girl slunk off, leaving the smoke-filled room and the clink of beer bottles.

My curiosity got the better of me.

I laid my hand on her hand and felt the tug of that electric shock again.

"But, mum, he *touches* me."

"Away wi' ye. Stop havering, bairn, and get to yir bed. I'll skelp yir arse in a minute."

So.

She had not listened when Kate had told her of the abuse.

No wonder she was bitter.

****

Sheena left the next morning, and gave me her phone number.

"You never know when you might need me," she winked.

I tried to smile back, but knowing that she had not listened to Kate, and that she had been physically abused as a result, made it difficult for me.

Kate would never tell me. I knew she would never talk about it. But I did not need to ask. I could accept now without my questions.

I wish I had been able to stop it. I wish I had been able to save her.

I wish I had been able to save her.

I began to sing 'Release' without knowing it.

****

I was sitting at the kitchen table, having a cup of tea and a smoke when I suddenly had the urge to read my notepad that I wrote my dreams in. Kate was reading the paper with a coffee and a croissant. She didn't start her shift until later.

I brought my notepad back to the table and began to read my garbled handwriting.

Why was I quoting obscure texts from the Bible?

Who was the woman putting her lippy on before a night out which saw her strangled to death by her own tights?

Who was the polite, sweet-talking stranger?

Something in my head was beginning to add up.

I went into the living room and turned on the computer.

Kate followed me in and said, "You left your cigarette burning." She hated my smoking but I just could not give up.

I was waiting for the PC to warm up and asked, "Who was murdered the other night?"

"Why do you want to know?"

"Jesus, can you just tell me without the Spanish Inquisition? You know by now I won't tell anyone."

She frowned at me. "Her name was Jean McPherson."

"And before that, six months before that, there was another woman murdered, and you are linking them. What was her name?"

She got curious and came over to stand behind me, to see what I was doing.

"Polly Deans."

I felt the surge inside me.

"Polly Deans, PD," I muttered. "Jean McPherson, JM. Helen Puttock, that will be HP."

"What are you doing, Jen?"

"They were both strangled, yes?"

"Yes, that's right."

"Found semi-naked or naked? Raped?"

"Yes, that's right, too."

"Oh God," I said. "And they both had their period?"

"Actually, yes to that."

"We have four months."

"Four months for what, Jen?" and then she looked at the computer screen.

It was Bible John.

Chapter Eleven

"But Bible John is most likely dead. And he hasn't been linked to a murder since 1969."

I took in the wisdom of Kate's words. "What about a copycat, then?"

She conceded that was possible. "Are you telling me, Jen, that you know the murderer?"

I squirmed. "Not exactly. But I saw his face in my dreams. And I remember it."

It's funny how I cannot remember something simple like buy milk at the shop, but I can remember a face I saw once in a dream.

"So, just let me clarify this. You are saying that because two women have been murdered, and who happened to both be menstruating, that another woman is going to be murdered? Because Bible John murdered three women and these first two had the same initials as his first two? Is that what you are saying?"

"Yes."

"And we have four months until the third murder?"

"Yes."

I waited an eternity as I watched her weigh it all up mentally.

Finally, she said, "How do I find him?"

At last.

She believed me.

We talked over what we knew and concluded we were looking for a needle in a haystack. I knew nothing of the man except what he looked like, and I knew nothing of the woman except that I suspected her initials were HP, as Helen Puttock was the final victim of Bible John. That we know of. I did know she had two children and came from Scotstoun, but that hardly narrowed it down.

But, this was different. In the past, I had seen things too late. This hadn't happened yet. I had a chance to change the future. I had the chance to prevent some woman from losing her life. We were on a countdown to a death. I remembered Rob pointing to his watch, and knew what he had meant now.

And then suddenly, Kate was just staring at me. I stared back. She kissed me and it was a kiss full of passion and love, and of course, I could not help but respond. Clothes were coming off and we were on the floor and she was on top of me, and the delights just kept coming.

And then she started to cry and would not stop. I held her, naked, in my arms and let her get it out. I felt the lump grow in my throat as she broke her heart.

"Katie, what's wrong?"

"I… uh… love you… uh," she snorted through her tears.

"I know you do, darling. I love you, too. Why you crying?"

"I… uh… don't know… uh… I just got this wave of love for you… I know… uh… that I should show you more… but I do love you."

"You don't need to show me anything, its fine," I hushed her.

I knew from the way she held me in her sleep that she loved me. I do not need extravagant gestures or flowers and chocolates. I need that small reach out of the hand to feel me next to her when she drifts off. That alone lets me know that she needs me beside her. Words are cheap. Her tenderness is priceless.

"It wasn't my father that abused me, well, not… uh… my real father. I had a succession of 'daddies'. My mother was a lush who went with anyone. I hated her."

Eek. I was not sure what to say. And sometimes, I open my mouth before my brain engages.

"What about your real dad, then?"

She laughed bitterly. "The last I heard, he was serving a life sentence for killing my little sister. Didn't mean it, of course. Came in pissed, she was crying, the noise annoyed him. I was seven. I've never forgotten that."

I remembered the child standing watching the coffin being lowered, before being led away by the peroxide blonde. That would be Sheena.

"And you don't know what became of him?"

"I don't want to." She sniffed up her snot. "I'm sorry, babe. Where were we?" and then she was kissing me again.

While my body can always respond to her, my mind can be in two places at once. Sometimes, three.

I just wondered.

****

"Right," she said, in copper mode. "I've been thinking. Obviously, I can't go looking for this woman while I am on duty, because I need you with me. And anyway, how would I justify it to my boss? My girlfriend had a dream? No. You said she got the bus from Scotstoun. Right?"

I nodded. She was so sexy when she was being all assertive. My mind started to wander to the night before. Yum.

"Well, I think what we do is work on what we know. We know she may have the initials HP, if your theory is right, and that she has two kids, and possibly a husband. We go to the library, I'll bring a map of the area and we go through the electoral register. Now I have considered the possibility that she might not be on it and, if that's the case, then we are going to have to do door-to-door in our spare time. I can flash my badge and you can see if you recognise anyone. How does that sound?"

It sounded perfectly logical to me. So that is what we did. We went to the library and we went through street after street, searching for the 'P' surnames, but found no woman who could be my 'HP'.

Then, we moved onto the next step, the door-to-door campaign. We agreed that a single mother could be using a different name, in order to claim benefits fraudulently and have a man in the house undeclared. This meant no doorstep unturned, or unknocked. We made a geographical list and I even did a spreadsheet, which impressed me slightly, and got me a kiss on the nose from Kate.

"Hi, my name is DI Coutts." A quick flash of the badge. "I need to ask if you know anything of the murder of Jean MacPherson."

We were invariably met with "Who?", "Whit?" or "Fuck off", at which point Kate would turn to me and I would apologise for disturbing them. The cue for me recognising the woman would be me asking if they were aware of anyone suspicious in the area lately. I felt a bit Juliet Bravo.

That wore a bit thin after two months of door knocking and constant abuse. There are only so many slams in the face you can take before the novelty wears off. And trawling the streets of a suburb of Glasgow in the pouring rain to be met by a chorus of disinterest was quite disheartening.

"Two months," Kate said, double-checking the doors knocked on our spreadsheet. We had to fit this in between her job, my job and having a life. When you think you have four months, you think you have all the time in the world. We were now half way through and no nearer.

"Jen, why do you think we have four months?"

"'Cause Google said it was four months between the second and third victim of Bible John."

"Do you ever wonder if this man is having the same trouble as us?"

"Meaning what?"

"We have been looking for two months for a woman in Scotstoun with the initials HP, and we have yet to find her. I can legitimately knock a door and show my police ID. He can't do that."

"Oh God, Kate. I think you're onto something."

Why had it not occurred to me before?

She put her pen down, neatly onto the papers in front of her. "Have you 'got' something?"

I shook my head. "No. But think. Whoever he is, he *wants* to be known like Bible John was. He did three murders and then vanished. Never found, right? So this guy, he studies that and he works them out. Perhaps the first two were random because they all had to tie in with the third, the actual person he knew. Maybe he knows HP and worked back, if you get me."

She nodded in silence. "We still have to find HP then."

****

For maybe the first time in my life proper, I felt like my gift was in reality a gift. I was, with Kate's help, on the way to preventing the murder of an innocent woman, I hoped. We had two months left to find her and I was confident when I saw her, I would know and that would be that. I never really thought beyond the point of recognising her because that, to me, stopped her dying.

It drew Kate and I close in a way we had never been before. I could see now why she was the way she was, after meeting her mother, and I knew how much she loved me. I knew she had finally accepted my dreams as messages and we were working together, as a true couple, for that higher goal.

So, even though I was trying to find a woman I thought might be murdered, I had never been happier.

****

I was in the dream of the young boy, tied to the chair and the smiling man came in. He turned on the camera, like before, and went to the boy, getting him onto the bed. And in the dream, I knew what was going to happen but I could do nothing to stop it, and I helplessly watched as his small face grew purple with death again.

I woke up and noticed I had wet tears on my cheeks. I grabbed my notepad and went into the kitchen, seeking the comfort of a boiling kettle.

Kate had already left for work. I do not know where she found the energy. She worked all the hours God sent, went door knocking with me to find a woman I had seen in a dream and still managed to find time to love me. I noticed, when I went into the fridge for the milk, that she had taken the packed lunch I had made for her. I had filled it with love heart shaped Post-It pads, with little messages on them, like 'Love you always', 'You're so sexy' and 'Cheeky bum'. I hoped I did not embarrass her too much when she went for a sandwich.

I got my cup of tea and sat down at the table, flicking open my notepad to a blank page. I began to write down what I could remember. When I had finished, I sat back to light a cigarette and get my morning nicotine fix and I had a flash of pain in my head. I pulled a face and the cat looked at me.

"In a minute, Jonah," I said, to the fattest cat in the land.

Slowly, I began to re-read. And slowly a picture began to form in my head as recollections and dreams and conversations linked up.

A little boy was missing. A little boy with four toes on one of his feet.

My student, Gail, had said her little brother had a toe amputated in an accident and she had been absent from class lately. Someone had said her brother had gone missing.

Gail. Gail. Gail.

I dragged on my cigarette.

Gail Dunstable.

The smiling man. The one with the camera. The one with Logan.

Simon Dunstable.

Bingo.

****

My classes finished that day at lunchtime, and I had written down Gail's address in my notepad before I left and made my way to Kate's flat. I had a spare key – she said I needed it in case I had to get in when she was not around. I think what she meant was in case Logan pulled any stunts, but it was nice that she had trusted me all the same.

I rang the doorbell, having climbed up three flights of stairs, and tried to get my breath back. I should exercise, but I hate it.

Logan answered, looking the worse for wear from a night on the town.

"Jenny, babes, come in, and excuse the mess. Coffee?"

"Tea. Two sugars. I need to speak to you." I followed him into the kitchen. It was a pigsty, and I was glad it was me who was here and not Kate.

She would have had a fit at the state of the place. Dirty dishes, empty take-away cartons, black bags of rubbish to be taken out.

"Logan, open the window, it stinks in here."

I went to sit down in the living room, realising upon first sight that it was not much better. He came in with our cups, draped in a shabby, once-white dressing gown. So, then I felt guilty for thinking badly of him for not tidying the place when he obviously had suffered such a hard life.

"Logan, do you remember when you first came back to Glasgow and we went for a drink, and you brought along that man, Simon? What do you know about him?"

"Simon? He's fucking loaded, babe. He's not around much but when he's in town, he gives me a buzz and we get together and he leaves me a load of cash." I must have looked shocked because he added, "Don't look at me like that – he can afford it and I always show him a good time."

"Where does he live?"

"How the fuck should I know? I just sleep with him."

"You must know something about him."

"And why do you want to know, Princess?"

Logan (or Lisa at the time) had not known about my ability. Or curse. And I had never mentioned it. I wasn't about to change that now.

"I have a student in my class. They have the same surname and she's been absent 'cause her brother is missing. I wondered if he knew anything about it. You know, to pass on my best wishes and that – if they are related, that is."

"Well, fucked if I know." He stood up, draining his cup. "I need to go. I have an appointment with the Jobcentre. Bastards. Feel free to stay and tidy up."

He flounced off into his room, emerging two minutes later dressed in red leather trousers and a leopard print jumper while I finished my tea. He came over and kissed me on the head, saying, "Text me," and left.

I was alone in Kate's flat. I had been there before, of course, I had stayed there many times, but I had never been a nosy parker. I respect people's privacy. Usually.

Sometimes I thought I knew Kate well, and at others not at all. Her mother made me curious. She said Kate was her eldest. She never spoke of brothers or sisters. She had said I was a keeper unlike… I didn't know, because Kate had shut her up.

I went into the bedroom that had been Kate's, opening the door and peering in, as if she would be lying on the bed ready to catch me. It was as perfect as the day we had left it.

I am ashamed to say I went through her drawers, every single one. I was surprised at the amount of clothes that she had left here. Like she would live here again one day…

I was beginning to feel a bit like a prying snoop in her cupboard, when I came across a photograph album, hidden way at the back under a stack of shoeboxes.

I took it out and sat on the bed and began to flick through. Then I stopped. Because my heart had begun to race and I had a sick feeling start in the pit of my stomach.

I started at page one. Two teenage girls, smiling at the camera. More pages of two young girls. My Kate being one.

Then they got a bit older. But it was still the same girl with Kate. Kate had her graduation gown on and the girl was beside her, arm around her.

More of them, with other friends in the pub. On a beach, somewhere warm. Certainly not Scotland.

I had started to cry.

Kate's life. In photographs. With another woman. A woman who was not me.

Near the end of the album, I turned a page, still choked with tears, and a card fell out. The front was a picture of sand on the beach and the words 'Kate & Elaine' had been drawn in it. I opened the card, my hands shaking. I read the words.

"Love you, K. Always and freva."

Up in the far right corner, like she did with all the cards I had sent her, Kate had written the date it was received.

It was just over a year ago.

Chapter Twelve

I am sitting on a bed, facing out to the three walls that I can see. There is a window in the wall to my left and a door in the wall to my right. The wall in front of me is my Wall of Glory. On the table in front of the window is my laptop and a glass of water. I look again at the wall in front of me.

On this wall there are newspaper cuttings. Some have been printed off the Internet, and some he has cut from actual newspapers. But, they all have the same theme. Dead women and Bible John.

I start to squirm in my sleep.

I flick some specks of imaginary dust off my trousers and stand up. I run my hand over the smoothness of my hair and check the parting is immaculate. I tighten the tie at my neck and raise my chin. I can manage a smile.

I look at the pictures in front of me. My eyelids flicker and I try to stop the blinking.

I look at my hands, perfectly manicured and neat, my nails tidy. I blow on them. These are my instruments of death. I do not need weapons.

I walk over to my table and I open my Bible. I read, "No temptation has overtaken you that is not common to man. God is faithful, and he will not let you be tempted beyond your ability, but with the temptation he will also provide the way of escape, that you may be able to endure it."

I smile to myself and feel the beginning of an erection. The word of God is my law. The word of God is all.

I am all.

I am the word of God.

****

I had limped home the day I had been snooping in Kate's flat and drowned my sorrows in a bottle of wine. I was asleep in bed by the time she came home. I only know she came home because I awoke with a cry in the middle of the night and she was snoring beside me, her hand on my thigh. I brushed it off and deliberately lit a cigarette, hoping the smoke would wake her up and annoy her. But it didn't.

I whispered to her as she slept.

I said, "I love you, and I hate you too."

****

I rang Damian and arranged to meet her. I *had* to talk to someone.

Her assessment, when I had told my sorry tale, was short and biting. "She's still in love with her ex."

"But she's never mentioned her to me!"

She laughed. "Why would she? What's she gonna say? 'I keep an album devoted to my darling ex-girlfriend and I can't talk about her because it hurts too much?' You need to wise up, soldier."

I could feel the beginning of tears prick my eyes. "She's not like that."

I would defend my Kate until the end of time. Even if that end of time was the end of our time. Which it might be soon. How would I know?

"You're only saying that because you can't bear to see any bad in her. I don't have your loyalty. I think she's a cunt."

I cringed. I hated the 'C' word.

"She's not. You don't know her like I do."

Damian smiled again. "Do you have a photo album of Julie hidden in your cupboard?"

"No." All my photos were in the same place that Kate knew about, and that she could see any time she wanted.

"Then you've answered your own question. Why hide something if you are not ashamed of it? Or need it to be kept secret?" She peered into me. "If you have nothing to hide, then you have nothing to hide. Simple as."

I remembered hiding my friendship with Rob. And I realised Damian was right.

I hid Rob because there was something between us, something I thought Kate would not understand and something I would not take the risk of telling her, to lose her. Is that what she was doing to me with this Elaine? But how could she? She lived with me. I would know. I saw her every day, she kissed me every day, I told her I loved her every day.

I thought my heart was going to break in two.

My Kate. Loving someone else. Not me.

I began to have trouble breathing, and even realising I was going to create a scene was not enough to stop me. I cannot breathe. I am seeing her with someone else and the pain is tearing me apart.

Damian has leapt around the table and has her arms around me. I had never known her be tender before.

And I begin to cry, in big huffing puffs that choke me and render me speechless. I do not believe my Kate would do this to me. Not my Kate that cried making love to me. Not my Kate that reaches for me when she sleeps. She wouldn't.

Would she?

I can't breathe.

I can't breathe. My darling. My baby. No. Please. No.

Yours are the only arms I need around me, they make everything else better. Why can't I be the same for you? Why can't I be your everything?

I can't let go. I can't let go.

"Eyes that told me so much

Lies

As words are woven

We'll never start, darling we'll never stop."

I choke with the snot in my nose, trying to breathe and Damian grabs me. She doesn't say anything but she doesn't have to, she is there and that is enough. When I manage to calm myself down, I blow my nose and wipe my eyes, knowing it is obvious I have been crying. But I know that Kate won't notice, because by the time she gets in from work I will be sleeping, or recovered somehow. She will never see this. I will never show my heartbreak.

And why should I? She does not know that I have seen her secret.

I hug Damian back and feel that nest of butterflies in my stomach begin to move. She runs her hands up my back, and grabs my head and pulls my face into her.

And then she kisses me.

I am immediately drawn back to the time that Rob kissed me. When I kissed him back.

I panic that history is going to repeat itself and pull myself away.

No matter what Kate has done to me, I will not do it back to her.

****

Kate comes in that night, as usual knowing I will have her dinner in the microwave, and I do not disappoint. I put a little more garlic salt in it than I normally would. Let Elaine kiss that, I thought.

I am so angry and hurt and upset and betrayed and guilty, that I have forgotten my dream. I am silently seething and cannot bear to sit pretending to watch the telly, while I know she is happily eating in the kitchen. I stalk in and she is feeding the cat while her dinner reheats in the microwave.

"I've already fed him. No wonder he's fat."

She continued to spoon food into his bowl, with Jonah trying to eat it before it was even out of the tin. She threw me a glance, but did not say anything. She had laid her papers out neatly on the table. It was our file that she kept meticulously, making a report after every time we had gone out. I lifted up the file, had a quick look and tossed it back onto the table, making a convenient mess of her neatness. As much as I had told myself to say nothing, I was spoiling for a fight and, as soon as I had seen her, I knew I would not be able to keep my mouth shut.

She sat down with her dinner and moved the file back into the pile. So that all the edges matched. My blood boiled. I seethed silently.

"I think we should go out tonight, even if it's just for a few hours. Tonight might be our lucky night," she said happily.

"Are you having an affair?" I couldn't contain myself and just blurted it out.

"What? No," she laughed, and continued to eat. That made me even madder.

"I was at your flat yesterday, I went to see Logan. I found your photo album. Nice pictures of you and Elaine."

She sighed and put down her fork. "Babe, she's an ex."

"An ex that sent you a card saying she loved you a year ago? A fucking year ago you were with me!" I was shouting.

"Sit down, calm down and let me explain."

"No, I won't calm down. What do you expect me to think? Bloody hidden away where no one will find it, your whole life in photos with that girl and her little love cards to you."

"Jen, I gave you a key to my flat because there is nothing there that you cannot see. I am not having an affair with some ex-girlfriend that I haven't seen for four years."

"How do you explain the card then?"

"She sends me a card now and then, Christmas or birthday or just out the blue. I honestly have no idea where she is."

"You expect me to believe that? Your nights away 'working' so you say. You could be seeing anyone!"

"But I'm not. This is ridiculous."

"It's not to me! It makes me feel sick to think of you with someone else when you are asleep next to me."

"I'm not with anyone else!"

I was on the verge of getting hysterical. "I don't believe you! I don't believe you! I'm just convenient for you and you are getting me back because I went with Rob. Never mind how much I hate myself for that. You go away God knows where and say its work and you can't discuss it. You have kept all your photos and cards from this Elaine, that you have *never once* mentioned…" The tears start to come. "I don't want you to love someone else."

And then I completely break down into a frantic crying fit. Kate comes to me and tries to cuddle me. I throw her arms off me. "Don't touch me!"

She rolls up the sleeve of her shirt. "Jen," she says, holding her arm towards me.

"What?" I snivel, blinking my tears.

"Take my arm."

"Why?" I still don't get it.

"If I am deceiving you, then you will feel it."

And, just like that, I knew I had been a fool.

****

In the dream, I can hear the telephone ringing. Then I realise it is the actual telephone and Kate has answered it. I am about to roll back into sleep, when I feel her jump out of bed and fish around the room for some clothes.

I sit up. "What's wrong?"

"We've found that wee boy that's been missing. I'm going now."

"The little boy who was missing… Oh God…" I say, as my brain slowly processes this. "I need to come with you."

And I am jumping out of bed to look for clothes, too.

"Jen," she says, coming over and placing her hands on my shoulders, very steadily, "I need you to stay here, darling. We *think* it's that wee boy, but we don't know yet. A body has been found badly burned. We need to let the right people do their work now." Her calmness soothes me.

"Kate, you need to look at his feet, you need to look at his feet."

"Why?" she asks, and already she has taken her hands off me and is finishing her hurry to dress.

"Because he is going to have four toes on his right foot and that's how you will identify him."

****

Kate leaves, and I know there is no point attempting to go back to sleep. I grab my notepad from the side of my bed and throw it across the room in a temper.

I could have stopped this!

I know it was all there for me to stop it. I should have read the signs better. I should not have forgotten to buy a new pad. I should have known when Gail Dunstable was missing from my class.

I should have known, and now a wee boy was dead because I was too wrapped up in the drama of my relationship. I had not been able to separate my life from the dreams I had and deal with them separately.

I sat down and cried. A wee boy was dead because of me.

I could have saved him.

****

Kate texted me later that day to say she may get home about ten, if she was lucky. I was not to worry, she added. I replied that both myself and some dinner would be waiting for her. I had gathered myself together over the course of the day and cried the tears that needed to be cried. It was another death in the long list that I had seen in my short life.

And I realised that HP from Scotstoun could still be saved, and I had to focus my energies on finding her and saving her life.

I had been here so many times before in the past, seeing the murder, the death, crying my tears. It would be easy to get swamped in that when I had the chance to do something to stop one. Didn't make me feel any better about the wee boy, but I couldn't change that.

Knowing Kate would not be home until late, I decided to continue with our door knocking on my own. I would just blag I was working with the police. Most people never even looked at Kate's ID. It would only take one sighting of the woman I was looking for and I would know, I felt sure of it.

"Hi, I'm investigating the disappearance of Jean MacPherson. Can I speak to your mum?" It didn't work when a man answered the door, but I diligently marked that on the spreadsheet as needing another visit. Kate would be so proud, I thought.

After an hour or so, I was standing along the landing of a block of flats. There were eight doors and I was about to knock on the last, when two actual police officers in uniform came through the landing doors. I tried not to look guilty and knocked on the door. They threw a glance my way and then went to their right. An elderly lady poked her head out of the door, said something to them and pointed to me.

Oh no.

"Madam, could we have a word?"

I felt the dread rise up from the pit of my stomach.

"We have reason to believe you have been impersonating a police officer and would like you to come with us."

"Am I being arrested?" I started to panic. Kate would kill me.

The officer smiled and said, "You will be if you don't come down the station of your own free will."

I nodded and began to trudge off with them. As we came to the landing doors, I heard a voice say, "Did you knock on my door?"

I turned and saw the woman from the last door I had knocked on.

It was HP.

Chapter Thirteen

Three hours later and I was still sitting in a police cell, where I had been deposited upon my arrival at Pitt Street in the centre of Glasgow. I had originally been taken to the local nick, but after an hour I had been moved without explanation. My feet were cold. They had taken my trainers off me – I assume in case I concocted some makeshift noose from the laces and hanged myself. I was trying to warm them up with my hands when the door opened, and an officer asked me to follow him.

God knows what I could be stepping my socks into.

I had already made up my mind that I was saying nothing without a solicitor present. Or Kate.

The officer walking in front of me led me down some corridors and then opened a door and waved me in with his arm.

Kate and another man were sitting in front of a table.

"Miss Keith," he said. "Please sit down."

I looked from him to Kate, but did as I was told.

Kate said, "Jen, this is my DCI."

"Hello," I stuttered, adding, "Sir", unsure how to address him.

"Jen, what were you doing earlier?" She saw me look at the DCI. "You can talk freely. I've explained the situation."

"I was only trying to help," I began to babble. "I know we don't have much time left and no one ever looks at your ID. I thought I'd be okay and get a few more doors knocked. I never actually said I was a police officer, so you can't do me for impersonating one."

"Jen, you're not going to be charged. It's okay, calm down."

A wave of relief washed over me. I could have lost my job.

The man spoke. "You are a very interesting woman, if what my DI tells me is true."

"That depends what she's told you," I answered, and he laughed a little bit.

"She tells me that you have dreams and know there is going to be a murder. She tells me that you helped our departed colleague, DI McLean, on a number of cases as an assisting psychologist and she tells me you gave her the clues to find Charlton Heston."

I nodded. "Yes, that's all true."

"Miss Keith, I have checked out every single thing I can find out about you and your involvement in these cases. I have no reason to believe you were ever involved in a sinister way, and the very fact that McLean, and now Coutts, both find you convincing, convinces me. There are things in this world that have no explanation. I do believe that, and I believe it would be completely foolish of me to let this opportunity go to waste. So, tell me about your dreams."

I was taken aback, as I had expected to be roared at, and charged with some offence. Instead, he was quite amicably stating he wanted me to help.

"Well," I began. "I get all sorts of dreams and some are absolutely rubbish. You know, just dreams that make no sense, like everybody else's. But other dreams are different and for years, I have written them down. Lately, I had these dreams where I would quote phrases from the Bible and I saw a woman being strangled. It made me think there is a sort of Bible John copycat murderer on the loose, so I told Kate after Jean MacPherson was murdered, and we thought the last woman to be murdered, the one I had seen in my dream, would have the same initials as Bible John's last victim, Helen Puttock. You see, the other two women strangled had the same initials as his first two victims as well. I had seen the woman's face and I knew she came from Scotstoun, as I saw her getting the bus from there, and the only way we could find her would be to go door knocking and see if I could recognise her."

"Yes. Coutts has explained that to me. What were you going to do if you *did* see the woman from your dreams?"

"Um, we hadn't quite decided on that yet. But I've had other dreams. That wee boy that went missing, the one with four toes on his right foot – I know who killed him, and he's going to kill Logan next."

"Logan?" he questioned and he looked at Kate. There was an imperceptible shake of her head. Almost so subtle that if you had not known her you would have missed it. But I did know her, and I didn't miss it.

"Our friend. I've seen him tied up. Simon Dunstable is the man who kills him, or will kill him. He killed that little boy and he filmed it. I saw it on his computer."

"Miss Keith, you don't need to worry about the Dunstable boy – we have people on that. I'm more interested in this Bible John character. You and Coutts have yet to find this woman – am I right?"

"No."

Kate looked startled. "No?" she asked.

"As your officers were dragging me away, she answered the last door I knocked. I know where she lives. We can stop her being murdered," I implored.

"Tell me, Miss Keith, how do you propose we do that?"

He was beginning to annoy me. "You're the detectives – you tell me."

Kate shifted in her chair uncomfortably.

"Okay then, we can have officers watch the woman. How are we going to find the killer?"

That was where I was stumped. "I need to sleep." It *was* two in the morning, after all.

"We haven't quite finished."

"No, I meant if I sleep then I can dream, and if I dream, I might get more details."

"Ah." Kate had sat very quietly throughout all of this. She turned to her DCI. "I have an idea, Sir…"

****

By the time we got home that night, it was after three in the morning. I had fallen asleep in Kate's car and she had had to wake me up when she pulled up at our flat. I threw off my clothes and left them on the floor, not caring, and got into bed.

I heard the kettle boiling and knew Kate was making me a cup of tea, so I tried to stay awake a bit to drink it.

I felt happier now we had a plan. And I had not been arrested. But something niggled at the back of my mind. Why had her boss not been bothered about the Dunstable boy? What did that look between them, when I mentioned Logan's name, mean? I knew if I asked Kate she would palm me off with a glib answer, so I quickly grabbed my notepad and wrote 'LOGAN' in big letters. That would remind me to think harder about that when I was more mentally capable.

Kate brought me my cup of tea and set it down on the cabinet beside my bed. She sat on the bed next to me.

"You're remarkable," she said, as I lifted the cup.

"Am I?" I asked, blowing into my cuppa to cool it down.

"Yes. Just when I think I can't be surprised any longer, you manage it."

She took the cup from my lips and set it back down on the cabinet. She took my face in her hands, and I gulped, mesmerised by her beauty yet again, despite my fatigue.

She began to kiss me, slowly at first, and then with more urgency.

It was a long night.

****

The next day, with matchsticks holding open my eyes, I fumbled my way through my lectures and then went for my swimming lesson with Damian.

After, we decided to go for a quick pint, which became two pints. She was so easy to get on with that the time just flew away between us. We laughed, I told her about me getting lifted by the police the night before and she had a proper mock.

"Oh Jen, only you!"

I accepted the ridicule in the good humour it was intended. I was just grateful she had not started on at me about Kate again and wanted to keep things jovial between us. I asked her again to come round for her dinner, and again she refused. I would wear her down eventually I thought, as we hugged goodbye.

I was in a good mood when I got home. I was not expecting Kate to be home that early, but I had spotted her car and was hoping she was after a repeat performance of the night before, minus the time in the police station. I popped my head in the living room but she wasn't there, so I thought she must be in the kitchen as the door was shut.

I opened the door quietly and stopped in my tracks when I saw her and Logan bent over the table, whispering to each other. They saw the door open and quickly sat up straight, like I had walked in on something I should not have.

Logan immediately put on his act. I was beginning to see that now, that he was all an act. But for what purpose?

"Jennifer!" he shrieked. "We were just talking about you."

"Oh?"

"You know it's our Katie's birthday next month? She is trying to talk me out of roping you into organising a surprise party for her."

The idea of throwing a surprise party for Kate had never even crossed my mind. I wanted to do something quiet and intimate, I knew she would like that. I could just hear the moans if I threw a big bash. But then maybe she thought I was going to. I was so tired and, after the two pints and an hour of swimming, that I could easily have slept. My poor brain was in meltdown. It was making me overly suspicious, and I shook my head to bring me to life a bit more.

"I have something else planned," I said, cryptically. "And I am saying nothing more on the matter."

He laughed loudly. "Well, I shall leave you both to it – things to see, people to do!"

He got up and kissed Kate, and pecked me on his way out.

"What did he want?" I asked, flopping into a chair by the table.

"Something wrong with the loo. I need to get a plumber as I'm the landlord. How you feeling?"

"I'm shattered."

Her face lit up with a cheeky grin. "No chance of seconds, then?"

I grinned back. "Every chance."

****

Later that night, we sat in Kate's car at the bus station that would take us into town from HP's house in Scotstoun. Her real name was Hanna Plewinski. She was Polish, and had lived in Glasgow for about twenty years with her husband, and now two children. They seemed a decent, hard-working family who kept to themselves and bothered no one. Hanna had a sister, Anka, who lived on her own a block away, and we figured it was probably her that went on the night out with Hanna, the one I had dreamt of.

The plan was simple. Kate and I would sit and wait at the bus station that I had seen in my dream and the night that Hanna and Anka got on that bus, Kate would radio her boss under the codename 'Operation Church' (I had thought it up as a reference to Bible John), and plain clothes officers would meet us and also monitor Hanna and Anka. This way, Hanna would never know and not have the anxiety of knowing she was the target of a serial killer, based purely on her name. And there was always the possibility that the killer did know her. If we alerted her, she might inadvertently alert him and we could lose him.

I don't know if I was entirely happy with this, but as a DCI was willing to stake his officers on the strength of a dream I had, I did not think I was in a position to bargain. Jen, the assisting psychologist. I was now officially on the books. Even better, I got paid for it.

My problem was the killer could not be arrested until we had actually caught him doing something. Which meant timing was everything. Timing would determine the life or death of Hanna Plewinski and she was completely unaware.

It was all or nothing.

Again.

****

When I finally fell asleep that night, I would have thought I was too tired to dream, but this was not the case.

I was behind the eyes of the killer, staring at his newspaper cuttings on his wall. I could feel the rage build up inside him.

Slovenly, slutty, despicable, whores the lot of them. I can hear the words in his head. Filth, sex-mongerers, diseased, evil… It went on and on and I began to feel an uneasiness in my stomach.

I could see what he wanted to do, as he pictured it in his head. He jumped up and ripped all the cuttings from the wall in a fury. He caught his breath and wiped the sweat from his brow. Dirty, dirty, dirty, I could hear in his head. He left his room, locking the door with a key which he then put in his pocket and went into another room, a communal bathroom. He washed his face and hands and looked at himself in the mirror.

And I memorised that face.

I was going to see it soon.

****

I was meeting Julie again, and as I waited for her, I lit up a fag. It just didn't taste the same outside. I smiled as I saw her coming to me, pushing the buggy with her little boy inside. The little boy that my Kate had wanted her to get rid of. That Julie had pleaded and cried to keep, crying because she knew she would never chose Kate over him and crying at her heartache for losing the woman she loved. Still loved. I chose to ignore all that.

It was nice being friends with Julie again. I was able to be myself with her, although I was careful not to mention Kate too much or the work we were now involved in. I think Julie realised this and saw that I was trying to spare her feelings.

But, inevitably, the conversation would wind its way back to Kate. It was, after all, the only thing we had in common any more.

"How is she?" she asked, and I saw the controlled effort it took to ask casually.

"She's fine. Enjoying her work."

"I've never met anyone so career-driven."

"Do you think so?" I asked, for it had never occurred to me.

"Oh God, yeah. She wants to get to the top. She won't care who she has to trample on to get there."

"What if she has to trample on me?"

She unconsciously moved Jack's hair with her hand.

"I just hope she doesn't have to."

****

We were sitting in Kate's car again. As I could not be specific about exact dates, we had been here every night for the last three weeks and were now past the 'four month' mark from the murder of Jean MacPherson. All I knew was that Hanna had got on the bus before it was dark, as I had been able to see the last glimmer of light in the sky. Every night, we had returned home when the sky was black.

I had dreamt the night before of the killer's rage again, building up inside him. It had been getting more frenzied in my head and I knew it had to be coming soon.

I still wasn't prepared though when I actually saw Hanna and Anka approach the bus stop.

"Oh Kate! They're here!"

My heart sank. This was it. The night it would all end. I had to hope it would end well for Hanna.

She grabbed her mobile and rang a number. "It's DI Coutts. We are go on 'Operation Church'. I need two officers on standby. I will be on radio channel two-three, I repeat two-three. All comms now via radio."

I watched Hanna laughing at the bus with her sister, as they stole nips out of a bottle of vodka from Anka's bag. I had never witnessed one of my dreams being replayed. It made me feel sick, but I had to see this through. I had to save this woman's life.

The bus came and Kate grabbed my hand. "You okay?"

I nodded. We followed the bus into town, not sure where their stop would be but finally, they got off and we hastily parked the car, following on foot. It was going to be a long night of drinking and keeping a distance.

We followed them from pub to pub, watching them get drunker and drunker. I felt so sorry for this woman. We could see her door from our position waiting at the bus stop, and she never went out. This was her chance to let her hair down, and she certainly was.

I had no idea where or who the other two officers were who were watching along with us but Kate would use her radio occasionally and nod to someone. It made me feel safer that this did not all depend on me.

We were walking a distance behind, as they laughed and reeled their way into another pub in the city centre of Glasgow. I saw the sign above the windows, 'Horseshoe', and began to get that familiar feeling of dread.

I began to breathe in heavily, something in the air catching my nostrils. I was completely and utterly panic-stricken. We walked in after Hanna and Anka, and Kate ordered two soft drinks.

I could smell blood.

"He's here," I whispered to Kate.

"Where?" she said, her eyes scanning the clientele.

"I don't know, but I can feel him… He's here…"

And there he was. With his nice brown suit, and perfect side parting, smiling his way over to Hanna.

The stench of blood washed over me in a wave.

Now or never.

All or nothing.

Chapter Fourteen

And in the dream there are furious hand movements, too quick for my eye and brain to process. I am in a large hall, filled with people, throwing their hands and arms all over the place. I am following one boy. Or I should say, I am seeing through the eyes of one boy. I can feel his mouth moving, and feel his fingers.

He is walking towards the toilets and passes a notice board on the wall. He opens the calendar pinned on there, and flicks forward to April.

Then he lets the pages fall back down. In the toilet, he goes into a cubicle and closes the door. He takes a powder from his front pocket and lays it on the cistern, smoothing it out into a little line with a bankcard. Then he rolls up a ten pound note and snorts it.

I feel like I can conquer the world.

He goes back into the main hall and begins to talk again, with his hands. I don't understand how he can talk using his hands and am confused.

At once, I realise he is using sign language and the silence of this dream tells me he is deaf.

As he begins to pass pleasantries with a middle-aged woman, I am hearing it in my head and I understand it all. I can now talk with my hands.

I can hear every word that my fingers spell. It was almost magical, the words and pictures forming in my mind as he used his body to tell them.

I wake up and, for a split second, the small noises I can hear confuse me. Kate breathing beside me. A car driving past in the distance. Then I get that it was a dream and I can hear.

I remembered to write this down.

****

We are sitting at a table watching Bible John (even though that's not his real name, it is how I identify him in my dreams) talking flirtatiously to Hanna and Anka. He is smiling and goes to the bar to buy them a drink. In my head I can hear "Dirty, slut, filth, prostitute, whore, slag." Kate is keeping a close eye on me, I have noted. I would admire the way she can be so clinical if I were not so terrified.

They get up to leave and anyone can see Hanna and Anka are both beyond the point of merry.

"Jen, some officers are going to take you home now. We are going to take it from here."

"No!" I protest.

"Yes, Jen. Don't worry, we will get him, but this isn't your job now – it's ours."

I gritted my teeth. "If you don't let me stay, I am going to scream and cause a scene and he will know."

I saw the quick flash of anger that flitted across her face before she said, "Follow me."

Which I did. As we left, I saw the two women and the man get into the taxi. Somehow I still did not believe it was all real. Or maybe it was all too real.

Kate nodded across the road and I finally saw two burly men jump in a car. Kate's car was also outside, and I don't know how it got there, but we got in and she began to drive and follow the taxi.

"Tell me again what happens."

I close my eyes. "Anka will get out, and they will drive on and then they will get out, and he will take her round the back of some garages and that is where it will happen."

I think I am going to vomit and swallow hard.

Before I know it, Anka is waving goodbye to the black cab and I wished I had listened to Kate and gone home. This is not my job. I am not a police officer. I don't know what I am – a messenger of sorts – but I am not brave and the terror is washing over me.

The cab drives on a little bit more, and we are both silent, and I know it cannot be far as Anka and Hanna live close.

Out of nowhere, I think of Rob and I can hear him saying, "You can do this, Jenny. You are saving a life, remember," and I feel reassured, comforted even. He has my son, my little blue eyed, blond haired boy who could smile his way into Heaven and I am filled with love.

Hanna has two children. Two children who need their mother. Two children whose life will alter forever if I don't get a grip and find my feet.

All or nothing.

I am taken back in time, and Nina Grainger has a gun and I am saying, "I choose you!" to my baby, Jonah.

I chose all and got nothing.

I am choosing all again.

Kate is jumping out her car and I have to hurry in my mind to follow what is happening now, because I have been lost in thought. She is talking into her radio and running and I am running after her.

They are going to be kissing behind the garages.

I can see Kate ahead of me, and the two plain clothes officers are side-by-side with her. They are conferring on a corner and, as I run to catch up, I am thinking, Hurry up, he is strangling her. Before I can reach them, they are running round the corner, into the darkness.

A darkness I have been in before. I run faster and my legs hurt, but I keep running.

I skid turning into the corner of the garages that I had dreamed of, and I see the two men on top of my Bible John and Kate on the ground leaning over Hanna.

I am frozen.

Kate shouts "Jen! Help me!", but I don't know what to do and I am scared. I think she might be dead and we are too late. The man is grunting on the ground as the officers wrestle with him and I see the struggle to put handcuffs on.

"Jen!" she shouts again, and I am reminded of Hanna's two children, tucked up in their bed, sleeping none the wiser, knowing their mummy will be there in the morning to get them up and feed them breakfast.

"Get her mouth!"

I am standing over the still body of Hanna Plewinski and Kate is pumping her hands on Hanna's chest. She means me to blow into her mouth and I get down on my knees, pinch her nostrils with my fingers and move her head back to open her airway. I let my lips touch hers and blow in. I can smell the blood on them.

I hear Kate counting. "Again!" she says, and I blow. I can hear the voices of the men, rights being read and I can hear one screaming for an ambulance.

I am too late.

I am about to lose control, thinking not another one that I could have saved, not another one to die, when Hanna chokes and Kate tenderly puts her hand under her head.

"Hanna, it's okay. I am a police officer, and you are going to be alright. Where is the fucking ambulance?"

I hear the distant blare of the sirens and pass out.

****

I come to and feel the shame of being a drama queen and that I have embarrassed Kate. But, she is nowhere to be seen. A paramedic is sitting with me and asking if I am alright and I say yes, all the while looking for my Kate. I see her in talks with the DCI, who has obviously arrived while I have been unconscious, and see also the amount of police panda cars in the area.

Bible John is smiling out at me from one. Hanna Plewinski is being loaded into an ambulance. Alive.

I have done it. I did it before, with the girl in the cemetery, and I have done again. I will sleep with a smile tonight.

****

A police car took me home and the female officer was awful nice, walking me up to my door. She had said my Kate was a great officer. I was so dead on my feet that I could barely smile at the compliment and opened the door to the smell of an overflowing litter tray and Jonah screaming at my legs for food. I went straight into the kitchen, opened the window, and cleaned the litter tray. I emptied the bin and took it down to the bin shed downstairs. I opened the lid and threw in my sack and felt a piercing pain in my arm.

I staggered back and let the vision work its way into my mind.

I am the eyes of new Bible John, fuming in his isolated cell. All I can feel is anger and hatred. Pacing back and forward in the cell. And the vigilance I had is not so noticeable here as he takes off his belt and begins to make a noose.

Or perhaps that was deliberate. Is that how the police view murderers? Low enough to be able to take their own life?

And he is hanging the belt from his light fitting, and around his neck it leaves no room for oxygen. My hands reach for my throat and I feel the asphyxiation start to take hold.

I pass out again.

****

As I come to, I feel cold and feel the last sting of the slap Kate has administered to my face. She is, once again, my saviour and gets me upstairs and into bed.

I have no idea what time it is, but I know it is early in the morning and I would normally be sleeping by now. I am overcome by all that has happened tonight, relief mixed with horror, and I start to cry.

She comes to me and holds me, silent in her solace. I cry into her shoulder and think how strong she is, how good she is. And then I remember Julie saying she would trample on anyone to get further in her career and I cry even harder.

She is my love, she would not do that to me.

But I have just helped her find another killer, so she can afford to be benevolent with her cuddles.

****

I barely saw Kate for the rest of the next week. I understood it was her job, and I did not complain. Hanna Plewinski had been discharged from hospital the next day, and had happily returned to her family life. She had no idea how close she had come to being a statistic. But I was happy that she could continue to be a mother to her children and a wife to her husband. I would live with the memory of my dreams if it meant she had her life.

Two nights after the capture of Paul John (Bible John), I had woken up again with the strangulation dream and insisted Kate phone the prison he was being held at. I knew she hated me waking her from her undisturbed sleep, but she had got up, put the light on, rang someone at her station and then rang another number.

"Yes, Mm hmm. Just check," she said, and looked at me, peeping out from the top of the quilt. I could see the goosebumps on her arms.

"Thank you," she said, and clicked off her mobile. "He's dead. You're right – he hung himself."

I would loved to have gone back to sleep, but sleep is such an enjoyable torture.

****

After my swimming lesson, Damian and I went shopping. She said she needed a new top, but was vague about why. I smiled to myself, knowing she had a boyfriend and did not want to tell me. I would play along.

"Here, this one," I said, pulling out a nice red vest top, with some black lips on the front.

"Try it on. He might like it," I teased.

She dutifully went into a changing room and came back out, saying, "Well?"

"Gorgeous," I beamed and went over to grab her, trying to move her in front of the mirror.

I felt her tense and heard "No!"

"What's wrong?" I asked, a bit lost.

"I don't do mirrors."

"Why not?"

"You can see the dead behind you."

****

"Still Life" by The Horrors.

It was playing in my head. In my dreams. I was walking along a path, amongst the grass, gravestones on either side. The weight of grief was pressing down on my chest, but I kept going, finding my way to the grave. Someone was holding my hand and leading me on, and I let myself be led.

And then the song in my head changed and yet again it was 'Summoning of the Muse' by Dead Can Dance, a song with no words but only music that wraps its way around your heart and encompasses you in its melancholy. My church song.

This time it is me standing by the grave, looking in on the dug out rectangle of dirt that awaits the coffin. I can feel the misery inside me. The loss. I look around me, but the faces are blurred. Every face is the same. Each body is in black and the face is obscured. None are human to me.

I know the tears are burning down my cheeks and I grasp the hand that holds mine as hard as I can. I turn to see who holds it and this face I do see.

It is Damian. Her sad eyes hold mine.

I wake up, howling with pain and tears, and Kate throws herself up in a daze until she comes to and realises it is only me and my dreams waking her once again.

But I cannot stop crying.

She puts her arms around me and tries to shush me, and I try to let her because I know, I know.

I know that I would never cry like that at anyone else's funeral but hers.

****

It was Kate's birthday. I had taken her to her favourite Indian restaurant and we were having a lovely evening. She had laughed and made me try a dish I was not familiar with, even if it was only a korma. She had a night off from driving. I insisted we get a taxi so that she could have a drink and enjoy herself, and really, that made it a bit easier for me to swallow the wine without her disapproving looks.

I had given her the presents earlier. I had got her some nice diamond stud earrings and a pair of boots, some perfume and a book I thought she might like. She had seemed really glad, and kissed me on unwrapping each one.

After our meal, I felt a bit full up and wanted to be home so that I could have a proper belch, when she grabbed my hands across the table. My Kate did not do public displays of affection much, so I soaked it in.

"Jen, thank you for a lovely birthday. It's been great. Great presents, great meal, great girl!" she grinned.

"Babe, you are *so* welcome, I just wanted it to be nice for you."

If you have ever had a bad dream that has followed you into the next day and ruined your mood, you will know, a bit, how I felt.

"It *was* nice, and now I want to do something nice for you, or to you. Fuck, I'm nervous."

Nervous? My Kate was never nervous.

And then she spoke.

"Jennifer Keith, will you marry me?"

Chapter Fifteen

I can hear… silence. This lack of noise is comforting and allows me to focus single-mindedly on the task in hand, which appears to be fiddling with some pieces of blue and red wire, and snipping bits with pliers. There is a mess of wires and bolts and screws and screwdrivers on the table in front of me. I am concentrating on splitting the blue plastic around the gold wires inside and feel my tongue edging out the side of my mouth. I look at my silver alarm clock. It reads seven.

The light above my head flashes. I get up and grab a bed-sheet and throw it over the table – just in time, as the woman opens the bedroom door and walks in with a tray. There is a sandwich and a glass of orange on the tray.

I move my hand up to my lips then pull it away. "Thank you."

She begins to move her hands in sign and I nod and say, "After I've eaten, I'm going to watch TV for a bit in bed. Good night." But I say it with my hands and face.

And then I am in the club. I see the old, small, fat woman with hairs on her chin coming towards me. I smile. This is my moment. Instead, she says "Victor got the most votes, he is going to get the trophy this year."

I don't believe it. Victor? Captain of the football team? Week after week, I turn up and I clean the kitchen and I hand out cups of tea and I wash the dishes, and I empty the tables and I sweep the hall, and I fix the things that are broken. I did a walk to raise money and made £1500.

But I can't play football.

I start to tell her this, and say, "but you told me I had it, you told me the committee were impressed." She throws her hands in the air. What can she say? It wasn't up to her, and I storm off into the kitchen.

I am back in my bedroom and I throw the bed-sheet off my table and sling it into a corner. Fucking Victor. I slump into my seat and look for the drawings. I look at them closely and lift a piece of red wire.

This *is* going to work, and they will see that I am the champion.

I wake up and start moving my hands. I have no idea what I am doing, and I have no concept of what I mean.

I lean over for my notepad and use the light of my mobile phone to write down 'Learn sign language' before I go back to sleep.

****

I could not stop looking at the ring Kate had given me. It was a beautiful plain diamond set in a silver band. It fitted perfectly, and every now and then, I would hold out my hand to look at it and feel a firework of love going off inside me. On her next day off, we were going to go shopping to get her a ring, and I could not wait to see her wear my ring on her finger, her promise to me. When she had proposed, I had immediately said yes, and started to cry tears of happiness while she produced the box containing the ring. I had forgotten I had wanted to belch, and we had stayed a long while in the restaurant, giggling after a few too many wines and being glared at by the customers, not used to seeing two women kissing and holding hands.

The next morning, she brought me a cup of tea in bed to wake me up, as she was going in to work later.

"Morning, wife-to-be," she smiled, getting in bed beside me and leaning over to kiss me.

"Oh don't," I said, turning my head. "I haven't brushed my teeth yet."

She laughed. "Think I've never smelled your morning breath before?"

I pretended to be offended and asked, "When are we going to have our engagement party?"

"Whenever you want, darling. There's a hall the boys use for events. I can find out about hiring it when I get to the office if you want."

"Great. I'll get to work on the invitations, and you can look over my list later and see if I have forgotten anyone."

"Sounds like a plan."

"So, when you said you had to be in work later, how much later is that?"

Her eyes twinkled at me. "I have about an hour – is that enough?"

"An hour is fine," I twinkled back, reaching over for her.

****

I had a whole Saturday to myself to do nothing but dream about my wedding day and try to organise a party to celebrate our engagement. When Kate left, I finally dragged myself from bed and had a fag in the kitchen while feeding the fat cat. He has to go on a diet, I thought, and went for a shower.

I rang Damian. "Can you do me a swimming lesson later?"

"Time?"

"Four?"

"Meet ya there."

I was going to have to tell her. She would see the ring, as she never missed a trick. I felt a bit scared, but if she was a true friend, I decided that she would accept my decision and just be happy for me.

I rang Sheena, Kate's mum. I had sat and deliberated it for a good ten minutes before I had punched her number in. She was Kate's mother, and she had the right to know she was getting married. I would sweet talk Kate if necessary.

"Um… Hi Sheena, this is Kate's partner, Jen. How are you?"

"Hello, hen, I'm fine, I'm fine," she boomed. "Is everything okay?"

"Yes, oh God yes, nothing to worry about. I just wanted to let you know that Kate and I got engaged last night, and we are going to have a party and well, I wanted to invite you to it."

"And Kate's okay with that, is she?"

I squirmed a bit. “She doesn’t know, at the moment. I will tell her later and I’m sure it will be fine. Please. I would love you to come.”

I could hear her hearty chuckle. “Tell you what, Jenny, you send me an invitation after you’ve spoken to Kate and I’ll come. Got a pen?”

I wrote down her address and thanked her. I would need to put a shimmy in my shake and get a move on. I skipped into the bedroom, floating on my happiness and looked for a cardigan. I saw my notepad lying open on the bedside cabinet and curiosity got the better of me.

I sat down on the bed and looked at what I had written. ‘Learn sign language’. I nodded to myself. Of course – the dream about the deaf boy. I wasn’t yet sure where it was leading, but it would not hurt to learn and it might be fun. I’d ask Damian to come with me.

‘Logan’, I had also written. I frowned. There was something not right with him and I could not put my finger on it. Yet. But I would. I had always liked Lisa, as he had been when I had first known him in my Uni days, but this new incarnation had yet to grow on me. There was something shifty and unconvincing about him, like that day I had come home and caught him and Kate whispering in the kitchen. I did not know if this was connected to Simon Dunstable, and I would need to speak to Kate about that when I remembered.

I had not liked the way her DCI had skimmed over me saying I knew the killer of that little boy. I named the killer and I told him Logan was next, then the look between him and Kate. It meant something, of that I was sure. Why would she not have told me later? Could she be hiding something from me? But she had asked me to marry her and that, to me, meant no secrets.

Then I remembered that I had met Julie a few times and immediately felt guilty. Whatever it was, I would have to trust her. But I would make sure Logan was safe all the same, just to be sure.

****

Sitting in the pub with Damian after my lesson, I took a big gulp of my pint of lager and tried to work up the courage to tell her about my engagement before she noticed the ring.

"I need to tell you something and I don't want you to go off on one, I just want you to be happy for me because I *am* happy, very happy."

She also took a drink of her lager and asked, somewhat sardonically, "What?"

"Kate asked me to marry her."

I saw her raise her eyebrows. "And what did you say?"

"I said 'Yes' of course."

"Hmm."

"And you *are* coming to my engagement party. I won't take any more refusals."

She leaned across the table at me, and in a very quiet voice said, "Are you fucking stupid?"

I felt the flash of hurt that her words cut into me. "No, Damian, I'm not stupid. I love her."

"She doesn't love you."

"She does!"

"What about the photos of the ex?"

"I asked her and I believe her."

"You just 'believe her'?" she echoed.

"Yes! I believe her. She offered me her arm, so that I could, you know, 'see' into her. That proved to me she was telling the truth and I was being paranoid."

She laughed, in a slow drawl. "Well, if I had a psychic girlfriend and I wanted her to believe me, I would do exactly the same."

"I don't see what you are getting at."

"She called your bluff, and you fell for it."

I did not know whether to be angry or burst into tears. "It wasn't like that."

"And are you forgetting something?"

"I must be!" I sulked.

"I told you, when you were asked, to say 'No'."

****

I left her in a bad mood and drove to Kate's flat. Logan answered the door.

"Can I come in? I was on my way home and I've been to the pub for a pint and I can't hold it in any longer. Honestly, I think I'm going to have an accident."

"Sure. Help yourself, sweetie," and he stood back to let me pass.

Just before I went into the toilet, I turned and asked him. "Everything okay? With the toilet now?"

He squinted his face and looked like I had asked him to quote Pi to fourteen decimal places.

"It's fine."

She had lied to me, then.

****

I fell asleep on the couch that evening, with the cat on my stomach. I should have been happy as I had started the day, but I could not shift the edginess I had felt since seeing Damian.

I could hear the song, turning round and round in my head.

I woke up when I heard her key in the door, and I said, involuntarily, "Loving you isn't the right thing to do."

****

I asked her about the little boy who had been found burnt to death, the one with four toes on his right foot, the one I had seen murdered in my dream. Gail, his sister, had never returned to my class. I didn't blame her. Kate said they were working on it.

"But I told you the killer."

"It's not as straightforward as that," she had replied.

I asked about Logan. Were they going to watch him, because I knew he would also be captured by this Dunstable man? Logan was a big boy, I was told, and could look after himself. Her lack of concern alarmed me.

I asked her about her blatant lie about Logan needing the toilet fixed. At that, she took me seriously and came to me.

She held my hands and asked, "Do you love me?" I nodded. "Then please, you have to trust me."

Didn't look like I had any other option.

****

It was the night of our engagement party. I was sitting in front of my mirror in the bedroom, putting on a bit of mascara and I felt elated, excited, delighted to show off my fiancée. I was watching my eyes in the mirror, mouth open as I flicked the brush, when suddenly Damian's words came back to me about mirrors.

"You can see the dead in them."

I quickly turned and looked over my shoulder.

At nothing. I half-laughed at my own silliness and superstition, and turned back to my mirror.

But it no longer held my reflection.

I saw a building explode into flames, debris flying through the air. I could almost feel the heat on my face.

I closed my eyes. No. Not now.

****

The party was in full swing. Kate was laughing and letting her hair down, swigging from a can of cider. I smiled and thought how sexy she looked when she did not know I was watching her. Her mother had come and, although it had been a bit frosty at first, I had grabbed Sheena's hand and got her on the dance-floor and when I looked back, Kate was laughing and shaking her head.

She had got her own back and invited my younger sister and her boyfriend up from Birmingham. They had arrived at the club we had hired with their bags, straight from the train, and I had run to give Rhona a hug. I had not seen her for a long time.

Damian had even come with her new girlfriend, Sasha, a brooding black beauty, almost Grace Jones-like. I had shook her hand and she had smiled tightly. I don't think she liked me, but it was not going to spoil my night. I secretly wondered where the boyfriend was that she never mentioned and had hugged Damian tightly.

"Be nice," I had whispered into her ear. "And thank you."

The night was just as I had imagined it to be, and Kate had even organised the DJ to play the cheesy kind of music that I liked. I was on the dance-floor giving it 'yee-ha' to Erasure, when the music quietened down and we all turned to the DJ. I groaned inwardly as I realised Kate had the mike and was going to make a speech, but I'd had quite a few drinks by then and wasn't as embarrassed as I would have been sober.

"Jen, Jen! Come up here," she spoke into the microphone.

A cheer went up and I danced my way over to where she was standing. She slung her arm around me.

"Everybody, my fiancée and I" – some wolf whistles were heard, the station lads I presumed – "would like to thank you all for coming. I am very proud to have Jen as my fiancée and to share this all with you tonight. And, to you, my darling, I just want to say that I love you and I will never abandon you."

And then she kissed me and I threw my arms around her and kissed her back, and the cheers grew even louder.

So, I was laughing, dazed by the intensity of the love I felt for my woman, when I turned to the opening doors of the hall and saw the blonde-haired beauty walk in.

It was Elaine.

Chapter Sixteen

I am striding down the street with purpose, gripping my holdall in my left hand. I stand at the kerb, looking left and right, then left again like I was taught when I was a child, and I march across the road. I approach the building and look at the sky, still dark from the night before but getting ready to break into morning. I see a few birds and wonder what it would be like to hear them. I will never know.

I fish in my pocket for the keys and I let myself in. I am practically the caretaker, and I am trusted. I punch in the alarm code and lick my lips. I push through the double doors and walk across the hall, to the far end, where the stage is. I walk round the side to where the wooden stairs are, and I get on my hands and knees to crawl under. When I think I am under the centre of the stage, I stop and open my bag, tenderly lifting out my creation. I get my duct tape and attach it to the flooring of the stage, above my head and then I look at my good alarm clock. Seven o'clock.

At seven o'clock their small, silent world will change forever, and I am the architect of this.

I crawl back out from under the stage, and wipe the cobwebs from my hair. I am done and dusted.

I grin as I walk back across the hall, set the alarm and lock the doors on my way out.

I look left, right, left and cross the road, beginning the long walk back to my home, as the sun begins to rise far, far away.

I will be champion now.

****

I heard Kate say, "Oh fuck!" as the DJ resumed his tunes and she followed my eyes to the door and saw Elaine, her long lost girlfriend.

I had two choices, I quickly realised. I could create a huge scene and embarrass myself and Kate, or I could keep my mouth shut, smile sweetly and keep my paranoia in check and see what transpired. I am fucking psychic, I drunkenly thought, I'll know.

"That's Elaine," Kate whispered to me, taking my hand. "We have to go say hello." I let her lead me over to Elaine.

Elaine. Taller than me, skinnier than me, bigger boobs than me, prettier than me. I felt sick at the back of my throat and swallowed hard. But she was so *butch.* I was a bit stunned that Kate had been into someone like that. She had walked in wearing a white vest top, and her left arm was covered in tattoos. She had two lip piercings, a nose stud, various hoops in her ears and short, spiky blonde hair. She had skintight white jeans on with holes at the knees and black boots, unlaced. I felt immediately uncool in my grey trousers and light pink shirt.

I'm a fuddy-duddy, I thought. I have never been butch or femme, or whatever the stereotypes are. I wear skirts, and in the summer when it's warmer I wear dresses, but I have old boots and jeans too. I wear a little bit of make-up and I get my hair cut every few months to keep it at a tidy length. I shave my legs and armpits and pluck my eyebrows now and then. I paint my toenails and keep my fingernails neat and clean.

In my head, I heard the words, "Fuck, she's as hot as ever."

But as Kate and I walked towards Elaine, I knew no one had spoken. I would not have been able to hear over the music. Which was now 'Spin Me Round' by Dead Or Alive.

"Elaine!" Kate said, welcoming her and giving her a hug. She leant back to me, taking hold of my hand again, and said, "Meet my fiancée, Jen. Jen, this is Elaine, an old friend of mine."

"Hey, Jen," she said, warmly and hugged me before I saw it coming.

Kate said, "What the hell are you doing here?"

"I'm in Glasgow for a visit, so I went to your flat and that guy said you were here, so here I am!"

That guy? Logan? Now why would an old girlfriend of Kate's, that she had a relationship with for so long, not know Logan, who was supposed to be an old friend? And come to that, why was he not here?

"Come and get a drink. Where you staying?" Kate asked. I was still stood, holding her hand, smiling like a silent statue.

"I'll book into a hotel, don't worry. Engaged, eh?"

"Fucking numpty." Again, I knew no one had spoken but I had heard those two words as clear as day.

"Don't be silly, you can stay with us. Can't she, Jen?" I nodded, helplessly. "Settled. Come and get a drink. Fucking hell, I never thought you would be here! What the fuck have you been up to?" I hated that Kate swore all the time.

As we were walking towards the bar, my sister Rhona came over and grabbed me.

"Come on, big sis, it's our song, we have to PARTAY!"

I gladly let Rhona lead me onto the dance-floor to boogie a bit to Adam and the Ants' 'Prince Charming'. When we were little and I had been a teenager obsessed with Adam Ant, I had taught her how to do the dance. It appeared neither of us had forgotten, as we strutted our stuff, much to the delight of her boyfriend, Mitch.

I was aware that photos were being taken, and that it would be plastered over every social networking site in the morning, but I didn't care. I had one eye on the bar, where I could see Kate happily chatting to Elaine and one eye on mastering the dance.

My little sister came up and hugged me and screamed into my ear, "Love seeing you so happy, big sis."

I could have cried. I hugged her back and shrieked, "Love you too, wee yin."

"Are you still psychic?" she asked, because, of course, she knew all about me, growing up in the same bedroom with me, and I wasn't unconvinced she didn't have a little bit of the fey about her herself.

I laughed. "Yes," I said into her ear.

"Good," she smiled. "There's something I need to talk to you about."

****

Somehow, later that night, me, Kate, Elaine, Rhona and Mitch had all managed to stagger into a taxi and get back to our flat. Rhona and Mitch were in the spare room and deposited their bags, and after getting two pints of water from the kitchen had hugged us all good night in a drunken good humour and gone to their bed.

Damian and Sasha had slunk off early, I had noted. I had spotted Damian watching me from afar, jumping on the dance-floor, hugging Elaine and whispering with Rhona. All I could remember was her saying, "I told you to say no."

Kate was getting some spare bedding for Elaine to sleep on the couch, and I was left awkwardly alone with her in the living room.

"Do you want a cup of tea?" I offered.

"No, thanks."

"What does she see in her?"

"I'm sorry. What?" I asked, bewildered.

She looked at me, blankly. "I think I'll just go to sleep. I'm fucked!"

Kate came back in then with a spare quilt and an old T-shirt and threw them on the couch.

"We are going to bed now. Make yourself at home. You know where the kitchen is. Come on, Jen," she beckoned to me. "Night," she threw in, as we left the room.

We undressed in that way when you have to concentrate really hard not to fall over when you are taking your clothes off because balance is a dangerous thing. When we had got under the duvet, she cuddled into me and said, "I love you."

"I love you too," I replied, but I wasn't finished or ready for sleep. I had a bone to pick.

"Kate, don't you think it's odd that your ex-girlfriend happens to appear at our engagement party?"

She was slightly drunk. "Mmm? No. She's always been the way she is, goes where she wants."

"And what does she want now?" I asked, uneasily.

"Says she's up for a holiday, to see her family."

"So why isn't she staying with them?"

"Jesus, Jen, her mum and dad live in Prestwick. It's not exactly a taxi ride from here."

"But the first thing she did was come to Glasgow, to your flat?"

"No, she's been to see her parents. She got the train up to see me."

"Babe, I'm scared you're going to end up with her again."

"Jen," she cooed. "It's you I want."

I just *knew* I was going to have a bad night, and I did not need to be psychic to see that one coming.

****

"Damian! Damian! Help me!"

I am screaming and Damian is running towards me. I cannot make out what she is saying but, as she gets closer, her words begin to make sense.

"I told you to say no!"

And then she is holding my hand and I am crying inside, outside.

My tears blind me, and the weight of grief is making my legs buckle. She puts her arms around me and holds me up. She says, "I told you I would never abandon you".

And my head is screaming, "No! No! It was Kate who said that! Where is my Kate?"

My legs go weak again and Damian is my strength. "Shush, my darling," she says.

****

I am barefoot, walking over the burning coals of a building destroyed. It cannot touch me.

All around, I can see blood, smell the burning flesh, see the parts of bodies strewn amongst the rubble.

I am the architect of this. I created this destruction.

I smile and lick my lips.

****

I hear a song, the words come and go and the music fills my head.

****

I am drowning. Drowning in the sea of love. I am filled with love and water. I am cold and happy and dying.

I am filled with the cold of the water, rising all over my body, until there is no more air and I have to gulp in the salt of the water and choke, choke on it.

But it brings with it the calm.

The now, find your peace.

This is my death. And, in the split second it takes, I understand that in my mind but it does not stop my body revolting against the influx of the water into my lungs.

"Find your peace."

****

I am standing on some steps and I am watching Kate walk away from me into the laughing arms of Elaine. She embraces her, and Elaine sticks two fingers up at me.

I have no response. All response in me is numbed by the horror of seeing the woman I love walk away and love someone else.

I feel sick at the bottom of my toes and my body begins to shake.

I try to shout, but in the dream my voice is caught in the back of my throat, and they walk away holding hands, and sneering at my love for her.

****

I wake up, realise I am going to vomit and run into the bathroom and get over the loo just in time. As I catch my breath, I feel Kate come in and rub my back, asking if I am okay. I gulp yes, through the rest of my dry retches and she stays rubbing my back until the sickness subsides.

I begin to shiver and she guides me back into bed, throwing the quilt over me and tucking me in. I continue to quake and she holds tight, her stomach in my back, her arm across me, her little feet rubbing mine.

"It's okay," she says. "It's okay, I'm here."

As I fall back to sleep, I hope she will always be there.

But I know that's not going to happen.

****

"Jen," she whispers, as I am dropping back into oblivion. "I'll always protect you."

I know she speaks from the heart, at this darkest hour, when nothing can be spoken but the truth.

"I know," I whisper back.

But I don't know.

****

The next morning, there was an amalgam of hangovers in the kitchen, all brooding over the boiling kettle. I would have to face the stench of coffee.

My sister laughed "Did I hear you puking, Jen, you lightweight?" And her and Mitch had laughed at me.

I had managed a smile, flopping about in my old blue pyjamas that I could not bear to part with.

Julie had bought me them, and parting with them would be like throwing her away and all that we had.

"Oh," I groaned. "I had some bad dreams." Then she shut up, because she had shared a room with me for many years, and knew what my bad dreams meant.

Elaine walked in then, and I thought, quite enviously, how good she looked in a morning. She did not have creases in her face like me, or scabby old blue pyjamas, or hair mashed up in a sleep frenzy.

"Cuppa?" I asked.

"Coffee, thanks."

Typical.

'I am fallen.'

I heard the song in my head, that had been ringing in my dreams and swung around quickly.

The faces gave nothing away but I had *heard* it.

I made her and Kate a coffee each and me, Mitch and Rhona had a cup of tea, then we all went into the living room to watch mindless Saturday morning TV and recover.

"My head hurts," Kate laughed.

'I'll rub it better.'

What?

Rhona was looking at me funny. "You okay, sis? You gonna puke again?"

"No, I'm fine."

Singing, 'Canny hold her drink.'

I turned my head rapidly from my sofa position, with Kate resting her head on me,

"Did you say something?" I asked, directing my question at Elaine.

She looked dumbfounded. "Me? No," and turned back to the telly.

"Babe, are you suffering?" Kate teased me.

'I'll show her fucking suffering.'

And then I knew.

"I'm fine," I smiled.

But, I wasn't fine. Not really.

I had just discovered something about Elaine, something that I did not like or know how to cope with, something that I had never had to deal with before.

'Fine. Jesus, what a fanny.' I could hear her thoughts.

Chapter Seventeen

Damian and I are sitting in a pub. No, it's not a pub, it's a large hall, and we are drinking Bacardi Breezers. In between taking mouths of our drink, we are talking with our hands and I realise we are signing and I can hear the words in my head. The hall is full, the bar is busy, the only noises that of scraping chairs on the floor and excited sounds, the occasional distortion of a thousand voices.

I am gingerly trying to tell Damian something with my hands, and I am painfully slow. She has picked up the flow of language from her brain to her hands much quicker than I have.

My eye is caught by the slightly overweight young man, collecting the glasses with a scowl on his face. He is the one who sits over his desk and fiddles with wires and a silver alarm clock, and diagrams on bits of paper, printed off the Internet.

He is the one who is going to crawl under the stage, set out before me with chairs and a table full of prizes. In the centre stage of the table is a gold cup. I watch him and see him eyeing this cup and feel the vibe of resentment that flows from him. As he moves amongst the tables, stacking the empty glasses with his left arm, I see him look at the clock, on the wall, high above the stage.

It reads 6.55pm.

At seven o'clock, it is all going to change and I am going to be there.

I have to warn these people.

But, my hands choke and the words do not come and the seconds keep on ticking.

****

My sister Rhona has cornered me in my kitchen, where I had gone to boil the kettle, needing a cup of tea but really needing time to think about what I know.

I can hear Elaine's thoughts.

Not all of them. I cannot hear her make sentences, but it's almost like the loudest thought in her head can be heard in mine. While I find this disturbing as it is like nothing that has ever happened to me before, I slowly realise that this could be a blessing, if I can keep my mouth shut after her nasty comments. I can accept she doesn't like me, but if she doesn't know me, how can she judge me? She is seeing the woman Kate has chosen to be with, and is resenting me purely for that. I get it. I begin to think a bit wickedly, which I can blame on the hangover. I could have some fun with this.

Rhona interrupts my amusing thoughts by saying "Jenfer", which was her name for me when she was little and couldn't pronounce Jennifer. "Can I ask you something?"

My shoulders sank. "Rone, I am *not* going to tell you if Mitch is unfaithful or if you are going to get happily married and have kids and a dog and live happily ever after, blah blah blah."

"It wasn't that, but am I?"

As I turned to frown at her, I saw the cheeky smile on her face and knew she was pulling my leg. Just what little sisters were meant to do.

"Yes. All's well that ends well. Do you want a cuppa?"

"Yes, but I need to know something."

I heard the change in her voice and knew it was serious. I walked over to the door, closing it.

"What's wrong?"

She looked at the floor. "When mum and dad died, did you… know it was coming?"

"No, Rhona, I didn't."

"You didn't dream about it before…?" she tailed off.

"I never dreamt about it before," I answered honestly. I went over and hugged her. "It's just one of those things, wee yin – don't be sad."

She hugged me back. "I'm not sad any more. I just always wondered."

No, I had not dreamt of the death of my parents before it happened.

I dreamt of it after.

****

In the summer between me leaving school and going to University, our parents had decided to take a short break for their twenty fifth wedding anniversary. I was seventeen and allowed to stay at home, but Rhona was only ten and had to go stay with our Aunty Joan. She lived in Solihull near Birmingham, and Rhona had been dropped off there on the way to their weekend break in Brighton.

They had driven from Solihull to Brighton on the Friday after arriving with Rhona on the Thursday, and had been involved in a major pile up on the Saturday night coming home.

No one could understand what they were doing coming home on the Saturday when they were booked in until the Monday morning.

Except me.

****

In the days before mobile phones and Skype, I had been lounging on the couch watching MTV, thinking I was in heaven. No parents, no annoying wee sister, music on, bottle of beer on the go. I was watching a procession of music videos and thinking how great it was that I had the freedom to fart on the couch, watching what I wanted without being told to watch my rubbish in my bedroom, when the phone had rang.

It was an old phone that you put your finger in and turned the number round to dial. My mother had liked them.

I looked at it and grimaced. I had drunk a few bottles and knew my dad would be able to tell if I was drunk and I would get a bollocking. But if I didn't answer, I would get it worse, so I slouched off the couch and walked over to the sideboard where the phone sat.

"Hello?"

"Jenny! It's your Aunty Joan. Your mum and dad have had an accident…"

Her voice broke and I heard the sobs. My legs began to shake and I put my hand on the sideboard to steady myself.

"What kind of accident?" I asked, sounding much calmer than I felt inside.

"They… They're dead, Jenny. Uncle Hugh is on his way up to bring you here. I'm so sorry, darling."

I dropped the phone.

And then it all went black.

I could see my mother and father drunk in their hotel room, the abuse spilling from their mouths like venom and I had seen that they hated each other.

"You can't keep it in your pants!" she was screaming.

"If you were more of a woman, I wouldn't need to look elsewhere," he screamed back.

"We're going home!" my mother had announced, and began to pack her bag, and he had said, "Fine" and began to pack his.

And so, they had got in their car and driven away, both in a fury, and my dad had caused a three-car pile up on the motorway.

My mother screamed, "Watch out!" and he couldn't, because his senses were too slow, hazy from the alcohol.

And that was that.

Four other people died.

I never told Rhona.

****

My Uncle Hugh had taken me back to Solihull and I had stayed there with Aunty Joan and him for a few months, until I had been ready to start my University course. I was able to get away and distract myself with a new life and studies. Rhona stayed with them.

I knew Aunty Joan had been given the toxicology results, and I knew she had shielded us from that. I knew anyway, but I would shield my sister.

She was my family.

****

While I had been talking to Rhona, Elaine had gone for a shower. Kate was still lying on the couch, sipping a coffee, unused to drinking so much. I think Mitch must have gone into the bedroom he and Rhona were sharing.

I knelt on the floor beside Kate and leant in close to her face. “Aw, is baby suffering?” I teased.

“Umph,” she managed.

“Let fiancée Jen make it all better,” I continued and began to laugh and nuzzle into her neck.

It was the way we played when no one was around, the nice bits of us that no one saw. They did not see her giggle because I had hit the funny spot on her throat that reduced her to a giggling mess and made me annoy her all the more. I began to throw my arms into it, tickling her sides and her giggles got louder as she tried to fend me off.

Soon, I was being pulled onto the couch and was half-fighting on top of her, half-kissing. And then I heard her.

‘God, do you have to?’

“Hey, Elaine,” I said, and popped my head up over the side of the couch.

She smiled and Kate tried to muffle her giggles, her politeness kicking in.

“Nice shower?” I asked, pleasantly.

“Yeah, great, thanks.”

She sat in the chair in front of the TV, half turned away from us. Oh dear, I thought, I do hope we are not making you uncomfortable in our own home.

Kate cleared her throat and tried to sit up a bit, and we fell over and across, with a bit of rib tickling in between, until we were both sitting up.

"What have you got planned for the rest of your visit then?"

"Oh, I dunno," she mumbled.

'Trying to get you back.'

I said, "I hope you are not going to try and get my Kate back" and laughed. She had turned sharply and Kate had laughed, still being in playful mood.

"Jen, I've told you we are old friends. You're my fiancée now," and she edged her face forwards into mine to rub noses.

'I'm going to be fucking sick.'

"Feeling sick, Elaine?" I asked.

She glared at me. "I'm fine." 'Fucking psychic.'

"Yip, that's me, the fucking psychic."

She glared even harder, and Kate's smile shortened a bit, puzzled.

That will show you, you blonde, skinny bitch. You do not come into my home and mess with me and my woman.

She might have been skinnier and prettier and have bigger boobs, but she couldn't read my mind.

One word. Winner.

****

I see the thin man walking in his high heels towards the door of the house and preen his hair before he rings the doorbell. He stands a minute and the door is answered by someone who recognises him and nods him to come through.

He minces his way into the room on the right and smiles affectionately at Simon Dunstable. He sees Logan and waves him over and throws his arm around him, introducing him to the older men standing in the circle, drinking brandies with him.

Hours later when they are all very drunk, Logan excuses himself for the loo.

My dream-eyes follow him into the toilet where he gets out his mobile phone and scrolls through his contacts, until he comes to the name he is looking for and hits 'dial'.

The name he was looking for was Kate Coutts.

****

I awoke from my mid-afternoon snooze to find Elaine had left (good riddance) and Rhona and Mitch had gone into town for a wander. Kate was sitting at the kitchen table reading the paper, and smiled up at me as I walked in.

"Head better, woman?"

I nodded. "Nothing that a cuppa and a cuddle won't cure."

"You stick the kettle on and I'll throw my arms around you," she romanced.

The radio was playing and, although I was not really listening, I was vaguely aware of it in the background.

"Shhh," she said. "I love this song."

I listened. It was 'Lurgee' by Radiohead, her favourite band.

She pulled me tight and sighed into my chest, where she leant her head.

"Do you know why I love you, Jen? One of the *many* reasons?"

"No, baby," I whispered.

"Because you never ask why when I need to hold you."

****

On the Sunday, Rhona and Mitch had been seen off at the train station with promises of visits and a little kick to my guilt complex for not making the effort to see her more often. Kate was still off work, so we went around the shops, had some lunch, and bought a few bits.

The simple things you do when you are in love.

"Where's Logan?" I asked her.

"Logan? Holed up with some bloke, no doubt."

"He didn't come to our party. Did you invite him?"

"Of course I did, but you know what he's like."

I don't think that was true anymore.

****

I am surrounded by trees and they are moving and the wind is blowing in my hair. The branches are swaying and the leaves are falling on my head.

"Kate!" I shout.

But, my Kate is not there. No one is there. I am alone in the dark forest, not knowing which way is in and which way is out.

"Kate!" I shout again.

Because, when all is lost and there is nowhere to turn, you scream for the one deepest in your heart.

"She's gone."

I do not know whether I have heard the voice with my ears or my mind.

I turn around and around and around, looking for the one who has said these words, but all I can see is the darkness of the moving trees, their shadows mocking me and holding out the moonlight that would guide me home.

"Kate?" I question into the black.

I see a small light and train my eyes in, as it grows and becomes a shape, the shape becoming a person.

It is Elaine. She is dressed like Joan of Arc.

"I am back. She will be mine."

"No," I protest meekly.

She continues to grow until she is towering over me, ten feet, twenty feet and the moonlight can shine in chinks off her armour.

She says "Tell me something I don't know."

I know that song.

And I know my answer.

But my dream changes, or I wake before I get the chance to say it.

I don't bother writing this dream down because I know I will never forget it.

The ones that leave scars on your heart cannot be unwritten.

Who has not carried a dream in their heart forever?

****

Jonah and I were pussyfooting about in the kitchen quite literally when the house phone rang.

I frowned because the house phone rang so infrequently. Nowadays everything was done by text, unless it was someone trying to sell you a loan.

I looked at the fat cat.

"Will we answer? Will we? Will we?" I sang.

It looked lazily at me and I thought how much cats hated humans – unless, of course, we were feeding them. I still loved the fat lump despite his prejudice and smiled.

"Oh, yes we will, oh yes we will," I sang on.

I lifted the phone. "Helllllloooo?" I sang.

"Hi, this is the Royal Infirmary in Edinburgh. I'm looking for Kate Coutts."

I instantly became serious. "Uh, Kate's not here – she's at work. I'm her partner."

"We have her mother here, and we need to speak to Kate. Can you take this number and get her to call us?"

"Yeah, yeah, of course. What's wrong?"

"We really need to speak to Kate, I'm afraid."

****

I hung up the phone and ran around the house in a panic, the cat making haste to where he would not be trampled on.

Sheena, Sheena, Sheena.

Where was her engagement card? I ran to the living room and found it, amongst the others on our table behind the couch.

Sheena, I said to myself, as I ran my fingers over her writing. 'To my girl, I hope you can finally be happy, love mum.'

Love mum.

Come on, Sheena. Let me in.

****

I can smell the dirt from underneath my nails. I can smell the filth from my underwear.

I am filth.

I let that happen to my poor wee girl. I let it happen to the other one.

I swig from the bottle of vodka and swallow down the gag, getting the alcohol into me. Numb me, make it go away. Make her love me again. Like she did when she was little and it was just us.

My little girl. I begin to cry. She hates me, she hates me. I will never hate her, she is my little girl and I sacrificed her.

No more.

This ends.

I will find my peace in this release.

****

I grab my mobile and fumble for Kate's number, programmed into my phone, my hands shaking.

Her mother has tried to kill herself and I don't know if she has or not.

"Release" I sing quietly to myself.

Chapter Eighteen

I look around me and see… nothing. There is only the grey landscape that I stand on that stretches for as far as my eyes can see.

I open my ears and concentrate, and the only sound I can hear is the beating of my own heart, bursting through the temples in my head.

I think into my head and there is emptiness. Not a single thought, not a single feeling, not a single emotion.

Nothing.

I am surrounded by nothingness, and the grey is working its way up my body. My clothes are grey, my skin is grey, the air is grey.

I do not remember who I am.

I feel… nothing.

There is nothing to hear and nothing to see but my eyes continue to search.

Then, it comes.

The colour in the grey. Far, far away like a small black dot. I zoom in immediately, focusing on the only infusion of life in this barren wasteland.

But who, or what, is it?

And as I begin to realise it is a person, I hear a faint echo of a piano key. As I strain to make my ears hear, I hear another piano key and listen harder, and one key becomes two until it emerges into a distant song.

All the while, I am watching the black dot, hoping it will grow and when I realise it is not going to come to me, I start to run to it. I run slowly, despite my whole-hearted effort to escape the desert of abandonment, and every step is a battle.

The song becomes louder and I can make out the words. It is 'Trust' by the Cure.

I am still running and it feels like I have run forever. I can see a woman standing with her back to me.

I think it is my Kate and try to run harder.

But I realise my eyes might be deceiving me, and it could be Damian.

I run and I run and I run.

There seems no way out of this nothingness.

****

I am running into my car, programming the Sat Nav for the Edinburgh Royal Infirmary and ringing Kate again and again because she is not answering her mobile. My hands are shaking and I fumble to get the keys into the ignition. Oh God, I pray, please let Sheena be alright.

I am driving and Kate is still not answering, and my heart is hammering in my chest, and soon I am parking the car and running into the hospital, trying to ask the reception where Sheena Coutts is and being directed to the assessment area. I have stopped running now, and have levelled out at a fast walk as I make my way into a curtained off area.

"Sheena Coutts," I tell the nurse at the booth, and she directs me behind a curtain at the far end of the room.

I walk behind the curtain and Sheena is lying with her eyes closed, her blonde hair stuck down on her head and a tube coming out her nose.

There appear to be monitors attached to her but I cannot take it all in and just whisper, "Sheena?"

"Katie? Katie? Is that you?" she scratches out from her throat.

"No, Sheena," I answer, reaching out to take her hand. "It's Jen, Kate's partner."

She seems dazed. "Where is my Katie?" she wails.

I remain quiet and softly slip my hand out of hers, as she falls back into unconsciousness.

I am better because I know she is alive.

I leave the ward and ring Kate again and this time she answers.

"Coutts," she says into her phone.

"Kate, it's me. Your mum's in hospital. She seems to be alright, so don't worry. I'm up at the Edinburgh Royal Infirmary."

"What's happened?" she asks, and I sense a lack of concern in her voice, like it is some con she is dealing with.

"She took an overdose. I haven't seen the doctor yet. When can you get here?"

There was a lengthy pause. "I'm working."

"Kate," I said, incredulously "Your mother has tried to kill herself. Don't you think you should be with her?"

"It's her decision. I don't see how it affects me."

I was appalled. "She is lying in a bed with tubes coming out of her, and she is asking for you!"

"It's not my problem," she said, calmly.

"It's not your problem?" I repeat and I can hear the anger begin in my voice. "It's your *mother*!"

"Jen, I appreciate your concern, but you don't know anything about us and I'm not coming to the hospital. I am working, and I am not coming off my shift for the drama that is my mother's life. I suggest you come home."

I hung up.

I stood, dumbstruck, looking at my phone, disgusted at the woman I loved.

I sat with her mother all night, and Kate never rang me once.

****

I stayed at that woman's bedside for two nights, until I knew she was out of danger and there was no damage to her liver. She had drank a bottle of vodka and taken a load of anti-depressants, and who knows what else. She had received psychiatric assessments but we all know the health service in this country is pushed to the limits, and I was worried about how easily she would slip through it, returning to this dark place again.

She wouldn't talk to me. She hid her face in shame and cried silent tears that slid down her cheek in a hurry to be gone.

When they discharged her, it was me who helped her into my car, drove her back to her house, went to the shops, got her some milk and bread and made sure her messages were stocked up. I asked her if there was anyone she wanted me to contact, and she smiled sadly and said no. After some arguing back and forth, I agreed to leave her – she would not come back with me to our flat – and I made sure she knew that if she did not answer her phone, I would be straight back up.

She walked me to the door and gave me a hug. "You are a good one, hen."

"I know," I joked. "I'm a keeper, eh?"

She pulled back and looked at me, face to face. "You watch out for that Elaine – she's a sneaky wee rat. Kate was always too soft with her, burned her in the end that one did. I know you won't, darling."

"I would never hurt her. I just wanted her to be here for you, and I'm sorry."

"The river runs deep in Kate. I'll tell you a secret. All you need to do with Kate is never question her – she hates it. Take her how she is, or don't take her at all."

She waved me bye from her window and I drove off, mulling her words. Take her how she is, or don't take her at all.

****

When I got home Kate wasn't in, so I fed the cat, made a cup of tea and went to bed to relax with a book, hoping she might stroll in the door. As much as I was angry with her for what I saw as the shocking treatment towards her mother, I also hadn't seen her for two days and I missed her.

I tried to stay awake but inevitably, I fell asleep.

In this dream, I was following Logan again, an eye in the sky, watching over events. He was standing outside the big house where he had met the older men, having a cigarette. I heard his phone vibrate and he pulled it out of the pocket of his skin-tight jeans and frowned, reading a text. He shoved the cigarette in his mouth and punched in a reply.

He spat out the cigarette and crunched it out with the high heel on his right foot, and after a quick glance around him, he made his way back into the house. I saw him bend over to take his heels off and carry them in his hands as he tiptoed along the hall and into a room. He knew where he was going and made his way into another room, which lay off the main one.

He came to a computer and switched it on, sitting down at the chair in front of it and nervously drummed his fingers on the keyboard, waiting for the PC to boot up. I saw him take a portable storage device and shove it into a USB slot and then begin to click on folders. Copy and paste, copy and paste, copy and paste.

This went on for some time until an error message pinged on the screen, informing him there was no more room available on his device. He quickly removed it, shoved it in his pocket and closed down the PC. He left as quietly as he had gone in.

Then he was back outside and was walking quickly, still holding his high heels in his hand and looking furtively over his shoulder. The house was still and quiet, and he was undisturbed in his mission. He walked to the edge of the garden, bordered by a line of thick trees. He cursed and shoved on his heels and began the delicate task of tramping himself through the undergrowth. I could hear him swearing under his breath and see him going over and trying not to fall. He did make his way through until he came to a wall, and he edged himself along the wall until he came to a wooden gate.

He knocked the gate, continuing to look behind him and around him.

The gate opened and my Kate stepped through. He handed her the USB device, saying nothing and she stepped back behind the gate, disappearing as quietly and quickly as she had appeared.

He cursed and tottered his way back through the hedges and tree stumps and muck, and slipped back into the house, again removing his shoes, now with mud caked around the heels. He tutted at the state of them and swore some more.

He swept up the stairs like a ghost, and went into his bedroom.

As he closed the door, a gruff voice asked "Where you been?"

"Smoke and a shit," he replied.

I woke up. The bedroom lamp beside my pillow was still on, and the book I had been reading was lying on top of the covers. I grabbed my notepad and wrote down the dream.

At the bottom of my page, I finished with 'Another liar.'

****

When I had got up the next morning Kate wasn't there, but I knew she had been in because she had left me a note next to the kettle.

'Saw you sleeping and didn't want to wake you. Be back about 7 tonight. Quiet me and you night? Missed you. Xxxx'

I felt that little jump in my heart that I always got when I knew she had been thinking of me.

I would never know what had gone on between her and her mother, and maybe it was best I did never know. Whatever it was, I knew it was not the greatest of childhoods, and I knew my Kate had overcome this and made something of her life and her career. I would take her as she was and not question.

But I would question Logan, and I went round to Kate's flat, where he was living, after my lectures.

It was four o'clock in the afternoon and he eventually opened the door, having come straight from his bed, it seemed.

Through his sleepy eyes and matted hair, he asked sarcastically, "Need another piss?"

I smiled just as sarcastically back and walked in past him. I was not waiting for an invite.

"I want to speak to you."

"Come in then," he said, shutting the door and following me into the living room.

"I want to know about you and Kate."

"Know what?"

"Oh, you know – how you met, how you kept in touch, everything."

"Oh I can't function without a coffee," he complained and swanned off into the stink of the kitchen.

I followed, now that I was like a dog with a bone. A bone that was being dangled in front of me and then inched away as I got closer.

"Late night?"

"Every night is a late night for me," he moaned.

"Really?" I asked. "Is that because you are downloading images from rich men's PCs and passing them to my Kate via a USB stick?"

He turned and stared at me. "She told you?"

Nail on the head time.

I was right then. They were involved in something and whatever that something was, it ended in Logan being kept in a dirty room with a blanket nailed over the window, gagged and bound. The same room where a young boy had been raped and murdered on camera.

Damian had said I needed to help Logan.

"She hasn't told me anything. She never tells me anything, and that's why I need you to tell me. I think your life is in danger."

He put his hand on his hip and screwed his face up. "Kate *hasn't* told you anything, but you think my life is in danger? Whatever I do, I am always careful and you don't need to worry, sugar."

Oh God, he was patronising me.

"Logan, I don't know what the hell is going on, but I know you are involved with some dodgy people, especially that Simon Dunstable, and I want you to promise me that you will stay away from him. This is important to me. I've never asked you for anything but I am asking for this one thing. Will you do it for me? Will you? Please?" I could hear the hysteria begin to edge its way into my voice and tried to remain controlled.

"Okay," he answered, all too easily. "I'll stay away."

Liar, liar, pants on fire.

****

As I left Kate's flat and got into my car, my mobile rang. It was Damian.

"Hi, babe," I answered.

"Can… can… you… come to me…" she falteringly sobbed.

I did not hesitate. "Of course. Are you at home?"

"Mm hmm."

"Give me twenty minutes to get there. I'm on my way."

I consider myself a good friend. I would like to think when I am in trouble or need a shoulder to cry on that my friends would do that, and I will always do that for them. I panic when a friend phones me and there are sobs cracking their voice. I swore at the traffic jam and wondered what was wrong with my good friend Damian. She pretended she had this aura of invincibility, that nothing touched her. The walls around her were to protect her but I knew, deep down, she was just the same as me. Too sensitive for her own good, she put other people before herself and never showed her pain.

And now that she was showing me her pain, I worried. Because that meant it was bad.

I pulled up to her flat, literally running out the car and up the stairs to knock her door. When she answered the door, her face gave away the problem instantly.

She had a split lip, black eye and blood encrusted around her nostrils. She spoke funny until I realised she could not breathe properly and was inhaling through her mouth.

"Oh my God, Damian! What's happened to you?" I cried, throwing my arms around her.

She held me tight for a long time, weeping into me.

"He found out about Sasha."

The boyfriend I had always known existed.

"Where is he?"

"I don't know – he left, I rang you…"

Despite my doziness, I can still be extremely practical.

"We need a joiner to change your locks and we need to ring the police. This is assault, for heaven's sake! I'll just Google it on my phone and we can get it sorted. Don't worry, I won't leave you."

Half an hour later we were waiting for a carpenter to come and change the locks. The police had been informed of a domestic assault and would send someone out "when an officer was available". I had texted Kate to let her know that I was going to stay the night at Damian's, because there really was no way I could leave her in this state.

I held her when she cried, I paid the joiner, I spoke to the police, I made her coffee and a sandwich. I listened to her as she repeated her tale over and over. Nothing was a surprise to me, only that she had not trusted me enough to tell me in the first place.

I went to bed with her and lay with her until she fell asleep. I myself also nodded off.

****

I am in a disco on my own and the music is pumping the floor, the vibrations rising up my legs and helping me find the rhythm to dance along. I do not know where my friends have gone, but finally I see my Kate, and I smile and make my way across the crowded dance floor to where she stands with her drink.

I look at it and think, that's a cocktail – Kate doesn't drink cocktails.

I walk over and say, "Hey baby", and she looks at me like I am a stranger. She turns away and holds the hand of the woman next to her. I see this is Elaine and feel the terror in my stomach.

"Kate, it's me!" I plead.

"I do not know you," she says, and turns away to kiss the spiky haired blonde.

I fade back into the crowd and when I look for her, she is no longer there.

All the faces are the same and the one who would stand out has gone.

****

I wake up and it is 5am and I have to get home. I have dread in me. I think to myself that I will not leave Damian long. I'll just nip home and feed the cat and give Kate a kiss and explain better than my garbled text messages. My fear from the dream will dissipate when I can hold her again.

I am running up my stairs, and the quicker I run, the more stairs there seem to be, but I get in my door and I run to the bedroom.

I throw open the door and see the lump under the covers.

Oh, how I have missed her.

I go to the side of the bed and I pull back the covers because I just want to kiss her head before I leave again, feeling better already.

As I pull the cover back, I see it is not my Kate.

Seeing who it is is like a bomb going off… A fleeting vision enters my head, but it passes. I am taken up by who is before me.

Elaine is sleeping in *my* bed, her head on *my* pillow, having eaten *my* porridge.

I am going to roar like three bears.

Chapter Nineteen

My Kate is smiling at me and I am smiling back across the short distance between us. I can feel my heart beating, as it does every time my eyes meet hers and feel the love jump inside me.

There is never a beginning and never an end to love. It just is.

You cannot pinpoint the moment when liking someone moves into loving someone, or when being with them becomes part of your soul and not just something to pass the time. But when the line is crossed, there is no going back. You cannot retract your heart.

It is all or nothing.

Love me back or don't love me back.

When there is emptiness all around and you see one sunshine in the smile of someone else, that is your lifeline.

I walked to my sunshine, beaming at me.

A metre between us, and the flying pane of glass hit me, splintering into tiny, tiny pieces, cutting me to shreds.

Ripping every limb, every sinew, every muscle.

Until there is nothing left on the ground but a bleeding heart.

****

I take my right leg back and I boot the lump on the bed, again and again.

At least, in my head, I do. In reality, I turn and strop off out the bedroom into our living room, where I see Kate asleep on the couch.

I am tempted again to bring back my right leg, but instead I roughly shove her awake.

Before her eyes have even fully opened, I ask, "What's she doing in my bed?", like she is Goldilocks.

I can feel the glass shards ripping into my body, waiting for her reply.

"Jen?" I could see her move the cloud of sleep from her brain. "Elaine turned up drunk, so I put her to bed."

"Couldn't she have gone in the spare room?" I seethed.

"Ours has a loo. I thought she might be sick."

I am not rational all the time, and when anger and fear mix in me, it is not a good combination.

"I'll find out myself if that's true," I say and strop back into my bedroom.

Elaine is still slumped under my covers in her stupor. I am not delicate and throw them back until I can grab her wrist.

I never hate anyone, but as soon as I touch her, I know I am going to hate her.

****

I am fourteen and I love her and I will do anything for her but she will not stand up for me.

We are standing outside the shops, laughing with the boys we always hang out with, and she is mocking me and teasing me, and poking me, and everyone is making fun of me.

"Mither's a drunk."

"Faither killed yar wee sister."

"Sister's mental oriental."

I grit my teeth and take it all. I take it all because I love her, and she is not like this when we are alone.

We are alone and she puts her arms around me and whispers that she loves me, but we can't tell people because they wouldn't understand and I don't ask questions. I just grit my teeth some more. I am used to being told how to feel.

Inside, I know exactly how I feel.

I am seventeen and sitting my exams. She wants me to come out and go clubbing and I refuse because I have to pass these exams, I have to find a way out of this life. And when she does come to see me, she is drunk and tells me I am ugly and thick and useless, and no wonder my dad killed my wee sister – he should have killed me.

I listen and I say nothing. I know no one wants me, but then she cuddles me, and I see someone who does want me and I let her kiss me and make it alright.

I am now graduating and the only person I want to be there could not tell me if she would come and I spend the whole time waiting for her to appear. Which she doesn't. Not until I am in the pub with my new friends, friends who believe in me and make me feel good about myself. But as soon as I see her swagger into the pub, I am reduced to being fourteen again and long for her approval.

I am older now and I have a proper girlfriend, who lives with me and is nice to me. Elaine comes into my life, absent for so long, and reminds me, without a word, how worthless I am, that my own mother did not want me. I feel like the small child, terrified of the man who will come into my room on a Saturday night and hurt me.

She says, "People who cannot look after children shouldn't have them" and Julie is asking me to be a co-parent. Julie wants us to be a family.

I can't do it and I harden my heart and I say to her "No." Elaine smiles in my head and congratulates me.

And Julie walks away and has her child. I see her once, driving past in my car, and she was smiling down at the baby in her buggy, and my stomach lurched and my legs wobbled but I kept on driving and I told myself I had done the right thing.

Despite her tears, and her pleading, I let her go. I would not bring a child into a world where depravity was commonplace.

I let go of Elaine's hand, I have held it mere seconds and seen so much. As I turn and see Kate enter the room, I grab her hand again.

****

"I love you."

"I don't love you."

"Yes, you do," she smiled.

"I love Jen." Her face is unreadable.

"She's not your type."

"You don't know my type," she answers, coldly.

"I am your type," she sleazes and moves towards my Kate.

Kate moves away. "You need to sober up and get some sleep."

"I need *you.*"

"No, you don't."

"I do. I've always needed you. You just never saw it."

"I saw that you could have had me and you fucked it up a long time ago. I'm happy now, and you're not fucking it up again. You can sleep here, but you're gone in the morning. I don't want you upsetting Jen."

"Jen?" she mocked. "She's a fucking drip. What the fuck are you doing with her? And engaged? Jesus, I near pissed myself when I heard that…"

Her words were cut off by Kate's hand grabbing her by the throat and holding her against the wall.

"You can't hurt me any more, and you won't hurt Jen. So, shut your fucking mouth."

She let go and Elaine rubbed her throat.

"So, she knows about…"

****

Kate threw my arm off and broke the chain.

"What are you hiding?" I snarled, because my anger and hurt had fused into some unfathomable rage.

"I'm hiding nothing. Come out the room and let her sleep it off."

"You can go fuck yourself!" I shouted and left the flat.

****

I went to Damian's. Which was lucky, really, because her irritated boyfriend was trying to kick in her door and did not take kindly to me trying to reason with him.

I phoned the police, wishing I could have a name to quote, but I knew Kate was in the flat and not on duty and I was trying to avoid them hearing Damian shout, "Fuck off, you cocksucker", at the top of her lungs.

The big, muscly, hairy thug turned to me and said, "Huv ye jist phoned the police, ya fucking lezza?"

I looked him in the eye and said, "Yes, frankly I have. There is no need for all these dramatics."

He grabbed me with his hand curling around my hair, and punched me in the face and I passed out.

And that told me.

****

I am walking in the dust and I can't see and I can't breathe, and all around me is smoke and it is covering everything. I cough and stand on something and I look down and see that it is a leg.

Just a leg. No body.

I go to walk on and think, hey I recognise that leg because it has a tattoo on it, and Damian has a tattoo on her leg and it looks just like it, and I begin to panic. I am bending over, to lift the leg and check the ink on it, knowing all the time it is going to be the same tattoo and hoping, at the same time, that it's not.

But it is.

And this is my fault.

I have led her here. It is the building where we learn our sign language every week and I knew, I *knew* the man was going to do this, and I have done nothing to stop it.

Like I did nothing to stop the murder of the young Dunstable boy.

I could have prevented that, and I could have prevented this, and in my dream I am holding her leg, and I begin to cry.

Was this what she meant when she asked me if I dreamt of her?

Through the rubble and the dirt and the smoke, I see one man.

One man who has saved me before and can save me again.

He points to his watch and says, "It's ticking, Jenny. Get a move on."

I have no time to spare any more.

****

When I came to, I was on Damian's sofa with her looming worriedly over me, and a nice policewoman asking if I wanted to go to hospital. I declined, but knew I was going to have a shiner in the morning. Her savage of a boyfriend had been arrested and was going to be charged with assault, if I wanted this to go ahead. Damian had said, "Charge the bastard", so I agreed to go down the local police station later that afternoon and make a formal statement.

After the police had left and we were sitting with a cuppa, she told me everything that had been going on with him. His name was Michael. And he was a first class tosser. Tried to control her, tell her what to wear and eat and see, but Damian being Damian, she had done what she wanted to do and suffered his wrath until finally he had lashed out at her, and then me.

And then there was the whole Sasha thing, which he had discovered from a card Sasha had sent Damian. It had pushed him over the edge, knowing a woman was satisfying his girlfriend.

"Good riddance to bad rubbish," she toasted. "I only put up with him because he let me drive his car."

I knew it was more than that, but I did not press the issue. It was her way of justifying that she had accepted an abusive relationship.

"Damian, there's something I need to tell you…" I began, and launched into my dreams about the man at the sign language club and how I thought he was making a bomb and it was going to go off and we had to stop him. I left out the bit about me finding her severed leg.

"So," she said, after some consideration. "Are we gonna be like Cagney and Lacey?"

I couldn't help but laugh. "I suppose we are, in a way."

“What are you going to do about Kate?” she asked and I felt the black cloud of doom hover above me.

“I’m going to let her come running to me for a change.”

But my notepad was in the flat, and I would need to face her at some point.

Just not right now.

****

Later that evening at our class, I pointed out the young man I thought was going to blow up the hall we sat in. Damian said she thought he was, “kind of cute”, and I shook my head in despair.

“When does the deed occur?”

“I’m not sure,” I whispered, as we tried to get to grips with the signs for colours and animals and places. “I think I saw something about a calendar in my dream, but I would need to check back my notebook.”

“Which would mean facing darling Kate,” she pointed out.

Kate had texted me earlier, asking when I would be back and to let me know that Elaine had left. It did not make me any less angry, but I knew I would calm down eventually, and she would logically say, “I did nothing wrong, I put her to the bed nearest a toilet in case she was sick, and I slept on the couch. It was *you* who stormed away, and I texted you as soon as my shift was over to tell you she was gone and you could come back.”

Logic was all very good and well, but I am not Spock and I live on my emotions. I knew I would go back though, and I knew as she put her arms around me and called me silly and gave me a kiss that I would grudgingly smile and let it go. Because I can never hold a grudge with her for very long. And she knew that too.

I walked Damian up to her door, just to make sure no one was loitering about, and then left because she insisted I go and sort it out with Kate. She was just fed up looking at my miserable face. I didn’t blame her – my face *was* miserable and I had been unable to concentrate in the class.

We had watched the man but learned nothing.

Kate must have been sitting in the kitchen, but came to meet me when she heard my keys open the door.

"Where have you been all day, and what the fuck's happened to your eye?"

I had forgotten about that. "Can I get a cuddle first?"

"Of course," she frowned, still unhappy at my black eye.

But then she put her arms around me and everything was washed away. I was in her arms, and nothing and no one could hurt me. I was in my bubble of Kate Coutts, the woman that I loved.

"Sit down," she said, leading me by the hand into the kitchen. "Tell me what happened, and I'll make you a cuppa."

"She's really gone?"

"Yes."

I told her what had happened when I had gone to Damian's. She swore a lot, and then phoned the station to find out what was going on. She didn't tell me but seemed satisfied by what she was told.

"Jen, I need you to do something for me."

"What, my love?" I asked.

"Please trust me."

I heard her mother's words echo in my head. "All you need to do with Kate is never question her."

I would heed those words.

For now.

****

In the middle of the night, my phone rang, waking me from a dreamless sleep.

It showed as a number so it was not someone I knew, and I lifted the phone and scuttled into the kitchen with it, trying not to wake Kate.

I answered, "Hello?"

There was no sound.

No words audible to a human ear.

But words audible to a psychic.

I could hear the thoughts of the person on the other end of the phone and that could only mean it was Elaine.

"Elaine, what do you want?" I sighed.

'How can she know it's me?'

"I know it's you, Elaine."

'She's a fucking freak.'

"Elaine, leave us alone."

'I'll never leave Kate alone. I'll always be in her life. I'm her first love.'

This was very strange having a one-sided conversation with someone's mind, and I was getting cold, wanting to get back to the warmth of Kate's back.

"I'm hanging up and switching the phone off."

She finally spoke but I had heard the words in her head before she said them.

"Ask her about Elizabeth."

Chapter Twenty

I am a fly on a wall and I am watching the girl – no, not a girl, I am watching the *man* put on his make-up and check himself in the mirror. He looks like an ordinary lad in his jeans and black T-shirt until he goes to his wardrobe and fetches out a pair of PVC trousers and a see-through vest top. After he has changed, he runs a hand through the unruly mop of curly brown hair, puckers his lips and fishes around the room until he finds his white shoulder bag.

He grabs his keys and mobile phone, throwing them in the bag, and leaves the flat, tottering down the stairs in some high heels and hailing a taxi when he gets outside. He does not speak to the taxi driver, only to give his destination, and he remains quiet and surly throughout the drive. He takes his mobile and punches in a text message and then switches it off, throwing it back in his bag.

He drums his fingers on the window, impatiently waiting for his destination to be arrived at. He pays the driver when the taxi stops, and fixes the smile on his face. He walks into the busy, upmarket Glasgow bar and searches the room with his eyes until he meets the eyes of the man he is meeting and smiles.

It is a fake smile.

And instead of tottering, he begins to mince over to the man who is smiling and holding court with his friends. He budges over on the sofa he occupies, and Logan slips in beside him.

Logan lets his hand fall on the leg of Simon Dunstable, who discreetly gives him a wink and continues to chat with his cronies. A bottle of champagne is brought over.

I am the fly on the wall again and I see Logan totter up to his flat and slam the door shut, kicking off his heels and going to the bathroom to wash his face.

When he has done this, he goes into the living room, unearthing a laptop from below a pile of dirty clothes, sits down with it and begins to type. I cannot see the words he types.

When he is finished, he lights a cigarette and turns the TV on, sighing to himself.

And in my dream, I switch from being a fly in this room to being a fly in another room.

But in that room, Logan is tied up and caught in the hunter's net.

****

I was already up and awake the next morning when Kate dragged herself into the kitchen and thanked me for the coffee that was waiting for her. My mind was running wild. Who was Elizabeth, and why did Elaine want me to know? I tried to tell myself that she did not need this before going to work, but if I did not ask, I would drive myself mad and get myself into a state. I reasoned with myself to be calm. Elaine was a stirrer, that much I knew – she wanted my Kate, and I was the obstacle.

I am not completely stupid and can see jealous and vindictive behaviour when it presents itself.

"Did I hear your phone last night?" Kate mumbled through half open eyes, sipping her coffee.

"Yes. It was Elaine." I saw her face sink and did not know if I should be happy or worried.

"What did she want?"

"To annoy me, mostly. But she said one interesting thing before I hung up."

Kate looked across her coffee cup and met my eyes. "What did she say?"

"She told me to ask you about Elizabeth."

I watched the pain cloud her face, as she set her cup down on the table. I felt the knot of dread begin to unravel in my guts and wondered if I should pursue this, but before I could say a word, she spoke.

"I should have told you about Elizabeth before. I'm sorry. It can't be nice for you, having someone ring you in the middle of the night and fire off a name you know nothing about. I *am* sorry, darling. Let me explain."

She put her head in her hands, elbows on the table and took a deep breath. I ached to throw my arms around her and tell her whatever it was would be okay. I just could not watch her suffer.

"Elizabeth is my sister. Not the sister my dad killed – my other sister. She lives in Edinburgh in a special home, because she's brain damaged."

"Oh my God, Kate, I am so sorry!" I wailed.

She smiled in an I-have-not-quite-finished way. "It was my fault, Jen. I was seven, Lizzie was three and Amy was just a baby. My mother and that specimen of a father had gone out and left me to look after them, and I couldn't. I had to give Amy her bottle and Lizzie had got up the stairs and she fell back down them. I couldn't get to her in time to bring her down, and she didn't listen to me. Fuck, she was only three!"

"Kate, it's okay," I said, instinctively reaching out to her.

"No, you need to know and I should have told you before you heard it off someone else."

I saw her steel herself and continue. "You have to remember, this is before we all had mobile phones. I didn't know what to do. I had a baby in my arms and a convulsing three year old who had just gone head first down a flight of stairs. I ran to the neighbour with Amy in my arms and she got an ambulance. Somehow, my mum and dad got back by the time it arrived, and I was told not to say they weren't there. They would have got into trouble, you see. Turns out that wasn't really going to be a problem in the next few months, but Lizzie got taken to hospital and we all dutifully sat by her bedside, until it was determined she wasn't going to die but she was never going to be the same."

"Oh, Kate," I squeezed her hand.

"We were trying to recover from that when the prick killed Amy."

A single tear escaped her eyes.

I could bear it no more, and jumped up and threw my arms around her, as she wiped the solitary tear.

"I'm sorry," I whispered.

"It's fine," she sniffed, bravely, and removed herself from my clutches. "I need a shower before work. Don't dwell on it," she said, as she left me in the kitchen.

Dwelling on it.

****

After my class that day, I drove to Edinburgh to check in on Sheena. If I am honest, I wanted to ask her about Elizabeth and Elaine. She seemed in good fettle when I knocked her door, and she made us a cup of tea and we sat down to chat.

After the pleasantries were out the way, I got stuck in. It has made me realise that I am not good at coping with what I don't know. You would think a lifetime of premonitions would arm me in some way, but when my emotions were at stake and it affected me, I had to blurt. I thought sadly of all the murders and accidents I had seen and been able to do nothing about, and I shoved it to the back of my mind. What's done is done.

"Sheena, can I ask you about something? It's personal and I know you might not want to talk to me about it…"

She butted in. "Look, hen, you're the only bugger that's shown any interest in me. You ask what you like, I won't be offended."

"It's about Elizabeth. Kate's sister."

"I know who she is, hen," she said, but not unkindly. "What do you want to know?"

"What happened, I suppose."

She sighed, and in that instant I saw Kate in her. Or her in Kate. "Jen, darling, I'm an alcoholic. I have been for years. Some months I am good, and some months I am bad. When I was younger and married to Kate's dad, he was as bad as me, and we didn't understand how to look after kids. Drink was the important thing. I left Kate with my babies and I shouldn't have. She was good, you know. She could have got me into a lot of trouble by saying I wasn't there, but she never opened her mouth."

She started to cry. "I have a lot to hate myself for. Wee Lizzie a veg, dribbling oot the side of her mooth. Amy…" she struggled. "Amy deid 'cause of that bastard," she spat. "It was just me and Kate, and I let her down." Her eyes wander off and I sit in silence, wishing I had kept my mouth shut.

"I didn't mean to upset you, Sheena," I apologised. "Maybe I should have asked you about Elaine instead."

"Elaine?" her eyes narrowed.

"Yes, the girl who used to be with Kate. She came to our engagement party, I don't know if you saw her."

"No I didn't, and she wouldn't come near me anyway. You watch out for her – she's a snake in the grass."

"I can hear her."

Puzzled, she repeated me. "You can hear her?"

"Yes, I can hear her thoughts."

She nodded. "Then if I was you, I would stop listening."

****

As I was driving back, I stuck my phone on loudspeaker and rang Damian. "Afternoon, sweetheart."

"Hey Jen, when we meeting?" It was like she knew what I was going to say before I said it.

"Tomorrow night. At the Deaf Club. I'll meet you across the road as usual about half six."

"You checked your pad yet for the date?" I knew she meant my dream notepad for the calendar date I thought I might have written down, when I had dreamt of the man putting the bomb below the stage of the deaf club.

Bloody Nora! "No! I will when I get in, I promise."

"See you then, bird."

I heard the giggle of the woman in the background that I took to be Sasha, and I smiled because my friend was happy.

****

I can feel the soft essence of the piano permeate my mind into my dream, and the keys striking remind me of a sadness and unhappiness I cannot put my finger on. A chord of heartbreak runs over my skin, sending shivers down my body, and I tremble in my sleep.

There is a flurry of women all singing a line, here and there, and my eyes are momentarily amused by the striking attractiveness of a few of them. And then I listen to the words, banging in my head, over and over, in the dream.

And then I see the youth. A boy I place about thirteen or fourteen, sitting on his bed with a big glass of vodka, judging by the empty bottle beside him, and a couple of packets of paracetamol.

Words echo in my head. And as the words are being sung in my head, the boy is necking the tablets, washing them down with the vodka and trying to swallow against the gag reflex that is kicking in.

His eyes don't open again and I feel my panic when I realise I cannot get to him and make him wake up. Why has he done this?

****

That day, I held onto Kate when I woke up and she held on back and when I said, "Just five more minutes" she relented, closing her eyes against me. I held her in my arms and looked at her beautiful face, eyes closed and I thought of all the sadness and unhappiness they held behind them, and I hugged her a little bit tighter. I closed my eyes and slipped into a sleep.

Rob was waking me up. "Jen, it's time – come on."

"Time for what?" I mumbled.

"Time for the next one," he answered.

"My baby, where is my baby?" Even though in my mind, I told myself Jonah was happy and in the right place with his daddy, I could not help that one moment of longing escape my lips, betraying my heart.

"I'm here, Mummy," I heard and I smiled, tears falling freely down my face, and fell back into my sleep.

****

It was time to go and meet Damian, and I left my flat and began a walk to the bus stop to take me into town, then I could walk to the Deaf Club. As I walked, I heard the matching footsteps echo my own and looked around to see no one in particular.

I kept walking and remembered I had to check my notepad, congratulating myself that I had put it in my handbag. I pulled it out and began to read as I walked, flicking back through my scribbles until I could find the one about the calendar in the Deaf Club.

But the footsteps grew closer, and although I could not see who could be following me, I did something I had never done before and I listened with my mind.

'Look at the state of it.'

So when I heard the thoughts in my head, I immediately knew it was Elaine.

I turned around and stopped walking, holding my notepad in my hand still.

"I know you are following me, Elaine – just step out."

And surely she stepped out from a tenement opening and smiled at me. A smile dripping utter hatred.

I can do utter hatred when my love is challenged, and I smiled back, a smile as insidious.

"What do you want?" I asked. I was going to be late for Damian.

"Fancy a drink?" she leered.

I sighed. "No, Elaine, I do not fancy a drink with you. I want you to leave me and Kate alone. We are not interested in your drama."

She laughed. "Kate and I have a bond, and someone like you could never break that."

I rolled my eyes. "Jesus, let it go – she doesn't want you. Be a sport, eh?" I turned to walk away from her.

She grabbed me and knocked my notepad from my hand. “Sport? Did you ask her about Elizabeth?”

“I know all about Elizabeth.” I was trying really hard not to show that I was shaking inside.

“What about last year?”

“What about last year?” I asked.

Then, she began to giggle. “Oh, you don’t know everything then.”

“I don’t know what you’re talking about,” I replied, as snootily as I could.

“When Kate met me, just after your boyfriend was shot.”

The words stung me like a million wasps all over my body.

When Rob was shot. When Rob died.

When Kate would not speak to me and I had my baby growing inside me.

She, my Kate, met *that*?

Despite telling me she had not seen her for four years?

That was two lies. She lied about the toilet in Logan’s flat, and now she had lied about seeing Elaine.

Her mother saying, “Don’t question her if you want to keep her.”

Kate saying, “Jen, you have to trust me.”

Damian saying, “She’s a cunt.”

Oh God, Damian – I was supposed to be meeting her!

My eyes flashed to my notepad on the ground and I saw the page open, staring up at me with a date circled in big letters.

2nd April 2011.

That was today.

Damian!

Oh God, she was going to the Deaf Club, and the bomb was going to go off and she didn’t know. I scrambled for my phone and tried to ring her, Elaine laughing at me all the time as my tears began to fall. I must save Damian and those people.

Her number was engaged. I tried again and still I could not get through, and my tears began to turn to the hysteria that I knew so well, when I could not save another human being.

"Answer your fucking phone!" I screamed.

I dialled 999. "Police." I waited. "A bomb is going to go off at the Deaf Club in Norfolk Street, and you have twenty minutes to get everyone out of there! Never mind my name, just evacuate the place! Norfolk Street Deaf Club. Hurry!"

I sobbed hysterically into my hands and sat down on the pavement.

Elaine had left me and I had not noticed.

My Damian.

****

The leg. It is her leg, it is her tattoo. It is my Damian's leg.

I could have stopped this. I could have stopped this!

Chapter Twenty-One

I am running. I always seem to be running, whether it is through fog in Ibrox or chasing a taxi to find my kidnapped lover. This time I am running for Damian, and I have found a taxi to take me to Norfolk Street where the Deaf Club is. Where the bomb is that is going to go off any minute and kill my best friend. I know her – she would have gone inside when I was late and ordered us two drinks.

If I had got into my car, I would have been there by now and avoided Elaine. We could have got people out safely and saved innocent lives. But we get the bus so that we can have a drink and feel less self-conscious with our amateurish signing in front of the people who use this to communicate, the way we use our voice and ears.

The panic is rising in me as we approach, and I see the blue sirens of the police cars before I hear them. The road is closed off and I have to get out the taxi and run towards the building.

And, only as I am running and gasping for breath, do I realise that the building is still standing. Which means the bomb has not gone off.

I run into a policewoman who stops me getting any closer.

"But my friend is in there!" I cry frantically.

"I'm sorry, Madam, you can't go any further."

"There's a bomb in there! You have to get people out!" I cannot suppress my hysteria.

My outcry has attracted the attention of another officer and he comes over to me. "How do you know that?"

"Oh Jesus, I just *do*!" I did not have time to go into the manner of my dreams when lives were at stake.

"Please come with me," he ushered me through their barrier and opened the door of a police car, beckoning for me to sit down. I did, but I kept my legs out the car. I wasn't sure if I could stand any longer.

"The club has been evacuated, and we currently have members of the Bomb Squad in the building. So there is no need to panic. Your friend will be okay. But I need to know how you were aware of a bomb in this building, when you have clearly just come out that taxi that drove off."

"I'm saying nothing until I speak to DI Kate Coutts and her DCI."

"Jen!"

I turn hearing my name and see Damian pushing her way through to me, pointing and being allowed to come over. I jump up and hug her, bursting into tears.

"Oh Damian, I thought you were dead!"

"Do I look dead?" she hugged back.

The officer was watching us.

"Can we have a minute, please?" I asked, politely.

He moved back but continued to keep his eyes on us.

"What happened?" I whispered. "I saw my notepad and it was tonight it was to happen, and I missed the bus and you didn't answer your phone."

"Calm down, Jen – it's alright, I'm here."

I nodded, trying desperately to be calmer. She put her arm around my shoulder. "I waited for you, and you didn't turn up and I know how anal you are about being on time, so I figured something had held you back and I would go in and get us a drink. It was weird actually, like when I spoke to you the very first time I met you. I had no idea what I was saying, but after it all made sense.

"I was about to step forward to cross the road when everything around me changed. I was surrounded by smoke and bricks and rubble and bits of bodies. It fucking knocked the shit out of me. But when I stood back, it went as quickly as it had come. And I figured that was how you must feel when you have your dreams."

"Is that why you didn't go in?" I asked.

"Partly," she continued. "I knew then something was wrong. Like, really seriously wrong. So, I got my phone and I rang the police and told them there was a bomb under the stage."

"*That's* why I couldn't get through to you!"

My brain went into overdrive. The police would trace the calls. One would be to my mobile and one would be to Damian's pay-as-you-go. Which, inevitably, led the trail back to me as her phone was unregistered. I would need to get to Kate. She believed me and would somehow sort this out for me. Otherwise, I could be looking at charges for bomb planting, or whatever it was called.

As I was figuring this out, the policeman came back over.

"We are going to need you to ask you a few more questions, Miss."

My phone began to ring. It was Kate. "Jen? I need you to come to my station."

"I don't think I have much choice in that," I replied.

****

Damian and I are in an interview room, waiting for my Kate to come in. It has been over an hour.

Finally, she walks in with her DCI and I say, "Kate! Did you get the bomb? Is it okay? No one died, did they?"

Damian remains quiet and I know, without looking at her, that she is glaring at Kate in the way that she does when she has no time for someone.

The DCI and Kate sit down and he asks, "Was it you that rang in the alert, Jennifer?"

"Yes," I say, nudging Damian with my foot under the table.

"We had two calls."

"I made a call, it will be on my phone. I can show you. I don't know who made the other call" I lie.

His eyes narrow, as he regards Damian. "Was it you?"

"Nope."

"I can check your phone," he says.

"I don't have a phone," she answers, just as cool as a cucumber. "Which you know, because you made us hand in our possessions when we got here," she smiles.

It's Kate's turn now and I have this feeling of the good-cop, bad-cop scenario. Unsure who is who.

"Jen, did you dream of this?"

"Yes."

"Why didn't you tell me?" Her voice is soft and caring. Good-cop.

"You have enough on your plate."

I saw the gritting of her teeth, emphasised through her cheekbones. Her lovely cheekbones. I was reminded of the first time I met her, when I had walked into this very same police station and given her the details of a girl I thought had been murdered. How I had felt giddy inside at how pretty she was, and admired the cut of her suit. I didn't think I would ever stop admiring her beauty, even if she annoyed me.

"I thought we understood each other, Miss Keith," spoke the DCI.

"Understood what exactly? That I gave you the name of a man who killed a little boy, and that he is still wandering the streets?"

His face reddened. Not with shame but with anger, and I knew I had hit a nerve. Kate stared at the desk in front of her and I could feel Damian watching me.

"I helped you get our Bible John, but the understanding seemed to end there. Whatever was going to happen tonight, I stopped it, not *you*. So don't sit there and give me platitudes. I want to know what's happening to that wee boy's killer."

"Go girl!" Damian muttered under her breath and I quickly turned to smile at her, returning a steely gaze to the DCI.

"I don't even know your name," I hissed.

"It's John Bailey."

Silence and the stand-off resumed. Then he spoke.

"I have to let you go and justify that. Now, I know you are not involved – so tell me, Jennifer, how do I prove that?"

"Find the caretaker of the club. His bedroom will give you all you need. We overheard him or something from going there to learn sign language. *You* make it up," I spat back.

"Very well. You can both go." I stood up to leave before he added, "But Jennifer, I will be coming to see you again."

****

When Damian and I got outside, she told me she had lobbed her phone after calling the police, so that it could not be traced to her.

"Not as daft as I look," she laughed.

After seeing her off, I got a taxi home, fed the fat cat, made a cup of tea, switched the telly on and fell asleep on the couch before my cup had even got cold.

It was one of those dreams where nothing makes sense and I jump from scene to scene, not knowing what is real and what is imagined when I wake up.

I hear a song, echoing in the background, all the time. Women's faces are flying around my head like the Queen video for 'Bohemian Rhapsody'.

I am walking down a corridor of white. White floors, white ceilings, white doors and I am dressed in black, in stark contrast. I move towards a door, my hand reaching for the white handle and I am about to grab it when I change my mind and curl my fingers back and move to the next door. I hold the knob and twist and am suddenly sucked into a storm and the white has disappeared. I am crouching in the heart of a forest, surrounded by dark and trees, and I look down and see the splashes of mud on my white trousers. Now I am in white, and around me is dark.

I jump at the crack of the thunder and look behind me. I see a building in rubble, in smoke, rebuild itself brick by brick, like watching a demolition video backwards. The last thing I see is the tattooed leg flying back into the mist.

That was Damian's leg and somewhere, deep in my subconscious I know I have saved her life, but put her life in danger in the first place. She is my friend, and she trusted me. She went along with me and I led her into trouble that could have killed her. But for her wits.

There is a crack of lightning above my head and the ground changes under me, and I am running, always running, up a wet road. The wind is pushing me back and I struggle forward. I can hear screams behind me but I keep going. I don't know why I keep going or what I am trying to reach.

Until there is another crack of thunder and I am sat in a car, with sore ribs and a bang on the head, and the cold is making me sleepy and I just want to close my eyes, and as I close my eyes, the water comes up across my chest and swallows my neck and face.

The song changes and I hear, 'Release'

This nightmare continues in circles all night.

****

"Jen! Wake up! You're sweating buckets, babe. Come to bed."

It is my Kate, and I do not know what time it is, but I am so sleepy and drained from the sleep that I have had that I allow her to put me to bed and cuddle into me.

As I drift off, I can't help trying to remember the reason I should be so angry with her, but I can't and I let the dreams overtake me again.

****

The next afternoon, when I had got home after my work was finished, I switched the computer on, went onto YouTube and searched the song 'It Does Get Better'.

What was the L Project?

I hit play and sat back and listened to the song that had been singing in my head. I knew the words before I heard them. What I did not expect was the outpouring of emotion in me when I watched the video right to end, and saw pictures of children that had taken their own lives for being bullied about their sexuality.

I cried openly, thinking how lucky I was to have had accepting parents whose only wish had been that I was happy. I never got abused or bullied and I sat and thought. I do not look like what people expect a lesbian to look like. I wear skirts, and the odd bit of make up. I have shoulder length hair,

I teach and am intelligent. I live with my girlfriend and no one is offended by us.

I cannot imagine what it is like to be taunted for loving who you love, or being the person you want to be.

And, as soon as I think this, I pass out and my head lands with a bang on the computer desk.

Everything is working in rewind in my mind. The little boy with four toes on his right foot is walking backwards with his mum into their home, and sitting down on the sofa. A girl walks in, and I know the girl – the girl was in my class – and she speaks and reverses back out.

And then the bang that echoes my head on the table. The mother walking up the stairs to a bedroom and the young teen lying on the bed, arguing back with her and she wags her finger and leaves the room.

I stay in the room and I look around with the eyes of the dreamer. Teenage boy. His walls are full of posters of boy bands.

A boy loving a boy?

****

"Jen, wake up!" It is Kate again, shaking me awake and she frowns. "You have a bruise on your forehead."

"I think I passed out and hit the desk"

"Why?" she asks but something inside of me is remembering my dream and I get up and go past her to find my bag, where my pad is. I had Gail Dunstable's address in there, I was sure of it and when I found it, I grabbed my coat and car keys.

"Where are you going?" Kate asked.

"I have to go see one of my students," I explained. But I knew I wasn't explaining and I could not put my finger on why. I would think about it later.

"Are you hiding things from me again?"

I doubled back and said "Am I hiding things from you? No, Kate, I am *not* hiding things from you. I have to see this girl because I think her brother is going to kill himself because he is gay. There is no bomb. There is no snuff movie. There are no lies. I am just doing what I have to do because I can't live with it. Is that okay?"

She looked down at the floor.

I left her looking and slammed the door on my way out.

****

I was in Gail's kitchen, having given my condolences to her family. Gail was talking non-stop about coming back to University and restarting her course, and would I help her.

I would help her, but I wasn't here for this.

"Have you got a teenage brother?"

"Um, yes, Nathan. Why?"

"Is he gay?"

In an instant, the defences went up.

"No. Why are you saying that?"

"Because I think he *is*, and I think he is going to take a load of paracetamol tablets unless someone tells him it's okay to be different."

"I think I'd know if ma wee brother was gay!"

My patience was at the end of its tether. I thought I had lost my best friend in a bomb blast. I had been hauled into a police station. I had not even begun to think about what Elaine said about my partner, Kate, and her meeting a year ago. I had the chance to save a life in this family who are devastated by the loss of their youngest.

The boy that I saw being killed and the killer I have informed the police of. They had their chance, as far as I am concerned.

I have had dreams for years and years, and when I started to help my friend Rob, things started to change slowly. It led me to Kate, and I have won some and I have lost some, but I am determined I am not going to lose this one. One child's death in a family is enough.

"Gail, you have to listen to me. I am telling you the truth. I get messages and I am trying to stop this happening!" I pleaded.

"Messages?" she looks at me horrified.

“Look,” I say, exhausted by it all. “I don’t care if you believe me or not, but I’m telling you the truth. Here,” I handed her a bit of paper, “Play this song to Nathan – you can find it on YouTube. Watch it together. Please, just do this one thing for me.”

She takes the paper from me, regarding it suspiciously. “Okay.”

I let out a large sigh of relief. “Thank you. Thank you, really.”

I get into my car to drive back to the flat and feel the tiredness washing over me. I can only hope and pray, yet again, that I have done enough. I have a good feeling though, and it makes me smile. Until I remember Elaine, and then the sickness washes over me. She saw my Kate a year ago? A year ago we had separated for a few months, and I had carried Rob’s baby, the one thing that had kept me going through my heartbreak.

Would she betray me with an old lover? Her mother’s voice spoke in my mind again.

“Don’t question her if you want to keep her.”

Oh, but I would question her.

****

As I opened the door, I heard voices coming from the kitchen and wondered who could be visiting us this late at night.

I was surprised to find DCI John Bailey sitting at my table, having a cup of coffee with Kate.

He smiled, as I walked in, and said, “Hello Jennifer. I told you I would be coming to see you again.”

Chapter Twenty-Two

I am kicking in my sleep. No. Not kicking. I am *dancing* and moving my legs and arms, having a wee shimmy to the music. I am on a dance floor full of bodies, moving around me, all swaying to the same beat, but the song I am hearing is not the one everyone else is hearing. It does not stop us as we bounce and swing with rhythm.

I am overtaken by music coursing through my veins and cannot find the proper way to express my love for this song in movement. But I try all the same. And when I find a lyric that I know, I begin to sing.

'Come Live the Life' by K's Choice.

I am here, I think, and am transported to a dark and wet road. I am here but I do not know what I am here for.

I think, 'I am here for her'.

I begin to dance again, kicking my legs in my sleep, and smile to myself because it is a nice dream.

Or, at least, I thought it was.

****

"Hello, Mr Bailey," I say, entering my kitchen because, in my home, he is just a man and has no power over me, despite his police badge. I do not wait for an answer and automatically go to switch the kettle on.

I notice Kate cannot meet my eyes.

"So," I say. "What is it you want?"

I know he is not here for pleasantries and wants something from me. I may as well know now, it is late and I am tired.

"What do I want?" he echoes. "I want your help to find a murderer, that's what I want."

I begin to pour the hot water into my cup and grit my teeth. I don't like this man, Kate's boss or not. I wait until I have squeezed the teabag and poured in some milk before I ask, "And what makes you think I can help you?"

"You helped Kate before."

"Yes. I helped *Kate*," I emphasise.

"You don't want to stop someone dying?" he asked, and it was the tug to my conscience that I could not say "No" to. Of course I would want to stop someone dying, and they both knew that. Which was why he sat smugly in *my* kitchen, with *my* lover, knowing full well I would never refuse.

I was already stressed and it did not take much to push me over the edge.

"Spit it out. I'm tired. You *both* know I will always help in any way I can."

He brought his briefcase up from below the table, and opened it. Taking out a file, he began.

"Two young women have been killed, both in similar circumstances, both with similar markings. Nothing has been released to the public, no one knows except us and the families. We have DNA, but that's useless unless we can match it to the killer and we can't. This is someone under the radar. We have run every lead and come up with nothing. So, I turn to you."

Like it was some honour.

"And what do you expect me to do?"

"What you have done before. Looked at a photo. Held something of the victim's."

Victim's. It made me remember that somewhere out there was a grieving family, and me being tired did not compare to the loss of a loved one. I gave in.

"What have you got?"

He smiled, knowing he would always win, and I remembered Rob. He had never been like this. He had treated me like I was fragile.

My heart ached.

"I'll come back tomorrow with the details – you look done in."

I tried to smile. "Thank you. I am."

He said his goodbyes and Kate let him out. As she walked back into the kitchen, I thought, two lies, and knew I was in for a long night.

****

She had gone straight into the bathroom to get ready for bed, but I had other things on my mind and had made her a coffee and myself another cup of tea. I waited, sitting at the table, for her to come in and find me.

After a shower she came in, her hair wet, and for a single moment I held my breath.

A droplet of water ran from her forehead down the bridge of her nose and I watched it in slow motion. A slow trickle of lust dripping down her. I felt the string attached to me down below give a tug and my stomach lurched. I wanted to stand up and grab her and kiss her hard.

Instead, I said, "I missed the bomb because when I went to go for the bus to meet Damian, Elaine was waiting for me."

Her face wrinkled. "What did she want?"

"She took great pleasure telling me she had met you a year ago. You told me you hadn't seen her for four years, so there's a bit of a discrepancy there somewhere, and I am guessing she isn't lying. Care to share?"

I saw her nostrils flare and, inside my guts a volcano erupted but I stuck to my guns. I *had* to know, to be able to trust her, to be able to love her.

"Fuck's sake, Jen, I have to get up in the morning. Can we do this tomorrow?"

"No! We can't!" I started to shout, and I knew, I just *knew*, I was beginning to get that hysterical way that she hated. "You either *did* or you *didn't* see her a year ago. A year ago, when we were not together, I might add, and so were free to do whatever the fuck you wanted. Like fuck your ex!"

"I didn't fuck her," she said, quietly.

"What then?" I screamed. "Just met for a quick drink, while I was out the way. That's convenient." I was full of venom and no logic would win me over.

"I'm not doing this tonight," she replied and turned to leave.

I jumped up from my seat at the table, and ran around, to grab her arm and pull her back. I wanted this fight finished.

As I grabbed her arm, she tossed her head around and our eyes met.

I say our eyes met but our eyes locked. I could not look away and the tingling began in my fingers until her eyes melted into mine.

****

'Come Live the Life'

'So come on, come on, come on
All is forgiven.
So come on, come on
Come live the life you're given.'

I would dance all night to this song but the vision is not so simple, and I am watching a young girl standing over the sink, moving her mother's hair as she vomits down the plughole. The young girl has a determined grace about her. She dabs her mother's forehead with a flannel and helps her to lie down on the bed. Then she sits in a battered chair, pulling her legs up to her chin and the silent tears fall.

They fall until the door opens with the daylight, and people come in and take her away in a car and drive her to another home, where she is given her own room and a television to watch of her own, and a clean towel to dry herself with after a bath.

But I can feel in her heart that she wants her mother and is soon back with her, and for a while, she has a clean towel there in her mother's house, until the blonde woman staggers in the door and falls over. The girl tries to get her up and this time, there are no tears.

This time, she is telephoning the people to come and get her and take her away.

Before she goes, she walks to a gate in a brick wall, and crosses herself before she walks in. It is a cemetery. She goes to a grave and she kneels down, pulling weeds out with her fingers, getting mud under her nails, but she does not notice and continues until the grave is tidy. It is only as she stands up and wipes a hand across her face that I notice the silent tears again.

****

She throws her arm back to free it from my grasp, and knocks me across the face. I reel back from the blow and fall to the floor. Immediately, she comes to me and I hear the apologies flowing.

I am in no mood for apologies.

"Get away from me," I murmur.

She stands back, frozen, not knowing what to do and I realise I have never seen her like this before. Kate always knows what to do. "Leave me alone." I say.

She steps back towards the door, and I see the silent tear make its way down her cheek.

She wants to bury all her secrets deep, down inside.
She looks at me and goes to bed.

I think Sheena is right. I should not question Kate.

I do not question my love for her, and I do not question her love for me.

But there are other things I question, and her honesty is one of them.

I will never get the answers questioning her though, she stores and holds onto her hurt and if I keep pushing for her truths, I will only push her away.

I will question Elaine.

****

I get back up and notice that John has left his file on the table. I presume this is 'accidentally on purpose' in order that I will look at it. I sigh and go to the fridge and find a can of Coke to pour into the bottle of vodka that is in the cupboard. I bring the bottle and two cans to the table, get my cigarettes and lighter from my bag in the hall, shut the kitchen door and sit down to read, after pouring myself a large one.

I open the brown paper folder and am confronted by sickening photos. I pull a face in disgust, but cannot take my eyes off the captured images. One is just a head. I thought briefly that the girl might have been pretty, but it was no longer that easy to tell. The eyes were closed, the lips puffed, the nose bent, dried blood plastered here and there, the lank hair hanging still. If the eyes had been open what last image would they have carried in them?

I flick to the next. It is what I assume to be the rest of the body, severed at the neck. Not tidily, I notice, like it has been hacked at. It is naked but what is obvious are the amount of cuts. Blade cuts all over the body, I lose count. There are then several close ups of various limbs, just showing the incisions. I continue to leaf through the photos and come to the next head. Similar to the first, and the body, again, covered in slices.

I think I see something that has my interest and I flick back to an earlier photo, taken of the first body at a distance, showing the surroundings. It looks like a deserted bothy, but chalked on the wall is a symbol. I think it is called a Pentagram. I write this down on my notepad. I begin to nod my head, remembering something I have once read, and believe it is actually called an inverted pentagram. This is meant to represent the 'dark side', frowned upon by many Christians, who see this five-pointed diagram as denoting the five wounds of Jesus on the cross.

I fast-forward through the photographs, gulping down the rest of my drink. I want to see if the second girl has this connection. I pour another drink, staring at a picture of her leg. It is a slim leg, shaved, I see from the knee to the ankle. It is covered in criss-cross patterns from the cut of a knife. I take another large gulp and find the photo I am looking for. It has the same Pentagram.

I look at it long and hard and realise it is not exactly the same. The angle of the point that should be at the top, has moved around, and I guess it is 72 degrees. A five pointed star will move 72 degrees in five turns to return to the same position. I gulp again and hiccup, a bit impressed at my arithmetic. I scribble a note.

Then I read the reports. I skip over them as they bore me a bit, and I don't know half the words they use.

Two words stick in my head.

'Ritualistic killing.'

I am a bit drunk now, and throw some more vodka down my neck. What can it hurt, I think, to throw my fingers across the photos and see if I 'get' anything? I am more used to my talent now and realise I have to control it, instead of it controlling me. I find the picture of the girl's head and I let my fingers stroke her hair. I stroke in a rhythm, up and down, up and down, up and down…

My head bobs, up and down, up and down, finally thudding onto the table…

****

Thunder boots. Big fuck-off Johnny Thunderboots. He pores over the book, taking delicate care and softly turning each page, to write elaborate notes into his A4 pad in red ink. This goes on for some time until he has had enough, and logs onto his computer. Johnny Thunderboots is his name, and he begins to type and soon gets a little box in the bottom of his screen. He expands and begins to talk to 'DeadSouls', and for some time they type back and forth.

The next night this is the same, and the next and the next, until it is weeks later and they have to meet.

Meet is meat.

Johnny Thunderboots thunders down the road in his black boots, inch high platforms reaching below his knees with silver buckles. The buckles shine. His long black hair breezes in the wind, and his dark make up masks his face, his body covered in black clothes and the long, black jacket sways in the wind in tune with his hair. He is nervous, excited, aroused.

He meets 'DeadSouls' and they wander off, holding hands and chatting, smiling, giving little kisses. It is almost romantic until he leads her into the makeshift hut in the woods and gets her on the ground, throwing his weight upon her. She is overcome with his passion and sighs happily. He gets up and brings the chalk from his pocket and they talk, and then he marks the upside down Pentagram on the wall. They turn and smile at each other.

Then, he knows – he knows it is right and he has been led here for a reason, and what he thought was correct. She needs to die. And then the great ruler, Satan, will give him power. He pulls the knife from the corner he has hidden it and her eyes widen when she sees it, but she relaxes seeing his smile.

Johnny Thunderboots smiles, a smile so pleasant and trusting, and then he throws his arm forward, driving the knife into her stomach. Her last expression is of surprise. He stabs her again and again until she no longer moves. He kneels down beside her and puts his head on her chest. There is no heartbeat.

He begins to hack in a saw-like fashion, retching here and there as he removes the head. Then he stands back and looks at the body. Cut it, he thinks, and he cuts and cuts until there is no patch of skin left untouched.

He takes his hand and rubs it over the severed neck, smearing blood on his fingers, sucking them and rubbing the blood on his face. He screams in ecstasy.

"You are a tower of strength to meee!" he shouts.

He is on a mission.

****

When I pull my head off the table in the morning, it thuds and my tongue feels like a carpet, but I instantly see the handwritten note from Kate, amongst my drunken scribbles.

'I'll be home at 7. We can talk then.'

It was 'Tower of Strength' by the Mission.

'You rescue me, you are my faith, my hope, my liberty
And when there's darkness all around
You shine bright for me, you are a guiding light
To me.'

Was it Johnny Thunderboots or Kate I heard in my head?

Chapter Twenty-Three

Five. Five points to the star. Five deaths. Five is the glory. Five is the number to hail Him and will see me high in the echelons of Hell. Where I deserve and long to be.

I know what I have to do. I have to make the sacrifices to the Dark Lord Lucifer, expelled from Heaven, our Lord Satan, and He will reward me.

I have made two notches on the goal I am set. Three more await me and I shall be free from the shit that is this life that their God has given me.

Fuck your God!

I get my book and begin to recite the words:

'Alham je deridsa
Alham je roka
Alham je roka
Ee sa mesa roka inhelmaja'

The wall of smoke around my candle begins to whirl, and I know the spirit is coming. I repeat the incantation, louder and louder. I throw some incense on the flame. It burns and I take a deep breath.

The moment of truth is approaching.

****

I lift my thudding head off the table and stretch my tired arms, retching at the sight of the vodka bottle and see a photograph of a dead girl's head. I feel the bile rise in my throat and make a dash for the toilet bowl, where I land on my knees and begin to vomit.

I hear the loo door opening and feel Kate lean over me, putting her arm around my back.

"You shouldn't drink on an empty stomach," she whispers, rubbing me.

I want to say that it is not the booze that is making me vomit but the picture of a head, and I realise that I looked at it last night and did not puke, so maybe she is a bit right. That doesn't change the fact that she has lied to me about Elaine, and as I think about this, I retch some more.

"You met that Elaine…" Vomit. "You lied to me." Vomit.

"Jen, I *arrested* her."

I take some deep breaths, spit down the bowl, and turn my head to her, thinking of my sick breath and trying not to aim at her.

"Why didn't you tell me?"

"It's confidential. I can't tell you who I have arrested. You need to trust me, darling." She leant over and kissed my forehead.

"How did she know about Rob then?" I ask, no longer caring about my breath.

"What?" she looked perplexed.

"She said, when I met her, that she had seen you when my 'boyfriend had been shot'."

"I don't know. I honestly don't know."

I looked into her eyes, so hard and blue and beautiful, and I felt the rise of another heave.

I turned back to the bowl.

I don't know what I hated more – my indecision or throwing up.

****

She had left me the note to say we would talk, thinking I would still be asleep by time she had left. She had been getting dressed in the bedroom and come running when she heard me being sick. When I had stopped heaving, she left me and I brushed my teeth. I threw some water on my face and looked at myself in the mirror. What a state. My eyes were bloodshot, black bags weighing them down, I had a spot coming on my chin and I needed to pluck my eyebrows.

I stare and stare at myself. I stare so much that all I can see are my eyes, and blackness folds in from the sides. I am looking at my two eyes, which change colour and shape until they are no longer my eyes, and then the light comes into viewing again, and it is not my face I am looking at.

I know these eyes. I would recognise these eyes anywhere because they are my Kate's eyes. I spread my vision and see her face looking back at me, blotchy with tears – she cannot breathe for her tears. I have never seen her like this, so full of heartbreak and misery and sadness. This time there is no solitary tear, but an avalanche streaming down her face.

Just as I am about to reach out, the face changes and becomes Logan. But both sides of his face are different, like someone has drawn a line down the middle. The right side has white powder all over, masking his skin tone, and he wears red lipstick, blusher, mascara, eyeshadow, his unruly mop of brown, curly hair set loose. The left side of his face is natural and free from all make-up. His hair is gelled and straightened, and sits neatly combed down on his head. There is even a slight show of stubble.

I am trying to get my head around this when he changes to Damian. She stares back at me, unsmiling, then her hand moves across, up her face from her chin to her forehead and then she is smiling. She brings her hand back down and the smile disappears. This continues until she finally changes to Simon Dunstable. Now he is smiling his charming grin and I stare at him.

I begin to scream as his face comes towards me, his teeth bared, growling.

I have seen the face of a monster.

****

"Did I hear you screaming?" Kate asks, when I emerge from the bathroom, slightly shaken.

"I thought I saw a spider," I reply absent-mindedly.

"John's just rang me. He's coming over, wants me here. Are you okay with this?" she asks, and puts an arm on my shoulder.

"Sure," I shrug. "I'll put the kettle on."

I am pottering in the kitchen when the door goes, and Kate goes to let him in. I know they are having a whispered conversation in the hall but I don't care. I am tired and hungover, and I have classes in the afternoon. I just want this day over, and it has only just begun.

"Good morning, Jennifer," he smarms as he makes himself at home at my table. "Ah I *did* leave the file here. Have you had a chance to look through it yet? I'll have a coffee, thanks."

"I'll make it. You sit down, Jen," Kate says.

"Yes, I had a look."

"Well?"

"The first girl was murdered in the south of England, the second girl on the west coast of England. Is that right?"

"That is right, yes."

"So, why are the Scottish police interested in them, then?"

He leant back in his chair. "That's a very good point and I will answer it. All I can say is we front a sort of 'special task force', answering to Scotland Yard in London. Kate's in it, with me and a few others."

Not really an answer, but all I was going to get and I accepted that.

"So, you believe it's the same killer, I'm guessing, because of the similarities in the MO – the head hacked off, the cuts, the inverted Pentagram."

"That's correct, but we don't know *who* he is, or where he will hit again."

I nodded. "He will hit again, I am guessing another three times and… Do you have a map of the UK?"

"No," he looked puzzled, and reaching for his briefcase, he added, "But I do have a laptop."

As he got his laptop out, Kate asked if I knew something.

"I have a hunch."

I looked at a map of the United Kingdom and sighed.

"Nah, I don't think I'm right."

John had lost his smarminess and was taken over by interest. "What are you thinking? Anything could help."

"It says in your report that these are 'ritualistic killings'. I think the killer has an obsession with the number five, seeing it as a magical number. Five points on the pentagram, right. I thought maybe he could be making five killings in separate parts of the UK to make his own sort of twisted diagram."

"Right, right," he muttered.

"What are you seeing, Jen?" Kate asked.

"I looked at those photos last night, and honest to God, they sickened me – they really did. I don't know how one person can do this to another, but I want you to catch him because he's not right and he is going to kill more girls. I did 'see' something."

"Tell us, Jen," Kate said, softly.

"He chats them up online – his name is 'Johnny Thunderboots', but I don't know what sites or chatrooms he uses. He's like – what do you call them now – an emo? A goth? He is tall and skinny, long black hair, black clothes, weird Marilyn Manson make-up – but his pride and joy are his boots. Huge, fat soles, black up to the knee with his polished silver buckles. I think he is interested in black magic and that sort of thing. He is reading old spell books and reciting bizarre words. I don't know what they are. It didn't make sense to me."

Kate looks at me awestruck. "You got all *this* from those photos?"

"Yes."

John has been writing some notes, while I have been speaking, and looks pleased with himself.

"Thank you. We can get our team onto chatrooms and that username. We can go through the CCTV again now we have an idea of what this Johnny Thunderboots might look like. What a stupid name," he mutters to himself.

He begins to put away his laptop, taking his file this time I note, and Kate comes over to me. "I'll be home at seven still. Fancy a takeaway and a DVD?"

"That would be lovely," I smile.

She kisses me on the lips. "I'll bring it home with me. Later, darling."

I walk them to the door and lock it behind them.

Tea. I traipsed back into the kitchen and saw Rob sitting down, where John had been moments before.

"Your cat wants feeding," he said.

There was never a dull moment in this house. I glared at Jonah sat on the work surface next to his bowl and sighed, reaching into the cupboard for his food.

"And to what do I owe this pleasure?" I asked, sounding annoyed. But in truth, I could never be annoyed to see Rob because he reminded me of my baby, and that always brought some happiness into my heart.

"I thought I would see how you were faring," he smiled.

"Oh just another ordinary day in the life of a psychic. My fiancée may or may not have cheated on me with her ex, her boss wants me to find a satanic killer and I can never feed the cat enough. How is Jonah?"

"The boy is fine. He is happy. I am looking after him, like I promised."

My heart skipped a little beat. I tried very hard not to think of my Jonah now with sadness, but to take comfort that he had a good man like Rob to be his dad and take care of him.

"You did well with the Deaf Club. It made a lot of people here happy."

I studied him. "When you say 'here', do you mean 'there'?"

He laughed. "Yes. My side. You saved lives."

I smiled proudly. "Did I really?"

He nodded. "You did well, Jen. I have been told to give you two messages."

Uh oh. I felt my knees buckle a bit and flopped into a chair.

"Okay. Go for it."

"The first is about your friend, Logan. And he is your friend, even if you can't see it. But he is going to be murdered. He is into something and he thinks he is in control and managing the situation. Logan is being played, and when these people find out about him, they are going to torture him and then kill him. You need to stop it."

"What's he into? What people? How can I stop it?" I flooded him with questions, my brain swirling with images of Logan tied up. The image I had seen in my dreams.

"That's all I can tell you." He held his hand up to stop me speaking. "That's how it works. The second message is about Kate."

I dreaded what he was about to say.

"Do you remember me telling you it was all about Kate?" I nodded, unable to talk. "It *is* all about Kate. You have to get to the bottom of her."

"And what exactly does that mean?" I spouted in frustration. "Oh, I know – you can't tell me. Thanks."

"I'm sorry I can't say more, but I don't know a lot. I'm not told everything either, you know."

I felt bad blaming him, knowing it was not his fault, and he was only trying to help me. "I know, sorry. Thank you for trying to help me."

"I will always try to help you, Jen," and his voice was full of the love I had taken for granted when he was alive. I felt my eyes sting with tears.

He abruptly stood up. "I have to go now," and walked towards the kitchen door to leave. As he left, his body became less solid and, as he faded to nothing, I heard the child's voice say, "Daddy".

****

I taught my classes that afternoon in a state of automatic pilot. All I could think about were the word's Rob had said. Logan is going to be murdered. Get to the bottom of Kate. I needed a room of quiet and a glass of wine to let it all sink in and try to work out just what exactly I was going to do about both of these predicaments. The 'other side' were telling me for a reason, and I was guessing this reason was because I could find a way to solving their clues.

I lay on the couch at five, thinking I had a few hours until Kate gets home and I reflected on how my life had been before I met her. Yes, I still had my crazy dreams, but life was so quiet. I had not dreamt that often or had strange visions, and since meeting Kate things had got progressively more and more intense. More murders to solve, more visions and dreams, more intricate messages.

So, as my heart became full with love, my head became full with death.

Was this all linked to Kate? The more I knew her, the more time I spent with her, the more involved I became in things that would never have touched my world.

It's all about Kate, Rob said. Get to the bottom of her.

Don't question her, Sheena said.

I knew from the times I had held her that Kate had been abused by a boyfriend of her mother's, that she blamed herself for her sister's brain damage, her mother and father too drunk to be responsible, and Kate had taken on that responsibility at a young age. That after Elizabeth's accident, her father had killed her baby sister, Amy, and had gone to prison, and she had never seen him again. I knew she was left to look after Sheena through the drunken benders, and that she had been in and out of foster care because of this. I knew she had a relationship over a number of years with Elaine, who had depleted her of any self-confidence, but she had clung onto the one person who had showed her love until she was finally old enough and strong enough to stand up to her. Then, she had a relationship with my ex, Julie. Poor Julie, who had wanted a baby, and Kate had refused to entertain the idea.

I could see why now. Every relationship in her life had been soured – a sister a vegetable for life and the other gone forever. Who could see having a child as a happy event, being brought up the way she was?

Any anger I had felt for Kate in light of the things Elaine had said vanished, as I saw her as a flawed but beautiful human being. She had dragged herself up, educated herself, made a career, and found a life with me. I knew she loved me, I never doubted for a minute when she held me and kissed me, gazing adoringly into my eyes, that there was anything other than honourable love in her heart for me.

What then? Where did I begin?

At the beginning, I thought. Mother and father. I know her mother.

Find her father.

****

The door knocked and I jumped up, thinking it was Kate carrying too many bags to reach her keys. I bet she has a bottle of wine for me, I thought giddily and ran for the door. Just as I reached it, I stopped in my tracks, at what I heard.

'I'm going to kill the bitch!'

Oh God, it was Elaine outside my door. I ran back into the front room to get my mobile and she began to bang. "I know you're in there! Open the door!"

I rang Kate. Please answer, I prayed. She did.

"Kate," I whispered. "Elaine is at the door, and she wants to kill me!" I squeaked.

"Calm down. Don't answer it. I'll be there as soon as I can and I'm sending a panda car. Just stay calm, it'll be okay."

"Okay, babe," I said, hanging up and creeping into the hall again.

She was looking through the letterbox. "Open the door, Jenny. I'm sorry for shouting, I just want to talk to you," she placated.

I inched closer.

'That's it, bitch. Keep coming.'

"Go away. The police are on their way," I threatened, half-heartedly, my voice shaking.

That set her off again and she began to hammer the door with her foot, kicking it. A small trickle of panic began to rise. It was an old door. Would it hold? Please Kate, hurry up.

'She stole my woman!'

I stood in my hall, counting the seconds.

If Elaine got in that door, I firmly believed I was dead.

She was going to stab me with the large knife tucked into her boot.

I would have to warn Kate.

Chapter Twenty- Four

The removal men have brought in the last of my boxes and I see them off eagerly. I am excited to be living in a new part of the country, leaving a cold trail behind me. I am renting this flat in a new name, with fake references, in a new town. I hate the Scots and Glasgow stinks, but I can blend in – just another loser in a city full of them. It is an indifferent city, open to anonymity. I am just another faceless and nameless nobody.

I lock my door and put the chain across, even though I am not expecting visitors. My mother and father think I am off writing a best-selling novel and continue to throw money into my bank account. The deluded rich bastards.

I spend an hour making my bed and organising my books in my bedroom. Everything in its place, and a place for everything.

I do the same in the kitchen. I am pleased that I had labelled the boxes for the room they belonged in. It is still daylight outside, and I pass more hours tidying up and being neat and orderly. I look out my window at the sun going down, and take a happy intake of breath. I need to make this place my own and bring my spirits and strength with me here.

I can wait a few hours for my ritual, until it is dark outside and the moon shines it's light into my room.

I light one candle on the shelf behind where I will be sitting. One candle is enough.

I get my salt and draw a circle in the middle of the living-room floor, three times, anti-clockwise. Inside the circle of salt, I draw a capital 'A' in salt, marking the abandonment of any law. Anarchy.

I take my seat below the candle and begin to read from *Necronomicon*, the Book of the Dead.

It prepares my mind.

As midnight approaches, I go to my bedroom and place the mirror in the centre of my circle.

I sit down outside of the circle and begin to empty my mind, willing the spirit to show me the way. A spirit no longer bound by the law of man.

With my mind empty, I began to recite the incantations I know so well, to summon my darkest Lord.

'Alham je deridsa
Alham je roka
Alham je roka
Ee sa mesa roka inhelmaja.'

I search the glass of the mirror and see the smoke begin to rise far away in the distance. I continue to chant and the smoke comes closer, swirling in patterns. I begin to see the colours emerge, dancing around like flames, and then the message is clear.

The next sacrifice is required.

****

I hear the voices outside my door. I hear Kate's and another man that I do not know. I hope she has read my text message about the knife in Elaine's boot. There are some words, and then our front door opens and Kate ushers Elaine in.

I stand frozen to the spot. What is she playing at?

"Kate. The knife. In her boot," I blurt, not caring that Elaine can hear and see me say this. I am reassured that she won't kill me in front of Kate.

Kate turns to Elaine, who is wearing unlaced brown boots that reach half way up her leg. Ample room to store a hidden weapon.

"Can you take your boots off, please?"

'For fuck's sake!', I hear from Elaine's head but she takes her boots off and there is… nothing. No knife.

I stare at her boots and then go over and lift them up with my own hands, checking inside them both, but still… nothing.

But… I was *sure* she had a knife. Could I have been wrong? I must have because there was nothing there. Maybe the stress of everything was getting to me, and I was imagining things that just were not there.

I shook my head, as if that would clear it of all the stupid thoughts it contained. Wishful thinking.

Kate spoke. “Right, let’s get this sorted out, once and for all. Kitchen everyone. Jen get the brandy out.”

We followed her into the kitchen and I got the brandy out and three glasses, pouring us all one. I resisted the urge to down my glass in one gulp.

We were sat, sipping, and Kate spoke again. “Elaine, what the fuck is going on? Why are you coming to my home and frightening my fiancée?”

“I didn’t mean to frighten her – it’s not my fault she’s a fanny.”

Blatant outright lie. I said nothing, wondering how this would play out.

Kate downed her drink, which I took as permission to down mine and did likewise. I moved for the brandy bottle and Kate’s hand stopped me, holding mine in place, frozen on the bottle.

“Elaine, *this* is the woman I love. I don’t know what is going on in your life but I will *not* have it disrupt mine, do you hear me?”

Kate let her hand on mine go limp and I clutched the bottle, quickly filling our glasses. Elaine had not touched her drink.

Elaine looked from me to Kate and I tried desperately to hear her mind, but it was just a jumble and nothing was loud enough to get.

“I hear you,” she said, quietly. “But I have nowhere to go and I don’t know who else to turn to. You are the only person who has ever shown me kindness.”

Kate lifted her glass and downed it again. I don’t think I had ever seen her drink as quickly. I almost moved to take her pulse, knowing it would be thundering in her wrist.

Thundering.

Thunder.

Like Johnny Thunderboots.

My head hit the table.

****

I am in a dungeon. No, not a dungeon. An underground disco. The heavy music is thumping and guitars are screeching and I worry that my eyeliner will have run.

The handsome tall chap who has been making eyes at me all night bounces his way over, the buckles on his boots shining bright. He introduces himself as 'Johnny' and we begin to talk. He makes me giggle.

He asks me if I know who Aleister Crowley is and I nod, and he asks me if I have read H.P. Lovecraft, and I nod. He smiles and I can tell he is pleased that I am not some stupid young lassie. He asks if I can keep a secret and I nod again.

He whispers into my ear, kissing it as he pulls away.

Oh fuck, he is gorgeous. I could get lost in his black eyes forever.

I nod, to his whispered question, and he leans in to kiss me on the lips.

Anything of worth is always sealed with a kiss.

****

"Jen! Jen!" I hear, as I come to, my head thudding with pains.

"I'm okay," I say, trying to remember where I am and what I have been doing, thinking I must write this down, I must write this down.

'Freak, haha.'

I snort at the sound of her voice in my head and desperately gather myself, determined not to make a show of Kate in front of Elaine.

"Does she have fits?" Elaine asked.

"No," Kate butted in. "She doesn't. It must be all the stress and lack of sleep. Here, have a drink."

She offered me some brandy and I did not need to be offered twice, throwing it down my throat in the blink of an eye.

It helped the banging in my head reduce, and for that I was grateful. I would ignore it until it subsided.

"How long was I out?" I ask, with fake jolliness.

"An hour," Kate replies. "At first I tried to wake you and nothing was happening, so I just let you sleep, and when I heard you beginning to moan, that's when I tried to wake you again."

An hour? I had been 'out' for an hour? It felt like thirty seconds.

"So, what you been doing?" I asked, feeling in my head for Elaine's thoughts. Zilch.

"Elaine's been telling me what's happened to her," Kate said, and I picked up on a slight slur in her voice. I quickly eyed the bottle of brandy and noted it was more than half empty. My Kate was not used to drinking, but seemed to have chucked a few down her tonight. Elaine's glass remained untouched. I would happily have shoved it in her face.

"Kate has kindly offered me her spare room to move into." I must have looked horrified because she quickly added "At her flat, to share with Logan. Is that its name?"

"*His* name," I said, a bit annoyed. Logan was not an 'it'.

"Elaine's got nowhere to stay, Jen, and it will bump up my rent. I have a spare room sitting doing nothing, after all," she admitted. I sensed a bit of sheepishness.

"Have you told Logan about this yet?" I asked. I could just imagine how much he would love another flatmate hoisted upon him and his untidy filth.

I could see Kate bristle a bit as she said, "It's *my* flat, and he will like it or move out."

I shrugged my shoulders. What could I say? It *was* her flat, and she could decide who lived there or not.

But I could be sly.

I yawned a tad overelaborately and stood up.

"I'm sure he will be fine, babe," I said, scratching my chair back and moving towards Elaine. I could pass her on the way to the fridge. "Shall I just defrost something for our dinner later?" As I passed her, I let my unseen hand delicately run over her back.

And then, everything went black again.

Just for a second.

A second is sometimes long enough.

****

I am sitting in a police cell. Fucking shit on a frog's fart. And where the fuck is Kate? She got me into this mess, why is she not getting me out of it? Bitch.

The door opens and a female copper walks in. I give her the eye. She looks as arrogant as I do. I have to admire that a bit.

"Do you know why you were arrested?" she asks me, like I am fucking stupid.

"Yes," I manage.

"Do you know *who* arrested you?"

"Yes," I manage again. God, no wonder the police never caught any criminals.

"My name is PC Grainger," she smiles. "But you can call me Nina."

I like the look of her.

I smile back.

****

"Yeah, take some chicken out. I'm gonna ring a taxi for Elaine," Kate says in answer to my question.

To me this time, long minutes have passed but they see no difference.

Elaine goes into her taxi and I have stayed in the kitchen, chopping some onions and peppers, defrosting some chicken thighs, and throwing it all into the wok. Kate comes behind me and puts her arms through mine, kissing into my neck.

"What a day," she says, really having no idea of the actual day I have had, only the day she has had.

I cannot hold this against her – it is not her fault – and I admire that she sat us all down to sort things out. She wasn't to know I would pass out and dream in the middle of it. I reached for the upper cupboard to get some Ibuprofen, as my head was still banging and she said, “I know this isn’t easy for you. I will make it up to you, I promise.” She kissed my neck some more.

I swivelled to face her and she kissed me, face on. I reached for the oven to turn off the hob.

This dinner would have to wait.

****

“Hi Sheena,” I warmly smiled, as she opened the door to my surprise visit the next day.

It was immediately apparent from the bloodshot eyes that she had succumbed to a bad day.

“Come in, hen,” she invited.

I walked in, hit by the smell, and without thinking, opened the window in her sitting room. I turned, seeing a few empty bottles on the floor.

“Sheena, are you okay? You know if you feel bad, you just need to ring me and I’ll come and get you. You can stay with Kate and I for a few days.”

“I’m alright, hen,” she gruffed, moving into her kitchen to make a cup of tea for me. “I just had a wee blip, it’s fine. I’m not going to top myself. Stop worrying. And I’m sure me staying with you is the last thing Kate wants.”

“That’s not true,” I defended. “We *both* want the best for you.”

She laughed bitterly, “I know Kate doesn’t want me, it’s alright, you know. Anyway, how are you?” she asked, bringing me a cup of tea.

It is true that a cup of tea made by someone else always tastes better.

I gulped it down, burning my mouth at times. “I wanted to ask you about something,” I confessed.

“Ask away, hen, I have nae secrets anymore,” she replied, sadly.

“Well,” I shifted awkwardly. “It’s about Kate’s dad.”

“What about him, darling?”

“I’m not really sure. Do you have any photographs of him?”

She blew out a puff of air. “Now you’re asking! You know, I don’t think I do. I’ve moved that many times that I’m sure I’ve lost them all, and good riddance to him I say.”

“Oh well, don’t worry about it – it was just on the off-chance.”

We chatted for another hour or so. I was careful about what I said, realising Sheena had a fragile mind, and I did not want her to worry any more than she had to. I left with promises of her calling me if she felt down.

As I walked down her path back to my car, she shouted, “Don’t forget my wedding invite.”

****

The next morning, Kate brought me a bacon sandwich in bed, a sure-fire way of getting straight to my heart. She had even put an extra sugar in my cup of tea, to sweeten me I’m sure. But I would let her, as it was nice to be spoiled once in a while and there were not many mornings we got to spend together lazily.

After stuffing my face, we decided we would go shopping for a new TV unit, as Jonah had been scratching the one we had, fat cat with no toys.

I wondered if I should tell Kate I had been to see her mum but I decided against it. Things were nice this day. We smiled as we argued about what unit would look better, and we went for a cup of tea in a quaint wee tea shop.

She took my hand and said, “We need to set a date, you know.”

My heart skipped a beat. I could not imagine a happier day than saying “I do” to her.

“I know, but you pick. You know my holidays are dictated by the Uni curriculum, so find what suits you. I love you,” I whispered, over the mundane pot of tea that sat in the middle of us.

She smiled back at me.

"I love you, too," she said and grabbed my hand.

It was a moment I did not want to be spoiled, but when that flash of pain hit my head, I closed my eyes and let what was going to be seen in my head just be seen and gotten over with.

****

I am sitting at my desk, thinking back over the last six years. There have been good times and there have been bad times, but I can smile now, for the bad times are over.

Eighteen years in prison, the best years of my life.

Without them, I would not be the person I am now. I would not have my brains, my looks, my contacts or my wealth.

I stand up and go look in my mirror.

Oh how good looking I am, I smile. I smile a bit more until I am bored.

I look at the TV screen in my room, noting the discomfort of the he-she and I smile some more. Think you could outwit me? Me?

I tighten my tie in the mirror and look how straight my nose is. It was never that straight.

I check my cheekbones, and see how they highlight my smile and I grin some more.

I am beautiful.

I am untouchable.

I am a monster.

Chapter Twenty-Five

The key of the synthesiser changes, one long note, a drum beat entering. I shift in my sleep, I know this song by Orchestral Manoeuvres in the Dark well. It is 'Joan of Arc'. If I could see myself, I would be smiling.

I am sitting in a room, bending over a large book, so large its pages fill the table I lean over. The room is empty apart from me, the table and chair and my book. The walls are painted bright red. I open the page of the book with two hands as it is heavy and I see the words 'Jeanne d'Arc' in gold script. I run my fingers over the words and smile some more.

As I touch the pages, I am transported to 15th century France, to a peasant house in the region of Lorraine. I am watching Jeanne the Maid, Jehanne La Pucelle, receive her instructions from God. She is going to fulfil the prophecy that France shall be saved by a maid from Lorraine. She is thirteen, listening to the voice of God in her father's garden. I am mesmerised by her piety and devotion, and utter belief that she is destined for great things.

I follow her through the journey of her short life, waving goodbye to her parents at the tender age of sixteen, her mother weeping, her father stoic. She goes to the uncrowned king, Charles VII, passes his tests and gains his trust to control his armies. She is fighting for all of France. She listens to God and tells her people she will be hit above her breast by an arrow, but she will still conquer and they fight for her at Orleans. Her predictions come true. The Maid of Orleans is born. A King is crowned.

But, as Napoleon now knows, victories will not last forever, and Jeanne was captured by the English. She kneels and opens her heart to God. And God speaks back.

A flash of red and I am turning the last page wearily, with heavy arms.

Deny, say the English. No, says Jeanne. We will rape you, they say. No, says Jeanne, resolute.

It will not matter in the end for she will burn.

I am standing in front of the stake she is tied to, built up with wood, the English baying for her blood. She is tiny, but the strongest woman I have ever seen. A charge of heresy is read out and the fire is lit. I begin to feel a horror inside me, wake up, I think.

But, I don't wake up and the flames catch the wood and it smoulders at her feet. I am being pushed nearer and nearer by the crowd, eager to see her agony. I feel the heat begin to tan my face and hear her last words of anguish, "Jesus, Jesus, Jesus".

I turn to fight my way out the crowd. I cannot bear this any more, but I get pushed back, and as I turn, I cannot help myself but look at her face, through the dancing of the orange fire.

I am rooted to the spot and almost on fire myself, but I cannot move.

Jeanne is no longer Jeanne screaming in agony.

She is Elaine. Laughing down at me.

I jump back and I am holding a burning book. My hands and arms being scorched. I scream myself awake.

****

"Jen, for fuck's sake, you're on fire!"

"What?" I scramble to come to, feeling hot all over.

"You are burning up, babe!"

I realise I have woken up Kate and that I am burning, not from a fever, but from the flames I have been standing next to in my dream.

"It was just a dream," I murmur. "Go back to sleep," I try to coax.

"I'm all sweaty from you."

"I'll get up for ten minutes and you can nod off – you won't even notice."

I slip out the bed and pad my way into the kitchen, my eyes still half-closed.

I flick the kettle on and hunt around the room through my slit eyes for my packet of fags.

What I would not give for one night, just the one night, without a nightmare.

****

The next day when I had got home from work, I rang Sheena and we chatted on the phone for an hour. About nothing in particular but I had come to care for her, and I think, in a way, she had come to care for me. She could not get the love of her daughter, and I was near as damned the next best thing. Maybe I should have felt guilty for going behind Kate's back, but I didn't. I knew one day she would come to thank me for keeping the bridge afloat between her and Sheena. Until that day, I would just struggle on with my battle to drag Kate across the bridge to meet her mother.

After hanging up, I rang Damian to see how she was. Michael had stayed away, which was good news for her and Sasha. She asked me if Kate and I had set a date yet and seemed relieved when I said no, we had not got around to it. Then she said something odd, which stayed with me all day, like a hangover.

"She won't marry you, you know."

I sighed. I knew Damian had a soft spot for me and disliked Kate but it was beginning to grate.

"She will, and I'm not getting into this."

"I would bet your life she won't."

"I'll text you in a few days to arrange a meet." I hung up.

I got up from the couch and wandered into the kitchen. She had said "I would bet *your* life", not "I would bet *my* life."

If it wasn't cryptic ghosts, it was cryptic friends.

I sat at the kitchen table, and opened my notepad, irritated that I had allowed Damian to upset me. Why could she just not be happy for me? I was going to marry the woman I loved – nothing would make me happier, and surely I deserved some happiness? I did my best in life to make people happy. I tried to save lives where I could. I never hurt anyone. I asked for nothing but love and respect. You would not have thought that would have been too much but apparently, it was.

Love and respect seem to go hand in hand with fear and hatred.

I took a bite from a cream cake I had found in the fridge and silently made a pledge that I should start doing some sit-ups or I would be a fat pig in a wedding dress. It was so silent that I had forgotten my pledge by the second bite. I flicked through my notepad and scratched my head. There were five things I had to puzzle over.

Simon Dunstable was the first. I truly believed this man was a monster, an evil human being, responsible for the death of at least one child that I knew of. I knew there was likely more that I had not seen, but I had been shown the young boy he had murdered for a reason. What was that reason? To link Simon to him?

I had told DCI Bailey about him, and he had not seemed interested. What more could I do? Hmm, I thought, I'll come back to that. It will reason itself out in the end. But, what if I missed another death? What if some poor child died because I would rather lie on the sofa and watch 'Coronation Street' than try to find a link?

And Logan. Where did he fit into all this? I know he knew Simon because we had all been for a drink together and I had dreamt of them. I had asked Logan to be safe. Or had I? I felt sure we had spoken and I had made him promise me to be safe, but I couldn't be sure. Sometimes it is hard to distinguish between dreams and reality when you have the brain that I do. I would have to trust my instinct and trust Logan to know what he was doing.

What could I do? He was an adult, he made choices, he knew the dangers. But would I forgive myself if he died? I tossed my head like Scarlett O'Hara, and vowed to think about that tomorrow.

Kate's father. Where did I start there? Did I just start to use the Internet to find out and old newspapers? Did I risk asking Sheena more because Kate certainly wouldn't tell me, and she was seven – what can I expect her to remember? I didn't even know why I needed to find him. Yet.

Then there was last night's dream about Joan of Arc. I love St Joan, and I have so many books about her I could recite her life in my sleep, which is practically what I did, but the dream I had and the books I had read were not the same thing. How much history can be lost in six hundred years? Did it mean my Aunty Joan was in danger? I would ring her. That was the second dream I had where Elaine had been Joan of Arc and vice versa. Well, with any luck, *she* would burn at the stake, I thought somewhat bitterly.

My pen rested on Johnny Thunderboots, tapping the pages.

I had an idea and ran through to the living room where the computer was, switching it on. As it booted up, I ran back to the kitchen, cursing at the killer cat trying to trip me up, and got myself an extra large vodka.

Let's play then Johnny, I thought.

****

About half past eleven, Kate walked in, surprising me. I had not even heard her come in, and the fat cat had not moved from lying on my lap as I sat at the PC, playing songs on YouTube and singing loudly to myself.

I turned guiltily when I saw her and gave her my best kitten eyes.

"Hey, babe," I crooned.

She laughed, and flopped onto the couch, asking what I had been doing.

"I'm going to find Thunderpants," I slurred.

"Thunderboots? Johnny Thunderboots?" she corrected.

"That's the one, my darling, my lovely woman." I can get a bit dramatic when I have had a few drinks and overly romantic. It seems romantic to me, anyway. "I've been sitting in a chatroom all night. You will never believe the rubbish they get away with. It's called, wait for it… I paused for the dramatic effect required… 'Hell's Den'." I giggled to myself.

Kate had picked up the remote control and was flicking through the stations as she asked, "And what makes you think you can find him in a chatroom? Isn't it a bit like a needle in a haystack?"

"Ah," I said, pointing my finger at her "But I am psychic, I *know*!" I had a laughing fit and peed a bit in my pants. "Oops!"

"If you were really psychic, then you would know what I need right now."

I bobbed my head, trying to get her into focus. "My beautiful, gorgeous fiancée, I will do whatever you want."

"Open your mouth," she commanded.

I opened my mouth.

"Stick your tongue out."

I stuck my tongue out.

"Ah," I said, the penny dropping.

"I think I know what you need." I smiled and went over to her.

You don't have to be psychic to know how to keep your woman happy.

****

I awoke during the night and sat up in bed, trying to remember why I was awake. Nothing. No bad dream, no nightmare, just a night where I woke up and needed a pee. I instinctively turned and saw Kate sleeping beside me, which comforted me more than a thousand cuddles could.

I got up and went to the bathroom and then headed for the kitchen, more out of habit than of any need.

As I stood watching the kettle waiting for it to boil, I felt a pounding in my head and rubbed my temples, reminding myself to lay off the vodka. I inhaled and smelled a scent I knew so well.

I turned on my heels and saw Rob sitting at my kitchen table, with a box of matches in his hand.

Strike one. I watched the flame burn and he blew it out.

"What do you want?" I asked.

He said nothing and took another match from the box.

“This isn’t fair,” I complained. “I don’t know what I am supposed to be doing. It’s the middle of the night, I’m hungover, my head’s banging and I can’t make sense of everything.” I was exasperated and at the end of my tether.

He held the match between his fingers and looked me steadily in the eye, trying to beam some message no doubt.

“I don’t get it!” I shouted.

He took the match, lit it and held it in front of us. We both watched in silence until it burned down into his fingers and died out.

“Can’t you say something? Anything?” I pleaded.

He reached for the matches and said, “It’s all about Kate.”

“Oh God, I know that!” I shouted back. “That’s not enough! I need more! I’m not clever enough to work out all this shit!”

“Watch,” he said and he held the match.

This time, he did not strike it, but just held it in his hand and I remembered the old soldiers’ tale of the three matches. First light they see, second light they aim, third light they shoot.

****

I do not remember if I passed out or went to sleep or what. I just know I woke up on the kitchen floor, and that I was cold and I was embarrassed and did not want Kate to see me. There was no further need to give her cause to moan about my drinking. I grabbed a can of Irn-Bru and went into the living room. I had not turned the computer off and went over to sit down and switch it off.

As my headache reduced and my eyesight cleared, I began to see I was still logged into the chatroom, and that I had several boxes of chat open. I began to work my way through them, systematically and close them down.

Until I saw the one saying, ‘Thunderboots: Hey Mrs Crowley’. That was my chat name.

I immediately froze.

It was him.

Chapter Twenty-Six

I feel love.

Even though I am not Donna Summer, I can still feel love. The mirror did not tell me about this. It said the next sacrifice must be made, but I realise not everything is black and white. Vic has been brought into my life to lead us, me and her, to a greater goal. Surely two souls are better than one for my dear Dark Lord?

I have found me in her. Where I go, she goes. What I think, she thinks. Together we unite for the purpose of worship.

She has looked into the mirror with me, and we have seen the same things. If there was doubt before, there is none now.

We are going to find our third sacrifice. And we are going to torture her until she willingly gives her soul to our Devil, and then we are going to kill her and cut her and smear the blood from her heart all over our faces. It will be beautiful.

Vic has shown me the way – she knows the words to type better than me. She, with her female mind, knows how to snare another.

I know we are pleasing our Lord.

That is all that matters.

****

I woke up and thought, Damn, he has an accomplice, scribbled a note on the book beside my bed and turned around to face Kate.

I watched her breathing, mouth slightly open, eyes flickering below her eyelids.

I loved this woman.

I would do anything for this woman.

Even if it meant dying.

I went back to sleep.

****

I had got up before Kate that next morning, and had her coffee waiting on the table, just the way she liked it. I had made her a packed lunch, complete with a secret note for her to find when she ate it, and had run to the local shop to get her a paper.

She came into the kitchen, and I went over and kissed her. She smiled and asked, absently, "What are you after?"

I put that fake innocent face on. "Can't a girl be nice to the woman of her dreams?"

She sat down, looked at me hard, and said, "I hope it's not me you dream of," before tucking into some toast that I had also prepared.

I frowned. "Why not, baby?"

"Last night, you were saying 'Kill her, kill her'. I hope *that* wasn't me!"

I attempted a small laugh. "Gee. Oh, did I? Oof. Sorry. Did I wake you again? I don't remember that."

Apologetic was going to be my new middle name.

She shrugged, opening the paper. "I poked you in the ribs and you shut up."

Ha, if only that was all it took, I would make her poke me in the ribs every night. But I got her off to work quickly and in a good mood, not a word mentioned about my vodka consumption the night before. I did a wee jig to myself.

"Right, Johnny Thunderboots, Mrs Crowley is coming for you."

Ping, ping, ping. Come on you bastard, grab.

****

Kate came home that evening with a bunch of flowers for me and asked what I had been doing all day. It was Saturday, after all, and I had no work, but being a bit sneaky, I had run around mad after she had left for work, and cleaned and tidied the flat.

I had chatted with Johnny all day. He did not just bite, he snapped my fingers off and I played right into his murderous, idiotic little hands. Oh yes, I loved the dark arts, I worshipped Satan, I would give my life for him, I just longed for a man to think like me.

I could almost see him and Vic clapping their hands with glee. I was going to trap him. I knew he would ask to meet me, and then I would and he would get caught, and that would be that. Another one bites the dust. I felt quite proud of myself.

After dinner, Kate said we needed to chat and I felt a tickle in my tummy.

But that was something else that was alright, because all she said was, "We need to set a date, Jen. I've checked my leave for next year and I can do a week at the end of February. I know it's not during your holidays, but I have to take what I can get, and if you request the time off now, surely the Uni will agree. It's your wedding, isn't it?"

Set a date.

I thought my heart was going to stop beating. Like a million small darts of cold had penetrated me and made me numb.

Marry my Kate.

I beamed. "I will sort my time off – let me get a diary."

The date was set for Friday 22nd February 2013.

****

I am walking down the aisle. The song playing is 'Hand In Glove' by The Smiths..'

I am giddy with excitement, my uncle on my arm. I see my Kate waiting for me at the altar. As I walk nearer, I smile at my friends. Damian, Becky, my sister and her boyfriend, my Aunty Joan. They all beam back at me. I close my eyes in happiness.

'Let me close your eyes
And I will take you all the way.'

I open my eyes and I am gliding up the aisle but something is wrong. That is not my Kate waiting for me.

My panic rises. Where is my Kate?

Damian grabs me, but I cannot be calmed down.

For fuck's sake.

I scream, "I am psychic! Why haven't I seen this?"

I am almost hysterical when I turn and see Rob sitting silently at the back of the church. I run to him and see he is holding a match between his fingers.

He says, "You *have* seen this."

****

But what *did* I see?, I think, as I wake up again, screaming from the horror of a dream I cannot comprehend. Not my Kate at the end of the aisle, I know that.

Who then? Who else would I agree to marry? Why else would I be walking down an aisle to pledge my heart to forever if it was not my Kate?

Unless…

No, that could not be it.

The feeling stuck. Unless my dreams lied to me.

****

I sat up in my bed and I breathed in deeply. I bit my tongue to prevent the tears from coming. I looked at my woman sleeping beside me, and I looked some more. Everywhere I went in life, I spoke to people. I met students, I wandered down the corridors of life.

No one.

No one but her stopped my heart. No one but Kate.

Kate who had lied to me. Twice.

You know what they say. 'Once a liar, always a liar.'

Kate, who kept her ex-girlfriend in her flat beside my ex-girlfriend, who was now a man. Could life get any stranger?

My Kate, who barely spoke to her mother, even after she had tried to kill herself. My Kate who had a brain-damaged sister, that I knew now she slunk off to see but would never talk about to me or let me in.

My Kate, who offered me her arm as proof of her fidelity. A double bluff?

Was I doubting my own fiancée? Did I value my own opinion that low that I could not trust my instincts?

What were they telling me?

I closed my eyes and let my hand slide under the cover until it was touching Kate.

I was going to hate myself for this in the morning, I could tell.

I did not take my hand away, though.

****

The bonds of love are hard to break, when it is the bond of the first love. You take them into your heart in a way that you never have with anyone else to come. Precisely because you do not know what is to come. The innocence makes the love stronger, seals that bond. You see the life before you both, happy as swans gliding on a pond. There are no waves.

And when that wave comes, it is not just a wave, it is a tsunami, washing over you and destroying everything that was once before your life. Washing away your love.

Nothing quite washes away your love, though. No matter the hurt, or the pain, or the betrayal, or the trying to forget.

Nothing will change that they are your first love and that mark is left on your heart, try as you might to scrub it. And scrub it we try.

Ignore. Ignore. Ignore.

Get out of my head. No longer scar me.

Take your sour lies and fantasy and give it to someone else.

I am wise now to your eulogies.

When the darkness creeps in, and there is no sound but my breathing, why do you torture me? Why do you seep into my mind, and weaken my resolve? Why is your face of love the only face I can see? Where is the face of your apathy and your hatred? Where is the face of your screaming abuse and wearing me down with your constant criticism?

Is that the face I see?

No. I see you when I have you at your weakest, when you want me most and scream my name in your ecstasy. You forget your lies then. I look at your happy face and I believe you. I *believe you.*

I believe you.

I believe you.

What an utter fucking arse I am.

Believe in love?

I would be as well believing in a pot of gold at the end of a rainbow.

But every night when I close my eyes, it is her face I see. Despite the historic lies and deception.

I hate this and I will not let it weaken me.

I will find a love to replace her. A love who is strong and supports me, who will not question me or ask me what I am.

I will find a love who will not question me.

No questions.

Why? Because if I am asked the questions, I will need to give the answers.

****

I withdrew my hand and went back to my computer screen. I tried to reason with myself as I typed to Johnny. Her first love was Elaine, my first love was Lisa, but that did not really count, so it must be Julie.

Did I have a Julie shaped scar on my heart? No, I did not. Did Kate have an Elaine shaped scar on hers? Oh, yes.

What kind of love surgeon did I need to be to erase that scar?

I looked at her ring of promise on my finger and hoped that would be enough.

****

I was meeting Julie later that day, having texted her for a cup of tea. I think I really wanted to see her little baby and give it a cuddle, and hope my little Jonah could somehow feel that I was really cuddling him. I also wanted to look at her and see what I felt inside, if anything. What demons of the past still haunt us when we see an ex-lover and can we conquer them?

But first, I had a date with Johnny. For two hours that morning we chatted and played in a sad, deranged way. Then it was time for his bed, as he slept during the day. I said I did too, as I was half-vampire – I surprise myself that I can even come up with half of these witticisms without vodka – but he fell for it and lapped it up. Or Vic did. I was not sure which one was typing, but it was six and half a dozen – get one, get them both. Strictly speaking I was saving her too, as she had not actually done anything apart from maybe abet, and was young enough to repent without a death on her conscience.

When we logged off, it was with reassurances that we would meet soon to burn some black candles and praise the word of the Devil. I felt a bit sick even agreeing to that. I am not religious, and I do not know if I believe in a God or not, but I certainly do not want to believe in a Devil that will make us take each other's lives.

I had a shower, singing some Simon and Garfunkel, fed the greedy cat and jumped in the car to meet Julie. I was disappointed to see that she did not have her kid with her, as his "Dad had him".

Over the course of the next few hours, whilst discussing all manner of mundane trivialities, I studied Julie. I looked at the way her hair stuck to her head where she had sweated and remembered I would always move it. I looked into her eyes and remembered how they would hold me entranced as she smiled and did a little dance in the kitchen as she regaled me with a funny story. I remembered the sway of her hips against mine when we put on soft music and candles and held each other close to dance.

I used to love her.

Used to.

I did not love her now. Not like that. I maybe loved her in a way that you did when you knew someone for a long time, and shared your life with them, but I was not in love with her. I would always want the best for her, for her to be happy, and I would never see her stuck but… but… But I no longer yearned for her smile.

As I was concluding this, she put down her cup and said, "Right, Jen, you forget I know you. What's going on in your head?"

I *had* forgotten she knew me. Seemed like I was forgetting a lot of things lately. Ever since I had met Kate, my mind had not been my own. Ever since I had met my Kate, my mind had been full of weird and wonderful dreams. And the odd bit of hot sex.

"Oo er," I hummed and hawed. "Well, I had this dream…" She groaned loudly but in good spirits, with a grin. "I had this dream about Kate and her ex, and it got me to thinking about the marks the people we have been with before leave on us…"

She interrupted "And you were looking at me, thinking 'What mark did Julie leave on me?', weren't you?"

"Yes, but in a nice way." I always have to be nice. It's just not in me to be nasty.

"So, what mark did I leave on you then?"

I inhaled and breathed out. I was going to be honest. "You made me doubt."

"Because you loved me and trusted me and I betrayed you?"

"No, not exactly."

"What then?"

"Because," I explained, "I loved you and trusted you and I couldn't see."

She nodded. "And what you mean is, you love Kate and you trust Kate and you can't see, so you don't trust yourself?"

It was my turn to nod. "Precisely."

****

When Kate came home from work that evening, I was sitting glued to the PC screen, typing frantically to Johnny. Things were moving along nicely. I had gained trust and I had offered to meet him. I was going to get this killer and make up for the

Dunstable boy. Not that saving one life can make up for another losing theirs, but I had to make some sort of psychic mathematical logic in my head or I would find it hard to go on.

When you are presented with a problem in life, there are two ways to deal with it. It can drag you down with the whys and wherefores, or you can make a logical equation out of it. Life does not work in logical equations, but it was the best I could do to cope with my guilt over that young boy's needless death.

"Can I get a cuddle?" she had to ask, and I felt bad then, for neglecting the woman I loved. She had worked all day and I could not drag myself away from the typings of a killer for five minutes to let her know I loved her.

I immediately left the PC and joined her on the couch, wrapping my arms around her. She still smelled as fresh as the first time she had turned up on my doorstep, with her offerings of wine and a smile.

I held her in my arms just a moment longer than I normally would have. Just long enough to let my love for her seep through me and into her, my psychic osmosis.

I inhaled her hair, and over her shoulder, I saw the words flicker on my computer screen.

'Johnny Thunderboots: Meet me tomorrow…'

Chapter Twenty-Seven

Kate has gone to the bathroom and I rush to the PC screen to type back to Johnny. I can feel my heart pounding with the excitement of knowing I am a step closer to snaring him. I agree to meet him and scribble the venue and time on a bit of paper, then shut down the computer and put the light out.

After brushing my teeth, I walk into the bedroom about to ask Kate something about the wedding, and I see she is lying naked on top of the bed. My heart that was pounding before is positively pushing through my chest. I stand and all I can do is look at her.

She has a small, unreadable smile on her lips, her eyes connecting with mine, taking me into her soul and telling me she loves me. She wants me. I lower my eyes, down the jut of her shoulder bone, to her small but firm breasts. My fingertips twitch as they remember the softness of her skin, longing to touch her. I see the hollow of her stomach and feel my lips tickle with the kisses that they lay there. My eyes lower some more, to the small triangle of hair and I feel a tug inside me. Her small, narrow hips that I love to hold, thrusting against me, and her slim, muscular legs, open slightly, teasing me with their invitation.

I do not need to be asked twice and quickly strip. I lie beside her and begin to kiss her, her hands gripping my hair and pushing her body round to mine.

This is the woman I love, loving me.

She panted, "Lick me", pulling my hair to get my head where she wanted it and when she came, it was my name she screamed, no one else's.

I almost cried with my joy.

****

In my dream that night, I was sitting on a school bus, wearing a girl's uniform. I looked at the badge on my blazer and run my fingers down the black and red striped tie. The bus had stopped and was picking up some more children in the same uniform as me, and as they got on, a few smiled at me, a few ignored me and they sat down. The bus started to move again and I wondered where it was taking me.

I looked at the window, trying to take in what I saw around me, never knowing when I might need to remember this, as the bus jostled me back and forth. I could hear the chatter of the girls behind me, drowning out some noise that in the back of my mind, should have been louder.

But I could not make it go louder and, instead, it was the voices that became louder and louder, without words making any sense. I had to get off the bus. The feeling would not subside, and as I stood up, I saw we were crossing the Kingston Bridge. The noise of the chatter was suddenly silenced by a lurching of the bus and a loud screech. I fell back down into my seat, thrown against the girl next to me, in turn thrown against the window.

In slow motion, I could see us tipping and the screeching was the bus scraping along the concrete edging. I knew, I just *knew* the way I always know, that it was not going to hold us and we were going to break through, and freefall down below. Straight into the River Clyde.

I had to get off!

As I tried again to push myself up against the momentum carrying us forward on our side, I heard a snap and then we began to tumble.

I screamed.

****

"Jen! Shush, it's okay!"

I heard Kate waking me up to soothe me, as she did so often these days.

I sat up and shook my head "No. Oh God!"

“What, babe? What is it?” she said in a small voice. It was the small voice she saved only for me, when she could not mask her love.

“A busload of kids is going to crash off the Kingston Bridge.”

Remember, I was thinking, remember!

“What?” Now she sat up. “When? How do you know? You dreamed about it?”

I shook my head, trying to clear the cobwebs and get some straight thoughts into it. I am not very patient when I feel like this and I snapped.

“Yes, of course I dreamt it. Gimme a minute to work it out.”

I retraced the bus in my head. “It is picking up kids…”

“Where?” she interrupted.

“I don’t know! I don’t know the whole of Glasgow!”

Very patiently, I noticed, she asked, “What *do* you remember, Jen? Any number on the bus? Colour? A uniform?”

I nodded. “Yes. A uniform. Black and red tie.”

“Do you know when, darling?” she whispered.

“Yes, I know now. What time is it?” I hated this, I hated this feeling of not being able to do anything, this horror at what was about to happen.

“It’s 7.29.”

“41 minutes, then.”

Kate jumped from the bed, and quickly grabbed whatever clothes she could find, speaking at the same time.

“What side of the Kingston Bridge? Coming into the city or going to Kilmarnock? Think, Jen. If I’m gonna fucking stop traffic, I need to be sure!”

“Into the city.”

“Get dressed, for fuck’s sake – don’t just sit there!”

I am frozen. I can’t go. I can’t see the carnage this is going to cause. Kate has grabbed my arm and is shaking me roughly.

“Jen!” she looks me in the eyes, “We can stop it. Move!”

She is throwing clothes at me and I am dressing, but I do not share her confidence.

“I can’t,” I whisper.

Kate grabs me again, roughly this time, and pushes her face into mine. "You *can*, and you are going to! Now, get fucking dressed and move!"

Somehow her words galvanise me, and I am soon sitting beside her in her car and she is leaning over me, going into her glove compartment. She is pulling out a blue siren that I never knew she had, but explains why we always went places in my car.

She is talking on her phone and driving with one hand, but I do not fear for my own safety. I know fifteen children are going to die, with seven seriously injured. A few will escape unhurt. How can I sit here so calmly and do nothing?

Kate snaps shut her phone and grabs my hand. "We *will* do this, babe. Stop worrying."

Stop worrying? You say that when you have dreams about people dying and there is nothing you can do. You say that when you see your dog, that you have loved all your small life, wandering out onto the road and you know what is coming. You know it is going to lean down to sniff a bit of stick on the road and that car is going to come round the bend and knock your dog into the path, and it is you, *you*, who is going to have to lay with it as a five year old, and pat its head until it pants no more.

You live with that! I don't want to live with this! I want a normal life!

"Jen!" I hear Kate say, and I snap back to the present, wiping away the tear for my first dog. "Think!"

I close my eyes and I hear the noise of the bus. "It's noisy, there is a noise about it – something not right, a screeching."

She is still driving, but it is not long before she pulls into the hard shoulder, and her blue light is flashing above our heads. We are watching traffic, and she is half watching me, searching for any sign, any half clue.

"That one!" I scream, glimpsing a girl sitting where I had sat in my dream, wearing that black and red tie. Kate needs no second telling and her car is skidding off, the light showcasing our arrival on the scene. She pulls beside the bus and I sit, transfixed, looking in.

For just a second, my eyes meet with a young girl, sitting looking out the window, her hands on her tie and then the moment is broken. I know I will find her again in another dream, another night.

I have lost what is happening, but Kate is beside the bus in her car, and is motioning frantically for the driver to pull over.

It's not going to happen, I think. They are all going to die. I put my hands over my face and begin to cry.

****

In that second, for a second is all it takes sometimes, my eyes close and a vision comes before me.

I wish I could stop this, I think, but I let my mind wander forward and a nagging voice of my conscience tells me that I do not really want it to stop. What if it stopped and Kate didn't love me anymore? What if she loves me because I can see these things that will help her career? What if it is all fake, and her lies are the only two that I have discovered?

My lids shut and the heat is what hits me. The warmth of standing in front of fire that cascades its flames into an enveloping blanket. I want to stay in this warmth, so far removed from the dream of the cold when I am in the water, being overcome by the numbness.

I let myself thaw and almost unwillingly open my eyes to see what is before me.

It is Elaine. Resplendent in her silver armour, she walks from the flames, untouched, towards me.

I put my hands over my ears, as I do not want to hear this.

'Are you ready for me, psychic?'

I shake my head, no.

'Get ready then, because you are going to burn!'

She throws her head back and laughs, and I am standing listening to the madness in her head, the justification for her lies, the vengeance she will seek. I believe she is completely unhinged.

I have looked madness in the face before and it is not pleasant, but easy to recognise.

That deluded self-belief, hidden behind a smile, but screaming out from the eyes. The conviction of the words leaving the lips, truth and lies, distorted into fantasy.

'My flames will eat you up!' her mind screams at me. 'My flames!' she sighs in contentment.

I have seen enough and shake myself from this vision, feeling a bead of sweat trickle its way down my cheek.

I felt those flames.

****

"Pull over!" my Kate is screaming, and I begin to hear that noise, the one that was loud in my head, that I knew meant something was wrong with the bus. It is getting louder.

I close my eyes. They are all going to die and I cannot stop it. I cannot do a single thing. My toes are tingling and my head is throbbing with the agony of the knowing, my eyes stinging for the tragedy about to unfold.

I open my ears, and the noise I hear, so loud in my dream, so loud a mere moment ago, is grinding to a halt.

I open my eyes and see the bus slowing down, and Kate still waving and screaming. I have not even heard her.

And then the bus is stopping and she is jumping out of her car and arguing vehemently with the driver, showing her ID. She reaches into her pocket for her phone and speaks, snapping it shut again.

"Wait here!" she is saying, as she begins to move on traffic.

She is truly talented. I am in awe.

No one has died. There are not screaming children lying at the bottom of the Kingston Bridge, crying over a lost school trip to the Lake District. There is no noise now.

I am sat in the passenger seat of Kate's car, and I am slowly realising that she has done it.

She has believed me and saved people from dying.

The noise of the bus screeching subsides in my head, replaced by the sirens she has summoned. I watch it all unfold, a bystander to this moment of history that no one but me shall ever have witnessed.

I watch my Kate argue and gesticulate, and they are removing the children from the bus, with another on its way. A tow truck appears and she nods and says something else but I cannot lip read and I know she is having to fight.

In that moment, that single instant, I see it is me she is fighting for, and I love her just a tiny bit more.

She gets back in the car beside me, and smiles, a smile of reassurance.

"You did well, Jen" she says and starts the car.

We drove home and I think, what if I had said nothing? What if she did not believe me?

What if.

My most hated sentence.

****

She made sure I was okay and then went back to work. I spent the morning in a daze, sat at the kitchen table, smoking cigarette after cigarette, my fingers trembling.

I had saved them. I do not know how but I had done it.

She had done it.

My Kate.

She had helped me save them and she thought I would help save her.

I lit another cigarette.

****

My phone rang. I saw Damian's number and smiled as I said "Hello."

"Jen."

"Yes," I replied, a bit perplexed. I knew it was her, and yet she sounded different.

"Don't go."

"Damian? What do you mean?" I asked.

"You can't go ahead with this," she said, in a voice that was hers, but not hers.

"Go ahead with what?"

I looked at my phone, waiting for a reply and the line went dead. I rang her number back, a bit piqued, and there was no reply. Again and again, nothing.

Go ahead with what, I thought?

And as I thought this, I looked down at my scribbled note.

'Meet Johnny!'

****

I sat down on the sofa, dazed by the events of a day that had not yet progressed beyond the morning.

It goes without saying that the fat cat lay on my stomach and I fell asleep.

And in my sleep, I met eyes again with the young girl who had been sitting on the bus.

She locked me into her and her lips began to move.

She mouthed a sentence to me.

When I woke up, I had a crick in my neck and no idea what she had said.

****

I rang Sheena and had a chat. She was off her bender and was taking each day as it came. When I hung up, she said, "Love you, Jen", and I felt a lump grow in my throat. I so wished she would have been able to say this to her own daughter, and not me, the psychic surrogate.

I rang Julie and she asked me straight away what was wrong. I can't even kid on that I am alright, it seems.

I assured her I was fine and we arranged to meet. She asked me how Kate was and I paused before I answered, feeling her love stream down the phone. I had no wish to hurt her or rub her nose in how happy we were.

"She is fine," I said, finally, and we left it at that.

I rang my sister and she prattled on for ages. Sisterly love knows no bounds, but I drew the line when she started to tell me how her bowels were playing up.

And then I fell asleep again, secure in the knowledge I had no classes today.

Kate woke me up when she came home, shouting my name as soon as she walked in the door.

I sprang up, trying to remember where I was, and thinking what did I dream?

But, I had dreamt nothing. I had a pure sleep.

"Jen, they took the bus to our mechanics, and you were right! The brakes were going, and the suspension. God knows what else!" I could hear the excitement in her voice. "They say it was a miracle no one died! Do you know how happy you have made me? Do you realise what you have done?"

I looked at her and saw the sheer joy on her face, her complete pleasure and I would never break that. I smiled back.

"You did it, babe, because you believed me."

She came rushing over, and held me tightly in her arms.

"You are *my* fucking miracle," she whispered.

I let her smile.

****

She fell asleep on me, as we lay on the couch watching 'South Park'. I tried not to laugh and wake her up but when I was sure she was asleep, I removed myself.

I had a date with Johnny Thunderboots.

Chapter Twenty-Eight

As I put my coat on, I stand over her, watching her sleep. My lovely Kate, who has again believed me and saved the lives of at least fifteen schoolchildren.

And one I can still see in my mind, one whose time has come, I know, and will pass into my dreams as I try to figure out why. Her eyes locked with mine and I will have to wait for that message, but wait I can do, as I have no more choice in this than I have in determining the weather. Which is rain. Again.

I am not entirely stupid and I write a note for Kate, telling her that I have gone to meet Johnny, and where I have gone. I know he is not going to kill me – at least not at this meeting – because I have not dreamt about it and I feel safe, trusting my dreams.

A shiver runs through me.

You have been lied to before, my head says.

It wasn't like that, my heart replies.

What was it like then?

She loves me and she has proved it time and time again.

My head said, But when it comes to it, will she be there for you?

I did not know the answer and slunk out my flat. My heart silent.

****

There is a song playing in my head.

'Burn baby burn!'

What does it mean?

****

I clunked down the road in my old Doc Marten boots that I had kept from my student days – thank God I never threw anything out. I had found a black crushed velvet skirt and threw on a Clash T-shirt. With a holey cardigan completing my ensemble, I thought I passed for an old Goth. I had overdosed on the black eye make-up and felt all Siouxsie and the Banshees.

I hailed a black taxi and told him where to go, a 24-hour cafe that Johnny had told me to meet him at. As I paid the driver and got out, I took my cigarettes out my bag and lit one for some inner strength. Because cigarettes have that power. I looked in the cafe window and saw him straight away. He was not difficult to spot, with only one other customer there, an elderly man swirling a cup of coffee.

I dragged some more, lurking in the shadows across the road, and watched him. He was sat bolt upright in his chair, watching the door. For me.

I took another drag, threw my cigarette away, and crossed the road. I need to pretend I am mad, like Kate Bush, I thought. A voice in my head said, ‘Shouldn’t be too hard’, and I tutted at myself as I opened the door, beaming a huge grin at Johnny.

He lowered his head, keeping his shy eyes on me, and a small smile curled on his lips. As I approached, he stood up and bowed, sweeping his arm in front of him. Then he grabbed my hand

“Mrs Crowley, I presume.”

I pretended I was on the wily, windy moors and gave my best madness-filled smile. “Johnny?”

“Indeed, Mrs Crowley – sit,” he commanded, in a soft voice. “I shall get you a coffee.”

“No! Tea!” What a pathetic Goth I make.

“Then tea it is, my dear,” and he swept away to the counter, where one bored looking woman stood playing on her mobile phone. I looked at his boots. Perfect shine on the silver buckles, an extra inch to his already dominating height. A pair of glorified moon-boots. A black jacket, maybe PVC, hitting his knees, swished as he walked.

He brought back over my tea and set it down for me, and laid out some sugar and some milk. Nice and neat.

I deliberately grabbed a sugar, messing the straight line and began to rip the packet, letting it empty into my cup. He watched me intently.

"I brought you a present," he said and reached into his pocket.

I began to stir, curious, and tried to focus on his mind. Maybe now that I could hear Elaine, I could hear someone else. But I did not hear anything from Johnny.

"What's your first name?" he asked, his hand still in his pocket.

"Annie," I said, plucking a name from nowhere.

"Annie," he said, again softly in his deep voice, and he handed me a piece of wood, that he had carved into two initials.

A and C.

Annie Crowley.

I reached over and took it, a trembling running through my fingers as I held the wood.

"How did you know?" I asked.

"My mirror told me. I have darker magic now to share with you, Annie," he smiled and I noticed then that his eyes were a blue so pale that they had to be contacts. No one had eyes that colour.

I was still sat with the wood carving in my hand, twisting it around. I sang Kate Bush's 'Wuthering Heights' in my head. It helped with the madness.

"When, Johnny?" I ventured, meeting his stare.

"I need you to pass a test, Annie, before I can share. I have been told this is the way to our unholiness." He leant over, took my hands in his, he was warm, and whispered. "I have spoken with the spirits, Annie, like we discussed. They have told me a great many things, but the most important thing they told me was that you are special. You have a force, they said. Do you have a force, Annie?" His pale eyes bored into me.

Show no fear.

"Yes, I have a force."

He snapped back, removing his hands. "Tomorrow. I will phone you. Give me your number."

He took his phone out and punched in the number I recited.

"Annie," he stood up, "You must go now, but I ask you to do one thing for me."

"Yes, Johnny?"

"You must cut yourself and bring a drop of your blood. It is required for our contact. Tomorrow…" He leaned in to whisper again. "The darkest Lord will meet you, Annie. Can you do it?"

I nodded. "I will do it, Johnny. I will."

He smiled, his pale eyes glinting in the false fluorescent light of the cafe. "Until tomorrow, then."

He took my hand, kissed it, and swept away, his buckles rattling as he strode off.

I sat back, flipping his woodwork in my hand, and sipped my tea with the other.

A good night's work.

****

I got out the taxi at the entrance to my close and ran from the rain to get into the stairs. As I climbed them, I wondered what Johnny was thinking and let myself into my flat.

As I opened the door, I heard Kate shouting, "Wait!" and she appeared in the hallway. "Fuck! Cancel that! She's in."

"Hi, darling," I smiled, looking not dissimilar to Alice Cooper, knowing my plastered smile was shortly about to be wiped off my face. I could smell that storm brewing as soon as I had seen the worry etched on her face.

"I'll speak to you in the morning," she said, gruffly, and snapped her phone shut. "We need words," she said and stormed into the kitchen.

I followed meekly and quickly tried to piece together what I thought might have happened.

So Kate had woken up, saw my note about meeting Johnny, had a paddy, rang her colleagues and then I strolled in the door, not a scrape on me. Not a victim of a devil-worshipper. I could see her concern.

"Now listen, babe, before you get your knickers in a twist…" I began.

She had been stood with her back to me, and swivelled rapidly. "Don't you fucking *babe* me! Do you know how worried I have been? I wake up in the middle of the fucking night and you are nowhere to be seen but that's okay because you have left me a Post-It saying you have gone to meet a murderer?"

The vein in her neck was popping right out.

"But I knew I would be okay, there was nothing to worry about," I tried to placate.

That was obviously the wrong thing to say as I noticed that little vein throb a bit more.

"Oh, *you* knew, *you* fucking knew, so it was okay," she stormed around the kitchen.

Even fat cat had moved, sensing a meltdown.

"I didn't know! For all I knew, you could've been murdered!"

"But I wasn't, babe!"

"Don't you call me *babe*!" she shouted, and threw my favourite cup across the kitchen, smashing it over my head where I had ducked. Fortunately.

I took a step towards the hostility, knowing it was her fear ruling her. My Kate never let fear rule her, and when it did, there was only one way to deal with it. Let her get it out her system and ask no questions. I was learning. Two years later. I am not the quickest when it comes to the minds of women, I readily admit.

I continued to walk towards her, noting the flaring of her nostrils and the controlled effort not to knock my head off. I put my hands at the top of her arms. "I'm sorry, I didn't mean to worry you. You needed to sleep and I knew I was okay. Don't you want to know what happened?" I would appeal to her curiosity and guessed that would win over her rage.

I was right.

She breathed out heavily. "What happened then?"

"I met him, Kate. It was fantastic. He is going to ring me tomorrow and arrange to meet again and probably try to kill me then, I don't know. I'm vague about that bit at the moment. But, we are a step closer."

She put her hand up to her head, covering her eyes. "You can't just go off on your own like this, Jen. I was worried," she said, and I heard the break in her voice.

"Come here," I said, pulling her into me for a cuddle. As she came into me, I saw the tears at the corner of her eyes, one silent tear again running down her face.

"I know," I agreed, in my most tender voice, kissing her hair and breathing in her smell. "I'm sorry. I really am. I won't the next time."

I heard her sniffle, and remained holding her close. I knew she would not want me to see her weakness.

My heart said, See, she does love you.

****

Later that night, when we were in bed and nodding off, I thought how sweet it was that Kate had fallen asleep with her head on my chest and an arm slung around me. Like she was trying to hold on to me forever. I would let her hold on to me forever; she completed me. Actually, I thought, no, it isn't that. I am a complete human being without the need for another person but I *want* another person to bring out the love in me, and she is the person who does that. My purest love.

I fell asleep and went to meet a murderer.

****

I can see Johnny and his girlfriend, in his room. He is sitting inside his salt circle and she is standing behind him, chanting from a book held in front of her. The room is dark except for the well-placed black candles, and the floor is clear. Inside the circle with Johnny is his mirror.

I am leaning over his shoulder, watching the mist swirl inside until the swirls began to take shape and form a face. An ordinary human face, with eyes so pale, like the lightest of light blue skies. Like Johnny's eyes.

The man in the mirror is speaking to Johnny, and he is nodding when he screams, "Fucking bitch!" at the top of his voice. I cannot hear what mirror man is saying, but something has upset Johnny. He motions to his girl and she puts down her book gently on the floor like a newborn baby, and leaves the room. Johnny is still listening to the words I cannot make out, when she returns with a sword.

The face of mist begins to laugh and I tremble as I see the eyes turning to red, glowing through the mist.

They mean to behead me.

****

I awoke with a start and checked the clock. 6.30am. Early enough to get up and have a fag. As I waited in the kitchen for the kettle to boil, Kate came in behind me, rubbing her eyes.

"You're up early," she croaked, her hair knotted on one side. She looked adorable.

I raised my eyebrows as if to say, you know why I am up early, and she nodded and said, "Right, right" and sat down at the table. I brought her a coffee over and sat down for a fag.

"What do I do if Johnny texts me today? Shall I arrange to meet him and then let you know?"

She glared at me, over the top of her cup, sipped and said "Yes. *Don't* go rushing off until I know and I can do something about it, please."

"I won't," I answered. "They are going to decapitate me," I told her calmly.

She spat out a mouthful of coffee. "What?"

"Oh," I said waving my hand, to wave away her concern, "I dreamt about him last night. They have this massive sword and I think they intend to cut my head off."

She shook her head. Unimpressed. "This doesn't bother you, Jen? You are not bothered in the slightest that some madman wants to kill you?"

I thought about it, taking a puff of my cigarette. "No."

"Unreal," she shook her head some more. "Well, it *fucking should*!" she screamed across the table at me.

"Alright babe, the neighbours will hear."

"I can't deal with this," she said, scraping her chair back. "I'm going for a shower." She walked to the door, before turning back. I was trying not to giggle at the knots in her hair, while she was being serious. "And don't, just *don't*, go anywhere without me, okay?"

"Okay. God, you're so sexy when you're riled."

She drew me a dirty look and slammed the door, while I had a small laugh to myself. Jesus, did she think I wanted to be dead? Not particularly, I wasn't going to do anything stupid. Really, I tutted, she got awful worked up at times.

To make up, I made her some sandwiches for work and put a love note in. She had grabbed them as she was leaving, and without saying anything to me, had just waved her finger. I knew it meant 'Don't you dare!'

After a shower, I rang Damian.

"What time is it?" she groaned.

"It's eight. Are you not up?" I chirped, cheerily.

"I am now."

I laughed. "What did you mean the other day when you rang me?" I asked.

"When?" She was still not entirely with it.

"You said, and I quote, 'You can't go ahead with this', unquote."

"No, I never."

"Yes, you did!" I insisted.

"I think I would remember," she insisted.

"Oh God, you don't remember, do you? That's why you had such a weird voice." I came out in goosebumps.

"Jen, what are you on about? Fill me in, I'm lost."

I told her what had happened, I told her about the bus crash and I told her about Johnny.

"Well, I must've meant Johnny then, mustn't I?" she questioned, like I had all the answers.

I would have to think about that one and I went into my bedroom and wrote it in my notepad.

I rang Sheena just to check everything was okay, which it was.

Around lunchtime I was sitting at work marking some papers, when I got a text from Kate, thanking me for my note in her sandwiches and asking if I had heard anything. I replied that I hadn't and went back to work.

I remembered the carving and took it out my handbag, throwing it from hand to hand.

I wondered how he knew the initials of Annie Crowley, a name I had entirely made up. Was it possible that he was getting messages in that mirror of his as I got them in my dreams? I realised it was completely possible that the forces we knew nothing of, the good and the evil, were in contact all over the world, and I merely tapped into a small part of that, and that if I was getting messages from the good side, then he could very well be getting messages from the bad side.

As I held the carving in front of myself, staring at it, my mobile phone beeped and I dropped it with a start.

It was a text from an unknown number. I read the text and rang Kate.

'We are on for tonight.'

Chapter Twenty-Nine

"Has he rung? When? Where?" I could almost feel her mind going into overdrive as she began planning in her head how to catch him.

"He sent me a text, with very clear instructions. I have to drive to the opening of Culzean Castle, leave my car at the gate where you pay, and walk down the dirt track to the opening where the castle grounds start. He will be waiting. He said I was to come on my own."

Tick tock, Kate, tick tock, went her mind.

"Culzean Castle? That's fucking miles away. Never mind. What time have you to be there?"

I told her midnight and heard her cursing. "It's going to be pitch black. I'm not happy about this, you walking in there. Can you come into my office? I'm going to have you wired up at the very least."

I agreed, hung up and began to pack my things away. This was going to be another long night. Maybe one day I would catch up on some sleep, but while there were maniacs on the loose and I had an equally deranged sleep pattern, there was nothing to it but get on with it.

I picked up the 'AC' carving and put it in my bag.

I had a feeling it was going to come back to haunt me.

****

"Okay," Kate said to me, "Are we clear?"

"Yes," I nodded, for the fifth time.

"Tell me it back."

We were sitting in her car, with two other men in the rear. There was another two unmarked cars sat in the lay-by, one of which I was to get in. In the event, I had to drive somewhere and they lost me, it had a tracker.

I began. "I'll drive to the opening of Culzean Castle, and leave my car at the paying booth, as instructed. There are already men in place, watching for my arrival and they will follow me unseen." She nodded me to continue. "I'll walk down the path and I'll sing a bit, then talk so that you can hear me through the wire. When I approach him, if I see any weapons I will scream at the top of my lungs and you lot will jump out and arrest him."

She frowned. I had added the ending to spice things up a bit. "Don't joke, Jen. You could be killed here."

I gave myself a shake and leaned over to kiss her. "I'll be fine," I reassured her and got out of the car, making my way to the one behind. The driver got out, saying nothing, and got into Kate's car.

I had an uneasy feeling that something was not right. Why would Johnny have told me to come on my own? Was he onto me? And why had he screamed "Fucking bitch" at the mirror? I had to shake this off, as I started the car and noticed for the first time, that I had jelly legs.

I began the engine and drove away, Kate flashing me as I passed. This was it, Jen, another now or never. Another all or nothing.

I'm saving lives, I told myself over and over, as I neared the turn in the road and skidded to a halt because my legs would not work properly and I went down too hard on the brake in an unfamiliar car. Get a grip, I thought.

I got out, looking around. I could not see anyone, but I guessed that was the point. I locked the car, putting the keys in my bag and taking out the torch Kate had given me. I flicked it on and began to walk towards the dark.

"I'm walking into the dark," I whispered. Then I started to sing a bit, knowing Kate would be having kittens at my apparent nonchalance. Oh well, if I was going to die, I might at least die singing some songs I liked.

I sang 'Annie's Song' by John Denver to steady me.

I was walking at a fairly steady pace, following the small light of my torch, and trying to remember that there were men in the woods following me. At that I heard a crack and a squirrel ran across my path. I screamed.

Then, remembering the wire, said, "It's okay, just a squirrel spooking me. Just a squirrel", but my heart was racing below my ribcage and my voice was shaking too now. I kept walking through the mud of the path, hardly any moonlight visible, a slight wind shaking the leaves of the trees. The perfect Gothic murder scenario. I gulped and kept going, seeing the gardens to my left, not far now.

I remembered the size of the sword and gulped, she was right, I *could* be killed. What was I doing? Was I mad? What was I doing here risking my life, risking police officers' lives, on the strength of my weird dreams?

I began to slow my pace, the drama of the situation overtaking me. I could feel my breathing begin to speed up, blowing cold in front of me. My legs seized up and I stopped, dead in my tracks. I could turn now and run, I could still get away. I needed Kate here to slap me and tell me to get a move on, that I could do it, but she wasn't here and I shut my eyes, trying to hear her voice in my head.

I heard another crack in the woods and opened my eyes quickly, scanning, but I could see nothing. Maybe it was another squirrel, or maybe it was Johnny watching me. Remember Jen, I told myself. Remember he is a murderer and he is going to kill again unless you do something.

I had to keep my head. In more ways than one.

After a few seconds, that seemed like an eternity in the black of this cold, wet night, I gathered myself and made my legs move and began to walk again, nearer. "I'm okay," I whispered to reassure Kate, and perhaps myself.

My Kate. I thought of her, trekking through the mud behind me, worried sick, determined to catch the bad guys, determined to save me. How long ago it seemed that she had put her arm around me in front of Lorraine to protect me. She had never stopped protecting me, and I resolved that I could not let her down but this was the last time, definitely the *last* time, that I was getting involved. Time to step back and let other people who knew better than me risk their lives.

As I thought this, I realised I could see a light glowing and my heart began to beat a tiny bit quicker. Get it over with, face your fear.

I began to speed up, nearing what looked like a parapet with a light inside. He would be there.

"I'm walking towards a parapet, and there's a small light glowing that I can see," I whispered again. "I can't see any shadows."

As I approached, I could see the light inserted about waist high on the brick inlay of the wall. It wasn't a candle and I began to jog closer.

Now or never.

All or nothing.

As I neared, my eyes darting from left to right, I realised there wasn't a soul around and I got a bit braver. As you do. Or not a soul that I could hear or see. I walked up to the little light, its orange glow enticing me. Inside us all is a light that directs us.

I stood in front of the battery-operated lamp and saw the piece of paper beneath it. "I'm at the light. There's a piece of paper underneath it, hold on, I'm pulling it out. I'll read it out… 'Annie Crowley, you deceived me. You are not she. She WILL die tonight while you stand here. Adieu.' Fuck!" I swore. "He's not here!" I shouted and the rustling in the bushes and trees gave way to burly men in bulky uniforms. I was pushed out of the way as they carefully bagged their evidence.

I stood helpless, watching, until my Kate emerged from the twisty bones of a tree and joined the gang of officers. They chatted amongst themselves as I moved further and further away, distancing myself from these events, again scared by the proximity of death.

I caught her eye and I saw the worry on her face as they all realised this killer had duped us, had played us right into his hands, and we had all fallen for it.

I felt those pangs of guilt begin, and in my head, I began my defence. How was I to know? What could I have done? And I felt so bad that she had taken all this manpower out from the realms of crime fighting to follow a dream of mine. How could I repay this? I wanted to scoop her up in my arms and apologise.

And then she turned again to meet my eyes, and what I saw this time, was not her concern.

It was her anger.

****

"She will trample on you to get to the top."

"Don't ask her questions."

"She's a cunt."

****

I began to move back, away from that flash I had caught in her eyes. I turned my back on her because I did not want her to see me start to cry. And I was going to cry. I was hurt. That look had cut into me and made me remember that life and love are fragile, balanced on the edge of events. Those events can turn and change the people we love into monsters, ruled by their obsessions. In Kate's case, her desire and drive to catch the bad guys sometimes overtook everything else she held dear, namely me. I knew deep down, she was only disappointed but it still hurt – it wasn't my fault, I had done everything I could to help.

I turned my eyes to the woods, and wiped away my tears with my sleeve.

That's when I saw the glowing red eyes. The same red eyes I had seen in Johnny's mirror. They were on me. I stood frozen with fear, a shiver running up my whole body. I felt the glare of pure evil drain every drop of my happiness. I could feel my legs begin to give way, even though there was a good fifty feet between us, this hatred sapping me.

And then a funny thing happened.

I felt the warm glow of love that I had felt from Rob when I had been mourning the death of my baby, circle around me like a force field and I gather strength. I knew him and Jonah were close and they were protecting me. But protecting me from what? I held my head up high and met the red eyes of that devil, its teeth bared, growling at me.

"Come on then!" I shouted. "Gimme your best shot!"

It took a step closer, and then I actually saw Rob and Jonah appear at either side of me, their faces determined and it stopped. My heart was again racing but I stood firm. I would *not* be beaten by the evils in this world, and I had angels on my side to fight with me. The three of us stood in the dark, a trilogy of goodness and love, facing a horror so great I would have nightmares if I did not already have enough horrors to dream of and keep me awake.

It was only when it suddenly turned its head and I saw Kate walking towards it, that I moved.

"No!" I shouted and began to run to her.

Split seconds passed. I ran, in slow motion, the demon growled at me, and its eyes burned into mine and then it floated back into the darkness, leaving a small red glow that only I could see.

I ran to Kate and grabbed her. I was sure it had been going to rip every limb from her body, and my relief let me forget her anger moments ago.

"Come on, Jen, we have to go," she said, and I realised she had not seen it. But, she had looked straight at it… Maybe we can only see the things in front of us when we open our eyes enough.

I turned back to where Rob and Jonah had been. They, of course, were also gone, but I still felt that circle of love. It would follow me for a while.

We got back to our cars and began the drive back to Glasgow, and I ran over the events in my head.

Johnny was on to me. How? Something in his mirror, some entity, had told him and he had tricked us. Was this the same entity I had seen in the woods? I shivered. Whatever it was, it was bad. But, it had been scared of me, I had sensed its fear when Rob and Jonah had stood with me and faced it. This thing was used to being obeyed and worshipped, not met by a wall of love. I shivered again. Johnny's note had said, 'She WILL die'. Who did he mean?

I got my bag and took out the wood carving. I held it in my hand, running my fingers over it. AC. Annie Crowley. No, that was the name I had chosen and they knew I was fake, so what then? Come on, come on, I willed myself.

Kate had not spoken since she had told me we had to leave, and she was driving with a grim look on her face. The other two officers were equally as silent in the back. I just didn't get her sometimes. I knew she was earnest in her devotion to her job but I was only trying to help, and do my public duty as a good citizen with a conscience. I did not set up wild goose chases on purpose, and surely she must know that.

I looked down at my hands and realised I was holding the carving in both hands, covering it completely. I felt my palms begin to tingle, and then the shooting pain hit my head. I dropped it, putting my hands to my head to cradle my skull.

I am in Kate's car and we are driving across the Kingston Bridge, locked beside a school bus and my eyes meet those of a young girl. She tilts her head and stares back at me. And the words unspoken in her eyes, that I can now see are, "Help me".

"Help me".

I know it is too late. I have not helped her, I have left her to the wrath of a demented murderer intent on pleasing a demon he sees in a mirror. My head is so sore that it falls forward into my lap and I grit my teeth, my hands gripping my hair.

And then it comes. As always.

Outside the school gates stands Johnny Thunderboots, smiling in his kindly, shy way. Head down, eyes up. The girl sees him and her step lightens, her face brightens. His head is pumping into mine.

Beautiful little Anne Crawley. Beautiful little girl. How beautiful her head will look on a plate. I want to please Him, I want to do anything for Him. He wants her and He shall have her. He has told me the psychic is a fake – she is not Anne Crawley, she is not the next sacrifice – but she is going to die after Anne does.

I smile at Anne and take her hand, the fucking fool, taken in by the older man who wants her. Stupid young girl, trying to annoy her parents. Oh, this will annoy them. This will crucify them and get their pathetic faces on the television begging for me to be found. But you won't find me. I have the Devil on my side.

I can smile as I take her to the place, the woman waiting for me with the sword. And then it is all okay as I lie her on the ground and take her head off. Twitched like a chicken and the woman and I laughed and hugged and run home to speak to my mirror.

I am shocked at his anger. I thought I had done well. He is disappointed and angry and growls at me. I get on my knees and beg and see the error of my ways. I am never so great as the greatness that I worship and pride is a sin. I want His love, I want His approval, I will do anything for that, and I listen. Although I am scared.

I am scared now.

"Jen!" I hear bringing me out of the vision.

I turn my burning head to Kate driving and attempt a smile. "Head hurts."

She tuts and goes back to driving.

She might be able to tut, but I have the glow of a demon's eyes burning me. How can I go back to anything after that?

****

We finally got home and I threw my jacket on the floor in the hall, scooping up the fat cat to say hello as it purred into my cheek. You can always count on the love of an animal. I went into the kitchen to feed it, and Kate went into the bedroom. We had ignored each other the whole way back, dropping her colleagues off, driving home, saying nothing about my headache.

I had a demon trying to kill me and I could not tell the one person I loved, the one person who might be able to stop it. What did that say for my life?

I got a can of Kit-e-Kat and scooped some into the bowl of the cat's dish, and then buckled to my knees on the floor, the pain of a vision knocking me down.

Burn baby burn.

As I was getting to my feet, the palm of my hand on my temple, trying vainly to relieve that pain, Kate walked in.

I saw her from the corner of my eye, standing in the kitchen door, watching me silently, on my knees in obvious pain. She turned and left me kneeling.

She left me. She still had her anger.

****

I had gone to bed after feeding the cat and having a cup of tea and a fag, and had mercifully fallen into a sleep that had not felt her crawl in beside me. And I think I was probably grateful for that. I think I was just grateful for sleep.

Until I was woken by the ringing of Kate's mobile.

As I came to, I thought here we go again and began to sing some Whitesnake. There is no reasoning with a mind that restraint has left.

I heard her. "What? Where? What fucking note? Fuck! I'm coming, I'm coming – gimme fifteen minutes."

I watched her jump from the bed and grab clothes. Another repeated night. Another murder.

She caught my eye and looked away. Guilt.

"Anne Crawley" I said.

"What?" she stopped, hopping on one foot with a sock half on.

"Her name is Anne Crawley. The dead body you have found."

She glared at me. "How do you know?"

I said, "She won't have a head."

Chapter Thirty

The woman is pacing up and down in Johnny's front room. He is cradling his knees in a corner of the room, shaking with a fear that has disabled his senses. In the middle of the floor, in a salt circle, sits the head of Anne Crawley. A murdered fourteen-year-old schoolgirl, who had escaped death when her bus that was destined to crash had been saved. And she had looked out the bus window and stared at her own grim reaper, knowing her end would come.

Vic Kavanagh had been taken in by Johnny Thunderboots' desire to please a dark lord, and found a love inside him for her. But now poor Johnny was weak, a slave to his inadequacies. He had meant to kill me, she thought, and now look at him. He cannot even look at a harmless head.

She continues to pace, her black leather trousers squeaking, the only noise in the silence. Her orange hair stands erect in a quiff and her face distorts in fury.

"Set the mirror up, Johnny," she barks at him.

"No," he whimpers from his corner.

"Do it, ya big Jessie!" she shouts, outraged at his disobedience. She cannot believe this Johnny that she had fallen in love with, so strong and dark and evil, has been reduced to a blubbering mess just because their devil had chastised him. Where was his spine? It was up to her, she saw this. She had led him to Anne Crawley, the little sister of an old schoolmate. She had made sure that fucking charlatan psychic would know they were after her, calling herself Annie Crowley like some sort of joke, despising them.

Her hair flows from side to side as she struts around the room. The five points would have to be disregarded, she decides. Johnny could not move after this murder, and they have unfinished business with the psychic. Looking at Johnny in disgust, she knows it is on her shoulders now. Always up to the woman.

She walks over to Johnny and lands a kick on his thigh. "Get up, ya fuckin' fanny!"

He raises his eyes to hers, like a beaten puppy, and begins to crawl along the floor, getting another kick for his troubles.

"Set it up," Vic orders him and he began the ritual.

Now it was her turn. And she wouldn't fuck it up.

****

I sat that night at my dinner table in the kitchen, smoking too many cigarettes and drinking too much wine. I was waiting for Kate to get home, and who knew what time that would be. When I had got in from work, I had immediately opened the bottle of wine I had bought on the way home and sat down with my notepad. There were too many things not adding up in my life, and I never seemed to have the time to deal with them, so I was making time. Whilst getting pleasantly drunk.

Okay, I tried to focus and start at the beginning. What was happening with Simon Dunstable and Logan? I was now completely convinced that Dunstable was going to kill Logan, just as he had done that little boy. Was he in the porn industry, making snuff videos? But more importantly, why were the police so unconcerned? I wrote at the start of my 'To Do' list to visit John Bailey, Kate's boss, and go over this with him again. Surely they could get a search warrant or whatever they did and have a look in Dunstable's house?

Johnny Thunderboots. Hmm, my pen tapped the page as I considered this. Johnny had had some sort of breakdown. Looking into the eyes of madness can leave you there, and that's what had happened to him. It was the girl now who was the danger, she had taken over the reins and they had a poor wee girl's head in their house. Anne Crawley. They had known I was lying; they had set me up and taken us off the trail to abduct Anne and cut her head off with their sword. Johnny's woman knew Anne's big sister – surely we could trace her or narrow it down? A ginger Goth cannot be too hard to disguise, I mused, slugging down another gulp of wine, screwing my face up at the slightly sour taste but swallowing nevertheless.

Let's face it – if I did not find her first, she was going to find me and cut my bloody head off. That was a bit of an incentive.

Tap, tap, tap. What had happened last night with that demon and its red eyes? It had meant to come after me but Rob and Jonah had appeared, my guardian angels, and it had turned to my Kate. Somehow, it had slunk back to whatever hell pit it had come from, but I knew it would not stay there for long. It looked me in the eye and hated me and that meant it feared me. But why? What could I fight a monster with? It scared the living daylights out of me and I was just grateful that I had not dreamt of it. At least, not yet.

My mobile rang, interrupting my thoughts, a welcome distraction. It was Sheena, Kate's mum.

"Hullo, hen," she boomed. "How urr ye?"

I smiled. "I'm good, thanks." No point saying I was being chased by a glow in the dark devil.

"Good, good. Listen hen, I found a wee photo of Kate's dad – it's a bit craggy and creased but it was all I could find. Do you still want it?"

"Oh God, yes. Yes, I do. Can I pop over at the weekend sometime? Do you need anything, I can get it on the way over?"

"No, hen, I'm fine – still aff the booze, so managing," she laughed. "Just send me a wee text when you're coming and I'll stick the kettle on for yir tea."

"Brilliant, thanks Sheena." I hung up. I realised she had not asked about Kate.

This made me think about Kate's dad. I knew there was a jigsaw piece missing somewhere, but I did not know what the picture looked like, or what piece I was searching for. All about Kate, Rob had said. Right, well, that went on the list too. 'Visit Sheena'.

The phone rang again, Damian this time.

"Are you alright?" she asked with a panicked alarm.

"Yes, why?" I laughed, realising I was a tiny bit drunk.

"I dunno, I just got a really weird feeling there. What are you doing?"

"I'm having a bottle of wine in the kitchen – go me!"

"Ha!" she laughed. "Your girlfriend won't like that, will she?" she poked at me.

"Well, she's not here so I can do what I like."

"Has she left you?" she asked, hopefully.

I tutted and sighed. "No, she has *not* left me, she's working. Anyway, when we meeting up? How's Sasha?"

"Mmm, she's delicious, like a gift from the Amazon. The things that woman can do. Last night…"

"I don't want to know!" I butted in, laughing. "Just text me when you have a spare hour, and I'll come see you."

I shook my head, and looked back to my notepad. While I had been talking on the phone, I had unconsciously doodled a pair of fiendish eyes.

I shivered and drank more wine.

I forgot about Elaine.

****

I am dreaming. I am walking up the path to the doors of a church, headstones of the dead welcoming me on either side. I look to the sky and see the rain waiting in the clouds looming overhead. I make my way to the heavy wooden doors, and my eye catches the stained glass windows to the left, Jesus holding his hands out, a bright halo above his head. It is comforting and I pull open the door with both hands, and feel the cold air rush out to meet me, sending a shiver down my spine.

I move through another set of doors into the heart of the temple. I see a large cross behind the pulpit, empty wooden benches on either side in front of me, their hymn books in place for the next service. Behind the cross is a huge stained glass enactment of Christ, carrying his cross on the trek to his death. As I bring my eyes down from this, I see a hunched figure in black, kneeling on the floor, in prayer. Like a nun.

I move towards her. I know it is a her from the curve of the habit and the bow of her back. I am curious and find myself standing at her side, watching the back of her head, listening to the quiet whispers of her prayers.

I strain to listen to what she is saying and slowly, I begin to hear the words in my head. Not with my ears, but with my head.

"God, give me the strength. God, give me the strength. Let me get her back. Let me destroy the lover. God give me the strength. Make her burn in her sin, let her sin burn her. Theft is a sin. God, give me the strength."

It continues on over and over, the same inane litany that makes no sense to anyone but her. I am about to turn and walk away when she finally notices me, and the voice in my head becomes silent.

"You came," she says, not lifting up her head.

"Yes," I reply.

"I knew you would come," she says, her voice barely above that whisper still. "In the end, you always come. Like moths to a flame," she laughed.

"Who are you?" I asked.

She lifted her head and I saw it was Elaine. But not Elaine. She had a strange hacked haircut, a fringe that slanted across her forehead, sides cut in straight lines behind her ears.

"I am Jeanne," she said.

I began to back away, edging towards the doors, never taking my eyes off her, as she never took her eyes off me.

And in my head, the song started.

****

"Wake up!" I heard as my chair was kicked, nudging me awake. I must have fallen asleep at the kitchen table again, I noted from the wet patch of dribble on my notepad. Kate had come in, found me beside an empty wine bottle and thumped my chair, unimpressed.

Showtime.

I stretched my eyes to focus, blinking at her, stood not even bothering to hide her annoyance.

"Hey babe, have a good night at work?"

Her eyes widened in fury, possibly at the slight slur still in my voice, but I was in one of those agitating moods and decided to continue to poke the hornet's nest.

"Find any dead bodies? Need the help of your psychic girlfriend? Promotion looming?"

A red flush spread across her face, and I silently congratulated myself on hitting a nerve. I was still a bit drunk. Which was no excuse – alcohol is never an excuse for abuse, but sometimes I just cannot help myself. There are only so many limits I can let myself reach before I snap.

"Was it just the one bottle of wine, then?" she fired back and I laughed outright. I knew she would hit me with the drink. My seeming weakness.

"Yes, dear, just the one tonight. Sometimes one is enough when you have the things in your head that I do."

"Pah," she guffawed, incensing me.

"Your mother phoned," I smiled sweetly, my venom hiding.

"What did she want?"

"Me, Kate – she wanted me. You know why? Because I give a shit about her, unlike you. I actually care and phone her and ask if she's okay, and does she need anything. I visit her and clean her flat and talk to her. That's all she wants, a bit of company."

Her lips pursed and I could tell she was choosing her words. "Do you think this is about my mum?"

"No," I said. "It's all about you."

"What's that supposed to mean?" she retorted.

"Everything is all about you, isn't it? *Your* mum, *your* ex, *your* job. When does something become about me?" I wailed.

She walked over to the table and banged her hands down on it, making me jump.

"Listen to me," she snarled. "*You* cocked up and made me look like a fucking idiot, and I have had to spend all day justifying that – did *that* ever occur to you? That I did all this because I believe you? I believe your fucking mad dreams and visions and headaches, and I act on them to save people's lives? And this is the thanks I get? I work fucking hard and come home to a pisshead fiancée?"

"Is that all I am to you?" I screamed. "A pisshead fiancée with mad dreams and visions? Well, you go fuck yourself. I will keep them to myself in future and then see how fucking precious your lot become when more people die!"

She stared at me, her hands still spread on the table, leaning over me. "Do you know what I did today?"

"No!" I stormed.

"I went to the registry office and booked our wedding and I paid the deposit on the hotel."

That shut me up.

"Do you know why I did this?" she asked.

Feeling a bit sheepish, I shook my head.

"I did it," she said, leaning farther into me "Because I fucking love you, and I believe in you. *Not* because I want you to help me get a promotion. I can do that on my own, thanks."

I felt sufficiently shamed and muttered an apology.

"What?" she demanded.

"I'm sorry," I said, a bit louder.

She stood back from the table and began to take her jacket off.

"So, how do we catch Johnny Thunderboots then?"

****

"Ask him, Johnny," Vic prodded, nudging him with the steel toe cap of her boot. Johnny made a small, frightened sound and cowed his head.

Oh, for God's sake, she thought, and kicked him out of the circle. Vic sat down, facing the mirror, watching the mist swirl, as Johnny slunk back to his corner.

"Tell me, dark Lord, how to slay the psychic," she spoke, her voice that of subservience and undying love. She ran her hands through her ginger quiff and waited for the answer. The lying psychic was going to pay the price for addling the mind of her Johnny and defying her great master. There was no greater pleasure than pleasing him and feeling the snap of tendons and sinew spliced by her sword of obedience. The charlatan's head would roll next, and she licked her lips, cracking her knuckles subconsciously, as she watched the mist form a pattern and became engrossed.

She watched the swirls grow and change, forming the face of the one they loved and feared and worshipped.

"My lord," she said, bowing her head, avoiding the glare of the red demon eyes.

"I will obey you in all matters. Show me the way to our justice."

The face in the mirror spoke, "Look at me," it hissed.

Vic raised her eyes and met the madness head on, an invisible string connecting the eyes of the demon with her psyche. Madness defines the chosen few and madness would define her. She nodded, receiving the message and she became complete. Her devotion to Johnny and her master were now her destiny and she felt no fear, no hesitation.

She smiled. "Burn baby burn," she said.

****

I awoke with a start and wrote this in my notepad, falling asleep quickly. I was awake long enough to notice that Kate had finally come to bed beside me, sitting at her laptop for hours after I had gone to bed. She still had her work shirt on, I thought absently, as I drifted off.

I could smell burning. Outside the room there was a fire. Where was I? What room was I in? I looked around trying to make sense, and began to choke, the black fumes curling under the door and working their way into my lungs. I threw my arm up to cover my nostrils and began to search for a way out, but the only way out was that door, where the smoke was coming from.

I would have to face the fire. I would have to burn.

I tossed in my sleep, the sweat dripping through my pyjamas.

There was a blaze coming.

Chapter Thirty-One

I walked down a grizzly Glasgow street, pulling the collar of my coat around my neck to keep out the battering wind. I have walked this path before, and it never gets any easier. I thought back to a few years ago, when I had trod the same pavement, weary from another sleepless night, seeing a girl battered in a cemetery. That had been the day I first met Kate, when she thought I was a head case initially, but not that much of a head case that she had ignored what I said.

I sighed as I plodded on. It had taken her a while to trust me, to believe that the things I saw were real and that together, we might be able to stop innocent lives. I had fallen in love with her, with her silent strength and ability to make me melt inside by a single look from her lovely, deep blue eyes. The way she drove herself on, never stopping, always trying to do the right thing – it made me love her more. The way she held back the secrets of her past and moved on, not letting them drag her down. The way her body buckled under my touch and she let her mask down, just for a second, to show her true vulnerability.

I thought of the way she would come in from work and plant a kiss on me, and then feed the fat cat, smiling without realising it, happy in our domestic bliss. How she would always know that I had a dinner for her in the microwave without asking, and shove it on for three minutes to heat it up, not needing to look inside. She never complained about what I made either, which was extraordinary considering my limited culinary skills. She never moaned at me; she never made me feel stupid or silly or inadequate. She trusted me, even when I told her Damian thought I was with the wrong person, she had just laughed, completely secure in her knowledge that I loved her and would never cheat.

Again. I would never cheat again.

So secure in her knowledge of my love that she would let her ex-girlfriend move into her flat and expect me to say 'heehaw' and accept this as nothing but the norm. It was not the norm. I do not know many other lovers who would accept this, although granted, I have led a sheltered life. But, she never even asked me. Two years we have been together and she never even asked me if I minded – she just blindly expects me to follow and trust her back. Which might be easier if I did not hear the thoughts of her ex in my head, in some sick telepathic joke. Elaine, who despises me for taking Kate from her. Although how you can take someone who was not theirs to take beggars even my boundaries of belief. They say love will always find a way. That doesn't take into account lunatic exes.

And why do I hear her? And why do I dream she is Joan of Arc? Joan of Arc was burnt at the stake. Joan of Arc said she heard the voice of God. I hear Elaine. What kind of demented message are my dreams trying to convey? Joan of Arc heard God. I hear Elaine. Joan of Arc was killed. I am going to burn.

I shook my head and tried to laugh off these thoughts. It's not nice to know that someone wants you dead. Like Johnny Thunderboots and his girlfriend, the deranged ginger Goth who wants to cut my head off with her sword of obedience. She might just do it too, if I did not get some clue soon enough about how to end this. I mentally chastised my dreams for not being a little bit clearer. Rob had told me before that I was being given enough clues to work things out, so why was it so hard?

Rob. I missed him. I missed going for a pint and laughing about some fat woman at the bar in a skirt that was too tight. I missed the way I would go for a pee and come back and a fresh pint of lager would always be waiting for me. I suppose he had really been my best friend. And the loss of a dear friend is always hard to bear, reaching up and grabbing you when you least expect it.

I felt a prick of tears behind my eyes, not sure if it was the wind or my melancholy, and swallowed hard. A fleeting vision of myself holding my baby in my arms flashed through my mind. A baby whose warmth would heat my breasts, staring up at me as he suckled on his bottle. A baby who would look to me for comfort when he had a sore belly, or wind, or just needed his mummy.

I felt a brick jam in my throat and let out a sob. I wanted to feel my arms around my baby, just the once. To hold him and kiss his forehead and whisper into his soft, pink ears. And then to see him stumble on his fat, wobbly legs as he attempted to take steps, grabbing hold of the furniture to help him on his way. As I leapt around, taking photographs that I could treasure for years to come and embarrass him with when he brought his first girlfriend home. Maybe to see him blow out the candles on a birthday cake, or whoop with delight that he had a Buzz Lightyear toy. To sneak in quietly to his bedroom when he was sleeping and watch him lie, with his eyes closed, breathing softly and think, 'My love, my love'.

There is no huger love than a mother's for her child.

I felt the pain of my love shatter inside me. I would never know this love. It had been snatched away.

A girl walked past me, my tears flowing unabashed, pushing her buggy, talking into a mobile phone. I envied her. No greener eyes there are than mine.

I would never have that love. I could love my Kate with all my heart, which I did and I would, but I would never know that bond of creation.

I wiped the snot from my nose, as I walked in the doors of Strathclyde Police Headquarters in Pitt Street and threw my hands down my cheeks to clean my tears. I walked up to the reception desk, seeing an officer approach with a smile. He looked about twelve.

"Hello, Madam, how can I help?" he smiled, all eager in his helpfulness. A new recruit I sensed and I did not need to be psychic to know that.

"I would like to speak to DCI John Bailey," I informed him, trying to appear confident, trying not to think of my Jonah, dead before he was formed.

"And who shall I say is asking?"

“Jennifer Keith.” He went off and I stood looking around, clearing my head of the things that hurt me, and focusing on the things that I knew I had to do.

After about five minutes he returned, asking me to take a seat and that I would be seen shortly. I was surprised, to be honest. I had not expected Bailey to see me, I thought I would be palmed off, but I took my seat and waited, not sure what I would now say.

Time passed. I sat in my seat, trying hard not think of things that made me cry, wondering why I had let my mind be filled with them today. The mind is a strange place and not always one that we can control. I should know that better than most.

“Miss Keith,” the voice said, bringing me out of my wanderings, and I looked up to see John Bailey, smiling at me from a door. I got up and followed him as he led me down the same corridors I had been the night I had found Hanna in Scotstoun. He did actually take me into the same room and sat himself down, extending a hand to a chair, my cue to sit also.

“Jennifer. What can I do for you? Coutts never mentioned that you wanted to see me.”

I shifted uncomfortably, aware of the fact that I was going behind Kate’s back. Being unfaithful all over again.

“She doesn’t know I am here.”

His smile thinned as he regarded me. I know he was a clever man – you surely do not get to be a DCI in a force like Strathclyde Police without some intelligence.

“What do you want then?” Straight to the point. I liked that.

“I want to know why you have not arrested Simon Dunstable. He killed that wee boy I told you about.”

He leant back in his chair, his eyes narrowing, and I could feel the scrutiny, as he deliberated his answer.

“You know this conversation is not being recorded, Jennifer?”

I nodded. “Jen.” I really hated being called Jennifer.

“And nothing I say here can be repeated or will stand up in court?”

I nodded again. He leant forward, putting his elbows on the table, stretching his arms in front of him, clasping his hands together. "I can't find him."

That took a slight second for me to process. "What do you mean? You can't find him?"

"We don't know where he is," he admitted.

"He *did* kill that boy. I *saw* it. And he is going to kill my friend, Logan too, if you don't find him."

Now he shifted uncomfortably in his chair. "We can't find Logan either."

I felt like the carpet I had been standing on had been whipped from under my feet. This was a day I had dreaded coming true. I brought my hands to my face in a silent prayer, thinking of my words. And then it all came flooding out.

"I *told* you this was going to happen!" I shouted. "I *told* you he killed that child, and that he was after my friend, and you have done nothing. I can't believe this is happening. I trusted you lot. I trusted my partner!"

There was no longer a smile on his face. "My officers are working around the clock to find him and I *told you* we had this under control and it was not your concern."

"It *is* my concern! I've seen a child killed and you have done nothing about it. And now my friend could be dead, and still this bloody man is walking free!"

"Your 'friend' is an undercover police officer who has been working on this case for more than two years, he does not need you to blow his cover!" he snarled at me.

2 + 2 = 4.

It started to make sense. Logan 'appearing' as he did in Glasgow, needing somewhere to stay, Kate being the benevolent friend from the past who allowed him to stay in her flat. Their whispering in our kitchen, abruptly altered as soon as I walked in. The lie about the broken toilet. The dreams where he was contacting Kate.

Of fucking course – he was an undercover police officer. His face in my mirror. One half wild and untamed, one half orderly. The dual personality. The hiding of the real person. So, who or what was Logan exactly? Was he really a transsexual who had joined the police, been used for his fetishes to snare a paedophilic murderer? Did it matter now? He was missing and I knew where he would be. With Simon Dunstable, tied up in a room with sheets over the windows and shivering with the cold.

"Can't you track his phone?"

"It's off."

"I don't believe this!" I moaned. "I need to get to Kate's flat," I said, abruptly, standing up.

The panic in my head was being calmed by the thought that if I could maybe hold something of his, I could get a bearing on him, and where he was. If he was still alive.

"Why Kate's flat?" Bailey asked.

My mind was working faster than my mouth. "I need to hold something of his. I need to find out where he is. I can find him. I can, I can find him. I don't think it is too late, not yet. I think we still have time. Yes, I'm sure we do. I had the dream months ago, and it has given me time for a reason. I need to go."

"I'm coming with you," he said, and I did not care to argue.

I had got the bus into town and I knew he would have a car. Quicker.

"I'll meet you out front," I said, taking myself out of the room and walking briskly down the corridors that were becoming too familiar to me.

I stood outside in the cold, the wind again battering me, trying to work out in my head all the dreams I had. I wish I had brought my notepad, cursing my notorious forgetfulness.

I saw Bailey pull up in his car, and I got in. I did not need to tell him the address and we drove in silence.

I was more than aware that every second could be counting towards Logan's death.

The clock ticked in my head.

****

'My name is Vic Kavanagh,' she wrote, stopping to suck on the end of her pen. I have to be smart, she thought. I have to be clever. I know they are going to find me eventually, the scum in their uniforms and they are going to arrest me, and blame me and Johnny for killing Anne Crawley. I am going to be one step ahead. She sat in her bedroom, momentarily stopping to sing along to her Marilyn Manson CD that was blaring, expecting her mother to come crashing through the door to tell her to turn it down.

'I love Johnny Thunderboots,' she continued. 'Johnny is my one reason for living. He gives me the strength to carry on in this otherwise dead end world in which I live. I would do anything for Johnny, but he has made me do things that I am ashamed of, that I would never have done if he had not forced me. Johnny worships the Devil and it scares me and if I do not do what he says, he is going to kill me next.

'We hear voices in our heads together, telling us to kill, to kill for the Devil. I am scared and I want to run away and never see Johnny again, but I know he will hunt me down and kill me, he promised me that.

'I have no choice but to go along with what he says and I do love him. My Johnny is a sweet man, except for cutting off girls' heads. He cuddles me and loves me like no one else has ever done before, he makes me feel like a proper woman and I love him with all my heart.'

There, she thought, sitting back. Once they arrest me, they will find this diary insert and they will think I am just a young girl being controlled. I might get a few years in prison, but I will get back out, and Johnny will take all the rap.

I have to go see him now, the useless fucking lump of a man, cowering in his corner, shaking at the devil we have conjured.

We have a psychic to behead.

****

I fumbled with my bunch of keys, my hands shaking as I searched for the one to Kate's flat. I let myself in, not bothering to see what Bailey was doing, but I knew he was there at my back, watching and waiting.

I went straight to Logan's bedroom. It was still a tip. Kate apparently did not mind mess when it was for the benefit of a fellow officer trying to trap a killer. My eyes wandered hopelessly around the room, clothes strewn everywhere, the bed unmade, the curtains still shut. I went over and opened them, hoping some daylight might make things a bit clearer. I started lifting up items of clothing, a sock here, a bra there, a boob tube elsewhere. Bailey was watching me from the door, saying nothing.

Clothing was not going to do it, I quickly realised, and began to search through his drawers, which were equally as unordered.

"What are you looking for?" Bailey finally asked.

"I don't exactly know," I said, still rummaging. "But I'll know when I find it."

"How?"

"I just will!" I snapped.

In the third drawer down, right at the very back, I found a box. This was going to be it – this box was going to give me a vision. I could tell from the vibrations beginning in my fingertips.

"This," I said. "Come on, into the living room."

I was surprised to find the living room much tidier than the last time I had visited, and mentally notched that one down to Elaine.

I sat on the sofa, and Bailey sat across from me in a chair.

"Now, let me explain this," I said, because he had never seen this before, and I felt I owed him an explanation. I had a feeling I was going to lose consciousness. "There's every chance I am going to fall asleep, because this is going to be a deep one. Don't panic. I could be out for two minutes or I could be out for two hours. I have no idea which. But I'm okay, I'm only sleeping. Will you wait?" I asked, suddenly anxious at the thought of waking up alone.

He nodded.

"Okay, I'm going to open this box and hold it, and then I will be off. See you soon. Oh, and if I say anything, keep a note." I had no idea if I ever spoke during my dreams, but it was always a possibility.

I opened the box, feeling the tingling grow in my fingertips, and saw a beautiful antique gold watch. I turned it over in my hand and read the inscription. 'To DM 18/01/12'. A family heirloom of sorts?

The pain shot up across my skull before I had a chance to think of this any further, and I instinctively put my hand up to the agonising sensation. Here we go, I thought, as I felt my eyes grow heavy and I leant to my right to lie down, as my eyes closed and the vision took over.

Logan is at the door of the large house I have not seen before. He stubs out a cigarette with his high heels, and waits for the door to open. He does not wear his usual grin and frowns at the man answering the door. I have never seen him before, but I think I have heard his voice in a dream, arguing behind a door. He has a distinctive American accent and a scar from his left eye reaching down his face to his jaw.

Logan goes through into the room he is accustomed to and, seeing Simon, makes his way to sit next to him. He puts his hand on his knee, and Simon brushes it off in annoyance. I can almost feel the prickle of his fear begin to creep in as he realises something is wrong.

"Frank, bring the photos," Simon says and Frank appears with a folder, laying it on the table in front of them. "You have been a naughty boy, Logan," he smiles menacingly.

Logan looks up to see another two large men stand guard at the door.

"Simon, I'm always a naughty boy," he plays along, still in character.

"Not this fucking naughty, you're not!" he growls, grabbing Logan by the throat.

He opens the folder and grabs frame after frame of Logan, walking into the police office, conferring with DCI Bailey over a cup of coffee in a sidestreet cafe, passing some object to my Kate. Photos of Logan all over the place.

Logan has no defence, knowing he has been cornered. But I know he did not expect this, not yet.

"What are you going to do with me?" he asks, a slight quiver in his voice. He knows exactly the kind of man Simon Dunstable is.

Simon lets go of his throat, saying, "We haven't decided yet", then punches him square on the nose, instantly bursting it into a bloody pulp. "Get him out of here," he nods to Frank, and the men at the door grab Logan, dragging him to a back room up the stairs. They kick him onto the floor and tie his hands and legs together. His ordeal will not stop at that, but for now this is all I see.

My mind darkens and I am watching Simon Dunstable get into a car. KY09 RTT. I feel my mouth move, and somewhere in the back of my beyond, I hope I have spoken this. He drives off, skidding on the gravel and my head flicks back to Logan, but I feel this is a different day. The room is darker and he has no clothes on now, sitting in his crouched position, not unlike Johnny Thunderboots.

For a fleeting second, I see a vision of Johnny Thunderboots standing in his silver buckled boots with his long coat flowing, and I fight to get back to Logan. My mind obeys and I see the blood on his thighs, knowing he has been repeatedly abused and tortured. Not just for fun, judging by the video camera set up in the room. My eyes are searching looking for some sort of clue but nothing, no way of knowing where this house is. No way of finding Logan.

The despair hits me and begins to rouse me from my dream. I open my eyes and see the room I am in is almost dark, but for a lamp in the corner, and I focus my eyes to see John Bailey still sitting across from me.

"What time is it?" I ask, rubbing my eyes.

He looks at his watch. "Just after ten."

"Jesus," I sit up. Kate will have been home hours ago and I've not done her any dinner or fed the cat. How long have I been asleep? I mentally calculate and estimate around seven hours. I must have needed it.

"Did you get anything?" he asks.

"Not really," I frown. "They must've had him followed because they had a file of photos of him, meeting you and Kate, and God knows what all else. He is in a house, naked, tied up but I don't know where it is. And I am pretty sure they are videoing their abuse of him."

"You said something."

"What? What did I say?" Was this a glimmer of hope?

"You said a car plate."

"Yes! I hoped I would! It's Dunstable's car. You can trace that through the DVLA, can't you?"

He smiled and nodded. "It's only a matter of time now. How are you feeling?"

No one ever asked me that. "I'm okay, actually. I think the sleep did me good. Come on, let's go get him!"

I had a renewed vigour with my hope that Bailey would now be able to get an address for Dunstable from the car, and track him down. Even if it was someone else's car, the net was closing in. I could feel it.

I stood up, about to make my way to leave when I heard the front door open. My heart sank. I would have to find some explanation for Elaine as to why I was in Kate's flat.

The door to the living room opened and Elaine walked in, stopping in her tracks when she saw me.

And in behind her trailed my lover.

Chapter Thirty-Two

'Tell her, tell her we slept together, tell her we kissed, tell her, tell her!'

As soon as I saw them both and heard the words in Elaine's head, my heart split in two, taking a bit of my sanity with it. I *knew* this day would come, I fucking knew it. I knew I could never hold onto someone like Kate. Someone infinitely more clever than me, more driven than me, more attractive than me. What could I offer but love and devotion?

Love and devotion are never enough.

It is the one who gets into your head when you are young and have not formed your vision of love that takes your perception and distorts it to their own. They are the ones we have to fight off for the rest of our lives. Their shadows casting darkness on any future love.

I felt the sob begin in my stomach, as though I had been punched. And still her words came flying fast in my head.

'Tell her, tell her I had you. Tell her you betrayed her. Just fucking tell her!' I saw Kate in my head, holding Elaine and kissing her, and the pain was too much for me to continue thinking. All I could think was, No!

After everything we had been through, to think she would betray me. Would she betray me? My heart kept silent, and all the while Elaine's thoughts were screaming in my head.

I caught Kate's eye and saw her look from me to John Bailey.

"What are you doing here, Sir?" she asked.

Not, "Are you okay, Jen? Let me explain why I have just walked in with Elaine."

That never ending well of tears, from which I so easily tapped into had begun again. Two rainclouds of misery that lived behind my eyes. I walked to make my way past them and

Kate grabbed my arm, stopping me as John spoke.

"We were trying to get a lead on Logan. Which we have."

Kate turned and looked at me, that look of, 'Well?', questioning me with her raised eyebrows.

"What are *you* doing here?" I shouted into her face, not even attempting to control my hurt or rage, or whatever it was that I was feeling.

She looked back at me stumped, and opened her mouth to speak but I had already pulled away and ran out the flat.

The fresh air hit me and I burst into great racking sobs that doubled me over and took my breath away. I let myself break.

My mind took me back to the dark days when Julie had left me. The emptiness of my flat, the lack of laughter, the silence in the bedroom. I did not know how I would get through that again. I looked up, trying to find a taxi. I wanted to be home where I felt safe, with my fat cat sitting on me and a large vodka.

I began to sniff up my tears and walk towards the main road, knowing there was a corner shop that I could buy booze at. Tonight I was going to get royally plastered.

After purchasing a litre of vodka, I found a taxi and soon I was home. I threw my coat on a hook in the hall, and went straight to the kitchen, pouring myself a very large vodka. But not before downing a neat one for good measure. I fed the cat and sat down at the table, where so much of my life seemed to pass.

Jonah jumped on the table, and even though he wasn't allowed, I let him stay there. Fuck her – it was my house and if my cat wanted to sit on the table, then he could. I got him a slice of ham from the fridge and let him eat it. He licked his lips and I tickled under his chin.

"You never hurt me, do you, Jonah? You just sit there and want to be fed and then you give me bumps and make everything all right. If only women were so simple." I started to cry again. "You know, Jonah, she's been having an affair with that Elaine behind my back. First Julie having an affair with Kate, ha! Now Kate having an affair.

"What is it with me and unfaithful women? Do I have 'mug' written on my forehead? Do I look like a pushover? Is my love not enough?"

The cat stared at me. I knew he understood as I gulped down more and more alcohol. Elaine's thoughts shouting for Kate to tell me. How long had it been going on? So, she was just using me, as I had been warned. Who warned me? Julie? Damian? I couldn't remember, as the vodka had kicked in and was giving me a warm glow.

"Well, you know what, Jonah? She can go and take a jump. I'm not doing it any more. I'm turning my brain off. I am going to ignore all these stupid dreams and predictions and let someone else worry about murderers and paedophiles and maniacs with swords."

My head fell on the table, as I let my heart break. Could I forgive her? Could I take her back into my arms, knowing she had held someone else that was not me? That she had kissed and touched and maybe even made love to them? That her hands had crawled all over Elaine's breasts and brushed her thighs?

Can I live without her?

Can I wake up every day knowing that I had her love and I lost it? Can I wipe the memories of her laughing into my eyes and make new ones, in time, with someone else? Can I remember to stop making her a dinner, can I remember to stop buying the biscuits she likes or emptying my ashtray after three fags because she says it stinks?

Can I? Can I walk to my job and walk back home again, empty inside, wondering what she is doing, is she safe, is she with Elaine, is Elaine treating her right, is she happy, does she miss me even a tiny bit?

I don't know. And I like knowing. For me, it is the knowing that she will always be there the next day and the next that gets me through. The knowing that she loves me and wants to marry me and be with me forever. The knowing that in her heart my name is written.

I thought I knew but the knowing has left me.

My mobile rang then, coming up as Kate's number. I ignored it. She hated being ignored. I couldn't answer anyway. I could barely speak through my choking sobs. Surely she must know how I felt. Why was she ringing and not bursting down the door to tell me it was all a mistake. Unless… Unless it was not all a mistake. And she was glad that I finally knew and she did not have to lie to me anymore.

The phone started to ring again and I lifted it and slung it across the room. It did not stop ringing. I got up and went into the living room and flicked on the CD player.

I began to sing in a haze of misery and alcohol. I realised I was dancing and singing the words to one of my favourite Bowie songs, 'Heroes'. And I caught myself in the mirror. Blotchy red face, hair dishevelled and a slight madness on my face. Kate wasn't going to walk in the door and laugh at me being silly and that thought immediately burst the tiny bubble of forgetting that I had tried to wrap myself in.

Was she ever going to walk through my door again? Of course, I told myself, she had belongings here, and surely we were not ending just like that – were we? Was I single again when I had almost been married? My legs buckled and I fell onto the couch, acutely aware that I had lost the power of speech and was beginning to slur heavily to the cat.

"She's gone, Jonah. She doesn't love me any more. She loves that blonde tart, her with the bigger boobs. Her that wants to burn me."

I said it again. "Herrrr that wantssshh to burn me."

I looked at the fat cat. Joan of Arc was burnt at the stake for hearing the word of God, so she claimed. And I dream that Elaine is Joan of Arc, and I could hear her thoughts. In some perverted way, the message was starting to seem clearer. This Joan was not going to burn – she was going to do the burning.

She was going to burn me.

I needed to write this down but my eyes were getting heavy. Not now, I thought, not now. I need to stay awake. I *need* to remember this.

But the vodka and the emotional drain of seeing Kate and Elaine had left me defenceless, and I fell over on the couch, trying in vain to keep my lids open.

The last thing I remember is the cat walking off.

****

I am sitting in the corner of the room in my underwear that I have been wearing for the last three days. There is rope around my ankles and wrists, and my joints ache from being stuck in the same position. But I have not given up hope.

I had hoped this day would not come, when Simon discovered my true identity, but I suppose I underestimated him, we all did. I should have known better. Kate should have known better, and so should the Guv. It was too late now. I had to hope that they knew I was gone, and were coming to get me because they were not going to keep me tied up forever.

The day is going to come soon when they are going to kill me. I am not scared. I thought I might have been when faced with death, but I am remarkably calm. I have been through worse things. Telling my parents I was going to live my life as a man and trying to make my way in the police force as a transgender were pretty bad. I am using these thoughts to comfort myself. To remind me that I am a human being and not an animal caged in a pen, fed on scraps and unable to bathe.

I think back on where I have been careless. I think back to the evening in the pub when we met Kate and Jen, and she did not hide she was a copper. We had agreed that, that she would be honest, otherwise Jen would say something and the game would be up. Better to be honest and go with the cover story of me meeting her at Uni and staying friends. I thought it had worked. Jen had fallen for it but Simon was a different kettle of fish. Simon who had insisted on meeting my landlord.

His eyes hid who he was, but I have seen the monster.

I have seen too much to live, I know that. I have to hope he cares in some small, meaningless sociopathic way. That I might be worth something to him alive. Maybe I can barter for my life and offer to appear in a film for him.

And we are so close to catching him. We have the evidence. I have taken it from his computer and passed it to Kate. The analysis has been done. The arrests were about to be made and he has slipped through our net.

I have to keep hoping. My work has not been for nothing, and my colleagues are this minute preparing to rescue me. How will they find me? I need to get them to my notes in the flat, hidden inside a tear in my mattress. Address, photos, car plates, names, numbers, associates – it's all there, waiting to be handed over.

I berate myself for not giving it to Kate sooner. They could have him by now.

I hear noises outside my door and stay as quiet as I possibly can. I do not want their attention; they torture me and burn me with cigarettes, needing to know what I have told. They don't believe me and the clock is running down. They cannot stay here forever, they know that. They expect to hear the sirens come rushing around the corner.

Still, there is only silence.

The voices fade, and my stomach growls with hunger. I do not remember the last time I ate. I am weak from beatings but my will is strong. I will fight to the end.

No one can hurt me any more, and death cannot frighten me. I will sit and wait and hope.

I woke up, my head hurting, and made myself move for my notepad. I had to write this down and remember this. Logan had written it all down in a book, hidden in his mattress. I staggered my way into my bedroom and grabbed my notepad, heading back for the kitchen, knowing my cigarettes were there. I lit one as I began to scribble what I could remember.

I eyed the glass of vodka and coke, thinking better of it, and got up to pour a drink of water. A shooting pain in my head caused me to double over the sink.

Oh no, I thought, not more.

****

I walk over and kiss Johnny, his tongue probing in my mouth, his hand automatically reaching for my breast. I grab his crotch and rub it until I can feel his hardness there. He will do anything for me when he is hard.

"Johnny," I whisper. "I need you to do something for me, my love."

We have been calm, and Johnny is slowly coming out of his catatonic phase. His fear has lessened as he has seen my strength and bravery grow.

He squeezes me. "Yes, Vic, anything for you," he pants.

"We are going to kill the psychic, Johnny – do you know why?" I said, still rubbing him, slower now, teasing a bit.

"Because she made a fool of us?" he guesses.

"No," I say, taking my hand away. "Because she made a fool of the Dark Lord!" I have a hint of anger in my voice, dismayed at his stupidity.

"Yes, yes, the Dark Lord, our Lord, yes," he says, fondling me with both hands now.

"Do you know how we are going to do it, Johnny?"

He stops moving his hands and looks at my face. "No, I don't. How are we?"

I smile and rub him again, soothing him. "We are going to walk right up to her door and knock it and she is going to let us in. But the Dark Lord wants her first, Johnny, then we get to cut her head off. Won't that just be grand?" I laughed.

Johnny laughed but Johnny was lost in his madness.

I was not. I am the ginger Goth that they will all fear and remember. My name will be written into history books as the one who held the sword of obedience and killed the heathen. That's all I ever wanted, to be noticed.

They will notice me now.

Parents who ignored me for a better looking and cleverer sister, a sister who outshone me at every turn, a sister who was not even ginger. Pamela this and Pamela fucking that. Pamela can do no wrong. I will show Pamela and my parents that I am a force to be reckoned with. They won't know the storm that will hit them. I hope they die of shame. I cried every night for attention, a bit of love and it went unseen. Pamela had a dance class, Pamela had a tournament, Pamela had a headache – poor Pamela.

You will see me now. They will all see me now and my lovely Johnny, my feeble-minded would-be occultist will take my rap.

And the psychic will die. Then my Dark Lord will be happy, Him who notices me and tells me how to do it. He will not abandon me. He will wait and exalt me to greatness.

I smile to myself and let Johnny undo my bra.

The ginger Goth is coming to get you.

****

I wake up again and feel fear prickle my arms. She means for there to be a confrontation. I write down 'Ginger Goth, sister named Pamela'. I know this can lead the police to her, surely, I think, my head pounding, barely comprehending what I have dreamt, but knowing I must remember. I must remember. Keep writing, I think, this is all going to make sense soon.

I am going to dread every knock at my door, no Kate to protect me now. A wave of pain washes through me as I remember her betrayal. I still cannot take it in and the alcohol is wearing off, leaving me hungover, miserable and heartbroken.

Two maniacs mean to cut my head off, my friend is missing and my girlfriend's ex-lover wants to burn me. Quiet day at the office.

I find two paracetamol in the cupboard and swallow, trying not to retch them back up. Sitting back down at the table, I check my notes.

Just as another shooting pain cripples me and I fall face first onto my notepad.

****

She sits astride her white horse, resplendent in beautiful shining, silver armour, holding aloft a small fighting sword. Joan of Arc at her finest, ready to do battle.

I walk up to the horse, which rears as I near, and she reins it down, patting it. She puts her sword in the sheath, draped over the horse, and lifts off her helmet. I see Elaine.

"Are you ready to do battle?" she asks, pleasantly.

"I am," I say, knowing not where my strength comes from but willing to fight all the same.

"Do you know what the battle is for?" she asks.

"I do not," I reply, calm.

"We fight for love!" she cries, as though she were a warrior on the field.

"I always fight for love," I reply.

"No, you fight for others, you never fight for yourself. This is why you will never win this battle," she explains.

I take a deep breath, puffing out my chest and see that I, too, am wearing shining silver armour.

"I will always fight you," I say. "I will always fight for right over wrong. I will always fight for love, and I will always fight for Kate."

She jumps off her horse and walks to face me. If I was ever afraid of her, I no longer am. She has no greater power than me, except the power that I have given her. And I am taking that back.

"Then let battle commence," she nods.

"Bring it on, bitch," I say.

****

When I wake this time, there is a feeling of dread inside me so deep and hard that I cannot ignore it. I have felt this dread before and know that the time has come. It is time for me to start facing the demons, one by one.

Strangely, I feel almost serene and ready for the fight. Whatever Kate has done, she had a reason and I have doubted her time and time again, only to be proven wrong. I am not going to doubt her again. There must be a logical explanation why she was with Elaine, and I will give her the chance to tell me.

Something in my dream has touched me, shown me the way to fight and steeled me for this battle.

I will apologise for my hysteria and she will moan a bit and then make me feel better, as only she can. She loves me; I know she loves me just as I love her.

I will not let a vicious little ex get in the way of my happiness.

I breathe in and out, feeling better.

I have to tell her, tell her that I am okay. I vaguely remember her ringing me last night and think back to what I did with my phone. I threw it somewhere. I begin to hunt around the kitchen, ignoring the cat's pleas for food.

I find it behind the kettle and see the list of missed calls from her and one text message.

I open the text from Kate.

It says, 'Baby, I'm burning'.

Chapter Thirty-Three

I looked at Kate's text, and read it again. 'Baby, I'm burning'. What did that mean? I felt that little pounding at my temple. Was my darling in trouble? But wasn't it me that was meant to burn? Elaine was coming after me in my dreams of her as St Joan. Not Kate. So why was she burning?

That feeling of dread that I had emerged from my dreams with began to grow. I had felt this dread before. The day that Lorraine shot Rob I had a similar feeling. Oh good Lord, no, please do not let my baby be in harm's way.

My hands started to tremble as I fumbled with the keys on my mobile to ring Kate's phone. I hurriedly put it to my ear and waited for the ringing to start. Come on, come on, I muttered to myself. It just rang and rang and rang. Okay, I told myself, she is busy.

Let me look at this logically. She was at Elaine's flat and John Bailey will have told her they had a lead on Dunstable's car and she will have gone to the station to check the DVLA records. Yeah, that sounds about right.

The pain in my temple really began to throb then, and I had to sit down. I realised I still had the phone at my ear and clicked off the call. She would see the missed call and ring me back when she was free.

I gritted my teeth, breathing through my nose, to combat the pain. Oh, it was no good. I was going to have to shut my eyes.

Thump. Head hitting the table.

****

Kate and John Bailey are bent over a computer screen as a green box flashes before them, printing data on the screen. Kate is poised with her little black book and pen, and quickly scribbles the address when the green box begins to move, revealing its secrets.

She smiles at John, and I see a look of pure happiness on her face. It is the happiness I only sometimes glimpse in her eyes when she looks at me. She has that look of 'Let's go catch the bad guys' on her, something I think she preferred to all else in her world.

They start their chase and get in Bailey's car, and I follow them in my head and I know I am seeing something that has just recently happened. No longer a vision, but a glimpse into the past. I have time in my head to meander through my thoughts and wonder why I am being shown this, as they pull out of the back of the station and make their way through the dark streets of Glasgow. Where it is raining again. Even in dreams, some things never change.

Kate went to the house to meet Logan and get a memory stick from him, I remember, seeing him standing at a gate and passing it on to her without a word. Why have they not been to this house?

Then my mind flips back a few days and there are armed police surrounding it, bursting in the door. My Kate and Bailey searching through rooms, guns in their hands, pushing open doors to reveal empty rooms with discarded furniture. Running up stairs, conferring in the hall and Kate kicking a door in temper. So Simon moved just in time. If only they had pounced a day or two sooner but he had eluded them once more and Logan's life hung in the balance now. A seesaw of good and evil, but which way would the see-saw fall? Who would land on their feet and who would be left high and dry?

I see the images fade into a blur and reassemble back to Kate and Bailey driving in their car, talking hurriedly between them. Kate is searching in her pockets for something and Bailey tosses her his mobile phone.

I can hear her on the car radio. "Drive round the back in case he does a runner. Unit four continue to follow us and park behind us. Follow on foot when we exit vehicle." Then she dials a number into the mobile. I recognise that number; it is her own. She has lost her phone.

I am trying to process this in my mind as I continue to watch them driving, their faces now tense. When did she lose her phone? Sometime between yesterday and the events of last night that I am unconsciously witnessing. But she phoned me last night, I think. No. Her number rang me last night – that's not to say it was her dialling from it.

'Tell her.'

Tell me what? Elaine in my head. Elaine has the phone? She is trying to fool me then. I cannot dwell on this now, as a scene begins to unfold.

Bailey has pulled up outside a nondescript terraced house, a panda car behind him. The officers in the panda car wait a moment, and then get out.

"Officers in position at rear."

"Let's go," says Bailey.

The four of them walk up to the door, the curtains shut, the house in darkness. There is a car in the driveway bearing the registration plate that I have murmured in my sleep.

Bailey knocks the door, the policeman's knock, and waits a few seconds before beginning to continuously bang. A voice shouts, "All right, keep your hair on. I'm coming."

A middle-aged man opens the door, wearing an open dressing robe, his fat stomach hanging over his tight pants.

"What do you lot want?" he asks, immediately unfriendly on seeing the uniformed police.

"We would like to ask you a few questions. Can we come in?" Bailey asks.

"Can't you come back in the morning?" the fat man says and I notice the scar on his face.

"No, sir, we cannot. I would like to come in. Now." There is no friendliness from Bailey either.

He is met with silence, as Scarface considers his options. "I'm going to give you until five to decide. 1… 2… 3…"

The door is opened and they go inside. The final officer closes the door and stands in front of it, barring any way out.

Bailey stands face to face and asks, "Is that your car in the drive?"

"Yes. And what? It's legit. I have the paperwork to prove it," fatty defends.

"We have reason to believe that this vehicle has been used in connection with several crimes, and I would like you to get dressed and come down to the station for further questioning."

"Am I being arrested?" he bleats.

"Yes. Constable, read him his rights."

PC Plod stood forward and gave him the spiel. "You do not have to say anything, but it may harm your defence if you do not mention, when questioned, something which you later rely on in court. Anything you do say may be given in evidence."

"Go get dressed, sir. Constables, go with him." The two officers took scar-man up the stairs and Bailey and Kate went into the main front room. They began to look under cushions, in drawers, cupboards, anything they could, for any sort of evidence, I assumed.

I jump forward in my mind to an interview room in the station I am becoming familiar with. Bailey is leaning over, hands on the desk, shouting at the man sitting silent with what looks like a solicitor beside him. My Kate is sitting, impassive. She speaks to the solicitor, who then speaks to the arrested man.

He is gesticulating with his hands, angry, but Bailey is having none of it and is shouting some more at him. The man breaks down, throwing his hands to his face, crying like a child. It is his fear. He is scared, more than scared, terrified.

Terrified of the monster.

Then he says the monster's name. That I *can* hear.

"Simon Dunstable."

Bailey leans back and looks at Kate, congratulatory. They have a witness. They are going to get him. They are going to capture the monster and put him in a cage where he belongs.

My Kate. Rescuer to the untimely dead.

My Kate.

My vision in this dream again fogs over, and I see my Kate. For she is *my* Kate. I can see that now. Why would I ever doubt her?

What has she actually ever done? My mind shows me myself with Julie and loving her and thinking I will never love another woman the way I love her, and then I see Kate and think, but I love her more. I see Kate with Julie and they smile happily, but I know my Kate's eyes. I know it is not all there. I know when she holds back.

I know her because I have the knowing.

It only takes one.

It only takes one special person to wipe out all the hurt and the deceit and the mistrust, and crawl around your heart when you are not looking to lock you in to their love.

Kate is my one. I know this. I have the knowing.

I think of how I have doubted her and I realise this is *my* insecurity, not hers. When you have been lied to once, you always think you are going to be lied to again. No one is different, no one is special, not when you have given your heart to someone that you believe loves you and then they trample all over that love, making a mockery of the things you have held sacred.

Like your heart. If the heart is not a sacred organ to be used wisely, then it is just a tool for fools. A fool who will take your love and use it against you like your enemy would, kicking you where you hurt most.

I am not going to be a fool any more. I am going to stand up for my love. I am going to fight for her. I see Elaine on her steed, shining bright and dazzling me, and I look down at my own armour and I stand proud.

This is one fight you are not going to win. I am going to be there for my love. And maybe I do fight for others before I fight for myself, but is that not the point? Who fights for themselves? Is it not for a greater love that we all fight? Did Jesus not die on the cross because He loved man, so the Bible says?

I will not put myself on any cross but I will open my mouth and I will throw a fist, if necessary, to protect the ones I love.

I wake up.

****

My eyes crisscross as I try to assemble the images, dreams, visions, and make them into a coherent pattern.

I need to get to Logan's mattress. There is evidence there that could convict people, and I realise this is crucial, because Simon Dunstable is on the loose.

I need to tell Kate all of this because… because… Because she needs to know; she is my partner, she is the policewoman who can stop things… Because I love her.

I love her.

I love her and I will do anything for her. I will die for her.

I remember her text. 'Baby, I'm burning'.

I grab my phone and ring Bailey's number, which rings and rings and rings. I should have known better, I think, as the pounding in my head begins anew, thudding.

But he answers, "Bailey". I know why he is tense.

They have got a lead on the number plate, they have followed it up, found one of the cohorts that Simon Dunstable has used in his game. They have arrested him and he has cracked and given them information they need. So the net really is closing in on the child murderer I have seen.

I can see it all now. A man imprisoned for many years, watching and learning from the others, standing beside them to joke and gain their trust and their secrets.

You can change who you are. You can change what you look like. You will always be a monster inside.

"It's Jen," I gush.

"I don't have time for this…" he starts, but I have to butt in.

I do not like swearing. "Fuck it and listen. Kate has lost her phone. I think it's with her ex, Elaine, who is going to try to kill me. Johnny Thunderboots has a girlfriend called Vic Kavanagh. She is a ginger Goth with a big sister called Pamela, and she knew Anne Crawley. They mean to come to my home and behead me.

"Are you listening and writing this down?" I ask, dramatically.

"Mmm" he replies, and I do not know how to take this. I will run on.

"Logan has notes of things you need and it is hidden in his mattress at Kate's flat. Can you tell her I am there and that I am sorry?"

"What notes?

"I don't know! I saw it in a dream last night. I am going to get them now. Just tell my Kate," I say, hanging up.

Every minute now is a race against the clock.

****

I put on my coat, from the hook I had slung it on the night before, and everything is clear.

I pull a wry smile at Rob telling me I have been given the messages. It is for me to read them. I have my glasses on now. I can see clearly.

Logan is going to die if the police do not capture Simon Dunstable. Soon.

I am going to die if the police do not capture Johnny and Vic.

Elaine is going to burn me.

Oh fuck, Elaine is going to burn me. I grab my phone, frantically searching for the time the text came from Kate's phone, knowing now that it was not my Kate but a jealous ex.

Hell hath no fury like a lesbian scorned.

That pounding began in my head and before I knew it, I was inveigled in another person's head.

'Fucking nasty skank. We always said we would be together, forever, no matter what. Look at her. All happy with a boring piece of shit. I am gonna get you back, Kate, no matter what.

'How can you look at me now and not know me, after everything we have gone through?

'Hey Kate, your girlfriend is sleeping on my couch.

'Look at her face contort. She hates it. I love it.

‘Kate she is at the flat, come see.

‘Oh you don’t believe me? Look, I took a photo on my phone. See the date and time.

‘Ha, she sees it now. Why is she so angry with me? Why is she questioning me? Does she not want me in her arms? We laughed about this when we were fourteen, how nothing would come between us. Her rage inspires me and her questions.

‘“How did Jen get there? Why is she asleep on the sofa? Has she said anything?”

‘I look at her, with her green eyes. They were never blue to me. Green eyes are the colour of demons. Like mine.

‘I tell her I cannot wake her sleeping beauty and revel in her concern and worry. When we get into her car, I lean across and kiss her. She pushes me off. I repel her. I will just try harder. She was always one for doing the right thing.

‘I tell her I want her. She says nothing. Driving with her lips pursed tightly shut. “I want to fuck you again,” I say. “I want to rip your clothes off and lick every inch of your body.” She tells me to shut up.

‘When we get into her flat, she sees her boss. I may have forgotten to mention this. It is nice to see the confusion on her face. Oh and the pain and hurt on Jen’s. That almost makes up for the fact that Kate has refused me, yet again.

‘Why does she refuse me? Because that simpering excuse for a woman has claimed her heart? And if she no longer exists, Kate will be free to love me. It seems so simple.

‘The girlfriend has run off. I thought I saw a tear in her eye. Such pleasure I get from this. Freak. She will doubt Kate, she will think Kate loves me.

‘Kate glares at me and I know she does not love me. This slices me in two. I thought forever meant forever.

‘She storms out with her boss. I can smile a bit. She never even noticed my hand stealing into her pocket, when I kissed her, to nick her phone.’

I blink my eyes open. Elaine is full of lies, I know this now. But I do not have time to worry about this. I have to get to the flat and get Logan's notes from his mattress. I have to save his life.

I fasten my coat, almost trip over the fat cat, grab my car keys and run down my stairs, slamming the door shut behind me. I get in the car, praying I have petrol in it, which I do, and set off for Kate's flat, drumming my fingers on the steering wheel at red lights. I have bitten my lip to the point of bleeding, and run my tongue over it.

My headache has gone, I realise, and I let some relief wash over me. This means my Kate is alright, and she is not in danger wherever she is, off chasing some criminals. I can only hope that Bailey has listened to me and passed on my message.

I park the car, unable to get a space in front of her block, and begin to walk quickly down the road until I reach the entry door. I use my key to get in and run up the stairs. I am puffing a bit by the time I get to her floor, and mentally make a note to cut down on the fags, like that is going to happen.

I push my key in her door and let myself in. It is quiet. I cannot hear Elaine in my head, and I make my way straight into Logan's room. It is still a pigsty. I throw the quilt onto a pile of clothes on the floor and take off the top sheet. I wander round, looking for a tear but cannot see anything obvious so retrace with my hands.

Still nothing, so I lift the mattress and instantly see the tear. Yes, I think, a small feeling of triumph flooding me. I am trying to hold the mattress up, bearing the brunt on my shoulder and reach in with my right hand and wiggle it around until my fingertips feel paper and I grab. It is only a small notepad, the kind you would buy at a newsagents. I push my hand back in to make sure I have not missed anything, but there is nothing else.

I move back, letting the mattress fall and open the notepad. It is all there. He has written down everything, in meticulously tidy handwriting.

Without sensing it, I am running my fingers over the writing and in my head. I am moving into Logan's mind.

It has been quiet for so long and I am fucking starving. Those bastards have not given me anything to eat. I suppose there will be less mess from my bowels when they finally kill me. I do not know how long I've been sitting here now and I'm not sure I can feel my feet any longer. I'm not even sure that I care.

I wish they would just kill me and get it over with. They haven't even been in to torture me. Something must be going on. But if they have been arrested, why has no one come for me? Am I going to be left here to starve to death, one less witness?

No. I have to stay positive. I have to trust my colleagues. I have to, or I will have nothing left.

I am almost dozing off when I hear a noise, a door banging downstairs. The thud of boots on the stairs. This is it. I am going to die now. They stop outside my door and I can hear them shouting at each other, but I am so weak that I can barely hear what they are saying and I let my eyes close.

And wait for the second of my life that is going to be the last one.

No!, I think. I have the address now, clasped in my hands. We can get to him. Just give me some time, I pray, unsure of who or what I am praying to.

At that, I hear the door slam behind me and turn quickly around. I am about the blame this on the wind, when the key turns on the outside and locks me in.

'Burn baby burn,
Disco inferno.
Burn baby burn.'

I hear the song in my head and know Elaine is outside, laughing to herself. I run to the door, shaking and turning the handle but it will not budge. I look to the window and immediately dismiss that. I am three floors up, after all.

I reach into my pocket for my phone and realise I have forgotten it. I must have left it on the kitchen table in my rush to get here. What is she doing out there? I can hear furniture being moved and banging, and all the while she is singing the same lines over and over in my head.

I am powerless and trapped and at the mercy of a jealous ex. This does not bode well, I think, frantically trying to work out a way of escape.

"Elaine!" I shout. "Can you let me out, please? I won't tell Kate, it's okay. No one need know. Just unlock the door, please?" I am almost begging.

There is no reply, just the constant repeat of her in my head.

The smell hits me. The smell of burning. The smell of flames. I look down and see the black smoke start to edge its way under the door. I hammer the door with my fists now.

"Elaine! Please open the door! There's smoke coming in and I can't get out! Elaine!"

I am throwing my bodyweight against the door, but it is solid and doesn't move.

I am going to die. She is going to get her wish and burn me to death. Oh God, no, I don't want to die, not like this. Not alone and without Kate beside me. I hammer the door some more in vain and scream her name, begging, pleading, cajoling. There is no bartering with madness, though.

The room is filling up and I begin to cough. I grab the quilt and stuff it at the space at the bottom of the door to try to keep the smoke out. Then I lie on the floor, remembering an old TV advert – smoke rises, doesn't it?

The quilt is beginning to burn. She has set fire to it somehow from her side. I am not going to get out of here. I am going to pass out from the smoke and burn to death in unconsciousness.

Time passes.

I am choking.

I close my eyes and wait for the second that is going to be my last one.

Chapter Thirty-Four

I am standing on the battlefield. Elaine dismounts and takes her sword from its sheath and comes towards me. I look down at my hand and see I also hold a sword.

We are going to fight to the death now.

She smiles, her madness seeping through her smile, reaching her eyes, glinting with hysteria. If it's not one madwoman trying to behead me it's another, I think wearily.

She walks over, stopping a foot away from me and raises her hands to the heavens, screaming. A circle of fire jumps up, trapping us inside its flames.

"Burn, baby, burn" she says.

"No!" I say and lift my sword for this duel.

When you fall in love, you don't see the duels that you have to fight every day. To get over the fear – what if they leave me, what if I get heartbroken? You fight the demons of their past, to win their love and show them that you are worth it, you are the one because it only takes one.

One right love to erase the wrongs of the past.

And now I shall fight again, I think, and swing my sword.

We duel, we thrust, we clash our metals against each other's, the wall of flames growing and making me sweat inside my armour, drips running down my neck.

I am growing weak and fighting harder and harder to hold off her advances as she moves to edge me into the flames. I defend myself once more, the sparks flying from my sword and I stumble backwards, stepping into the flames. The heat immediately sears me and I scream.

My feet are melting and adhering me to the ground, surrounding me in the flames, and I know I am going to die now and Elaine is going to win.

She has taken her helmet off and is laughing at me, a maniacal giggle. I try to get up and feel the scorching pain in my hand as I press down on the fire.

I am about to close my eyes and give in when I hear another horse approaching. I look up and see it leap over the flames and land, then rear. Another suit of armour steadies the animal and jumps off. She takes her helmet off and I see with delight that it is Kate.

She has come to do battle for me and save me. She comes to me and pulls me from the flames like I am a feather, weightless to her strength. Her touch instantly cools me and I catch my breath when she smiles at me. That beautiful smile, reserved for special moments, that only I ever see. She is showing Elaine that I am the recipient of her love, that I am the one she will fight for, will rescue, will stand side by side with.

She holds my hand, her gauntlet gripping mine, and walks over to Elaine. With our hands locked, we push her and she falls over. Kate smiles at me again, and leads me out of the circle of flames, untouchable, with our love to protect us.

I cannot help but turn back, like Lot's wife, and see Elaine smouldering, burnt by her own flames.

And I realise it is not me who has rescued Kate, her belief from her own nightmare, but Kate who has finally rescued me.

****

I wake up in a hospital bed with an oxygen mask on, and feel that my hand is being held. I focus my eyes onto my Kate and try to muster a smile, the movement causing me to break into a coughing spasm.

I can see she has been crying, and my heart breaks with the love I feel for her, and my shame that I could ever have doubted the one person who truly loves me. The woman who lives with me, sees all my faults and still only has nothing but devotion shining from her eyes at me.

"Don't speak, baby," she says. "You've inhaled quite a bit of smoke but you're okay, don't worry. And yes," she smiled. "The cat's been fed."

I knew she was trying to make me feel better, and the tears sprang into my eyes. It is hard to be faced with a wall of complete and utter love and not marvel at how wonderful it is, how lucky you are.

"Jesus, Jen," she broke down, and I saw how hard she had been struggling to keep it together, to stay strong for me. Sometimes even Kate did not always win the fight. "Why is it always you? Do you know how close you were to being dead? I couldn't…"

Her voice gave up and she started to cry, putting her head down on the bed, on top of her two hands that were clasping mine. She cried so hard I felt my hand grow wet.

She looked up at me, her eyes red, her face plastered with tears, a few blotches beginning to show. She never looked more beautiful to me than when she revealed herself.

I ached to say something to her, to make it better, but I felt like a weight was laid across my chest.

"I couldn't live without you," she went on. "I have no idea what goes on in your head half the time, and I'm not even sure I want to know, but I fucking love you. You're my world."

I nodded. I wanted to say "It's okay, baby, I know."

"This is the third time you have been in hospital, and I don't know how much more I can take. You need to start letting me look after you. I'll protect you," she smiled, through a mist of tears.

"Elaine," I croaked, and immediately began coughing again.

She knew what I meant, and I knew making her talk would detract from her pain.

"She's in custody, charged with arson and attempted murder. Do you want to know what happened, how you got out?"

I nodded, very gingerly, frightened I would bring on another spasm of choking.

"I got your message from John through my car radio. He asked me to ring in, and when I did he told me what you had told him on the phone and that you had gone to my flat. So, I raced over but the fire brigade were already there. I think a neighbour had seen or smelled smoke and had called them. Of course I was frantic and went bombing up the stairs, flashing my badge to get through.

"The firemen had already bust my front door down and had the hoses on in the hallway. Half my furniture was up in flames. I don't actually remember how I got in but I did, and made them burst the door to Logan's room because I knew that was where you would be. Ever trying to be the good citizen you, eh?" she smiled, and her eyes sparkled from her tears.

I nodded as best I could for her to go on.

"The place was black with smoke. It was hard to see, but I was screaming for them to check his room, knowing you were there. And there you were, my lovely, passed out on the floor, clutching a notepad to your chest." She buried her head on the bed again and I let her.

I knew she had to get this out of her system, and it had to be now. My Kate was never one for looking back at the past. Why would she look at her past when the future could only be better?

I looked at the back of her head, watching the quiet movements of her sobs and let my own tears run freely. How could I have doubted her?

She had lied to me twice.

And now I could see why.

She had lied to me about Julie but I didn't care. It was her past and had no bearing on us, or our relationship. Maybe she did think I would save her in some nightmare she had, but it did not stop her looking at me with love in her eyes, it did not stop her being there every single time that I needed her. It never made her unfaithful, like Julie had been; it just made her more sensitive to the hurts of the past that continue to haunt us in our present, and I could never blame her for that.

And she lied to me about Logan. But that was her job and now that I knew the full extent of why she had lied about that, I would never hold that against her. It could have put his life in danger, and maybe mine, if I had known what had really been going on. That Logan was an undercover police officer, sent to Glasgow to snare a murderer, a perpetrator of a possible paedophile ring, a cold-blooded killer.

My Kate, protecting me in every way she could from the pains in life that she bore and that I did not need to. Her strength, shown in my dream when she jumped the flames and saved me, was quiet but always there, like the morning sun rising.

She had done nothing to make me doubt her; she had quietly gone about loving me. Maybe sometimes so quiet that I could not hear, but I had so many other voices in my head, how do you ever know what is the right one to listen to?

The one.

You listen to the one. I knew that now. I had the knowing.

She lifted her head, sniffing and wiped her eyes and nose.

"Sorry," she said. "It's just hard sometimes to…" I squeezed her hand, again trying to tell her that I knew. "To think what could have happened. God, thank fuck you phoned John."

She looked at me, searching my face.

"Shall I keep going?" she said. I nodded. "I got the paramedics to come in and get you, and while they were attending to you, I searched the rest of the flat. I knew Elaine had to be there somewhere and hey, guess where the mad fuck was? Lying in the bath, fully clothed. I punched her in the face, I couldn't help myself, and then I called for back up and had the bitch arrested. I couldn't do it. I couldn't face the paperwork, having to write her name again and again – it's bad enough I'll have to go to court and testify.

"Fuck. Shit, are you okay? Is this upsetting you?" I squeezed her hand again.

What about Logan?, I thought. Had they got him yet? I tug on her, keep going I will her.

"You don't need to worry about her any more. And I got my phone back. She must've nicked it from me, I saw the message she sent to you." She shakes her head. "You think you know someone, and all the time, they are as mad as the March hare. But she won't get away with using madness as her excuse; this was premeditated. The boss will make sure she goes down for a long time. She will never hurt you again."

Logan, darling, Logan! I think, somewhat ironically, if only she knew sign language I could have finger spelled his name out to her. A language I had attempted to save lives could have saved another one.

"Logan!" I can bear it no longer and shout it as best I can.

I see her inhale and avert her eyes. My heart sinks.

"I came here with you in the ambulance, and I read Logan's notes on the way. While you were being treated, I rang my boss and I told him what was in it. There was another address, different from the house I had gone to where Simon Dunstable entertained with Logan. I got a call a few hours ago to say we had found him, but darling, he's not in a very good condition. He has been starved of food and fluids, beaten and tortured. He was unconscious and he has not come round yet. We don't know the full extent of the damage yet. But he's not dead, and while he's alive, there is always hope."

There *is* always hope and I did not fear. I *knew* he would live. It was alright now. I never saw him dead and he wasn't. Logan was alive because I had found his notes in time, and the right people had believed me. They had sprung into action, and with every second counting, had found him in time. As he had always believed in his heart because he had hope, too.

I smiled. Perhaps this could be a good day, after all.

"We are still looking for Simon. He has disappeared but we will get him. No one can hide forever. His scar-faced crony has blabbed his mouth off. We have all the evidence, just not him. But, if I have to hunt the corners of this earth for the next fifty years, I am going to get that fucking scumbag, don't you worry."

There it was. Her grit and determination, her passion to get the bad guy and her unwavering belief that she would.

Some of the things I loved about her. I looked into her eyes and held her gaze, and I felt it, that mental connection you get with someone when your love goes beyond the physical and the mental and becomes all-encompassing. It surpasses the ordinary to become extraordinary, to be the love that you never think you will find, except in books. But it was real, and it was mine and hers. When your breath is taken away by the sheer depth of that emotion that words will never properly describe, and all you can do is marvel at how lucky you are to have finally found something that makes your life matter.

She made my life matter. She believed in me and she loved me, and she would always be there. That was all I needed.

Kate's phone rang and she took one hand off mine to search for it in her jacket pocket, where it always absent-mindedly dwelt, and she flipped it open. I saw her face scrunch into the concerned look she wore all too often these days and say, "I'm on my way", before flipping her phone shut.

"I have to go, baby, but I'll be back later. Try to get some sleep, okay? Do you want me to bring anything?"

I shook my head. She leaned in and kissed me on the forehead and before I could stop myself, I grabbed at her arm.

Sheena. Sheena.

A fleeting image of Kate's mother and the moment passed.

"I love you," she said, as she left the room.

I fell asleep and dreamt I was a man.

I am nineteen years old and I am walking down the street, smoking a cigarette, puffing out my chest like the hard man I am. I see my girl and smile. She is getting it tonight. It's Friday and her ma and pa will be at the Labour Club, and we will have the house to ourselves. Apart from that annoying cunt of a wee sister, but I have a bag of sweeties to bribe her with. All is well and I go over to my girl and plant a smacker on her cheek. She's only fifteen and loves that I am the older guy, looking out for her. We stand and prattle with her mates until it's time to go back and babysit her wee sister, and we walk back to her tenement, holding hands.

Her parents are waiting, edgy at the front door, moaning at us for being late, desperate to get to the pub for their pints of bitter and gin and tonics. Her faither gives me a look and tells me to behave. I smile, ever the gentleman, and think I could cut him in half.

We get in and I check the fridge to see if her old man has left any beer and find a bottle, which I open over the dish-laden sink, the stench of tomato sauce momentarily nauseating me. I see my girl follow me in and look at the pile of dishes, apologising with her eyes at the mess, and rolling up her sleeves to begin to tidy up. Her parents are filthy alcoholic pigs.

I sit in her old man's chair and switch on the radio, lifting his paper. I can take my time to read and relax while she cleans up. Her wee sister comes in and rushes over to give me a cuddle. She knows I always have a wee treat for her. I lift her onto my lap and take out my poke of sugary delights, seeing her face light up. There is nothing nicer than seeing a smile on the face of an innocent, I think, bouncing her up and down. She will go to sleep nicely for me now, and I take her off to bed, tucking her in and saying she can eat the rest of her treats in the morning if she sleeps all night and doesn't get back up.

My girl is finished with her chores when I come back into the living room, stale with old tobacco, and I walk over and kiss her. She opens to me, so pure and full of adoration. I could do anything to her, I think, but I won't. Not yet. I'll make her mine first.

I take her into her parent's bedroom and lie her down. She is shy, but she knows this has been coming and she doesn't protest too much, a small whimper and tensing, but my whispers of love relax her and I have my fill. When I am done, she brings my beer in and goes into the loo to wash herself. She says she hurts a little, which is a shame, because I am going to have her again in a bit. I am going to teach her what I like and how to pleasure me, and she is going to do it all because she is my girl now and there is never going to be any getting out of that.

I moan in my dream.

"What do you mean, you're fucking pregnant?" I scream at her. Stupid bitch. Did I have to do everything? She's crying and saying sorry, she doesn't know how it happened.
"Well, I'll show you how it happened", and I push her onto my bed and say, "This is how it fucking happened!" before I rip her pants and ram myself into her.

She will move in with me, and she can clean my house while I go out and earn a living to look after her and the wean. It's the way of the world. I can get a job at the shipyard in Govan. I know a gaffer there and he owes me one.

Her parents are not pleased, but we quickly arranged a ceremony at the registry office and got hitched. My hair was perfect in its Teddy Boy quiff. I bought her a new dress that would hide her bump. We all got pissed and her old man slapped me on the back. He made me feel sick. I was not going to end up like him. I was going to do better for myself. I would have a nice house, and a nice car and nice clothes. I wouldn't stink of bitter and roll-ups.

Five months later and I was holding my daughter in my arms. A little scrawny mass that looked at me with quiet eyes. I would name her Katherine, after my mother.

Five years later, and I am worn down by the drudgery of my life. Get up, go to work, go for a pint, come home to that moaning face wife and a wean that shies away from me. No wonder I am never in.

No fucking wonder I dream of a different life.

****

When I was discharged from the hospital, Kate took the day off work and spent it chasing around the flat after me. It was all very kind of her, but I would have rather she had been out there looking for Simon Dunstable or Johnny Thunderboots and his ginger girlfriend. I could tell she was distracted, and every now and then, she would go into the kitchen on the pretence of making me a cup of tea, but I could hear her squawking down the phone at some poor recipient.

She came back through to where I was lying on the sofa, resplendent with the remote control and plonked another cup of tea down. She made a shit nurse, but her heart was in the right place.

"Do you want anything, babe – a sandwich?" she asked.

"Yes, I do want something. I want you to find my Butterfly Explosion CD and put number five on and sit and hold my hand through the whole song, and then I want you to piss off to work – you're doing my head in," I laughed, trying not to cough a bit.

She gave me that pretend irked look and went over to the CD player to do as she was told. I loved it when I found a song that made me stop everything I was doing to listen to it and be mesmerised, and what better way than to be mesmerised, both with music and a beautiful woman. My senses of sight and sound were fulfilled.

She knelt on the floor and lay her head on my chest. I stroked her hair as I let the waves of guitar and love wash over me. Love is not something you can seal in a moment, but if it was, I would have sealed it right there in that instant. That one moment where everything is right in the world and all you can feel is a softness inside that takes you to another place. A moment you would kill for.

A moment that is always over way too soon.

As soon as I had managed to cajole Kate into leaving me, and that I would be fine, and yes the door was locked, my phone was right next to me, and no, I wouldn't let anyone in, I rang her mother.

"Sheena, it's Jen. How are you?"

"Jen, bloody hell, are you alright, hen? I've been trying your phone, but it keeps going to answering machine."

I knew she would've seen on the news what had happened. Kate had tried to keep it out the papers, but reporters love a good story and a cop's lesbian ex trying to burn to death her new girlfriend was just too good to pass. Luckily, Kate had kept them away from me and the hospital, and had only just given me my phone back after blocking a load of numbers, which I hadn't even known I could do.

"I'm fine, Sheena, honestly – it's all a mountain out of a molehill. Can I come and see you today?"

I knew Kate would absolutely kill me if she knew, but it was something I had to do. There was a pulse beating in the back of my mind, and I knew it was connected to Sheena.

"Aye, hen, of course you can. I'm going nowhere. Are you sure you're up for it?"

"Yes. I'll see you in an hour."

"Right then, I better go get some milk for the tea, Jenny," she laughed.

I threw the blanket off me and shoved my phone in my jeans pocket. I looked at the packet of cigarettes with a deep desire and craving – it had been days since I'd had a fag and Kate had said I couldn't have any, but by God, I was gasping – and grabbed them, shoving them in my handbag. I looked around for a lighter and realised she had hidden them, or thrown them out – but I had a car lighter, I thought, that would do. The wiles of a desperate smoker will always outdo the un-infested brain of the non-smoker.

An hour or so later, I was pulling up at Sheena's house, a bit lightheaded after my first smoke and thinking that it did actually smell a bit, but oh, that was so much better, even if my mouth did taste like an ashtray. I'll be fine after the second one, I thought to myself, and tottered up the path.

She greeted me at the door, with her usual overpowering hug that made me cough a wee bit and induce a load of apologies, before she sat me down and went to make a cup of tea. I wanted to see the photo of Kate's dad that she had found for me.

We made small talk until I could stand it no more. I knew it wouldn't be long before Kate rang to check I was okay, and she would have a pink fit if she knew I had left the house.

"Sheena, do you remember saying you had found a photo of Kate's dad? Would it be okay if I saw it now?" I asked, almost meekly.

But I was scared suddenly and I did not know why. I don't like not knowing the reason for a fear. 'Confront it' was always my motto. Hiding never solved it, and hiding never lasted. Fears always find you.

"Sure, hen, I'll go get it. I put it in the drawer for you."

She heaved herself from the chair and went into the kitchen, where I could hear her riffling in a drawer, and then she came back, clutching a ragged photo.

I took it from her, thanking her, and set my cup down on the table in front of me. I held the photo in two hands and looked at it.

A young man and an even younger woman on their wedding day, black and white, battered and torn. I focused my eyes and they began to get nearer and nearer to the man's. Until I could see him in colour, standing before me, the arrogance never lost in his smile.

"Will you shut that fucking wean up?" I screamed. It was always the same. Every night. Screaming, crying. How is a man supposed to get any peace? The woman was on me, grabbing at my arms but I was going to shut it up. Little Katherine standing watching me with her cold eyes as I toss the wean to the other side of the room, drunk, screaming words I don't remember.

I killed her. I killed my own kid and I went to Barlinnie. The Bar-L. The best move I ever made. That is where I shared a cell with a man who would teach me all I know.

"Be who you want to be, and when you believe it, others will," he said. "There's money to be made in films and kids. Look into it when you get out, give me a call."

I watched his ass, literally, and he remembered that. Your ass is all you can look after in the clink. I watched and I learned; there was nothing else to do. I threw off the old me and embraced a new man. I read books, I learned, and I read more books.

I told my wife to forget me and rejected her pleas to visit me. She was part of the old. I would not be looking back.

When I got out, I went to see my new friend and he greeted me with welcoming arms. His ass had never been penetrated because my size had seen off any suitors. A man does not forget that sort of kindness and he showed me how to make money. He taught me how to speak without a thick Glasgow accent and when I was ready and had enough money, he sent me to his specialist and I had my surgery. No one would know me now. I truly was a new man.

We parted on good terms and I went my own way to set up my own business. I hooked up with another man I had met in jail, my scar-faced friend and we started to film. Prostitutes at first, who would do anything for some money and a bit of junk. I sold my videos to a contact in Amsterdam and that went well for a while and I made a bit of dosh.

I could afford the nice clothes and nice house and nice cars that I had dreamt of, but I couldn't be with a woman again. I was sickened at what they would do, how they would degrade themselves. I began to like my prey a little more delicate and fresh.

And then the money really began to roll in. I can rub my hands with glee as I see the small, pathetic, tear stained faces crying their last desperate cries. It never takes much to shut up a wean.

And they all shut up eventually.

"Jen! Jen! Wake up, doll!"

I flicked my eyes open to see the frantic face of Sheena. I had passed out, I knew.

I looked again at the photo, still gripped in my fingers.

Kate's dad.

Simon Dunstable, the monster.

Chapter Thirty-Five

I looked into Sheena's eyes, the sad, wrinkled eyes of a sixty-year-old alcoholic, fighting for every day to stay off drink and to find a way back into the closed heart of her eldest child. She had married a monster, still a child herself and had paid a heavy price. I would never know the demons that drove her to drink away her life and any chance of happiness. The procession of man after man, trying to find one to fill the void. A child brain damaged, a child dead, a child who hated her. What kind of chance did this poor woman ever have at life, all because when she was fifteen a beast laid his eye on her and decided she would do?

I wanted to put my arms around her and call her mum, and tell her she could have one person to love. I think having one person to love would have made it all worthwhile for her. Some people in life need to be loved, and others need to love. Sheena was a giver of love. You could tell by the way she never wanted anything back. Maybe I saw her through rose-tinted glasses. I hadn't lived with her, I admit, but time changes people. We learn lessons or we repeat our mistakes – it's as simple as that. I think I could see that she was trying to learn and make amends.

So, I would have to be gentle. Her hold on sanity was fragile, and I could not break that feeble grip.

"Sheena, you've never heard off Kate's dad?"

"Naw, hen," she said sadly, sitting back down, reassured that I was not about to collapse again. "When he went to the jail, he wouldnae let me visit him. I tried for a good few years, but there's only so much rejection you can take, you know." Her gaze drifted off into the distance, remembering.

"Was his mother called Katherine?" I asked.

She looked at me, surprised, that same look I had grown used to seeing. Then I saw the penny drop, again as I so often saw when people realised how I knew. "Aye hen, Katherine is his mother's name. Bless her."

"She's dead then?" I don't know what made me ask that and the words were out before I had a chance to stop myself.

"Not that I know of. I go see her every noo and then, she's not too far away from me – well, a wee bus ride but I've got ma bus pass noo. Eighty nine, she is," she admitted, with a hint of pride.

"Where exactly is it she lives? Could you write the address down for me?" How do I tread cautiously?, I thought. I didn't want to alarm her.

"What's this all about, hen?" Her eyebrows knitted together as she regarded me.

"Sheena, you are going to have to trust me. Will you trust me?" I pleaded, softly insistent.

I saw her lift her chin to face me. "If Kate trusts you, then I trust you."

"What was his name when you were married?"

I don't think it was the question she was expecting but she answered. "Ian. Ian Coutts. Why are you asking all these questions? Has something happened?"

I resisted the urge to get up and hold her arm and see what she saw. Some things are best left unseen.

"Do you still love him?"

Her eyes didn't lie. "Aye hen, I suppose I do. I was married at sixteen, pregnant with Kate. I fell in love with good looks and a swagger. It didn't last long, hen – he was a bastard. Never happy. The hoose was never clean enough, the weans never quiet enough. His temper could turn on the toss of a coin. I don't know how many black eyes and split lips I had, but you keep going, don't you? That's what you did in those days. You take the punch and you change the wean's nappy, and you hope the next day is a bit better."

I felt the outpouring of sadness in her voice and there was nothing I could do about it. A life ago she made her choices, as we all do, and sometimes those choices haunt us for the rest of our lives, shaping us and creating their own future of despair.

"Did he ever hurt Kate?" I can't help myself. I have to know.

"No," she says, lowering her eyes. "He never touched the weans until…."

Until he threw your baby across the room, killing her, I finished in my head.

"I'm sorry," I say, with real sympathy. I know what it's like to lose a child you love. I can remember my vision of her and Kate standing over the small coffin being lowered into the ground, and realise it never goes away. You learn to get on with life, but you never forget. Always in your heart there is that tug and emptiness for the memories that should have been created.

And occasionally, you will see someone walk past and a small, insignificant gesture will trigger some false memory. A trick of the brain. "That was the day Jonah first went to a zoo." I would never have those memories and my heart ached gently, as it always did. But I'd also never have the scene burned in my mind of my small child being thrown against a wall. How could you continue to love a man who would do that?

She stood in the rain, holding Kate's hand, watching her baby's coffin being lowered into the muddy ground. They had stood alone and faced the pain together. In their pain they had turned away from each other, and forgotten the reason they had stood alone together. United in their grief, a monster drove them apart, divided in their loss.

Apart in their grief, a monster could bring them back together.

As I dithered in my mind, twisting and turning over the possibilities and consequences my words could incite, I saw a figure from the corner of my eye.

Rob was leaning against the frame of Sheena's kitchen door, his handsome smile gone, and a resolute frown in place.

"You're right, Jen," he said and only I could hear him.

Sheena looked blankly, staring ahead at her window, locked in her nightmares. I tried to subtly shrug and tilted my eyebrows up, as if to say, 'What? What am I right about?'

"They need to be united again, and you can do it."

How?

"Remember, it's all about Kate." Yes, I *knew* that! "There are things written that cannot be unwritten. Events that have to happen, and you're the catalyst to set off this chain reaction."

I began to feel the familiar gnaw of dread. I shook my head. What if I didn't want to be this spark? What would I be setting off?

"You don't have a choice, Jen – this is pre-determined. Like Jonah being here. Like me being here. There's nothing you can do about it. You have to tell Sheena what happened to her husband, and you needn't worry about how she'll cope. It's not her time yet. She has a purpose to fulfil. And if you don't tell her, it won't change the future. The path will just alter and adjust, but you have been chosen for this. Whether you like it or not, you have accepted this."

I sat for a moment, watching the loneliness on Sheena's face and moved my eyes back to Rob. I nodded.

Now he smiled. "Your work is nearly done for a while. But I'll be seeing you again soon. One more thing – you need a mirror."

How ridiculous, I thought, I have mirrors all over my flat. Mirrors that I could barely bring myself to look at, Damian's words ringing every time I went near one. "You can see the dead in them." If I had ever disbelieved, I no longer did. I had seen too many dead.

Rob spoke again. "There's a shop called Boon's – it's down an alley at the bottom of Argyle Street. Go in and ask for a scrying mirror. And do it today."

I rolled my eyes. Jesus, these ghosts never ask for much, do they? Tell your girlfriend's mother that her child-murdering husband had plastic surgery and built an empire based on snuff movies and child pornography. Oh, and go fetch a mirror. I wondered sarcastically if he could add a bottle of wine to this list.

"One last thing," he added. Wine, I thought hopefully, because when this day was over, I was going to need a large glass. "Don't buy anything else. No matter how much you're offered."

He laughed, seeing the exasperation plain on my face. "I am amazed by you, Jen. Your trust in me goes beyond life and death."

It has to.

"Do what I've told you." He turned to leave. A ghost who wanted to make an exit. He looked back over his shoulder. "Jonah says, 'Hi mummy'."

That was all it took. The tears blinded me in seconds and when I blinked, Rob had gone, disappeared back into his world I can only glimpse in my dreams.

My baby, my baby, I cried out, screamed in my head.

Sheena turned, catching my distress and pushed herself up from her chair. I fleetingly noticed that she had aged. Somehow, in my mind, she was always that peroxide blonde, drenched in a cemetery, twenty-odd years ago.

She held me in her arms and I sobbed for a child lost. My child that I sometimes found in my dreams. That made dreaming a risk I was prepared to take if it meant one glance of my beloved. My boy. That I would never hold.

Sheena said nothing, but continued to hold me as I struggled to regain my composure.

A strange thing happened then.

I was holding myself, smelling the Dove soap on my skin and thinking how I longed to hold my baby once more. It took me a few seconds to realise that I was Sheena. I was inside her head, but I was still me and the confusion became a fog that love would have to lift.

I shut my eyes. Sheena shut her eyes.

I let my mind roam.

I heard it all. Every last beautiful thought, every last poisoned image. I let the incoherent jumble find its way into me and I listened. An echo.

Echoes that could open a heart that was closed.

My little girl. My Katherine. Thirty six hours of pain, a screaming agony, worth it for my firstborn. My little girl. That I would do anything for. That I would die for.

Thump. Hit me, bastard, hit me. I stand in front of the cot. Hit me again. Don't you hit my Katherine. I stood it all for her. I would stand anything for her.

Then, my Elizabeth. My beautifully shy, absurdly funny Lizzie, who followed Katherine everywhere, pulling on her pants until we all laughed. Even him. He could not touch Katherine, but Elizabeth was bounced and coddled and loved. Her smile could melt the coldest hearts and he loved her. I never saw him so happy. He was never the same after her accident – it changed him and not for the better. The one good thing he had held onto was gone.

And lastly, my precious Amy. The jewel to complete my crown. My trinity of love.

I felt a strangled sob begin in my throat. Sheena's throat.

How did I go so wrong? How did I let them all down? Drink? Was it the drink? How many times can you be battered and raped before you shut down and the numbness takes over? It numbs you to everything, even the love of your kids. There was no way out – there never is. You get married, you stay married, that's how we were brought up. He throws a fist, you take the punch.

My poor Lizzie. I thought it was her that went first but Katherine had already left me by then. Where had I been? Out on some drunken escapade, trying to keep him happy, trying to keep the money coming in from him to feed my girls. My Katherine, the sensible, quiet, contained one, looking after her sisters.

Coming in the door. Running. A neighbour shouting for us. My Lizzie lying there. A crumpled heap at the bottom of the stairs. On floorboards because we couldn't afford carpets. Her eyes rolling in her head. Her arms and legs, twitching and jerking in movements unfamiliar.

Brain-dead.

I opened my mouth to scream, and in that instant my eyes met Kate's, standing over her fitting sister, holding baby Amy in her arms, and she silenced me with one cool stare.

Her eyes told me I had failed her.

Oh, child, if you think I failed you then, that was nothing, was it? When I stood there, like a statue, and let him take our Amy.

I can't say the words, even to myself.

I held your hand in the rain, when we said our goodbyes and you looked at me with those dead eyes of yours. I knew then I would never be good enough for you. No matter how often we went to see Lizzie, trying to make her remember, trying to make her smile, trying to get anything, something from her.

I wonder just who is the brain-dead daughter.

All I had to hold onto was my Katherine, and she turned away at every chance. I could never embrace her again. She looked at me with those eyes, the same way she had looked at him. It killed me – the pain overtook me and the only way I knew to get rid of that pain was to drink, to numb away my agony.

I tried to reach out but she was too far away.

My little girl. My Katherine.

Echoes of the past, playing out, over and over. Never resolved. Seeking an ending. How do you end a lifetime of agony? How do you take this damage and undo it?

In my own head, I thought, Give them a bond back. Give them the love back. The bond between a mother and child is never truly broken. Despite time, despite pain, despite distance.

There are not many things in life you can take for granted but you can always count on your mother's love.

Make her see again, I thought – me, Jen.

I was yanked back into Sheena's head, an invisible, psychic tug I was powerless to resist.

The years have passed, the distance has grown between us but the pain, the pain has never ended. I would do anything, *anything,* to make up for this lifetime of anguish. To have my child, my daughter, hold my hand and tell me she loved me.

Her honey hands.

I've seen her hide her broken heart,. I've seen her be abused. I've seen her hate me and loathe me and despise me because I was too weak. I wanted her to love me and then I could love her back.

I only wanted someone to love.

I just looked in the wrong places, fuelled by appetites I didn't know how to control, and men who promised me love and gave me a void.

There was a void inside me and it filled with the love of my children. And when my children were taken away, I was emptied again.

Now, emptiness is a way of life, but while I have my Katherine, I have hope.

With hope, anything is possible. Dreams can be realised.

My dream is to have my Katherine love me again. Like that one day, when she was by my side and we stood united in grief.

I could die happily knowing she forgave me.

My head snapped back to my own, tears still running down my cheek, mingling with Sheena's.

I knew now.

I had the knowing again.

I took her face in my hands and I spoke to her. I told her how Ian Coutts became Simon Dunstable. How he took pleasure in the suffering of others to make money and feed his deviant desires. I told her of all my dreams and visions, ignoring the awe on her face. I told her about a young boy tortured to death and I told her about my friend, Logan. I kept telling her in spite of her cries and sobs, because she had to hear. I told her she was going to make a difference.

That difference would win back Kate's love.

And that was all it took.

There is a thin line between belief and despair.

Between love and hate.

Between hope and oblivion.

Where there is hope, there is belief, and where there is belief, there is hope.

I had given Sheena hope. There was no better gift I could have given her.

****

I drove home after checking my phone for messages from Kate. There were none, and I was relieved. I was already drained, and comforting her through her fears was something I could do without. She was better off occupied at her work, searching for that bad guy.

That bad guy who was her daddy.

Without realising where I was going, I headed into the city centre of Glasgow and found myself parking in the St. Enoch centre. I walked, in the rain, a weight removed. I followed my instincts down Argyle Street, Rob's words in my head.

Find a mirror.

You can see the dead in mirrors.

Why would I need to look in a mirror to see the dead when I could see them without effort in my dreams? I trusted Rob. He looked after my son in the afterlife.

There is no greater trust than that.

I found the shop called Boon's. It looked decrepit and run down, cobwebs in the corners of the windows, thick with years of dirt and dust, making it impossible to see in. A worn sign bearing the word 'Open' did not invite, but dared you to step in.

I stepped in, jumping at the bell, ringing over my head as the door opened. To my left and right were displays hidden behind locked glass doors, a counter connecting the walls of wares.

Behind the counter was a closed door. I had no interest in finding out what was behind that door. My eyes roamed and I realised this was no ordinary shop, and I became sure if I walked down this same street tomorrow that it would no longer exist.

Because magic and the supernatural have a deadline.

I peered through the glass doors to my left, shelf upon shelf of oddities. A rabbit's paw that looked like it might twitch, a jar of liquid with eyeballs staring back at me, a wand with secret writings etched on it. An embryo floated and moved under the green glare of the fitted lights, its oversized head mocking me.

"Can I help you?" a voice said, startling me. I jumped again. I had not heard the door open or seen the wizened man appear at the counter.

I gathered myself. "I need a mirror," I said, trying to hide the edge in my voice.

He regarded me, with his rat eyes. "Any particular type of mirror?"

"Just… a mirror," I replied.

His eyes narrowed into a sort of smile and he clasped his hands together, in prayer, in front of his chest. "I have the very mirror for someone like you. One moment, please," he said, retreating into the sanctum behind his door.

I shivered. This shop gave me the heebie-jeebies. I tried not to look around and focussed on innocuous incense sticks.

Within minutes, he returned, tenderly holding a mirror, with black glass, about the size of my face, framed in gold. "This is a scrying mirror. It's ready for you. It's £75."

"Take Visa?"

After I had paid, and he was putting my mirror in bubble wrap, he said, "I have something else that might interest you."

'Don't buy anything else. No matter how much you're offered.'

"No thanks. I'm done here," I tried to smile.

"No one is ever done here in one visit," he grinned, and I saw he had no top teeth. "Let me show you. You'll want this one day." It was almost a sneer.

I grabbed the mirror and began to walk backwards, toward the door. He pulled a skull from under the counter.

"This is for you. I've been saving it."

I shook my head and turned, grabbing the door handle, my hand slipping and twisting.

“You’ll be back one day, Miss,” he said to my retreating figure, as my grasp finally took hold, and I opened the door to flee.

I could not get home soon enough, via the corner shop for a bottle of wine. I’d face Kate’s wrath for that one, but at this point, I didn’t care. When I got in I opened the bottle, pouring a large glass, fed the fat cat who was determined to trip me up, giving me seven years bad luck from a shattered mirror – as if I did not have enough bad luck already.

I took the wrap off the mirror and looked into its black reflection.

A scrying mirror. I had not asked for that. I had asked for a mirror, but I had seen one of these before.

A twinge of light shadowing my outline. It was very much like the mirror Johnny Thunderboots had.

Oh God, Johnny Thunderboots. I had forgotten about him. How could I keep forgetting? When would I learn the lessons of the past?

I rang Kate. Typically, no answer, so I sent her a text message. ‘Hey babe, no rush but can you pop home when you have a minute? X’

I sat back on the couch, eyeing the mirror that I had leant against the CD player, wondering why I needed it today.

What more could happen in a single day?

I sipped some wine and decided when I got up for a refill, I would go find my notepad and see what clues were floating around. As I sipped, no, guzzled my wine, the door knocked. She’s forgotten her keys, I thought, and absent-mindedly got up, talking another gulp of my wine.

I trotted down the hall, eager to tell my girlfriend of the revelations I had encountered today.

I opened the door to the grins of Johnny Thunderboots and Vic Kavanagh.

Chapter Thirty Six

When you open a door, you never know what is waiting for you on the other side. You might think you do, but nothing is ever the same from when you closed that door behind you. Everything changes the moment the latch catches at your back. Things, people, images you thought were certain and immoveable become blurred, flipping into a different reality. A reality you can only see in your dreams.

And if you are me, your dreams become your reality and you open that door, unleashing monsters and demons. Nothing ever prepares you for that. No one tells you that opening the door to your dreams can unleash your nightmares.

How do you face a nightmare?

When you fall in love, you open the door to your heart. A door you closed at the end of the last failed relationship. Slammed. But then everything changes when you fall in love. You forget the pain and the hurt, the heartbreak and the rejection. A new love creeps in, different from the last, and the room behind your closed door has changed. Your unalterable heart has altered. How can it be? How can the object we treasure most deceive us and slyly change behind our backs?

Because behind every door, a love lies. You just have to open that door. Was I brave enough? A heart broken by Julie, sleeping with another woman in my bed, taking my love and throwing it in the rubbish bin. I thought I had slammed that door shut forever, until a smile, the cut of a well-tailored suit and a hidden vulnerability became a key to unlock that padlocked door. Because it was padlocked, and nailed, and stapled, and who could get in there? Who could take magic wiles and find their key?

My Kate. That's who.

I never knew she was waiting for me when I had opened the door in my old blue pyjamas and inhaled her perfume.

I never knew.

Is the knowing the quiet voice of the heart?

For a long time I have questioned many things, but I can question no more. I have allowed her to find her key and let it mould itself in the shape that my heart required to open it. How many people can say that? How many people can know that one person will always be there for them, no matter what?

Lovers come and lovers go, hearts fall in love and hearts break and hearts mend. But it only takes one to hold that special key, unlocking all the chambers of the heart. When you know someone has that key, you love and trust implicitly. You trust with your life. Sometimes your life is all you can trust with, and when your life is on the line, you have to trust that the people you love will stand beside you.

What meaning has life if you stand alone? We all want someone to stand with us, to confirm we are not alone.

I wish I had known that when I opened the door to my heart, to my flat.

I opened the door to the grinning faces of Johnny Thunderboots and Vic Kavanagh, their grins extensions of their madness. I think that is when I passed out.

****

It is my wedding day. I am standing at the altar, the butterfly explosion evident in my stomach, fighting the weakness in my legs. Standing in the front of the registrar in the dress of my dreams.

Of my dreams!

My thin veil masking the fear on my face. Why should I be scared to get married? You love, you marry. Isn't that what people do? Why this fear then? Standing at the altar is what I have worked towards with my love for Kate, and I have no doubts in my mind about spending the rest of my life with her. So, what then? What frightens me so much?

I look around me at the seated faces. My sister and her boyfriend, Logan, my aunt and uncle, Damian and Sasha. I let my eyes rest on Damian.

"I told you to say 'No'," she mouths.

I felt my heart rise in my chest. Why would I say 'No' to the woman I loved?

I continue to scan the room and realise there is no sign of Sheena or Kate. I hunt with my eyes, trying to find them and my panic begins to rise. I see Rob, sitting alone at the back. He takes a match and strikes it off the pew in front of him.

"Third strike and out," he mouths and disappears.

It is time to wake up.

****

I wake up to find myself lying on my living-room carpet and, as my sight begins to focus, I home in on the fat cat, who is watching me from the comfort of an easy chair. I look across the floor and see the familiar shine of some buckles, buckles that reach from the ankles to the knees of Johnny Thunderboots. Beside them stand some black baseball boots, scuffed and worn. I tilt my head and squint up at the two figures towering over me. A baseball boot is brought back and then rapidly forward, landing on my stomach.

I cough and curl up with the pain and wrap my arms protectively around myself.

"What do you want?" I choke out.

"To kill you," says Vic. I'm dealing with a sadistic ginger bastard, I think.

"Go on then, you ginger fuck," I spit. For which I get another kick in the ribs.

She leant down, closer to me. "Do you think I am going to make it that easy for you? Oh no," she laughed and I wanted to punch her in her sick, little face.

"Johnny, set the mirror up," she said, and he obeyed like an obedient lamb. He went over to the chair next to my TV and opened a rucksack they must have brought in with them. I watched him remove their mirror, the one I had seen in my visions, the one a monster had spoken to them from. That red-eyed monster that I had stood against in the woods the night Johnny and Vic were killing Anne Crawley.

I had forgotten that beast.

How could I keep doing this? Forgetting everything I was being shown. I should know by now that I was being shown these things for a reason – warnings of things to come.

Holy shit.

I tried to pull myself up to my knees, holding onto my sofa, and got another kick in the gut for my trouble. But I didn't fall down this time. I just knelt, holding myself partially up, glaring at Vic.

Vic was dressed from head to toe in black. Now there's a surprise for a Goth, I thought. Baseball boots, skinny jeans when she was just that wee bit too fat and a My Chemical Romance T-shirt that gloriously emphasised that ring of fat resting on her hips. There were chains around her neck, most notably an inverted cross. Nice touch. Strands of leather wrapped around her wrists but not enough to hide the scars of self-harm. For anyone else, I might have felt a shard of pity but this girl was a murderer and what struck me was that she *enjoyed* it. A light had gone out in Johnny's eyes since I had met him in the café, and he had given me his carving, but that light, the light of madness, shone bright in Vic's.

And the hair. Oh, the hair. The ginger quiff. Layers of lacquer perfecting its curve on top of her forehead, her sides and back shaved close. What an odd little creature she was. And she was little, not even five feet tall, I guessed.

An odd little *dangerous* creature, I reminded myself.

Johnny was taking a tub of salt from his bag and spreading it around my chair, where he had leant the mirror against a cushion. Vic crossed her arms, watching him, her tight mouth puckered.

Then she spoke. "Think you could deceive us, Annie Crowley? Did you think we wouldn't find out? Don't you realise yet that we have the Devil on our side?"

I saw Johnny quickly throw a glance at her as he continued to make his circle of salt around my armchair. He was terrified.

"We should have been perfecting our cycle of death – five perfect murders for the five points of the Pentagram. Instead you tried to fool us, and we have had to stray from our path. Momentarily, of course. Our Master will have his five.

"Did you enjoy your trip to the woods? Did you like our note? We killed Anne Crawley while you were prancing about in the dark, but we heard you met our Master – didn't we, Johnny?" She looked over to him, a triumphant sneer on her face.

Johnny nodded, unable to speak and I thought I might be able to work on him and his weakness.

"Johnny, you don't have to do this!" I pleaded. "You can walk away now before things get out of hand."

"Shut the fuck up!" Vic screamed, running at me and punching me in the mouth. My head fell back onto the couch, and I felt the blood begin to trickle in my mouth. "Don't you speak to him!" she yelled. "Johnny, look at me, you pathetic sack of shite. Are you gonna let her beat us, Johnny? Do you want to face the Master's wrath? Do you, eh?"

I heard him say, "No" quietly, in his clipped English accent as I rested my head on the couch, breathing through my nose, fighting the explosion of pain in my face.

"Well, man up, you fucking prick! She met you and told you lies. Remember, Johnny? The hours you spent on that fucking stupid piece of wood for her? How your fingers were blistered and red raw? Because *you* wanted to do something nice. Sap!" she spat, goading him, the veins in her white neck throbbing.

Johnny straightened himself to his full height and I noticed a little bit of the light had returned to his eyes. Then he turned to me and punched me on the cheek and my lights went out.

****

I am standing in a never ending, narrow corridor lined with doors on either side, as far as the eye can see. Everything is bright white, except for me. I am glowing orange.

I know I have to open a door. Something or someone awaits me but what if I open the wrong one? Can I close it just as quick? Does my life alter because a door is opened? Do my choices change?

My heart beats with fear. Or excitement. Opening the door to the unknown both excites and terrifies me but I will be brave enough when I have to. I stand trembling, my hand poised to hold a handle, my reflection igniting an orange shadow, and as I step to open this door, I hear a knocking further down the corridor. I immediately leap back and begin to take slow steps forward, listening intently.

It is almost like walking down a corridor of my life, always scared to open that door, liking my life as it is, scared of change and the unknown. Until a knocking grew so insistent that I could no longer ignore it. My heart crying out to be loved.

I stop at the door, shaking from the battering fist behind it. My life will change when I open this, I think.

“Jen, it’s me, Kate. Let me in,” I hear.

My lover. Waiting for me to be brave enough to love her. But it’s not just loving her, is it? It’s opening myself and when I open myself to love, I open myself to everything. Every joy, every pain, every delight, every beauty. I open myself to the forces of good and evil, to my dreams and visions, suppressed for so long because once you open your eyes, everything is visible. You cannot unsee. You cannot unlove.

I stand at the door, the knocking continuing. I am ready to take this step, and with a deep breath, I yank open the door.

I am greeted by smiling eyes.

It is me. I am behind the door.

I wriggle with the pain in my head, a thumping, pounding pain and slip back into unconsciousness.

I am shivering with the cold. The icy darts of freezing water piercing every inch of my skin, blue now. Where am I? What has happened to me? I close my eyes and hear the words of that song, ‘Release’.

I have to let go. I have to let go of the hurt and the pain and know that eventually everything has worked out all right. She forgave me and she let me love her.

I close my eyes, the water stinging and stealing my tears. It is over.

I open my eyes again in my dream, and I am standing in a churchyard by an open grave. I can feel warm tears on my cheeks and my hand being squeezed. I look to see who is holding me up and see Damian smiling sadly at me.

"Three strikes and out," I hear Rob in my head.

"No!" I scream.

****

I wake up on my floor in front of the armchair where Johnny's mirror rests. It is black and still. My left eye is closing over, where he has punched me and my mouth feels swollen. I am poked in the ribs by the boot of Vic.

"Are you back in the land of the living, sleeping beauty?"

I grunt in response, running my tongue over my teeth to check they are all in place.

"Tie her hands, Johnny," Vic barks, like the dog she is.

I realise then that they really are going to kill me in my own living room, in front of my cat, who remains on the other armchair, watching slyly. I try to get up and am kicked in the stomach again by Vic, knocking the wind from me, and flattening me. Johnny grabs my arms and I struggle as he tries to tie my hands together. I am trying to get up, flailing my arms, trying to beat him off.

I haven't seen that Vic has left the room until I catch her come back in from the corner of my good eye. I stop struggling as soon as I see what she is carrying.

The sword of obedience.

Somehow it always looked smaller in my mind, but when I saw the light shimmer on the sharpened blade, I gulped hard and felt my legs go weak. I would have buckled had I been standing. I saw a flash of the heads of Johnny's victims, of Anne Crawley's last grimace. I was next. My blood was going to run down that shaft. As I stared, mesmerised, I never noticed Johnny tying my hands.

There was no knight in shining armour coming to rescue me this time, leaping from her horse to pull me from the flames. Oh Kate, I screamed in my head. I never got the chance to say goodbye to you, my darling. To tell her of the happiness she had given me in the time we had been a couple.

I prepared my mind for my death.

"Now you pay attention, psychic. Johnny, get her onto her knees. This is the…"

"Sword of obedience," I finished and she threw her ginger quiff back and laughed, a sharp hyena-like giggle.

"Yes. The sword of obedience. The sword that's going to cut your pretty little head off."

"You must hate being ugly," I taunted her and her face convulsed into a sneer of fury.

"Say the words, Johnny. Say the fucking words!" she screamed, her cheeks burning red with rage, her hair standing on end, eyes bulging.

"Vic, maybe we should…" Johnny stammered, torn between right and wrong. His redemption had come too late.

"Say the words!" she screamed again, approaching me. She lifted the sword over my head, and pressed the blade against the back of my neck.

Oh, God help me, I said in prayer, not knowing if I believed and no longer caring, as I felt the heavy blade nick my skin.

I heard Johnny begin his chant.

"Alham je deridsa
Alham je roka
Alham je roka
Ee sa mesa roka inhelmaja."

I am kneeling with my hands tied in front of me, Vic standing to my right, holding her sword on my neck, and I try to twist my head to see what is happening to my left, to the mirror. These are his summoning words that I have heard before. I should have looked them up, found a counter-spell or whatever but, as usual, I had floundered my way through my days, and now my head was going to be severed.

The one thing I could not help but think was that it would be my Kate who found me, walking in from her shift to see my decapitated body and my head, wherever it landed. My poor darling. No loved one should ever have to see such a sight. I would try to die with a smile on my face. I felt the sting of my tears as I saw how her heart would break, knowing she would blame herself for letting me down, that she had not protected me. How could she ever get over this?

I turned my head a bit more, now unable to see out of my let eye, and noticed the smoke beginning to swirl in the dark glass. I watched, fascinated, seeing the cloudy swirls grown denser and thicker and felt my insides shudder when I saw the start of two red eyes forming.

Holy Mary, mother of Jesus. The demon in the woods was coming back for me. I am on my knees, hands bound, a sword weighing down on me. There is nowhere to run, there is no way out. I will have to face the monster. As I steeled myself to my destiny, I felt a strength inside me grow. I will not go down without a fight. No beast is having my soul.

That is promised to my Kate. I can hear a gurgling and Johnny falls to his knees in worship. He can't look, I think, he can't look at it – he's too scared.

The eyes are becoming clearer, and an outline of a face is being defined. It's going to speak soon and demand my head shall roll. I closed my eyes and prayed for a miracle.

And then a miracle happened.

I heard the key turn in the lock before they did because I am accustomed to the noises of my flat.

"Here!" I screamed, getting another kick. I felt Vic turn to the door because the sword scraped along the skin of my neck, cutting me some more.

Damian walked in, quickly followed by Kate running into her back, because Damian had stopped mid-step, astonished by the scene before her. I saw Kate reach under her jacket and pull out her gun, training her aim on Vic.

"I'd put that fucking sword down if I were you," she said.

"And I'd put the fucking gun down, if I were *you*!" Vic spat back.

"You'll be dead before you raise that sword," Kate countered.

"I don't need to raise it. I'll just fucking slice. Wanna try? Wanna be brave, pig?" Vic taunted. Seeing Kate would never risk my life, she continued. "Empty the bullets, put it on the floor – slowly – and kick it away." Kate did what she was told, her eyes never leaving us for a second. "Good. Stand next to the chair with the cat, pig, and you, dummy – you just stay where you are. This gets better and better," she said, licking her lips with glee.

"Johnny, wake up, fucking moron." He raised his head, opened his eyes, helpless in his terror to do anything but obey her. "There's five of us, Johnny. It's the magical number. Can't you feel it, Johnny? Can't you feel something massive is going to happen?" Johnny's eyes peeled helplessly around him but I realised Vic was right. Something massive *was* going to happen – I just didn't know what yet.

"Start the incantation, Johnny. Get our Master here. As he has commanded."

Were they going to try to summon a demon? In the flesh? Wasn't that what the mirror was for? I saw Johnny stand up and reach into his back pocket for a bit of paper. He cleared his throat and began, as Kate and Damian remained like statues, in this bizarre drama unfolding. I heard Johnny start his gibberish, reading from his scribbles.

"Hetra brog hollo dranko grennda
Anou esee brog hollo ubastrap
Brog hollo, brog hollo
Brog hollo, brog hollo."

I heard Kate say, "What the fuck is this?"

I turned to look at her as much as I could, and for the first time, saw my own mirror leant against the CD tower, in the middle of where Kate and Damian stood. The black glass was clouding, just like Johnny's. I began to see four red eyes come into focus.

"Kate! The mirror!" I mumbled as loud as I could through my fat lip. Everyone turned to look at my mirror, just as there was an almighty bang of breaking glass. Johnny's mirror had exploded. Glass flew across the room. A piece must have hit Vic, because I felt the tension ease from the blade on my neck and immediately took the opportunity to crawl across the floor, until I was next to Kate. As I turned on my knees to see what Vic and Johnny were going, I gasped, maybe screamed – I don't remember.

Their demon was standing in front of my chair where their mirror had leant. Johnny had fallen to his knees again, dropping his head in reverence. Vic stood, open-mouthed, still holding the sword, now resting its tip into the carpet.

A naked man. Muscular and hirsute. Normal but for those red eyes and horns jutting from the forehead. A demon.

It spoke, a low guttural growl.

"Johnny, stand, my servant, where your woman stands and hold the sword out."

Johnny jumped to his feet, scampering to Vic and taking the sword from her, as she gave no resistance, moving wordlessly to where Johnny had knelt. An unholy trinity.

"Jennifer Keith and your two women. You can kneel in front of me in worship, or be damned."

I answered. "I'll take my chances," I said, pulling myself up. Aching in my ribs, my jaw, my eye, neck smarting. I looked at Kate, the dilemma of this supernatural event conflicting with all her logical reasoning and then to Damian, who just stood in awe. I was about to speak when my own mirror exploded and I fell backwards with the force, feeling glass cut through my shirt, lacerating my arm.

I looked up to my Kate and followed her eyes.

To Rob and Jonah standing where I had been.

Rob, standing tall, his back straight and my boy. My boy! Six or seven? Holding his daddy's hand, his blond hair flopping into his eyes but his face was grim and determined.

The demon roared.

"Mummy, we need to join together," my Jonah said and I scrambled to him, as I always would. My baby.

Kate's jaw had dropped open and, as I got to my feet and found my legs, I went to her, taking her face in my hands. "If you really love me like you say you do, then now is the time to stand beside me."

I saw her blink and nod, all the while aware of the demon growling at my back, and I went to Damian, holding her face, too.

"Damian, my friend, unite with us." She nodded her approval, gritting her teeth.

Then I stood to face the demon, Vic and Johnny, opening my hands to those beside me. We joined hands and hearts – Kate, Jonah, me, Rob and Damian.

"You want five, devil? I give you five!" I shouted.

It raised its arms and threw its head back, roaring an animal scream. It brought its head back down and grinned, with its pointed teeth shimmering.

"You dare face me?" it questioned.

Rob whispered. "Be strong, my love," and I heard Kate gasp, loosing her grip on Jonah.

"No!" I said, but not to the demon, I was speaking to my lover. "Kate! You have to stay strong. You have to trust me. It's going to try to break our bond – don't you see that? Trust me, darling, love will get us through this."

The demon laughed but I sensed Kate was still holding my baby's hand. You laugh when you're scared, don't you? A laugh to cover your fears. It was scared of us.

It spoke. "Look, Katherine, how she holds her lover-boy's hand and her bastard child, never born. Is that what you want, Katherine?"

Oh no, I thought. It's going for her weaknesses. Would I trust her with my life? Her nightmare standing in front of her – the man I betrayed her with and my dead child, the result of that betrayal.

"I don't know what you are," she said. "But you're not real."

It growled again, changing its face to that of Simon Dunstable, and changed back.

"Don't you know me yet?" it asked.

"I know you are a bastard from Hell," she replied and it laughed.

Rob squeezed my hand, getting my attention. "Jen, we don't have much time. Do it!"

Do what?

"Think Jen. Of all the love in your life," he said and then I knew. The knowing was with me once more. The knowing never leaves me.

I turned to my Jonah and smiled, his blue eyes crinkling into a smile back at me. My beautiful, blond haired boy, full of love for his mum. The bond of motherhood that can never be broken. His little hand holding onto Damian, my best friend, always there with her opinions, whether I liked them or not. I smiled at her and she winked back.

I turned to my right, the hand that held Rob's and met his eyes. A man who loved me. I would never love him like I loved Kate but I would never forget his friendship and his kindness and his unquestionable belief in me. I would never forget that he was the father of my child that I loved beyond life and death, or that he would look after my Jonah in the nether worlds.

And finally I looked at my Kate, dumbstruck by the events before her, but nevertheless, holding the hand of a ghost of a man she had despised. She held his hand for me and her trust filled me with joy from my toes to the hairs on my head. I looked into her eyes, nodding my head, and she nodded back. She got it.

We all stand together and face our demons.

This all happened in a split second, but time moved slower for me, as I calculated in my mind.

"Come on then, devil. Catch me if you can," I said.

It snarled its teeth at me and took a step forward, and as it stepped forward so did all five of us, united in our love. It faltered and I felt the strength in me grow.

Love.

Jonah, Kate, Damian, Rob, all standing tall with me. How can you defeat love when all you have to fight it with is hatred and fear? Two small emotions will never overcome the hugeness of love.

I felt a force grow around us, inside us, inside me and I pushed it out, towards the demon, saliva dripping from its teeth, as it began to burn and smoulder.

Love does burn. But only when you won't accept it.

Push, I gritted in my head, push! And we all took another step forward.

"We are the five," I said. "Five of love, life and death, united. You'll never beat us. Because you can never beat love!"

It moved forward again, until its nose was almost touching mine, and I could smell its foul breath. I locked eyes, knowing I would never let a monster of hate defeat me when I was surrounded by so much love and goodness.

"We forgive you," I said, and the smoke that burned it became flames, forcing us back, still holding tight. I watched as it growled and snarled, flaming and burning, finally disintegrating to ash before our eyes. Before I had a chance to assimilate this, Vic, who had remained still throughout this brief stand off, moved towards Johnny, who was standing holding the sword, immobile.

She means to grab it and come flailing, I thought, and as I thought this, I saw the fat cat leap from his position on the chair and run to her legs. My fat cat that was forever trying to trip me up.

Vic saw him too late and stumbled to avoid him, falling forward with a daintiness that belied her awkwardness. She fell forward, impaling herself on the sword of obedience, and I gasped with horror as I watched her body slide down the blade, until her weight took them both to the floor and Johnny threw off his grasp. For a second, I thought he might have pushed it into her.

He fell again to his knees, overcome by hysterical giggles, a slave now to the master of madness. I would worry about him in a minute.

I felt the bond break and knew that Kate and Damian had let go, leaving me holding the hands of Jonah and Rob.

Rob smiled at me. "Beautifully played, Jen."

I almost felt anger for a moment, but too many emotions were flying around my head and my one prevailing feeling was for Jonah. I let go of Rob, swivelling around to bend down and threw my arms around my baby. I would never see him at six or seven, and this was my one and only chance to hold him. I felt his solid little shoulders, his tiny little hands make indents into my back as he hugged me back.

"I love you, baby," I sobbed.

"I love you too, mummy."

What words could ever be spoken that would mean so much? My beautiful little boy, dead to me until I died and we were re-united. I held on tight, knowing these precious seconds would end and I would soon be left with that gaping hole in my heart. I leant back and smiled through my tears.

"Don't you ever forget me, Jonah."

"Mummy, I'll never forget you. I'm waiting for you."

Just as I thought my heart would splinter and shatter into a million pieces, Rob came by my side, taking Jonah's hand.

"One more time, then that's it. Goodbye, Jen," he said, and they walked out the living room door, my baby smiling back over his shoulder at me.

I jumped, feeling a hand on my shoulder.

"Jen, was that…?" Kate asked, stopping, not sure what to say.

"That was Jonah, Kate. My baby that I lost."

She threw her arms around me and cried, and I held her tight, strong and certain of all things good and right. My little love was always there in my heart, and I knew we would be together when the time was right, but the time for living was now, and having faced my death, I knew that better than most.

And to live, I had to love my Kate.

Damian stood where she had stood the whole time and, as I held Kate, I said, "Damian, are you all right?"

Her eyes glazed and unglazed. "What? What am I doing here?"

Kate lifted her head from my chest, wiping her snot, and turning to Damian, saying, "You were waiting outside the door when I got here. Don't you remember? You said 'I told her to say no'."

Damian looked aghast, the colour draining from her. "I was at work," she stuttered. "I had a dream about you last night but…"

"Damian," I said softly, "Go home. Forget. We'll clean up." She turned and left, as Rob and Jonah had.

"Darling, how are we going to explain this without sounding mad? You did see them, didn't you?"

Kate nodded, saying nothing, and got on the floor to retrieve her bullets and gun.

Johnny was still giggling madly. I couldn't help myself. I walked over and kicked him hard in the guts. I had a swollen mouth, a black eye, a cut arm, and aches all over my ribs. One kick helped me feel a bit better. Not to mention the red line of blood across the nape of my neck, where a sword had rested. A sword that pointed up to my ceiling, holding the dead body of Vic Kavanagh, a thin trickle of blood drying on her chin. I couldn't look.

Kate came to me and took my face in her hands. "This is what you're going to say…"

****

Hours later, I sat at my kitchen table, stroking the fat cat that may or may not have inadvertently saved my life, its hunger assuaged by tuna flakes. I was having a black tea laced with whisky.

I had given a statement, repeating the words Kate had told me to say, and John Bailey had patted me on the shoulder. He had believed us, but what choice did he have? How could I have said a dead policeman and my dead baby had come to life and stood with us against a devil, our only weapon being love? Who would have believed that?

Johnny had been taken away in handcuffs and Vic's lifeless body zipped into a black bag. It would be the last smile from that deviant ginger fuck, I thought.

Kate came in, as I gulped at my tea, throwing back the last mouthful, scraping my chair back to replace it with a vodka and coke.

"Are you okay, baby?" she asked.

I grunted, assuming it was a rhetorical question and filled my glass with alcohol. She wouldn't dare criticise my drinking today if she knew better.

What a day. What a fucking day. What more can happen in a day, I thought. Surely I can sleep now. And as I thought it, I knew I was tempting fate.

A day contains many doors.

I heard my mobile ring on the table and saw Kate lift it up. She handed it to me, saying, "Why would my mother be phoning you at this time of the night?"

I shrugged. "Hi Sheena, it's Jen."

I listened. I asked her to repeat and listened again. I thanked her and hung up.

"Kate, your mum has Simon Dunstable."

Chapter Thirty-Seven

"What do you mean, my mother has Simon Dunstable?" Kate asked, perplexed.

I threw back a gulp of vodka and coke, figuring I was going to need plenty more before this night was over.

"Sit down," I told her, returning to my seat at the table. My whole body ached and I was tired. I didn't know if I could get through any more trauma today; and then I looked into Kate's inquisitive, trusting eyes and knew that I would. Because it was going to have to be for her.

"Jen, what's going on? If you know where he is, I have to tell the DCI right now. You know how long we have been looking for him. What do you know?" Her tone was not harsh, and she spoke softly but firmly. Her mind was back on ground where it was comfortable, searching for the baddies. Not holding hands with ghosts and battling demons with horns and red eyes.

My darling, that I knew would throw this memory to the back of her mind because it was easier to pack it away than have to think of the horrors that lie beyond the realm of our realities – like she had done all her life, and how could I blame her for that? If I had seen and experienced what she had growing up, I would have done the same. It was a testament to the strength of her character that she had emerged a rounded human being, still capable of love. I admired her strength.

"Jen, you're worrying me. Will you say something?" I heard the small, hidden tone of her fear and I snapped out of my head.

"I need you to listen to me, darling. There's something I need to tell you and you're not going to like it, but I can't do anything about that," I began.

"Jen, for fuck's sake, will you stop babbling in riddles and spit it out?" she said, exasperated once more by my procrastination.

"Okay. The reason your mum is with Simon Dunstable right now is because he's your dad." I sat back, waiting for the outpouring of her explosion.

Instead, she laughed. "No, he's not, Jen. Jesus, you can be fanciful at times."

She made to stand up. "He is, Kate. I've seen it."

In days of old, she might have scoffed, but days had changed and her eyes had been opened.

"What have you seen, Jen?"

"I've seen it all, my darling, I'm so sorry." I watched her wrestle with herself and her own demons, her emotions no longer hidden, playing out on her face. I put my hand across the table to hold hers and gave her a squeeze.

"Tell me it all, then," she said, very quietly.

Where did I begin? I hardly knew where the beginning was any more.

"I had dreams about that little boy that went missing. The one with four toes. What was his name, anyway?"

"Joe."

"Joe. Right. I dreamt about Joe and the men that did 'stuff' to him. I saw Simon's face, and then Logan came into the bar with him and I almost died because I knew then what he was. But I didn't have any proof, did I? And you always bang on about needing proof – you can't just go arresting people because I've had a bad dream. Am I talking too fast?"

"No."

"Well, I had more dreams about him, mainly to do with Logan. You were in a few, too."

"Me? What was I doing?" she asked.

"Oh, getting a memory stick from Logan."

"You *saw* that?"

"Yeah," I nodded. "I see a lot of things, darling, I just can't tell you them all at the time. Or until it makes sense to me. Which is usually too late." I frowned.

"It wasn't too late for those kids on that bus," she pointed out.

"It was too late for Anne Crawley though. She was on that bus. I looked into her eyes and saw Death. I just didn't know it would be Johnny and Vic killing her."

I thought back to the dead body of Vic, lying on our carpet with a sword jutting out her back. I thought absent-mindedly that we'd need a new carpet, as I'd never get the stains out.

"Jen," she gently nudged me, seeing me veer off course. She was used to me rambling away in my nervousness, although she was taking this news a bit too well for my liking.

"Sorry," I apologised. "Where was I? Oh yeah. So, I saw you meet Logan, and I saw the awful tortures he had to go through. I never knew if you were going to get to him in time. I had to leave that to fate.

"I started to wonder about people's histories – I don't know why." I stopped short of telling her that Rob had said it was all about her. "And I visit your mum. Usually once a week.

"She's lonely, Kate, and she loves you. It's all tied up in this, I think."

I watched her face harden at the mention of her mum. "*What* is tied up in this?"

I took a large mouthful of my vodka and coke. "There is some pre-determined act – I'm not exactly sure what, just that something is meant to happen and I think it involves you and Sheena."

"Go on."

"Well, as I said, I'm not exactly sure what, but the more I think about it, the more it becomes clearer. Kate, I've been inside your mum's head and, believe me, it's not somewhere I would want to go by choice. She's haunted by regret and tortures herself.

"Her grief is never ending."

"So it fucking should be," she snorted.

"No! It doesn't have to be like this. Do you ever get that feeling when you're lying in bed with me, just after we've made love, and I'm curled in your arms, where you think you're so happy you could just burst with love? The world, even full of misery and murder, can't touch your happiness because you have one person? One person who makes it alright, who makes pain and suffering disappear, and you just want to share that with the world? You just want everyone to be as happy as you are. For your mum, *you* are that one person."

She shifted in her chair. That meant she was not entirely happy with the way this conversation was going, taking her out of her comfort zone of black and white. I could see her fingers nervously tap the tabletop.

"Shouldn't you be telling me where this murderous bastard is so that I can go and arrest him?"

"Not yet," I said. "You need to understand first. Give me your hand, darling."

"No!" she said, pulling her hands off the table, away from me. She was so scared to let go, which made me want to be so much gentler with her.

"Kate, you can't stay locked inside yourself forever. Let me help you, darling – it's the only way."

"What are you going to do?" she asked, and I realised I had no idea. I had just been going to hold her arm and see what happened. I trusted that whatever ability I had would do the rest of the work for me. "

"I… I… I just want to try something, and I need you to trust me. I won't hurt you."

I saw her look at me, look down to my hands then to her own. Slowly, she moved her arm towards me.

"Just be quick," she whispered.

I ached with my love for her. I wanted to scoop the pain from her trembling hear and throw it in a furnace.

I felt the pain begin in my head, even before I had touched her, my tingling fingertips reaching to crawl around her wrist. I closed my eyes and went in search of Kate.

When I opened them, I was in the familiar white corridor, burning orange, listening for a knock that I knew would come. And when it did I ran, no longer locked in my own dreams, only desperate to unlock someone else from their nightmares.

I pulled open the door, no hesitation this time and I saw my Kate waiting for me, dressed in white. I held out my hand to her, and she took it, being pulled into the corridor with me. I did not have to speak – our communication was done with our eyes, the gateway to our souls.

I don't know if she heard the song in my head, but she gave my hand a soft squeeze, as I stopped in front of a door. A door just like all the other doors, winding down this never-ending corridor. But not the same at all. Behind this door lay secrets.

Now is the time for our strength, I thought, pushing the door inwards. We have to take a step in, we have to be prepared to face whatever has been locked away, because only by facing our fears can we put them to bed.

As we moved in, the door slammed shut behind us and Kate let me go, frantically trying the handle to re-open it. Of course it didn't budge and I went to her, slowly taking her hands off, back to holding mine and turned her to face forward.

I looked at a giant TV screen in front of us and looked to Kate. I had to look down because she was no longer my Kate. She was seven-year-old Kate.

The TV flashed into life and we began to watch.

Sheena stood in front of a door, shouting "You'll no' touch her!", and we see the drunken father raise his fist and brutally bring it down on her, steaming in with his boot when she fell to the ground, until exhausted, he staggered back down the stairs looking for more drink. Sheena crawls onto her knees, slipping into the bedroom of her sleeping child, the seven-year-old Kate *oblivious in her dreams.* She lies on the floor, crying, the blood drying on her face.

The scene switches. Sheena and Ian are in the pub. He is laughing and joking, the big man, downing his pint.

"I want to go home," she says.

"We'll go hame when Ah'm ready."

She drinks the drinks he puts in front of her, sneaking glances at her watch, until finally he has had enough and they make their exit. They walk home, his arm possessively over her shoulder, until they hear the woman next door screaming for them and they both break into a run.

"It's your Lizzie!" she screams. "She's fell doon the stairs."

They run in and see Lizzie lying at the bottom of the stairs, her head banging on the floorboards as her body spasms. Ian falls to the floor, cradling Lizzie in his arms.

"My Lizzie, oh my Lizzie," he sobs, while Sheena has run down the road, to the phone-box, to ring for an ambulance. As she runs back to the house, she goes to Kate who, seeing her approach, turns her back and takes Amy into the kitchen. The silent tears run down Sheena's face, tripping over the bruises.

The scene switches. We see young Kate playing in her back garden, chalking the pavement with faces and scribbling over them. She looks up to see her mother at the kitchen window, watching her. Her mother waves, smiling, and Kate turns back to her doodles. Her mother opens the fridge, taking out a bottle of beer, and walks through to where the father sits smoking, reading the racing pages of his newspaper. She sets the bottle down beside him, lifting the last empty for the bin. Amy cries in her cot and he glares at her over his paper.

"Shut that wean up!" he growls.

Sheena runs to the cot to cajole the hungry baby with a bottle but she won't take and her cries become louder. He is watching as he necks half his bottle, frustrated by the incessant wails, and continues to seethe. He finishes the bottle, ordering another one, and Sheena runs with the baby to do as she is told, shushing it as she goes past him. This scene plays over and over, with him getting more and more drunk, the baby more and more distressed. Kate has come to look in the window, as his frayed temper finally snaps and he leaps from his chair, grabbing Amy from her cot, shaking her, as he screams for her to shut up. Sheena runs in from the kitchen, as his fury peaks and he throws Amy across the room, her small head cracking on the bare wall, her body thumping to the floor, as her cries are suddenly and finally quiet. He stands still as Sheena screams and runs to the baby. Kate, watching, turns away and runs. She's known the number 999 for a long time now. She waits as the blue sirens arrive, her eyes caught in the revolving blue. One day, she thinks, that is going to be her. A dream is borne as a nightmare unfolds.

"My father killed Amy," she tells.

The screen clouds and clears. Kate is walking away in the rain, holding her mother's hand, looking back at the hole in the ground where the coffin of her little sister now lies. At home she shuts her bedroom door and lies on the bed, holding a doll of Amy's. Downstairs, Sheena sits weeping at the table and before long, pours her first drink.

Then Kate is older. She is banging the bathroom door, in a different house because they moved, unable to live in a house that held tragedy in every wall. Behind the door, Sheena lying on the floor, shaking hands holding a razor blade ponderously over her wrist.

"Mum!" she hears, as the tears trickle down, again and again, over and over. The word saves her, and she puts down the blade.

Cloud and clear. Sheena cuddles up to the man on her sofa, drinking neat vodka until she passes out. He makes sure she is asleep and then begins the lustful creep up the stairs to the bed of Kate. Until Sheena gets sick of his fists and moves on.

Care workers sitting with folders and clipboards, looking in her fridge. Temporary care, they call it, until she can sober up. They take Kate away and they bring her back. Kate turns her back and Sheena turns to drink. The cycle of pain.

Cloud and clear. We are looking at Ian Coutts, older, hardened. He is lying on an operating table with felt-tip pen lines on his face, marking the cuts. Frankenstein's monster. A new hairline is put in. Muscles are worked on at the gym. Contact lenses to change eye colour. A new accent. A transformation complete.

A new man, a new family. A woman with two kids. He is disgusted with his lust for her flesh but returns time and again, until she utters the words, "I'm pregnant", and he moves on, to reinvent once more, leaving the mother of Gail Dunstable to have Joe on her own. A child he will return for to erase his own creation, knowing somewhere that the cycle has to end with him. No more monsters.

The money changes hands. The prostitutes are beaten and filmed and murdered. The cars get bigger. The risks get higher. But he is untouchable.

The TV switches off and does not come back on, our viewing is over. Kate is my Kate again, and I lead her to the door, which now opens with no resistance and take her back to the corridor of doors, knowing now which door next to take her through.

I took her to the door that I have stood behind and usher her in, to where another screen awaits us. I hold her hand tightly. Now I am going to show her love.

A flash of colour and we see me traipsing to my flat's front door, in my old, blue pyjamas, opening to Kate holding a rose for me. To our first date, at the cinema, when her hand crept shyly to mine in the darkness. To our first kiss in my kitchen, my back against the fridge. The first time we made love, fast and frantic, overtaken by desire and passion. The day she moved in with me, when we carried box after box up from our cars and sat unpacking, amalgamating our belongings into an order her neat mind could cope with. Having midnight baths, surrounded by bubbles and candles, laughing with our growing love. Her arm around me as we left a darkened room to confront Lorraine. Me making sandwiches for her lunch and smiling as I sneak in love notes to her, her smile when she found them. The days and nights of happiness, small and simple pleasures. The way our bodies curled into each other in our sleep. Her belief in me growing stronger. Her agony at my hospital bedside. Her silent tears. Her silent fears. My arms enveloping her, wrapping her in my devotion. Wherever she was, I was, and whatever she is, I am.

I felt her hand squeeze mine and turned to face her. She was like me now, no longer white but burning orange, alight with passion, desire and love.

No matter the pain, there is always one love to wipe it away. There is always one love that made the life before worthwhile because it led you to this place.

She nodded. She was ready.

I opened my eyes, and for a split second saw that orange flame still burning in her eyes. There were trails on her cheek where tears had fallen and run away.

"How… How did you do that?" she asked, her face pale.

"Did you see it?" I asked, excitement growing.

"Yes. Yes, I saw it. I don't understand…" she said.

"You don't need to – neither do I. You just needed to see, that's all," I replied, energised by this discovery. A bond between us, formed through our moments of love, had let me open her eyes.

"I don't know what to think any more, Jen. About anything."

"You just have to let go of your hate, my darling. Close the door on it, and open another to love," I smiled.

"Is your head like this all the time?" she frowned.

"No," I laughed. "Or I really would go round the twist."

She smiled back, her tenderness evident. "Why is… that man… with my mother now, after all these years?" she asked.

I creased my brow. "I'm not sure," I said, slowly.

"We have to go to her, Jen, don't we?"

"Yes, I think so."

"I'll ring Bailey, tell him…"

"No! It has to be just us!" She looked at me. "I don't know why – it just does." I felt the beginning of a small throb at the back of my head. "Get me to the car and don't go in without me. I'm going to pass out."

I remember her driving us on the M8, and then it was back to my dreams.

****

I see Sheena getting off the bust and walking along the road, making her way into the heart of a run-down council estate, her headscarf shielding her hair from the rain. She is holding a carrier bag full of shopping and humming to herself as she closes a gate behind her and makes her way down the path. She punches a number in to a pad on the wall, which open its box to give her the key to get in, and she closes the door behind her, laying her bag on the floor.

"Katherine, it's just me, Sheena," she shouts in, as she takes off her headscarf and jacket, hanging them on a coat-hook. "I'll just put your messages in the kitchen. Do you want a wee cup of tea?"

"Aye hen – c'mere a minute," the elderly voice shouts back. Sheena sets the plastic bag down on the worktop and walks through to the living room, seeing the handsome stranger sitting on the couch.

"Hello," she smiles. "I'm making a brew. Can I get you a cup?"

"Yes please, Sheena," he says, smoothly.

"How do you know my name?" Then she laughs. "You been telling stories again, Katherine?" she asks, but a glimmer of doubt has crept in. That voice, so familiar.

"It's Ian, Sheena! My Ian! Look how different he is! He had a wee accident with his face and had plastic surgery, but ye cannae tell," said the old woman, proudly.

"Ian! Jesus, I would'nae have recognised ye. Where have you been all these years? Yir mither's been worried sick about you," Sheena lied. Inside her chest, her saddened heart began to beat. But not with love.

He smiled and stood up, leading Sheena into the kitchen.

"I'll just help Sheena with the tea, ma," he said. "I need a place to stay, just for a few days. I'm in a wee bit of bother with the law," he laughed, the old Scottish accent surging to the surface.

"What kind o' trouble?" Sheena asked, knowing full well.

"Never you mind. I just need a few days to get ma money together, and then I'm away."

"Where ye going?"

"Europe. Mebbe America. I've no' decided yet. I'm waiting on a contact sorting me some travel documents. Can I stay at yours? For auld times' sake?" he smarmed.

"Don't you even want to know about the weans?" she asked.

"Lizzie's still a veg in the hospital and oor Kate's a dyke poliswummin."

"You've seen Kate?" she asked, with astonishment.

"Aye, but she didnae know it was me and I'll be keeping it that way. She never liked me anyway."

"D'you blame her?" Sheena retorted.

"Listen, doll, I'm no' here to fight. I just want a bed for a few nights. Can you do that?"

"Aye," she grumbled. "Ah suppose so."

He beamed, flashing his new teeth at her. "How is oor Kate?" he asked, amiably, as Sheena made the tea.

"I don't know, I don't see her. She left hame at sixteen. She couldnae stand being near me."

He went and put his arm around her.

"Aye," he sighed, "It's hard being a parent."

They sat with old Katherine and had their tea and then he gave his mum a cuddle and took Sheena back to hers in his smart car with leather seats. At hers, he goes for a bath and Sheena rings on her mobile.

Maybe she has made a lot of wrong decisions in her life, but this time she has got it right.

****

I wake up and Kate is still driving.

"Are we there yet?" I ask.

"I don't know where she lives."

"What?" I said, still trying to shake myself awake.

"I don't know the address," she repeated.

"Oh," I realised and fumbled for the Sat Nav. "It should be stored," I said, fiddling until I found it and set the route.

"I just headed for Edinburgh," she said.

"He's at your mum's house – he's on his own and he knows who you are," I remembered.

"How? Did he recognise me in that bar with Logan?"

"I don't know, but I imagine he's had you checked out over the years. He's not the kind to let it go."

"Does she still love him? My mother."

"I don't know. I don't think so."

"He was always her weakness. Even when he disappeared for days on end and came home smelling of tarts, she forgave him."

"That was a long time ago, Kate, and Sheena's had time to reflect."

"Hmm," she grunted.

We sat in silence until we pulled into Sheena's street, seeing his big, shiny car sat outside, shameless.

"Are you ready?" I asked. "He's going to know as soon as he sees you that you're there for him."

"I'm ready," she said, grimly, and we walked up to the door. I knocked and waited. Another door, another drama.

Sheena answered and said "Come in" and there he was, sitting in her chair, watching TV, like he had sat there all his life. And perhaps he had, the ghost that never went away.

"Hello Simon," Kate said, going in first.

"Hello daughter," he smiled. "Come to see your old man. Lovely. Sheena, put the kettle on."

Kate remained standing, so I stood by her side and Sheena disappeared to make the tea.

"I'm here to arrest you, you murdering bastard," Kate said.

He laughed. "Why did you never like me?" he asked. "You never liked me, even before Lizzie and Amy had their accidents. Do you just not like men? Is that why you're a dyke?" he sneered at her.

"Ian Coutts, also known as Simon Dunstable, you have the right to remain silent. Anything…"

"No you fucking don't!" he shouted and leapt up from his chair. Just as quickly, Kate drew her gun and he stopped, mid-step. "You wouldn't shoot your daddy," he drawled.

"Just fucking try me," she answered.

Sheena walked in and he turned to her. "You set me up!" he screamed at her.

"Aye!" she screamed back. "You're no' taking another wean oaf me!"

He lunged at her, knocking the tray from her hands, grabbing her by the throat.

"Get your hands off her, or I'll pull the trigger," Kate warned.

Sheena's face grew purple as he applied pressure to her throat and Kate took aim, firing into his leg.

He stumbled back, letting go of Sheena, who I ran to to help steady.

Kate took aim again. "No!" I shouted. "Don't kill him!"

Kate looked at Sheena. "Mum?" she questioned.

"Do it," Sheena choked.

"This is for Amy," Kate said, shooting him square on the forehead.

He was dead instantly. Ding, dong, the monster's gone.

Kate said "Mum?", and Sheena went to her and they embraced, united again by love.

It was over.

****

Of course there were questions. It was a long night as siren after siren pulled up and we recounted our stories. It was quite an overwhelming story, even for DCI John Bailey to believe. Simon was Kate's dad?

We explained over and over that we had been going to visit Kate's mum, and she had phoned us to say her dad was there. When we had arrived and Kate had realised who he actually was, she had tried to arrest him and he had gone for Sheena and she had shot him.

Bailey believed us, because all he cared about was that Dunstable had been caught. He was no longer able to go on with his life of depravity and torture.

He came over to us and whispered, "This is going to be in the papers, you know. I'm suggesting you two take a holiday. I'll ring you, Kate, if I need to. Go. Get some sleep and take off tomorrow."

Sleep. I could think of nothing nicer. I tugged Kate's sleeve and we stood up. She gave her gun to Bailey and went over to speak to her mum.

"Thank you," he said, quietly, to me.

“For what?”

“For keeping your mouth shut. You could cause us a load of embarrassment,” he said.

“What?” I joked. “‘Psychic tells cop girlfriend where murderer is’?”

Turns out, I was not that far from the truth.

Chapter Thirty-Eight

I had barely been out the house in the last three months, but today Damian and I were going for the final fitting to my wedding dress and her bridesmaid dress.

Three months ago, Kate had shot dead her father, Ian Coutts, or Simon Dunstable as he had renamed himself, while had had attempted to strangle her mother. I had given my statement and been left alone by the police, something I think I had to thank John Bailey for. Kate and I had gone away for a few weeks, renting a cottage in the north of Scotland, where we barracked ourselves away from the world, shunning the television and newspapers. Our return to civilisation had brought the constant knocking of my door, the ringing of my phone, harassed by journalists when I went out for cigarettes.

Somehow they had gotten hold of details of my ability and were not prepared to let this go. A united front was maintained by Strathclyde Police, who denied any input from me, Kate remained stoically silent and I scuttled to and from the paper shop as little as possible, with as many fags as I could carry in one go.

I was on 'indefinite leave' from my job and found the monotony of my days draining. All I had to focus on was my wedding, and I threw myself into this with an energy I didn't know I possessed.

But I was sleeping, you see. No more bad dreams. No more nightmares. No visions. No reflections in mirrors. Nothing.

I think a part of me missed it. That knowing.

I waited for Damian to turn up and went to answer my mobile when I heard The Exorcist's ringtone play. My little joke to myself.

Before even looking at the caller display number, I answered and said "Hello," in what I thought was my funny voice.

There was a slight pause, and in that instant, I knew I should have hung up.

"Is that Jennifer Keith?"

"Yes…" I said, hesitantly.

"You don't know me but…"

I interrupted. "Look, I don't know who you are, and I don't want to know, but whatever it is, I can't help you."

I'd had a million of these phone calls in the last few months and eventually each crank gave up, until they were replaced by a new one. I had thought it was dying off.

"Jen, Rob told me to ask for you," the woman said.

That got my attention. Three months of silence was as much as I could bear, I was ready to grasp at any straw, however short. To me Rob equated Jonah and I would always grasp for my son.

"Who are you?" I asked, with a slight trepidation. But also with a slight excitement. I realised how much I had missed this, the search for the knowing.

"I'm Rob's older sister. My name is Moira and this is about my son. He's going to go missing."

"So he's not missing right now?"

"No, but when he does, you're the one that will find him."

"And you know this because…?"

"Because Rob told me."

Oh yes. How stupid of me.

"Did Rob tell you anything else?" I asked, trying to hide the sarcasm in my voice. As much as I loved and missed my gift, I knew it would not be hard to read back and piece together my history and Kate's to a dead policeman called Rob. I am not altogether thick.

"He said, 'Don't let him strike the third match'. I don't know what that means. Do you know what that means? Oh, and he said 'Jonah says hi Mummy'. I don't know what that means, either." I heard her sigh.

I heard myself sigh. I would get sucked in, I knew, because my belief in the goodness and honesty of people, coupled with my desire to help, always won me over. And as I said, I missed the knowing.

"It's fine, I know what it means," I replied with resignation. "Give me your number. Keep an eye on your son in the meantime. How old is he anyway?" Sucked in.

"He's twenty three."

"Oh, so he's not a child?" I was confused.

"Not exactly. He's challenged. Hadley has some delicate needs."

I didn't want to know. Not now. The timing was not right. This would come up again, of that I was completely sure, and this time I'd be prepared. I took down her number and said I'd be in touch.

I went into my bedroom, writing the details in my notepad with her number. It was time for me to start learning from my mistakes of the past.

As an afterthought, I added three words.

'Circus of horrors.'

I didn't know why. It's for later, I thought. My future.

****

My future that belonged to Kate. I had stood in my wedding dress, just a plain white, shoulderless dress, and closing my eyes, saw myself standing beside her, reciting the words we had written for each other. I had a long chat with Damian, in the pub after our fittings, and I could sense she was finally thawing to Kate.

I had told her everything that had happened, jogging her memory about our confrontation with Johnny and Vic, which was oddly vague in her mind. I think Damian was not quite herself that day, but some force had known I needed her there and had guided her to me.

Like it had guided her at the Deaf Club. There are some things in life you don't question, and I would not question this. Sometimes you have to accept there are no answers that our worldly brains can process. There are movements behind our movements. The invisible hand that pushes towards a destiny already decided. Cover my eyes and I will still blindly take the path that is written for me. Close my ears and I will still hear the same voices.

I looked at Damian over our pints of lager, as she gushed about Sasha, her Amazonian lover, and I thought of the pages of a book.

You open a book not knowing what it contains, having bought it because someone or something has told you that you will like it. You don't know what it contains until you begin to read, and if it suits your style, you get sucked in, you want to know how it ends. That is the pull for us all – to know the ending.

It is like falling in love.

We all want to know how it ends.

I watched Damian talk animatedly about her girlfriend, and saw how happy she was, finally free of the shackles of her man. I watched her eyes sparkle and the corners of her mouth curl, and I wondered how it would end.

Does happiness always have to end?

No, I thought and I smiled back at my friend, happy in her happiness. Not if you work at it.

Not if you don't take it for granted. Not if you wake up every morning and say, 'This is the woman I loved yesterday, the woman I love today and the woman I will love tomorrow'.

Love has many flaws but knowing it is not one of them.

I take Damian's hand and tell her I will see her on Thursday evening, prepared for my wedding on the Friday afternoon. She kisses me on the cheek.

"Maybe I was wrong," she says.

"Wrong?" I ask, having forgotten.

"Maybe it is okay that you said yes," she winks and walks away.

'I told you to say no!' I hear the screaming in my head.

I would never say 'No' to my Kate. Never.

She was the one. She whispered my name in her sleep. When she looked at me now, it was with a newfound respect, having seen what I can see. It made her understand me more, and if Kate can understand something, she can cope. She came in from work, exhausted and devoid of thought, throwing herself onto the bed, and always, always her arms reached out for me. She was no longer afraid to reach out.

What else if there to be afraid of when you have faced your fear?

****

It was the night before my wedding, and I was jangling with nerves. What had I forgotten to do? I must have forgotten something – this was me, after all. I ran through an imaginary checklist in my head, muttering as I wandered from room to room.

My dress was hanging up, invitations sent, cars booked, reception sorted, rings with Damian, passport renewed. Kate had the flights details packed safely in her case, and a taxi to take us to the airport had been reserved.

I felt her grab my shoulders and turn me around to face her. She was trying not to laugh at me biting my lip.

"Jen, calm down. Everything's in order. Nothing is going to go wrong. I have planned with precision like a military operation," she said, grandiosely.

"You're making fun of me," I sulked.

She laughed and gave me a kiss. "Of course I am."

I threw my arms around her and hugged her tightly. "I love you."

"I love you too," she whispered into my neck. Pulling away, she said "Now go enjoy your last night of freedom with Damian, and don't get too drunk. I don't want you staggering down the aisle," she joked. At least, I think she was joking. There may have been an element of truth in there.

"You will turn up, won't you?" I asked.

Kate was going to spend the night at Sheena's in Edinburgh. I had offered to drive her up, but she'd had none of it. She had bought Sheena a car to help her get about and to be able to visit us more often, and they would drive down separately in the morning. Damian would take Kate's car back to our flat and collect Jonah as designated cat-sitter while we were on our honeymoon. As Kate said, she had planned it with a military precision.

She was seeing a lot more of Sheena now, and they were slowly trying to rebuild a relationship. I knew it was not easy for Kate, but she was trying to put the past behind her and forgive her mother. They had even gone to see her sister Lizzie a few times.

It made me happy to see them interact, Sheena fussing over Kate, and Kate swatting her away like an annoying fly, affectionately. You could see how happy Sheena was just knowing Kate was prepared to let her in, and she had been almost paralysed with joy at her wedding invite, especially as we had asked her to lead us up the aisle.

"Of course I'm going to turn up, numpty," she scolded and pecked me on the lips. She walked to the door, lifting her case, "*Don't* be hungover," she warned.

I made a face. "Be gone. Text me later."

This was it. The last time I'd see her until she turned up at the hotel and we walked down their made –for –the occasion aisle.

I took a deep breath and went to join Damian in the living room, with a little vodka – but just a little one.

****

I went to sleep that night still sober, full of excitement. This time tomorrow I would be married. Kate and I would be spending our first night together as wives, wherever the surprise destination was that she had arranged.

I thought of my Kate, as my lids grew heavy. "Tomorrow," I thought. "Tomorrow it'll be all over."

How little did I know.

****

I was at a disco. I stood alone on the dance-floor, circled by empty tables, facing a wall of speakers and an empty DJ box. Then the first song began and I started to dance.

'And under strange skies
We cling on lost trails.'

I see Lorraine, possessed by my child, hold a gun and shoot my friend Rob in the head.

'Eyes that told me so much
Lies
As words are woven
You'll never stop
Darling, we'll never start.'

I see the face of Simon Dunstable leaning over a tied-up Logan. The grave of little Joe Dunstable, still waiting for its headstone, a small rectangle of dirt in the grass.

I am shouting at Kate. I cannot hear the words but the rage is plain on my face.

I am in my bed and I turn to see Kate's back and I move to her and put my arms around her. I hold her like I will never let her go.

I see Kate with Elaine, laughing together at our engagement party. I feel the thud in my heart.

Elaine is whispering to Kate, one thing. She says, "Don't worry. I'll never tell." And, in my dream, I feel my distress.

I trust my Kate, I tell myself, and my anxiety lessens. She loves me. I have seen this. I have nothing to fear any more. There is no threat to us.

I see a boy hanging from the top of his stairs and time moves in reverse. He takes off the noose and returns to his bedroom. As time restarts, he plays a video on his computer and his mother comes in to cuddle him. I smile to myself. A life not lost.

Elaine is teasing me with a lighter, shoving the flame back and forth to my face. “Burn, baby, burn,” she sings to me.

I am still dancing to myself, and I notice the tables and chairs have got closer to me. The floor is smaller, but I still have plenty of room to twist and turn, and I dance to myself like there is no tomorrow.

Kate is with me again, holding hands with Jonah, facing Johnny and Vic. She is believing in me and, with her belief, I will always win. I will always be loved.

Has she found her peace now? Now that I have saved her. I have taken her hurt away and given her mother’s love back? I have saved her, like she knew I would in her nightmare.

That’s right, isn’t it? I brought her and her mother back together. Simon Dunstable, her father, was dead. It had all been about her. Rob had been right.

I twirled and danced, until the dancefloor melted away and I was left singing to myself.

‘Find your peace.’

****

I woke up with a sore head and padded the familiar route to my kitchen for paracetamol. Damian was eating toast and drinking coffee. I noticed with some jealousy that the fat cat was sitting on her lap, purring loudly.

“Morning,” I said, grumpily. “Looks like you have a new friend.” I glared at Jonah.

“Morning. He slept with me all night, didn’t you, gorgeous boy?” she cooed, tickling under his chin. Seeing me reach for the tablets, she asked, “What’s wrong? Got the nervous runs?”

“No! I have a headache.”

Thump, thump, thump. I have had this headache before. It might go away, I try to reassure myself. It could be wedding day nerves.

Damian has made me a cup of tea, and I sit down at the table, ignoring the look from the cat, having been deposed from its comfy throne.

"You won't forget to take the cat, will you?" I asked her, staring back at Jonah.

"No, I'm going to forget and leave it to starve. Not that it couldn't do with losing a few pounds," she added.

"Hey! Leave the fat cat alone. Only I'm allowed to mock his oversized frame." Now I could smile at him.

She smiled. "I'm going for a shower. Drink your tea. And have some toast."

She kissed my hair on her way past.

The day of my dreams was finally here.

I half-heartedly ate some toast, staring blankly towards the window, watching a 'V' formation of birds fly across the sky, destination known.

I lifted my phone and rang the company who were sending a car for us and told them to cancel. I would drive myself. My sister and her boyfriend and my aunt and uncle were checking into the hotel we were getting married at this afternoon, and I wanted to spend some time with them before the madness kicked in.

This is what I told myself while my head continued to thud. Go away, I told it, *not* today.

"Damian!" I shouted to the toilet door. "We're leaving at twelve, not one! Okay?"

"Yeah, yeah, twelve. Got it!" she shouted back.

I had to get organised. I ran to my bedroom and laid out my dress. My case was already packed for the honeymoon, but I grabbed my rucksack and threw in three pairs of jeans, three pairs of socks and three hoodies. For Kate and I. In case we needed to change. Three for choice.

I was muttering to myself again, caught up in the destiny of the day. Allowing the movements behind the movements to guide me. I acted without reason or thought. I acted with the knowing.

Or perhaps it was the knowing of the unknown.

But what is worse? To know or not to know?

When you fall in love, would you want to know how it ends before it has even begun? Or would you rather take the journey?

Maybe before I would have answered that I would have liked to take the path of my life, not knowing where it took me – but now? Now? Now I would need to know. I would choose to see the heartache in front of me and nip it in the bud. I would choose not to waste years of my life, and more importantly my love on someone who was not worth it.

I think back to my time with Kate, from that very first meeting in an interview room in Pitt Street, when I admired the cut of her suit, to her turning up on my doorstep, wearing a scent I knew all too well, and kissing me with her soft red lips. When she moved in, after hours and hours of us talking about stereotypes and knowing we were different, that we would last. And my betrayal of her. The worst and best thing I had ever done. I broke her heart, but I discovered a mothers' love. Kate finding out I was carrying a child, hating me and loving me, unable to forget, willing to forgive. Sitting by my hospital bedside, blinded by her tears, love apparent on her face, unhidden. Not hidden unlike so many other memories of my Kate. Finding out she had been my girlfriend's lover. Julie left me for Kate, a woman she would never understand but that she would love all the same, and when it came down to it, a woman she would not choose over her unborn child. Just like me, although my choices were stripped away by invisible hands that wrote my destiny. That took me down dark alleys, firing shots into my belly, killing my unborn.

My beautiful, blue eyed, blond haired baby, Jonah, who was so confused by the time lines of life and death, that he took control of Lorraine, to get me back, to take his revenge. A revenge that had meant killing his own father. But love confuses the smartest of us at the best of times. Who could blame my innocent baby, whose life and lack of, had already been pre-ordained?

Already decided that I would almost die from smoke inhalation to find a diary that Logan had hidden in his mattress, in order to save his life.

Already decided that Kate and I would be in the right place at the right time to stop a modern day Bible John from killing his third victim.

Already decided that I would hear a song lyric and give a young boy's family some insight that would stop him taking his own life.

Already decided that an unhappy deaf man would try to plant a bomb and that we would stop him.

Like we would stop Johnny Thunderboots and his sadistic accomplice, Vic Kavanagh, from killing more. That we would stand up to evil and all we would have in our defence would be love.

Is that now what we only ever have in our defence? If love will not stand in your corner, what is left?

****

My head was still hurting as I sat in the car with Damian driving, biting my lips. Chewing my nails. Rubbing my temples. Go away headache, I demanded. It made no difference. That pounding kept pounding. That sneaky feeling of the knowing that was trying to creep up on me, my mind betraying me, I would *not* have it. *Not* today. No.

I sent Kate a text, asking her to let me know when she was leaving, telling her I had gone early to meet my family. Damian held my hand, as she drove, and I smiled nervously at her. It was not the hand I wanted to be holding mine.

I thought of a dream that I had. I was standing at a grave, tear after tear falling down my cheek, Damian holding my hand. My heart was breaking for a life that was gone.

We pulled up to the hotel, and I got out the car, hitching up the train of my dress and shivering with the cold. I looked up at the sky, so grey and unforgiving, and I prayed to a God I was still unsure of for a bit of sunshine.

We were met in the entrance hall by our organiser, who quickly filled me in on the details of my marriage to come, but I was only half listening. I looked around for my wee sister, a friendly face. Maybe that would make the thudding disappear. I found her, and we hugged, and we chatted but it didn't help.

Thump, thump, thump.

I nodded in the right place, smiled when I was supposed to and held a glass of champagne that I did not want to drink. Every now and then, I'd look in my clutch bag at my phone to see if Kate had texted.

Friends and family were beginning to arrive. I saw a few of Kate's colleagues and waved.

I could not stop the battering in my head. I needed quiet. I left the bar area and walked through the hotel lobby, along the corridor to where our ceremony was going to take place. I went into the room, quietly closing the doors behind me.

I saw the room in front of me. Chairs to the left, chairs to the right, each seat with a specially designed service sheet laid on it. I walked down the centre of the chairs, my aisle, to an empty table at the top. This is where it would happen. This is where I would be married.

It was the day of my dreams come true.

Thud, thud, thud, pounded my head.

I said that again, slower this time. "The day my dreams come true."

I put my hand to my temple. Did I want to know? Did I want to see how it ended? In my years, I had tried my best to lead a normal life, to ignore that I saw things. Rarely and only recently had I attempted to use my gift to my advantage. Sometimes, I was frightened and sometimes, it made me sad but the more I had accepted it, the better I had got and I had started to 'see' earlier, while there was time to change the outcome.

And then I knew.

It had all been leading to this day.

My phone beeped and I grabbed it from my bag. 'Hi, babe. We've just left. Mum's car wouldn't start, so we are coming in mine. Ask Damian if she'll drive mum to ours and she'll get the train home tomorrow. Can't wait to marry you!'

I turned and saw Rob sitting at the back of the room, holding the match in his hand, poised to strike the box held in the other.

"Don't you dare!" I screamed, running out the room in search of Damian.

"We have to go!" I said, pulling her from her company.

"What?"

"We have to leave! Now! Come on!"

"Jen, I thought you wanted this…"

I stopped and looked at her. "I need you to drive, and if I'm wrong, I'm wrong, but we have to go now."

She considered me for a moment, then said, "Let's go."

We ran to my car and while she manoeuvred out the crowded car park, I loaded the Sat Nav. Destination: Sheena's.

"Do you want to tell me what this is about?" she asked.

I closed my eyes and felt the cold surround me, the waves of intense pain washing over my body, a million darts of agony piercing my flesh.

"I'm going to save Kate."

That was it. It was all about her and I had to save her. She had been right, and I had been too scared to see the end that I had ignored the signs.

No longer. I would not let my Kate die.

We drove in silence and every time we turned a corner, my heart leapt, hoping for a glimpse of Kate's car. We were in the middle of nowhere, the heart of Scotland, all windy roads and lochs. I could not even get a phone signal, not that she would've listened to me. I could hear her in my head saying, 'We'll be fine. It's just your nerves, darling.'

It was not nerves. It was my knowing.

And I knew, as soon as we went up that hill, came round the curve and saw the road before us that it would happen now. I saw the stretch of road in between the loch and the forest.

Then I saw the dot appear in the distance. The dot that was Kate's car.

"That's Kate's car," I pointed to Damian. "Hurry. We have to get her to stop!"

"I'm going as fast as I can!" she wailed. "Have you seen the state of this road? It's been gritted but it's still slippery."

"Slippery, yes," I said, far away. "Like you would skid to avoid a big deer if it ran out in front of you."

Then we both screamed.

I had dreamt of this. The stag ran from the dark of the trees, from the soft mud of the forest floor to the harsh solidity of the road, and we saw Kate's car swerve, as the animal panicked and bolted back to where ecosystems it knew would protect it. We saw the car swerve and skid and drive through the flimsy fence that guarded the waters. We saw the nose head down into the dark and, even in my terror, I began to rip myself free from my dress, knowing what I would do.

"Kate!" I screamed. "Hurry up, Damian! Hurry up!"

And she drove, too carefully, as I ripped at my zip, tearing the dress from my body, kicking my shoes off. As the car slows to a halt where the fence has been broken apart, I throw open my door, stepping out of my dress, and I run, diving into the water.

The first thing I feel is the cold. The icy darts cutting into every inch of me, terrorising my muscles, but I have no time for my pain. I try to focus my vision through the swirls of the darkness and I swim deeper, knowing this is meant to be and trusting that the instincts that guide me will take me to her.

I remembered, a long time ago, Damian had asked me, "Have you started your advanced swimming yet?"

It was all for this moment – everything had led me to this fixed point.

I keep swimming and I see the car, bright in its red frame, calling out to me like a beacon. I can see my Kate struggling with her seat belt and I swim to her door, using both hands to grab the handle and pull it open against the weight of the water. She has got herself unbuckled and leans for Sheena's belt.

I cannot save them both.

Sheena's eyes open, and her hand grabs Kate's. In that moment, she is free. She has found forgiveness – she has known her daughter's love and these last few months have wiped forever the pain of her life. It has all been worth it.

'Release.'

She lets go of Kate's hand and opens her mouth to the black of the ice water. I pull on Kate's dress and she resists, knowing her mother is drowning. This time, I am stronger and I yank her from the car, letting my body take her weight and I cup my left arm under her armpit and across her chest. Then I swim up, with every last ounce of will that I possess, until finally I have our heads about the water and I am scrambling to the edge. She is limp in my arm and somehow, I don't know how, I get her out and I am shaking her.

"Breathe, damn it! You breathe for me, Kate!"

She did, vomiting water, and I dropped my head onto her chest.

"It was all about you," I whispered.

I looked up and shouted for Damian. She wasn't in the car.

"Damian!" I shouted again.

The seconds ticked by, and Kate began to shiver. I remembered my rucksack in the boot of the car. I realised, feeling her tremble, that I was holding her in only my bra and pants and moved up to get my bag, with warm clothes that I had known to bring.

As I stood up, Damian's head splashed through the surface, bringing Sheena's body with her. She had jumped in after me. My life-saving swimmer best friend had meant to save me, as I had meant to save Kate.

She swam to me and I pulled Sheena's lifeless body from her. Her face was white, her lips blue, but she had a peace around her. I began the CPR that Damian had taught me and when she crawled out, her new suit ruined, she took over the chest compressions while I blew in the air.

"She's dead, Jen," she said, sadly.

"No! Keep going!" I cried.

"Jen, she's gone." It was Kate. "It's okay, you can stop."

I looked from Kate to Damian to Sheena. I had packed for three because I had known it would come to this. I just hadn't wanted to see.

I had always known.

****

I am dressed in black at the funeral of Sheena Coutts, held up by my best friend Damian as my beloved Kate reads a passage over the grave. There is no barrier to my grief, and the tears fall in fat, heavy drops, smothering my face in their salt.

Sheena has finally found her peace and my Kate, so brave in her heartache, takes a handful of dirt and throws it on the coffin.

She walks to my side and my hands go to her. My hands will always go to her. As I embrace her, I see Rob behind the faces of the bereaved and he nods, throwing away his match.

I did it.

I saved her.

And, in saving her, I saved myself.

Epilogue

Circus Of Horrors

I have gone to bed with Kate, who is not my wife and never will be. We decided, in light of what happened on what was supposed to be our happiest day that we would forget the whole marriage idea – at least until it meant something more than a piece of paper. I did not need an empty ceremony to be committed, and I did not need a pretend marriage to know that Kate would always love me.

The passion in her kiss told me I had her heart.

She had asked me if I had known what would happen to her mother.

"I only knew the ending when it was the end," I told her.

And life goes on because it has to.

So, I went to sleep and I had a dream because that, too, would go on.

****

I dreamt I was in a big top. I was standing in the sand at the centre and the crowd were clapping me, looking up.

I looked up and saw the trapeze swinging with a corpse tied to it, the black tongue hanging from the mouth.

I turned behind me and saw the lion cage, with the lion lazily gnawing on a bone. A human leg.

I turned the opposite way and saw a woman, star-shaped on what looked like a lifesize dartboard. She was pinned to the board by the knives that had been thrown. Her head drooped onto her naked chest, her long hair covering her breasts.

I turned again and saw the welcoming neon sign that read 'CIRCUS OF HORRORS'.

I turn and mumble in my sleep and I dream I am in bed but my room has objects flying around, floating in mid-air. I am being haunted but I am not afraid.

I get up and go to my bedroom door. When I open it, there are two elderly women waiting for me. The one nearest to me is alive, and the one behind her shoulder is a spirit. She hands a folded note to her mortal friend, and she takes the note to give to me.

I open the note. It reads, ‘Keep the name Ishinnie alive.’

I wake up.

What, or who, is Ishinnie?